RAVEN SISTERS

ALSO BY GABI KRESLEHNER

Rain Girl

RAVEN SISTERS

Franza Oberwieser's Second Case

GABI KRESLEHNER

TRANSLATED BY ALISON LAYLAND

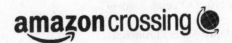

Previously published as *Rabenschwestern* by Ullstein Buchverlage GmbH in Germany in 2014. Translated from German by Alison Layland. First published in English by AmazonCrossing in 2016.

Published by AmazonCrossing, Seattle

www.apub.com

ISBN-13: 9781503934504
ISBN-10: 1503934500

Cover design by Shasti O'Leary-Soudant

Printed in the United States of America

RAVEN SISTERS

1

She glanced at the clock. She had two hours. It was enough time—plenty of time. Should she?

She had seen the little bottle reflecting the shop's display lights as she'd walked past. Her eyes had briefly lingered over the shelves, but she had not allowed herself to stop and give in to her impulse. Now her heart began to beat faster, and she closed her eyes to intensify the feeling. She liked the feeling, the prickling. The stirrings of excitement. She felt hot and cold all over and forgot all fear. Every fiber of her being was drawn into the shop, to the shelves of perfumes, surrounded by the silent, glittering bottles.

She paused for a moment, all her senses alert. She listened and watched. Sniffed the air. She finally reached out a hand.

She loved it as she always did. Loved the feeling, the prickling. The coolness of the bottle sent a current through her fingers the moment she touched it. It passed through her hand and burned into her skin like a brand.

That was why she did it. Again and again. It was not too often, but whenever her eyes fell upon the subtle sparkle of a bottle, whenever the sparkle of a bottle gently touched her heart, whenever it spoke to her in a suggestive whisper: *I'm a possibility.* Then she could not help herself.

She looked round, sniffed the air like an animal, eyes alert, ears pricked, heart thumping madly, taking in all there was to be taken in . . . Voices, movements in the aisles, gazes brushing over her . . . *dangerdangerdanger* . . . Once her heart was calm, once its beat had returned to normal, then she took her opportunity and stepped into the breach between the untouched bottles. She was a tigress, a lioness, a predator stalking her prey, following a scent. A scent she believed she remembered from her childhood, one that had completely eluded her, leaving her in despair during her years of adulthood, those years when certainties had still failed to become certain and she had fallen into a pattern of searching and failing to find.

. . .

Later, in the peace of the bathroom, she opened the little bottle with trembling fingers, let its scent flow out, and immediately . . . the spell was broken and it lost the magic that just a moment before had set her heart alight. Not the evocative scent she had hoped for—no, never.

The disappointment grew less with time, with experience and detachment, but it was always there, forcing itself into her memory as a bland taste, a misunderstanding.

She left.

She moved quickly, broke into a run, the image burned into her retina of the bottle she had dumped in the trash, still trying to give out a last sparkle, a final spray from among the cigarette ends, half-eaten sandwiches, apple cores, and crushed cola cans that finally buried it.

. . .

Sometimes she imagined how it would be if someone caught her red-handed as she haunted the aisles, approaching her with rapid footsteps and determined eyes. She knew she would defend herself. All she had learned in her self-defense classes in the sports center would finally pay off, and she would bring her assailant up short with a perfectly aimed kick, the toe of her shoe precisely targeted at privates that were protected by nothing but a thin layer of fabric, defenseless against a sharp-toed shoe and its devastating effect.

Lilli wondered how it would feel when her shoe landed in that spot; she wondered whether the cry of that unfortunate scent-bottle guardian would freeze her blood as the pain froze his.

She knew that she would run away then, despite the pain that flashed through them both. No, no one could snatch them from her grasp, the sparkling bottles, the dispensers of relief, the trophies of her intrepid quest.

．　　．　　．

Lilli smiled shakily and breathed deeply. Still thinking of the bottle in the airport bathroom trash, she leaned back to look at the departure screen. She would be home in a few hours. Home, whatever that was.

She smiled, a little lost, a little shocked by the thoughts that sometimes fluttered inside her like ghosts, vague and translucent but clear enough for Lilli to recognize that there was an abyss.

She thought of how her hand had wrapped around the bottle, how she had felt the pointed top digging into her palm, how the coolness faded into a faint warmth, a warmth that did not penetrate into her fingers.

Suddenly she was freezing. Shivering, she drew her coat tighter around her. The dark purple velvet was really too warm for the season, for the warmth of the early September afternoon, but she felt cold and she loved the coat. She loved its straight lines, which were beautifully softened by the supple velvet. She had discovered the coat at the end of the London summer in the tiny Soho boutique of a still-unknown designer. She had pressed her face against the sleeve and was

3

immediately absorbed by the softness and security of this dark purple haven. She had to have the coat whatever the cost. It had not cost that much, tidy sum though it was. But the money didn't matter. She suspected she would wear it until it hung from her body in rags.

Various other items in the shop had caught her eye, but none interested her as much as she interested the designer. The moment he saw Lilli, he assumed a rapt expression, reflecting the very same fascination she felt for the coat.

Would she stay and be his muse, he'd asked. Her features, her hair, her figure, her legs . . . ohhh . . . it was all so . . . Would she stay? *What is your name, miss?*

She'd smiled with a hint of pride mixed with a hint of perplexity, pretending not to understand. She was a tourist, she explained, and *very bad in English.*

By the time she finally left the shop, he'd added a pair of boots to the coat. They were dark gray and soft suede, high heels, over the knee. They fit so well, so lightly, that she walked as though her feet were winged. She'd turned back once and saw the designer at the door, giving her a bow and then raising his hands in applause. He'd called after her, *Stay! Please stay! Come back, my dear!*

Lilli laughed and began to run, waving to him with the full force of her good fortune, jumping into the air, imagining the world turning beneath her—unstoppable and continuous—and sensing the pulse of life all around her.

Back home in her tiny apartment, she'd twirled before the mirror in wonder, thinking, *Wow! Such elegance! If Mr. Greenow saw me like this at the office, he would bow and say, "My dear, you're the best!" and for once actually mean it.*

That evening she knew with certainty that she didn't want to become a lawyer. A small feeling of satisfaction had mounted in her, coupled with delight at the thought of flying home soon.

Her internship had been good. But the city had been even better. Huge. Loud. Glittering. Simply London. She had immersed herself in the city, in its strangeness and its freedom, and it had felt good. Three months had passed quickly, a series of flying visits, every morning starting with the shimmering of the dark coffee she brought to Mr. Greenow's office, which was received with a sigh of gratitude and the same words every day, *You're the best, my dear.*

Mr. Greenow had studied with her grandfather, and it was to that fact she owed her three-month internship in his office, where major cases were handled—revenue matters, business affairs, homicide investigations—the type of cases that made the life of an attorney so varied and exciting.

She had smiled as she participated in negotiations, sitting next to the tough young lawyers—all of them tigers—and listening to their confident voices. But every day she became increasingly aware that it had absolutely nothing to do with her.

It didn't make her sad. On the contrary, it gave her certainty. That surprised her. The consequences would be bitter—three years gone up in smoke. *A waste of a degree course,* she thought as she sat in the departure hall at the airport, London Stansted. Mr. Greenow would now be saying those same words—*you're the best, my dear*—to someone else.

But her internship had been good, and the city even better. She'd have to tell her grandfather that being a lawyer was just not for her. It was really not her thing at all. There would be something else, although she was not yet sure what it was.

She sighed. She wished she knew what the future would hold. But there was one thing she did know. She knew what her grandfather would say, the aging attorney who had wanted her to succeed him, to be the one to inherit his law firm since his own daughter had disappointed him: *You're like your mother,* he would say with a hint of contempt in his eyes. *You don't know what you want. You get carried away by stupid ideas.*

No, she thought, and couldn't help grinning. She was not carried away by "stupid ideas." In fact, there were no ideas at all for the moment. She felt . . . light. And she also felt a connection with her mother, which surprised her since they were, after all, so different.

She was hungry and wandered through the rows of counters that lined the airport in a cheerful array. Outside, airplanes landed and took off. She thought of the exhibition she had seen a few weeks ago. It was of a German photographer's work, titled *People at the Airport* or *Waiting Photos* or some such. Lilli had been unusually touched by the photographs, as if they were familiar. Perhaps it was the way in which the camera had portrayed the faces—the eyes—as though it recognized them. Lilli wasn't sure why, but she hadn't been able to forget the photographs or the photographer. But of course she wouldn't forget the photographer—she already knew her name, Hanna Umlauf, which she had always found strange-sounding and beautiful. She also knew her face. Her portrait hung on her grandparents' wall next to that of her mother.

•   •   •

Her cell phone rang. She took it out. Her mother. *Not now,* she thought as she slipped it back into the pocket of her velvet coat. *I'll be seeing you soon enough.*

The ringtone stopped, to be followed a short time later by a beep announcing a text. Lilli sighed.

Lilli, darling, I'm setting off for the airport soon. So looking forward to seeing you! It's been ages since we saw each other. Have you grown?

Lilli couldn't help laughing. What a question! *Yes, I have,* she thought. *I have grown.* She texted back. *Yes, I've grown.*

"Two salmon sandwiches, please," Lilli said to the girl at one of the food counters, "a bottle of water, a slice of chocolate cake, a coffee, and an apple."

She enjoyed the look of surprise on the girl's face. She thanked God for her healthy appetite and her even healthier metabolism, which disposed of all she gave it in no time at all. She sat down and ate and drank, satisfying her hunger and thirst.

London Stansted. So. She'd gotten this far. As always, she had given herself up to the inexorable logistics that characterized all airports. The map of the systematic processes had taken her under its spell, but now that she was satiated she waited in the row of seats in front of the gate, and snuggled into the purple velvet of her coat. She realized with a shudder that not everything was as perfectly straightforward as it sometimes—only sometimes—seemed.

. . .

Boarding was due to begin in half an hour. In just a few hours, she would be in Munich.

"May I have this seat?"

Lilli nodded without looking up and felt a large man sitting down beside her, filling all the nearby space. She sensed a tall, strong body, visible from the side as merely silhouette, and saw a large pair of shoes next to her own. They astonished her. Her own feet were not small, size 9 as they were, but these . . . these were flippers!

Lilli grinned to herself and felt slightly flushed. That was indeed what they were, flippers. Such huge shoes, at least size 14, probably even 15! Now those were what she called big feet. How sure-footed a man with such big feet must be!

Yes, thought Lilli with deep conviction. *Yes*. She nodded to herself, unable to take her eyes away from the feet. He must be successful in everything he touched, everything life threw at him—everything. Nothing could affect such a person—not cold, not heat, nothing. A man like that wouldn't chase around after an elusive scent or seek out security in a purple coat. A man like that carried around his own inner security.

She finally tore her gaze from the giant shoes and the equally large feet and turned toward the man himself as if to ask him something . . . But what? Suddenly, he stood and walked away, leaving her staring after him without so much as a glimpse of his face or knowing anything about him. She merely saw his feet clearly before her, those feet that went through life anchored on solid ground, like mountains, or hills, at least (she mustn't exaggerate).

Lilli finally closed her mouth, which was still hanging open with her unasked question, the question she could not even form into words, the question that now lay somewhere in the mysterious center of her brain.

Crazy, she thought with a self-satisfied sigh. *Boy, am I crazy. But there it is. That's just how things are sometimes.* She grinned just as she heard the announcement that the flight was delayed for another hour and a half.

2

She's always been like that, Gertrud thought. *She's had that arrogance since she was a child, and I know who she got it from.*

She looked at the clock and then at the arrivals board and then back at the clock.

She could have got in touch, Gertrud thought. *Surely she could have sent a quick text from London. I needn't have rushed if she had.*

Ah, well, another hour and a half to go. Lousy delay. I might as well have a coffee.

She turned and wandered around the huge concourse, then sat down in a bistro and ordered a coffee. *Oh, Lilli, you little devil. I love you so much. How I've missed you. Should I have told you the truth? Has the time finally come?*

She stirred her coffee, following the dark swirls with her eyes, and trickled in some sugar. She thought about the events of the last few days. It had been only a week. She'd immediately suspected that the world would be turning differently from then on. Faster. In the wrong direction: backward into the past, where no one wanted to go. Not Gertrud, at least. No way. There was no damn reason for the damned past. But he saw things differently. The man who had suddenly appeared.

"I'm Tonio," he'd said with a smile. "And you're Gertrud. Forgive me if I gave you a shock. I know how much I resemble my father."

Then he came out with some cock-and-bull story about how he had watched her coming down the avenue that led to her house, how he had silently prayed for her to stop. How he had thought, *Stop! Wait for me. Turn around!* And despite herself, she'd actually stopped. He'd started walking toward her as if drawn by a string.

She shook her head vigorously, bringing her thoughts back to the present, and realized she was shaking. If the recent past could shock her so deeply, how would it be if she delved deeper into the past? She suspected it was bound to happen; it sure as hell was bound to happen.

"Can I get you anything else?"

She looked around, and her gaze fell on the huge clock that hung above the counter. It had gotten late. She'd lost all track of time. The London plane must have arrived by now, and the luggage carousel would be turning.

"No, thanks. I'd like to pay now, please." She looked at the waiter and noticed he was staring at the table, at her coffee cup.

"But you haven't even . . ." He indicated the coffee that stood untouched, getting cold since he'd brought it to her. She waved him away, pressing a five-euro bill into his hand. She left without waiting for the customary polite protestation. He stared after her, shaking his head, eyebrows raised.

As she dived into the tumult of arriving and departing passengers and those waiting to meet them or see them off, the jumble of voices blended into a monotonous hum. *Now I'm late,* she thought, and had to grin. *Now she'll be the one waiting for me with disapproval all over her face. I'll take her into my arms and press her to me. I'll feel her resist at first and then gradually relax.*

Yes, Gertrud was late. Slightly. Lilli was already through the barrier, standing there waiting. Her stubborn little girl. She *had* grown. Grown up. Elegant. Gertrud was amazed. *How beautiful she is,* she thought. *Why didn't I ever notice that?*

"Mama," Lilli said. "Hello, Mama!" She allowed herself to be hugged, and Gertrud noticed that she had warmed toward her a little.

3

Gertrud stood on the terrace, a last glass of wine in her hand. The children were in bed; Moritz had been asleep for two hours, and Lilli had just gone. Christian was loading the dishwasher. She heard him banging around and thought of the meal and the relaxed atmosphere they'd enjoyed. Their little boy had quickly become tired, and after he'd clung to Lilli, wheedling a promise from her that she'd still be there in the morning, his father had managed to persuade him up to bed.

"I've missed him," Lilli had said quietly, with a smile.

Gertrud nodded. "He's a little treasure, isn't he?"

"Yes," Lilli said. "Yes, he is."

A light breeze blew up, carrying the scent of ripe damsons. Lilli smiled. "Damson jelly? Like every year?"

Gertrud smiled, too. "Of course," she said. "You can't just leave the fruit to rot."

"No," said Lilli. "You can't. Can I help you? In return for a few jars?"

"Oh yes, that would be lovely! Of course you'll get some." They were silent for a moment, then she added, "Will you be staying here awhile?"

"No," said Lilli, "I want to go home tomorrow."

Gertrud felt a pang of regret. "But I could take care of your laundry for you. You could relax and have some peace and quiet to settle back in."

"No."

"But you—"

Lilli shook her head, cutting her off. No discussion. There was a brief pause.

"I went to her exhibition," she said finally, and waited for Gertrud to freeze, to coolly arm herself as she always did when the name *Hanna* was mentioned, although that was hardly ever. It was a taboo, a red-hot coal no one touched. No one ever spoke about Hanna, no one. The photo on her grandparents' living room wall was the only evidence that she'd ever been part of the family.

This time Gertrud didn't freeze. She took a sip of wine and looked at her daughter wearily. "Well? Are they nice, her photos? Did you like them?"

"Yes," Lilli answered in surprise. "Yes, they're wonderful!" She hoped Gertrud would say more, but she didn't. She merely stared out into the darkness of the garden.

"Mama," Lilli said, tentatively touching her arm. "Mama!"

Gertrud shook her head. "No!" She heard the vehemence of her own voice. "No, don't ask me. I can't tell you anything. Maybe someday, maybe . . ."

She trailed off. Lilli nodded, stroked Gertrud's arm, stayed silent.

Hanna, Gertrud thought, *always Hanna.* She began to shiver in the darkness of the terrace.

"Maybe I'll shut up shop and fly out to Greece for a few days," she said. "It would be a good time to do that. Could you look after Moritz while Christian's at work?"

"Sure," Lilli said.

13

Christian came back out and refilled their wine glasses. Lilli told them about London, and time passed. Gertrud now found herself standing alone on the terrace with her last glass of wine, waiting for Christian to come up behind her and embrace her, waiting for him to trace the lines of her neck with his lips. She would give him a gentle shake and say, *It's late. I'm tired.* And she would leave without turning back, knowing that he was standing there with drooping shoulders and a resigned expression, wishing she were on the moon or in hell or wherever.

She shrugged. There was nothing she could do about it. It was as it was. And now Tonio had come back. For some mysterious, crazy reason he was back in her life, and somehow also in Lilli's and probably also in Hanna's. Which would mean that Hanna was also in Gertrud's life.

He had just approached her on one of the last mild evenings in August, when the fall was starting to make itself felt in the air. She had been walking down the avenue toward home, wearing a dress of copper and stone, the bronzed moons of her breasts swaying to the rhythm of her steps, black-red shadows falling from the canopy of the maples—a harmonious picture, precious and rare.

He'd told her he started walking toward her as if drawn by a string, silently praying for her to stop. He'd thought, *Stop! Wait for me. Turn around!*

And then she actually had stopped. She'd turned her face to the light, closed her eyes, and taken a deep breath, breathing in that early hint of fall, amazed by the moment of joy and peace.

"How strange," he said, touching her arm lightly. "In my thoughts I asked you to stop. And now you really have."

He grinned, embarrassed and nervous, cleared his throat. "I must have powers of hypnotism."

She stared at him, shaking her head slightly.

"What . . . ?" she said, faltering, taking a step back. He seemed to enjoy her bewilderment and shock.

"I know I resemble my late father." He looked a little remorseful. "Maybe I should have warned you so I wouldn't have given you such a fright."

She stared into his face, his eyes, taking in his hair and his clothes. This was no ghost, no illusion—different from her memories, but even so . . .

His father?

She felt her blood run cold and saw her past open up before her, a gaping abyss.

"Can I take you for a coffee? Or would you prefer tea? Perhaps a glass of wine?"

He talked away in embarrassment, his breath close to her face. *What insolence,* she thought. *What insolence!*

His lack of respect for her space irritated her, made her angry. She took a step back, shook her head silently, and stared with fascination at that remarkably familiar face.

It can't be true, she thought. She stared fixedly at his mouth, the lines of his cheeks, the gray of his eyes. The familiarity was almost enough to choke her.

"Who are you?" she asked breathlessly. "Who are you?"

"I'm sorry," he said, gnawing nervously on his lip before finally giving her his first name and surname. She only remembered the first name. She'd never heard the surname, but his first name shocked her afresh. It was clear that it was no coincidence that he was there for her, for Hanna, for the distant past.

"Like my father," he said, and she finally sensed the way he shifted with embarrassment. She thought, *Like his father. What an idiot—can't he see it's obvious?*

"You knew him, didn't you?" he asked, hoping for her assent.

She shook her head hastily, cleared her throat, and said, "No."

It's not possible, she thought again and again, shaking her head. But she could handle it, or at least do her best to.

"No," she said, louder than necessary. "Leave me in peace. Stop bothering me!"

She turned away.

"Please," he said. "Don't just go! Let me explain! Please!"

But she had already walked away. He followed her and pressed a piece of paper into her hand.

"My cell phone number. I'd really like . . . Please call me. Please! In a few days, a week. Whenever you want to!"

She stared at him and then at the note in her hand and then back at him, before finally leaving him standing there. At home she got out the old photos. She was alone. Christian was visiting friends and Moritz in bed. It was one of the last warm nights of the year, the summer on the wane. She wasn't happy about it. Perhaps she suspected that . . . No. She suspected nothing. There was nothing to suspect.

She stared at the photos: Hanna, Tonio, herself. *How young we were,* she thought. *How young.* She felt a slight longing for those days.

So, Tonio. Tonio again. With a dull taste in her mouth, she went to the window and leaned out into the night. She felt a churning in her stomach. *Shit,* she thought. *Shit.* But it was already too late.

Later, she lay helpless on the sofa, finally coming to terms in her heart and her head with what was logical and obvious. He had spoken of his father, his dead father, mixing the past with the present in such a way that nothing felt right.

So he deceived us, she thought. *He deceived us, the bastard. Hanna more than anyone, but also me somehow. He fucked around with others, who knows with how many, and had a son, who knows how many, and he even gave him his name.*

This boy is not coming into my happy life, she thought, feeling helpless that he had casually appeared as if it were nothing. *He'll ruin everything.*

She jumped up, went back over to the window, and looked out into the night. The darkness was soft, like down. There was nothing to get hold of.

Ah, well, she thought finally as she calmed down. *Ah, well, if that's how it's to be.* Time seemed to stand still for a fraction of a second and she turned . . . *backbackback . . . backthenbackthenbackthen . . .*

4

Twenty pounds! Franza groaned. *Twenty damned pounds! Twenty stupid pounds!*

They simply didn't fit. If only the weight would vanish. Just like that, without fuss, like the snow in spring. Why couldn't it be like that for her?

Franza sighed and then smiled. She was stuck in a ridiculously cramped dressing room. That in itself was bearable when absolutely necessary. But what was so much worse was that she was stuffed into the jeans. And that . . . that was unbearable. Or difficult, at least. She could just manage by holding her breath and pulling her stomach in.

Or like raspberry ice cream in the sun, she thought, daydreaming a little. *You lie down in a sunbeam, and soon you begin to melt. After twenty pounds have gone, you're done and you stand up, take a deep breath, shake yourself off, and make sure everything's still in the right place. Double-check your bust, your stomach, your backside are right where they should be. And then you go into that boutique and the sales assistant doesn't give you a pitying smile because you've arrived twenty pounds too soon. She smiles sincerely and warmly because she knows that the jeans, those stupid jeans, will cling to you like a second skin and that they'll be just perfect for the right shirt, the right blouse, or perhaps even the right jacket—that crazily expensive jacket that's hanging out front in the display window. She'll know she's going to make an amazing sale.*

Franza grinned and slowly released her belly muscles, relaxing. She was amazed to find that somehow it was working.

"Do they fit?"

The shrill, squeaky voice rang into the cubicle, and Franza noted its shrillness with satisfaction. *At least that's fair,* she thought. *At least this Barbie girl has a squeaky voice.*

"I'm still not sure," she said, pushing the cubicle curtain aside and taking a few steps out. Away from the mirror, the world already looked a bit different, a bit better. *Ah, well,* she thought, *it's not so bad, they're only one size too small. Two weeks' starvation and they'll fit as if made for me. And a few gym sessions.*

She closed her eyes with a sigh.

Well, sex, perhaps. Hot, wild sex. She preferred that to the gym. Much preferred it. After all, life was there to be enjoyed, in all its facets. She thought of Port, such a good lay. She wanted him even then. She longed for him to be there, tearing those damned jeans from her flesh. Then she thought of how he was at an audition right then and in the evening had a monster production. He wouldn't be available until late that night, and then he'd be tired, incredibly tired . . . perhaps the gym was the better option after all.

With a sigh she thought of the fresh-baked cookies in a tin in her bag. She knew their scent would leap out as soon as she removed the lid. *Felix and Arthur will be happy,* she thought as she twirled back and forth in front of the mirror.

"Excuse me. That jacket in the window, that light-brown leather jacket—I'd like to try that on."

The sales assistant coughed politely.

"I'm very sorry," she said, "but I'm afraid we don't have it in your size."

Franza turned and looked her in the eye with her best Detective Inspector expression. Even as she did so, she feared it would make no difference.

"You're afraid you don't?" she said. "Would you mind taking a look?"

"Yes, if you like," said the assistant with an almost imperceptible sigh. "I'll gladly take a look."

She went on a search for the right size.

Stupid cow, Franza thought. *There are plenty of women like me!* Her size wasn't really all that excessive.

"You're losing it, Franza," she muttered. "What are you doing in a boutique like this?"

She had not had any particular plans—just a little shopping expedition to buy some of that delicious pasta they stocked at the delicatessen on the corner. Nothing was happening at the station. She had to make the most of it. It didn't happen very often, and she was accruing overtime like the dust bunnies in her living room.

Yes, she had time, so much lovely time, so she'd wandered through the mall from store to store, up the escalator, past the windows until that jacket had suddenly appeared before her—the leather jacket she'd just discovered they didn't have in her size. The light-brown marvel had smiled at her, calling her in through the door, and that was why she had squeezed herself into the jeans, as she had no intention of trying on the jacket in her old baggy pants.

Enough already. She went back into the cubicle, sat down on the stool, carefully unzipped the jeans—her stomach enjoying its newly regained freedom—and waited for the assistant to return. Perhaps she had found something after all. But Madam was taking her time.

Fair enough, Franza thought. She took the opportunity to peep out and look around unseen. There were few people in the store, which was hardly surprising given the prices. The store sold jewelry, perfume, and shoes, as well as clothes. Everything was arranged in tastefully minimalist quantities in prominent positions. Boredom gradually set in, and

Franza wondered what the assistant was doing—polishing her nails, picking her nose, catching up with a thousand friends on Facebook?

Suddenly, the door opened, and a young woman entered and looked around. *Wow,* Franza thought. Stylish. Sweet girl. Purple velvet coat, over-the-knee boots, hair neatly pinned, an intelligent, direct gaze.

I know her from somewhere, Franza thought. *Where do I know her from?* She ran through criminal records in her mind's eye and then reprimanded herself with a shake of her head and a faint smile. Idiot. What would a young woman like this be doing among that set of hardened criminals?

Although . . . Franza continued to watch her in amazement, becoming more uneasy as the seconds went by. The young woman suddenly seemed to be full of desire; the velvet of her coat almost glowed with anticipation. She was practically sniffing the air, carefully turning her head from side to side to sense any lurking danger. Franza quickly ducked out of her line of sight.

It was the small, delicate, sparkling bottles of perfume that had caught the girl's eye. Franza saw her hand hover above the bottles for a drawn-out moment before her fingers closed in. A final quick glance around the store seemed to give the girl confidence, and the bottle vanished into the depths of her purse.

Franza sat on the stool, a little shocked, a little amused, a little amazed. She had caught a little shoplifter—a little kleptomaniac, in fact. The way she'd behaved indicated both a compulsion and that it was a repeated act. *Yes,* Franza thought, *repetition, compulsion.*

Franza heard the sound of the door. The girl had gone just as she came, silently, unobtrusively. The assistant, on the other hand, was still nowhere to be seen. It was as if she knew the police were on the premises.

OK, Franza thought, and jumped up. *Let's get to it. Let's do our duty.* She felt her instincts awaken, wild and predatory. She rushed out after the girl, through the door and out into the mall. As she ran, she heard the assistant yelling after her, "Hey, what are you doing?" Franza was wearing an expensive pair of designer jeans, and the assistant couldn't help the fact they didn't have the jacket in her size. If she didn't come back immediately, she'd call the police.

As if the little thief had also heard the shrill voice, she turned and saw Franza approaching. Recognizing the danger, predator against predator, she broke into a sprint toward the escalator, toward the exit, toward safety. Despite the high-heeled boots, the girl was fast, incredibly fast. Franza suddenly realized that she was not wearing boots, not even shoes, nothing. She had nothing on her feet except a pair of thin cotton socks, her shoes still lying next to her purse on the floor of the dressing room. For a brief moment Franza felt embarrassed and hesitated. As though her embarrassment had transferred to the young woman, she, too, faltered and turned around. She glanced at Franza's stockinged feet and slowed. The escalator came into view, and they hurled themselves onto it. Franza felt the ribbed step digging into the soles of her feet and realized how ridiculous she must look, chasing after a girl in her stockinged feet, the fly of her jeans open.

What an idiot, she thought and stopped and bent over, her hands on her knees. *Why do I get involved in things that don't concern me? A young madwoman lifts perfume from a stupid, totally overpriced store. Can't I just let it go?*

She took a deep breath, raised her eyes, and looked ahead. The young woman was standing twenty yards away at the entrance to the shopping mall, looking at her. Franza shook her head and gasped for breath. *Is she crazy?* she thought as she began to run again. *Is she crazy? Surely she isn't waiting for me!*

Yes, she was waiting. She passed through the revolving doors, then stopped to watch Franza.

"You're not in bad form," she said with a small grin, "for your age."

"Oh," Franza said as she tried to steady her breathing. "You think so?"

The young woman nodded.

"After all, we've just run through half the mall and you've got nothing but socks on your feet." She grinned again and looked scornfully down at Franza's feet. "Why?"

Franza raised her eyebrows, still a little annoyed at the lack of respect and the ridicule from her adversary, although inwardly she had regained her composure.

"Why what? Why am I running after you, or why am I running after you in socks?"

"Both."

"Hm." Franza considered for a moment. "You know why I ran after you. Why in socks? Well, sometimes life's just like that."

The girl smiled, and Franza felt a vague feeling of sympathy, of concern.

"Good answer."

"You think?" said Franza. "Thanks."

"Can I go now?"

Franza paused for a fraction of a second, then nodded, looking into the girl's thoughtful, alert eyes. "Who's going to stop you? I'm certainly not. I should go back and fetch my shoes."

"From the shop?"

"Yes, from the shop. A crap shop it is, too."

The girl laughed. "I know. Why do you go there? You don't need to."

Don't need to! Franza couldn't help grinning, but her face immediately turned serious again.

"What about you?" she asked. "Do you need to? How often do you need to do that?"

The girl's face suddenly turned bright red, and all at once she seemed really small, a sapling unable to withstand the wind. She shrugged. "It's nothing to do with you! Or do you want to send me to a therapist?"

Her scornful smile was back in place, but it was shaky. Franza felt a desire to take her in her arms and rock her gently. But of course she didn't.

"No," she said instead. "I've no intention of sending you to a therapist. That's something you've got to do for yourself."

The girl was silent.

"But that . . . that's going to take a while, isn't it?" she continued carefully.

The girl shrugged again. Franza reached out her hand.

"Franza," she said. "And you?"

The girl cautiously shook her hand.

"I know," she said. "You're Benny's mother. You're a police officer. That always amazed me."

"Oh!" Franza was surprised. "You know Ben? How?"

"From school. We were in the same class. I have to go now."

She withdrew her hand from Franza's and walked away.

"What's your name?" Franza called.

The girl turned once more. "Lilli," she said. "I'm Lilli."

Then she was gone, swallowed up by the crowds. Franza stood there for a while, lost in thought.

"Lilli," she murmured and recalled her eyes, light mottled brown.

She turned back into the mall, rode up the escalator, fielding with confidence the looks she attracted in her socks and unzipped fly, as if it were the most normal thing in the world.

The sales assistant was standing outside the door of the store, an aging Barbie gesticulating wildly as she talked to a police officer, who was holding Franza's purse in one hand and her official ID in the other.

"Oh," said Franza to the assistant. "I see you've called in reinforcements."

She smiled at the police officer, whose relief was plain to see. He must have recognized Franza from her photo.

"Thank God," he said. "All's well that ends well. What was the matter, Inspector?"

Franza shook her head and smiled. "Nothing, my friend. False alarm. You can give me my things back now."

"I'm sorry," he said, pressing them into her hands.

"No problem." Turning to the assistant, Franza added, "I'll make myself presentable now."

She went into the store and the dressing room, took a last quick look at herself in the jeans, then dragged them down and slipped into her old pants, which would do for a while longer.

The sales assistant had followed her and was now standing, a little bewildered, outside the door.

She cleared her throat. "I didn't know that . . . you . . . were a police officer . . ."

"No problem." Franza took a deep breath as she savored the comfort of her old pants.

"Will you be taking the jeans?"

"No," Franza said. "I won't be taking the jeans, as I assume you don't have them in my size."

The assistant fell into an embarrassed silence, probably feeling uneasy now that she knew Franza was a police officer. She was probably thinking of the traffic offenses she had committed, or the occasional joint she smoked . . . no, probably not. Barbies didn't smoke joints, certainly not aging Barbies. The most Barbies did was to take turns a little fast, causing the tires to squeal and making them laugh out loud. Apart from that, Barbies were good little girls, well adjusted and pretty. On Sundays they went out on the town with Ken and ate . . . well, anything but sundaes. Franzas, on the other hand, enjoyed sundaes. Franzas sinned occasionally, sinned like crazy, without so much as a bad conscience.

Precisely, Franza thought with satisfaction. *That's the way of the world.* Sometimes you just needed the simplicity of a clear worldview.

Franza left the store and the mall and went out into the sunshine. She walked with a swing in her step, thinking of nothing, of everything, of nothing.

5

Backthenbackthenbackthen . . .

Back then the world was small, yet huge. Enormous. Much bigger than today. Big houses, people, trees, sky. The perfect size for those giants whose bellies were level with your head. From a child's perspective, with your head at hip level, voices were from above, looks from above.

Mama had baked cakes and as always wore that necklace, with the little balls, around her neck, the balls she said were called *pearls* and very, very valuable. Gertrud must take care and not be too boisterous when she threw her arms around Mama's neck or the necklace could break and then the pearls would get lost.

Mama rarely baked. It was usually Sabine who did that with the weekday chores. Mama did the chores on weekends, as well as she could, but she was a doctor and not particularly good at housework.

Today was the weekend, a special day. Today Gertrud would be getting a sister, and that was why Mama had baked a cake.

Three days ago, Mama and Papa had come to Gertrud's bedside, given her a cuddle, and Mama had asked, "Gertrud, would you like a sister?"

Gertrud had just turned seven, and yes, she really wanted a sister, a little doll that she could mother and drag around with her sometimes, and then when she cried hand her back to Mama or Sabine or even Papa.

Her reply was full of enthusiasm. "Yes! Yes, I do! When?"

She peered at Mama's belly, but Mama's belly was as flat as ever, so it was going to be a while.

"At the weekend," Mama said with a smile and stroked Gertrud's head, delighted at how easy it had been. "This weekend!"

Gertrud was amazed. How could that be possible? Three weeks ago her best school friend's mama had had a baby, but it had taken a long time, many weeks and months. Brigitte's mama's belly had gradually grown bigger and fatter and had then finally spat out the baby, Brigitte's little brother. And now it was going to happen so quickly? Gertrud was amazed.

Perhaps, she thought, God had blessed Papa with a little magic and all he had to do was click his fingers and the baby would appear and Mama didn't have to get really fat. Perhaps it was because Papa was an important man, a man who always went to work in a suit and tie, a man who had offices in the town where he helped everyone who came to him and where the rooms were so tall and so wide that the world seemed a little bigger and Gertrud was paralyzed with awe.

"What a good girl," Frau Umlauf, Papa's secretary, would say every time Gertrud visited, as she stroked her hair.

"Do you remember Hanna?"

Gertrud looked at Papa. "Hanna?"

He nodded. "Yes, Hanna. She was here once. The daughter of Frau Umlauf, my secretary at the office. Don't you remember?"

Yes, Gertrud remembered. Hanna was a thin, pale girl with carroty hair. Anyone who had hair like that was to be pitied. She had been to their house once because Gertrud's father needed her mother at work. So Sabine had gone to fetch the child, so she wouldn't be home alone.

At first, although they were a similar age, the two girls had not known what to make of each other, but Sabine had finally managed to get them to play together.

"Hanna's a poor little girl," Mama said. "She has no one left anymore, so she's coming to live with us now. You have to be nice to her."

Gertrud was amazed. She couldn't say a word—at first. Later, she couldn't stop asking questions.

Hanna had no father. Gertrud knew sometimes people had no father. But Hanna had no grandma or grandpa either, and no aunts or uncles, no one at all. That happened, too. But now Hanna had no mother. Her mother had not died exactly, but was effectively dead. She'd collapsed like a stone and now she just lay there like a stone. It had happened two weeks ago in the office, in the middle of taking dictation.

"Isn't it dreadful?" Mama asked, stroking Gertrud's hair. Gertrud nodded and snuggled up to Mama's belly and Mama's bosom and put her arms around her neck. She thought she should be careful with the pearl necklace so the pearls didn't roll away.

That night Gertrud slept badly, waking up in fear several times, dreaming of mamas who simply collapsed and didn't get up anymore. Three days later, Papa drove off and came back with Hanna. She had nothing but a small suitcase and a doll called Helga, with blond braids. She was given the room next to Gertrud's, which Mama and Sabine had quickly prepared and which would be made much more cozy over the coming weeks. Hanna didn't talk much that first day. Mama and Papa made up for it by talking more, perhaps because they didn't really know what to say. In the evening Papa called the social welfare office and reassured them that everything was OK and that he would see to the paperwork as quickly as possible. He was an attorney, and it wouldn't be a problem at all.

• • •

When everything was dark and quiet in the house and everyone was asleep, Gertrud woke in fear again. She climbed from her bed and crept out onto the dark landing, something she had rarely done. She slipped along to the next door, opened it, and darted into the room and into the bed in which the little girl lay—the little girl who had no one left in the world. She jumped when she felt the strange body next to her and then immediately put her arm around Gertrud's neck, hugged her close, and began to sob—softly, but sobbing all the same.

"Shhhh," said Gertrud. Hanna slowly calmed and stopped trembling. Gertrud said "shhhh" once again, then stroked her carroty hair that shimmered in the moonlight and thought how pretty she was, so pretty . . .

They eventually fell asleep, the children, the little girls, the sisters who weren't sisters but who eventually became sisters. They embraced each other in their sleep and became one another's support, anchor, burden.

I have a sister now, Gertrud wrote in the red book she had been given for her last birthday. *A sister is for life. My sister is called Hanna.*

It was lovely to have a sister, someone you could share everything with, all your joys, all your pain. It was horrible having a sister, someone you had to share everything with, all Mama's caresses, all Papa's kind words.

29

6

Tonio stood on the hill, observing the house. He knew he must be a bit mad to be observing them—spying on them—like this, but he did it anyway.

"You have to stop this," Gertrud had said after he'd called her for the third time, asking her to meet him. "It's going nowhere. I can't tell you anything about your father. I knew him, sure, but not particularly well. He's dead, leave him in peace. Enjoy your inheritance and just get on with your life."

He called a fourth time.

"If you don't stop harassing me, I'll have to tell the police," she said.

But she had not called the police, which emboldened him and gave him confidence. He continued to follow her, approaching her on the street. He could see she was beginning to unravel; panic taking an ever-increasing hold of her. But still no police.

So my gut feeling's along the right lines, he thought. *There's something in the air, something . . . bad from when my father was still alive. I have to know what it is. I just have to know! Perhaps this is his legacy to me, his gift. Perhaps it will be my downfall, this knowledge, but I can't have it any other way. I owe it to him, my father. I owe it to myself!*

No, he couldn't have it any other way. He was Tonio's son. He bore his father's name and looked like him. His father had never even seen him. His mother had been a mere one-night stand for this man, not even a brief affair. There was no connection between father and son, nothing—only the name and the resemblance. It was probably a curse. Gertrud was probably right that he should merely enjoy his inheritance and be done with it. A father like that was owed nothing, absolutely nothing.

Tonio remembered the day, just a few weeks ago, when he had finally gone to pick up the letter from the notary's office. It had been an awful day. There'd been another death on the ward before his shift ended. He got in his car and revved the engine. Over by the pond Rasmus stood smoking, staring into space, his face vacant and expressionless.

Asshole, Tonio had thought, amazed at his own anger, which was out of all proportion, based on nothing but that dumb grin Rasmus always wore on his face. He was such a suck-up. He needed a good beating. Tonio wished he could hold him down and let him have it!

As Tonio turned out of the parking lot, he saw Rasmus getting smaller and smaller in the rearview mirror. Once Tonio could no longer see him, he finally did what he had been longing to do all along: he stuck up his middle finger and yelled at the windshield, venting his anger not only at Rasmus, but at them all, the whole world, the temples of shopping, the fitness centers, the sales talks, the peace and harmony—all of it. If he was hoping for relief or release, nothing of the sort came. The air remained dull, and the rain that had been threatening all day finally came down from the sky, turning the day so dark and oppressive it seemed as though the world were about to end.

At the traffic light Tonio stared at the circle of red that seemed to hang from the sky. When he narrowed his eyes, the red blurred into the gray of the sky, boring into his vision and his body as the wind whipped the rain through the car's open window. Tonio felt the cold, sharp bite of the rain lashing into his face, his arms, his brain. He wished for the end, and he waited and waited, but the end didn't come.

As if from a vast distance, he heard the angry blare of a horn from the car behind him. The light had long since changed to green, but he was glued to the spot, nailed in place. *Assholes,* he thought. *You're all assholes. Up yours!*

And he thought of Rasmus again and the constant grin he used to keep the world at bay. He thought of the hospital and the ranks of the sick who lay there, some of them close to death. He wanted to—needed to—get away to another life. He thought of the puke, the pus, the succession of running sores.

Behind him horns blared, lights flashed—rage, irritation—new, different sores. He flung open the car door, leapt out, and gave them all the middle finger. He spun around and yelled, "Shoot me; why don't you just shoot me?" Then he ran off across the junction, arm and finger still aloft, while brakes squealed and horns blared. The car stood abandoned at the light, its door still open—a nuisance, a lump in the throat, a stomach ulcer.

He saw a sign for the U-Bahn and stumbled toward it and glided down the escalator into its cathedrals of silence. He boarded a train, and the strange silence that reigned there calmed him.

He'd once seen a young man take a running leap into the rumbling path of a train, the darkness of the rails. As the young man vanished, Tonio thought of blood, of spilled brains, of pulped flesh, and turned away, leaving behind a knot of passengers who suddenly seemed united in their horror, their screaming, their gawking.

"Retards," he had muttered. "Fucking retards!"

There's no getting away from it, he thought as he got off the U-Bahn and lost himself in the crowds, with their umbrellas and dark-colored hooded jackets. *There's no getting away from this town, it craps out its viscous, sticky slime into your brain, then releases you, but only a little; you jump like from a trampoline, flung into the air, and it pulls you back and starts the shit all over again.*

• • •

"What's up with you? I thought you drove?" asked Kristin when he arrived home dripping wet. "What's the matter?"

"Nothing," he said. "Why should there be? Don't bug me."

He went to the bathroom and lay down in the tub. As much as he wanted to, he couldn't switch off.

Shit, he thought. *Shit, I'm losing control.* It was all getting too close, eating into him—the hospital, his ward, the cancer cases, the half dead. Their eyes were already misted over with visions of the next world, the existence of which he seriously doubted.

But he couldn't tell them that, and when they spoke of going over to the other side, entering a new life—be it white, red, or yellow, whatever kind of world they envisioned—and reached out for his hand in search of his affirmation of their hopes, he sometimes thought he would die himself of despair and shame. He had absolutely none of that damned hope.

There were no lines anymore. He felt it. Everything penetrated his thoughts, his feelings. He wasn't even free at home. There was no hope of washing it away in his bathtub or in his washing machine. Later, he knew, the images would seep into his sleep, his dreams. Like spiders, they would spread their webs, and he would finally be caught, a sticky package of prey, a chunk of meat that they would suck dry. Once he was spent, they'd spit him out and head off in search of new victims.

That was how it was. A slow suffocation. Burnout. The exhaustion, the vague fear burrowed into him, coming at him in constant waves, breaking over him and making him tired and lethargic. The waves robbed him of his breath and blocked his thoughts.

He shuddered and noticed that the water had grown cold. Kristin stuck her head around the doorway.

"Are you hungry?"

He nodded, wondering at her placatory voice and her kindness despite the way he'd snubbed her earlier. When he came out of the bathroom, she had already begun cooking.

"Did you pick up the letter?"

He was curt. "You ask me that every day. What do you care?"

She looked up, brushing a lock of hair from her brow with the back of her hand. "The card states that it's a notary's letter. That means it's important. Who knows, maybe it's an inheritance."

He barked out a brief laugh. "Me? An inheritance? You'd like that, wouldn't you?"

She threw the knife on the table and turned on him, eyes blazing. "You know what? I don't have to take that kind of thing from you. It's my area of expertise, in case you've forgotten. I know that if it's a lawyer's letter it won't be just a parking ticket."

"OK, OK," he replied in a soothing tone. "It'll be fine."

"Go and pick it up," she said sharply. "You've got fifteen minutes until they close."

"OK, fine." He sighed. "If it makes you happy. Will you lend me your car?"

She asked no questions, merely got her keys from her purse and threw them over to him.

When he returned, the letter in hand, she had set the table. He smelled fresh pasta, salad, and seasoning, and felt his stomach tighten with hunger.

"Open it," Kristin said.

He opened it, and there it was in black and white: He'd had a grandfather in a town on the Danube, two hours' drive to the south. He'd died and there was a will to be read. Tonio's presence was required.

Tonio and Kristin stared at one another.

"You do have an inheritance," she said. "I knew it!" She shook her head in amazement and laughed. "When? When's the will going to be read?"

He looked and got a shock. "In three days. Only three days!" She shook her head again.

"Because you took so long to pick it up," she said. "Idiot! Idiot!"

They eventually calmed down a little, convincing themselves that he would be left a few books or some old records and that would be the end of it. They finally ate the pasta, which had gone cold, and over a glass of wine, she asked about this grandfather. Tonio knew nothing. His grandfather had never been there for him, and why would he when there was no father?

Later, he slept with Kristin, or rather tried to. Somehow it just didn't happen—too much wine, too many thoughts.

"Shit," he said and rolled off her. What a load of crap.

"Hey," Kristin said, stroking his back. "It happens."

He shook her off roughly, then stood and opened the door to the terrace. It was still raining.

"What's up now?" Kristin asked impatiently, and he suddenly knew she would leave him. If not today, then tomorrow or the next day. Soon, in any case.

"Nothing," he said. "Doesn't matter. Leave me alone. Don't keep asking me about things that don't concern you."

"What?" This time she was seriously shocked. "How messed up are you? And how drunk?"

She jumped up, pulled on a shirt, slipped into her jeans, and ran from the room.

Tomorrow then, he thought and made a bet with himself, wagering a bottle of deadly absinthe. He imagined the persistent sharp taste the drink would leave on his tongue and thought the mark Kristin left behind on his life wouldn't run anywhere near that deep.

He went back to bed and waited for his mind to still, but it didn't. There was not a trace of stillness.

Kristin was banging around outside the room. *What the hell is she doing?* he wondered impatiently, longing for a drink to shoot through his body. The banging of the front door shot through him instead. *Ah*, he thought, *today. So I've lost my bet. A pity about the absinthe.*

*   *   *

In the morning he found her key in the kitchen with a note asking him to pack up the rest of her things and leave them outside the door.

Nothing else.

He went into the bedroom and opened the wardrobe, his eyes gliding over the few clothes that hung on hooks and lay on the shelves in there. Then he took a large shopping bag, threw all her belongings into it, and put it outside the front door. There it could stay until Kristin came to fetch it. Then at last it would be final.

A brief guest appearance, he thought, *only six months. The intervals are getting shorter.* He was surprised to feel a slight hint of regret. *Alone again,* he thought. *No one waiting for me when I come home, no smell of morning coffee, no fresh bread.*

He shrugged, picked up the wine bottle that was still on the table from last night's dinner, and poured the last drop down his throat, instead of coffee. It tasted lousy, and he pulled a face, but it suited the emptiness he was feeling and the fact that Kristin had left.

Oh well, he thought, *there's always Degenhard.* She would always take him back; her love was big and hopeless, and life didn't always throw up a beautiful woman around every corner.

*   *   *

The sky was scrubbed clean after the night's lingering storms, and Tonio was dazzled, closing his eyes as he stepped out onto the street. He looked around for his car, and then he remembered.

He closed his eyes again, balled his fists, and swore. It was the last straw! He'd be late again. The head nurse would bawl him out again, and Rasmus . . . The car had probably been towed to some godforsaken corner on the edge of this godforsaken town. Hassle, nothing but hassle.

He began to run. He was sweating, and he felt the moisture in the air clinging to his skin in a sticky film. He stopped suddenly. In front of him was the hospital. The glazed entrance doors, the elevator on the left. Oncology on the seventh floor, where Rasmus waited with his eternal death-defying grin—even though death could not be defied—along with Frau Beurer, who would maybe miss Tonio although she did not have long left to live, and the little girl who had been brought in the day before, with her blue eyes and thin, spindly arms.

Tonio took a last glance at the entrance, at the revolving door spinning and spewing out a small crowd of people who quickly dispersed in various directions.

Here goes, he thought and tried to start walking again, but it didn't work. It was as though his feet were stuck to the ground. *I'm stuck,* he thought and wondered at the fact that this didn't surprise him. *There's no going on, not in this direction.*

He stood there for a short while longer, then turned on his heel and retraced his steps back to where he had come from, back to his apartment. He locked the door, threw some more clothes into a bag—this time his own—along with a toothbrush, a comb, tissues, and on top of them all, the letter. Then he left. He stepped onto the street. Heading for the rail station. Heading to a new life.

Let them tow away his car. Let them curse him at the hospital because someone would have to cover his work. Let Kristin come to the apartment door sobbing and full of regret. None of it meant anything anymore. He left. To a new life. He was heading south to whatever awaited him—records, books, a fancy pen, whatever. Another life, come what may. It was the moment that always came, sooner or later. All it required was a little courage.

As the train drew away, Tonio stood by a window that couldn't be opened and stared out at the trees rushing past like flapping sheets.

• • • •

He settled into a cheap hotel by the station and explored the town for two whole days. He spent hours walking along the Danube.

On the third day he went to the address stated in the letter. When he entered the office, there was no one else there but the lawyer and his secretary. He was stunned. Everything had been left to him; there was no one else. He was the sole heir. He was stunned. Tonio was given a key to an apartment and a savings book with money—not a great deal, but enough to live on for a while if he was careful.

"All the best," the lawyer said as he shook his hand. "Enjoy it!"

"Yes," said Tonio. "I will!"

He left with an incredible feeling in his gut that would stay with him for the next few days. It felt like the hint of a smile, peace, the calm before the storm.

He got directions to the apartment and entered the building. It was an old building in an old residential area imbued with the stuffy atmosphere of its residents, who resembled the patients Tonio had until recently cared for day after day. He unlocked the door to the apartment, still stunned by what was happening to him, and closed the door behind him. He leaned against it and looked around a tiny dark corridor that stank of stale sweat and cat piss. Once his eyes had grown accustomed to the darkness, he carefully felt his way to the other rooms—kitchen, bathroom, living room, bedroom. It was crammed with furniture—cupboards and dressers all stuffed with things, essential and nonessential alike. The abundance took his breath away.

He sat down on the sofa, closed his eyes, took a deep breath, and wondered at his situation. For the fifth time he took out the letter the lawyer had given him, the letter from a grandfather to his grandson. A grandfather he had never seen or even known about. He gave the few lines another reading, understanding as little as he had the four previous times.

Eventually he began to search the apartment. He found things. Photos. Letters. Copies of police reports, translated from Greek into German, and his grandfather's meticulous notes recording the events, each day as it happened, with a precision that bordered on obsession, from the report of the death to the transportation of the body and subsequent burial.

A little later Tonio went back to the hotel, checked out, and moved into the apartment.

•   •   •

The days passed, a week and then two. The summer ran its course but still held a clear intensity. As Tonio wandered through the neighborhood, people began to greet him. He returned their greetings.

He began to clear out the apartment, slowly but surely, beginning with the clothes and the shoes. Getting rid, rid, rid. Underwear, dusty curtains, newspapers, books, moldy food, ancient toiletries. He smashed up furniture and household appliances and disposed of them in the bulk waste facility, then bought cleaning supplies and scrubbed floors, windows, walls, tiles.

He hardly kept anything. Just a mattress on the floor, the kitchen cupboards, the table, a chair, the record player, and a few records. The emptier the apartment became, the more freely it seemed to breathe.

He found little time to eat, fetching a pizza from the corner stand, snacking on bread, drinking water. The world shrank right down and became a tiny island that fit effortlessly into the apartment. *Finding my way back to health by following the footsteps of a grandfather,* he thought derisively.

When everything was cleared out and Tonio had finally gained a sense of calm inside his head, he retreated to the mattress and stared into the eyes of the two men he'd known nothing about.

He still hadn't given them their names. They were nameless, fixed to the wall with rough tacks, clearly visible from his mattress, looking at him with their dark eyes. He gradually began to feel them.

The younger one, his father, dead long before his grandfather, who'd spent half his life without his son—no, Tonio calculated, longer than half his life.

He began to talk to the father, to tell him about the hospital, about Rasmus, about Kristin, about his mother, who lived way up north and whom he hardly ever saw, perhaps once a year if something cropped up.

More days passed, and eventually he pinned up the women, placing them on either side of his father. He didn't give them their names either. *Later,* he thought, *perhaps later.* The violins howled from his grandfather's record player, wailing like ghosts, scratchy and much too slow. Upstairs, the neighbor banged on the floor with a broom because the music was too loud and it was three o'clock in the morning.

Then there were the letters. Love letters. *Florid,* he thought at first, *florid and dripping with platitudes.* But the more he read them, the more beautiful he found them, losing himself in the words again and again. He never wondered how the letters had come to be in his grandfather's possession, his and hers—they were as they were, as it should be.

... *dear hanna* ... *dear tonio* ...

That was the way their conversations always began, their dialogue intertwined like grasping fingers.

. . . *dear tonio . . .* she wrote. The days were empty. She was waiting for him, her beloved, with every fiber of her being, wherever he was, whatever he was doing. She was longing for him, she missed him as soon as he left the room. His body was her pitcher, her jug, her soul had found its place in him as had her heart. Without him she was a *small soft thing* that fell apart, unraveled . . .

He wrote back. . . . *dear hanna . . .*

The days were empty. He was waiting for her, his beloved. With every fiber of his being. Wherever she was. Whatever she was doing. He was longing for her. He missed her. He had always missed her. All his life. Always. As soon as she left the room. Her body was his pitcher, his jug. His soul had found its place in her and his heart had finally awoken. He fell apart without her. He unraveled without her. It was as if he had never lived before. *As if I'd never lived before . . .*

Crazy, the younger Tonio thought. *You were both completely crazy.* He wondered how it must have felt and realized that he had never experienced such depth of feeling. It must have been . . . incomparable. The violins on the record player penetrated to his marrow, like plaintive summer days. . . . *dear hanna . . .*

Tonio ran his fingers over her face—her radiant, young face framed in red hair—then over the other face: Gertrud. He wondered what his father had been to her, what role she had played for him and how remarkable it was that all these events had come so late into his own life.

A notion began to grow in Tonio, a desire to know more—to know everything. He had to know. The letters were the key, a key that he would send on once again.

It was easy to find their addresses. Gertrud still lived in the same town, and Hanna had not changed her name. He sent one of the love letters to Hanna. Then he approached Gertrud as she walked home.

He noted from her shocked reaction that the trail was still hot. She tried to shake him off, but he refused to give in and began to spy on her, to follow her. He sat in the café opposite her pottery shop. When she arrived at nine to open up, he was sitting there over his first coffee, looking over at her as she set up the stand on which she hung mugs and jewelry. The weather was still good, and she kept a table outside the door to work, creating little figurines and beads. It was a clever tactic, he thought, a good way of attracting customers.

It worked. Tourists stopped to talk to her and look at her wares. She explained what she was doing—smiling, friendly, cheerful—and they often went away with pottery fresh from the kiln.

Tonio didn't like it when people stopped to shop. They cut off his view of her. He wanted to see her clearly. He paid his bill and looked for a better position, daring to get closer. He pretended to browse the newspapers and magazines at the newsstand, hung around on the corner smoking a cigarette, all the time acting as if it were all coincidence, as if they were all completely normal moments of his life. Acting as if it were not as though time had stood still, as though everything was starting anew.

He wanted to watch Gertrud brush her brown hair from her face, watch her pin it up so it didn't get in her way as she worked. He wanted to watch her push her hands into the cool clay, kneading it and shaping it. He liked the way her face revealed her concentration and the way the clay left traces on her arms, her T-shirt, and her jeans, sometimes even her face when she distractedly reached with a clay-covered hand to brush away the lock of hair that kept falling over her brow.

He came again the next day.

The waitress, a good-looking woman around fifty, was pleased to see him. "You must really like us, you were here only yesterday!"

"Yes," he replied with a smile. "I'm visiting a friend."

He glanced across the street, and she followed his gaze.

"Oh," she said. "Gertrud."

"Yes, Gertrud."

She raised her eyebrows, let out an "Aha!," and left him in peace.

Once he had drunk his coffee and paid, he crossed the street and approached her. Gertrud looked up as his shadow fell on her, and she stiffened a little.

"What do you want?" she asked brusquely. "There's no sense in this."

"Talk to me," he said. "Tell me what happened."

She sat still for a moment, her eyes closed. "It's not your fault, but your father was an asshole. If that's what you came to find out, you know now."

"Why?" he asked.

She shook her head. "I can't say any more. I don't want to. It was so long ago. You're churning everything up again."

He sensed she was softening. And he probed deeper. "Because he loved Hanna? And not you? I found letters. I've sent one to Hanna."

She raised her face slowly and looked at him with empty eyes.

"Go," she said. "Please stop bothering me."

She said it in such a way that he knew he had no choice. So he went. She stayed sitting there, doing nothing, feeling nothing, thinking nothing. She had hoped so much that . . . but it would have been far too much, tempting fate, too much . . . No one deserved that, least of all her.

"She'll come," she whispered. "So you're going to come, Hanna."

The café owner stood on the other side of the street, watching.

. . .

There was a storm that night. Lightning flashed across the sky, splitting it open.

43

Gertrud hunched on her bed, staring at the photos that kept appearing out of the darkness in the harsh light of the lightning flashes. They had been children, then teenagers, and then young women. Then life had separated them.

I'll start counting, she thought, *and if it doesn't strike this house within fifty seconds, then Tonio's son will have provoked a storm and nothing will ever be the same again.*

She took Tonio's photo in her hand and looked into his face, the face that had suddenly come back into her life with an inevitability that took her breath away. Lightning did not strike the house. She nodded and murmured softly to herself, "Then that's how it's going to be."

And that was how it was.

7

I received the letter . . . *dear hanna* . . .

Everything comes to an end. You shut it away in a dark corner in your heart. You don't interfere with it. Perhaps it darkens the soul, but that's life.

You don't interfere with it. No.

But now, since I received that letter, I've had the feeling that the world is awakening. The old world that I'd shut away—the world that had nothing to do with me anymore—it's awakening. The ghosts . . . the black birds . . . The stories like grains of sand trickled through my fingers, then scattered and vanished.

But now it's all come back.

And the birds fly, swooping upward. I hear their wings beating, I feel the rush of air. I've felt them since I received the letter. They want to fly. Now. Yes.

. . . *dear hanna* . . .

So I was. Yes.

8

"My wife has vanished," the man said.

He was trying to keep the anxiety out of his voice, but Felix Herz heard it all the same. He leaned forward in his chair and stirred his coffee. He watched as his colleague, Hansen from Missing Persons, tried to calm the visitor.

"Why don't you sit down?" Hansen said. "Would you like a cup of coffee?"

The man nodded, sat, and gratefully accepted the coffee placed before him.

"So," Hansen said, "let's begin at the beginning, Herr . . ."

"Belitz," the man said. "Jonas Belitz."

"Well, then, Herr Belitz, what has happened, exactly?"

Belitz took a drink of his coffee and tried to gather his thoughts. "We actually live in France, my wife and I, but she's originally from this town. She spent half her life here." He fell silent, as if he'd lost the thread, but then continued. "Something must have happened about two weeks ago—I don't know what—but she changed very suddenly."

"Changed in what way?"

Belitz hesitated and briefly closed his eyes as if looking inside himself. "I don't know how to put it. It was as if she was afraid of something.

Then last Tuesday she told me she wanted to come here. She had something to sort out."

"What was it?"

"She didn't say. She only told me the name of the hotel where she would be staying. It was enough for me. My wife travels a lot with her work, so it's nothing unusual."

"Then why are you so worried?"

"Well, at first we spoke on the phone every day, or sent texts or e-mails, as we always do when one of us is away. But she's not been in touch for two days now, and I can't get hold of her. Not on her cell phone, not over the Internet, and not at the Babenberger, the hotel. When I called and asked about her, they told me she checked out two days ago. That's why I've come here."

"But you said your wife was from around here. She's probably gone to visit relatives or friends, decided to stay with them, and simply forgotten to tell you."

Jonas Belitz shook his head vehemently. "No, she would have told me. We're very careful about things like that."

"Hm . . ." Hansen tapped his pen on the sheet of paper that lay before him.

Peter Hansen, chief inspector of the Missing Persons department, had been a good friend of Felix Herz's for many years, often dropping in to his office for a coffee.

"But you understand none of this necessarily means anything?" said Hansen.

"But it does." Belitz was agitated. "I'm sure it means something! Listen to me, it's very unusual for Hanna not to tell me where she's going! We're in touch every single day! Please, I'm asking you, take me seriously!"

"Of course we are," Hansen said in a soothing voice. "All I meant was that we quite often find that people in these cases withdraw a little and then reappear after a few days. You really shouldn't worry too much at this stage. Do you have a photo of your wife with you?"

Belitz nodded and drew his wallet from his coat. He took out a photo and handed it across the table.

"Oh," Hansen said in surprise when he looked at the picture. "Rather a . . . young woman!" He cleared his throat as he passed the photo over to Herz. "I'm sorry, I didn't mean to . . ."

"No." Belitz shook his head. "You're quite right. Some people might wonder what such a young woman is doing with an old man like me."

He smiled slightly and then fell silent. Felix studied the photo. The woman was in her early to midforties, with an open, intelligent face, light skin, short red hair, and radiant blue eyes. The man sitting opposite him at the table was at least twenty years older than she was, gray haired, tall, gaunt but elegant.

Felix frowned. "She looks familiar to me somehow."

"Hanna Umlauf," the visitor said, raising his head. "The photographer. The photo artist."

"Oh yes. That's right. I saw some photos of hers recently in the paper. She takes really striking pictures."

A smiled flashed across Belitz's face, along with a slight blush of pride, a tremor of happiness that momentarily lightened his fear. Felix was touched. Like a father, he thought, who was proud of his daughter. Or in this case, his wife, who was young enough to be his daughter.

Felix cleared his throat. "Could it be, perhaps, that she . . . How can I put it? You said yourself that your wife travels a lot. That means meeting a lot of people, including other men. Maybe—"

"No!" Belitz's voice was resolute and sharp, and for a brief moment Felix found him unlikeable. "No, I'd know. And if that were the case, there'd be no need for her to *disappear*. She could simply *go*."

"All right," said Hansen. "When was the last time you spoke to her?"

9

She looked at the chrysanthemums—orange, yellow, red—and touched the petals. There were still a few hours to go—a few hours' grace. Still a few hours until life would begin to leak from her with every drop of blood that flowed from her veins, staining the floor of her kitchen.

She knew nothing. Had no idea. How could she? She looked at the chrysanthemums—orange, red, a couple of yellow ones. She loved chrysanthemums, loved their warm, vibrant colors. Those in her garden were particularly beautiful, lit up by the mild freshness of the day, lit up by Moritz's warmth, his bright child's voice when he said "Mama."

"Will you be here when I come home tomorrow, Mama?"

"Of course, darling. I always am."

Then his smile, his hug, his rough child's lips on hers. He was out through the door.

Gertrud smiled, and her eyes moved again to the chrysanthemums and the basket beneath the damson tree laden with juicy blue-purple fruit. Suddenly, she felt a tightening in her throat. She looked up, paused, listened . . . it was as if she sensed . . . as if she saw. Fleeting images, like lightning flashes: an onion falling from the table, deep red jelly, a biting pain, tears, release, death.

She shook her head rapidly. *No,* she thought. *It's summer, still summer.*

But the images persisted in her head, crept into her heart. She thought of Christian, of her work, of the children. She stayed for a long while on the terrace, fending off the images, defending herself. But the clock was ticking. It had all begun and would all come to an end. Self-defense would be pointless.

There were only a few hours. She looked out over her garden. She loved chrysanthemums and asters, and in spring, the tulips and the lilacs. She was less fond of roses. Roses distorted reality, roses pretended and put on a show, and when the leaves fell, they fell immediately, decisive and certain.

She looked out over her garden and resigned herself to the coolness of the change, accepted it like a quiet, constant blow to the breast. She looked into the transparent sun, thought of rain, of drizzle in a park. She listened to the music drifting out of the open living room door—Norah Jones, Sinéad O'Connor, Tracy Chapman. She saw the car turn into the drive.

Later, she would rinse the blade and lay it down next to the sink. Later still, it would fall with a quiet clink beside her on the floor. She was already barred from the world of the living, from those who were able to maintain her happiness, who held it in their hands, fiercely determined not to let it go.

10

Franza stood in the garden of her house, which, if everything went according to plan, would not be hers for much longer.

She looked around. It was all growing wild after nine months without care or nurturing. It was as if the garden knew there was no longer anyone here who wanted anything from it.

Everything had gotten a little strange. Franza could feel it as she walked across the overgrown lawn, as she ran her fingers over the leaves of the rose bushes.

She was thinking about how she and Max had finally made the irrevocable decision to sell. It had been during those days the previous winter when it had become ever clearer that Ben was not going to return, that he would stay in Berlin.

After Marie's death, she and Max had fetched him home. They'd traveled to the capital and brought their son back to his childhood home, and the thing she had hoped so fervently for, but hadn't truly expected, had happened. The house gave them sanctuary and allowed them to grieve. They were able to support one another in safety. While Ben grieved for Marie, his first great love, who had been murdered, Max and Franza grieved once again for themselves and their love, which had not worked out. They grieved for the house they would lose, for the world that had not turned out the way they had dreamed in their youth, and for the fact that Ben had been forced to learn this at such a young age.

Ben eventually packed his things and returned to Berlin, to the city in which he had hoped to settle with Marie.

"Are you sure?" Franza had asked him on the day he was due to leave, standing on the station platform as they waited for the train to arrive. She knew what his answer would be before he opened his mouth. The answer was clear; there was no doubt.

Long after the train had departed, she was still standing on the platform.

"We didn't do everything wrong," Max had said, hesitantly putting an arm around her and encouraging her to lean on him.

"No," she said. "Not everything. Coffee?"

She raised her head and looked at her husband, who had not been her husband for some time now. He nodded with a smile.

"Coffee. Yes, of course. Coffee. And cake."

"No. No cake. Look at me."

He sighed, throwing a covert glance at her hips and realizing that he still felt a twinge of longing for her, for her hips that had always been so wonderfully soft, offering him security that he still missed every now and then.

They drove home, and he made the coffee while she got out fresh-baked cookies, a new recipe that had not turned out quite to her satisfaction.

Then they had sat on the couch, contemplating the dusk slowly gathering in the garden, and talked about Ben as a baby, as a small child, as a teenager, and about how he'd had to learn about grieving. She'd smiled and laughed over the memories, felt renewed anger and sadness, and was finally calm.

She worried about her son, feared for him, but she sensed the strength he had suddenly found in himself. She sensed his courage simply to live his life, without a plan, without a supporting framework. She secretly admired her son's immediate return to his life. It was working. Not entirely without a hitch, but it was working. It made it easier for her to let him move away and to sell the house. Things were going well for him, her Ben.

A car swept up and stopped. High heels clicked on the asphalt. The prospective purchaser had arrived. Franza went to the garden gate to let her in. This young woman with her firm handshake, large mouth, and shining eyes didn't fit in this tired garden or the house beyond it, with its paint flaking off in places. She was too young, too pretty, too sharp.

Her blouse was tight across her breasts in just the right way, her skirt reached to just above the knee, and her stilettos were high and pointed and no longer clicked but sank deep into the lawn, which didn't seem to bother her.

"Uh-huh," she said, looking around. "So this is the object of desire."

She laughed a little foolishly at her own joke, and Franza forced a small smile so as not to appear impolite.

Since the beginning of the year, Franza had been living in an apartment in town, in a neighborhood close to the river and the wetlands. Two months later, Max had found an apartment four blocks away from her, and they'd put the house up for sale.

At first it had felt like the collapse of an old order, as if years of their lives had simply been wiped out and replaced by a deep pain. She knew Max felt the same, but neither of them admitted it to the other.

The house sale dragged on. It was more difficult than they had anticipated. A constant stream of people came to view it, but they always managed to find something that didn't suit them. The garden was too small or too big, the house too old or too modern. There were too few rooms or too many.

They probably found it too expensive and were seeking to drive the price down with their petty faultfinding.

And now here was another prospective buyer.

"Yes," Franza said. "It is."

She studied the young woman's face, as if to discover what was going on behind it, and noticed the beginnings of a pimple to the right of her top lip, a blackhead blemishing the surface of her skin. It immediately made her feel less old and ugly, and she began to smile.

"Welcome!" She extended her hand. "Are you here on your own? Couldn't your husband spare the time?"

"No," the young woman said apologetically. She looked like an attorney or a banker, at any rate, something to do with finance, with facts and cool objectivity. "He's stuck in a meeting, but he's going to try and get away."

Her gaze swept over the garden, and Franza had to smile. *She's already looking for faults,* she thought, *for something she can use to bargain with.*

"Well," said the banker, "it's a little unkempt, isn't it? Quite a bit of work to do."

She turned and looked at Franza, aggressive, observant, ready to fight for every cent.

"Law firm? Bank?"

The woman frowned in confusion. "I beg your pardon?"

"I was just asking what your profession is," said Franza with a smile, thanking God or whichever power was out there for her composure and calmness, which grew as she aged.

"The former," said the woman in the garden a little sharply, raising her eyebrows and allowing her eyes to glide slowly over Franza, who knew she was not looking her neatest that day.

Franza nodded. *She's probably thinking I'm a frustrated women's libber,* she thought, *and of course that I'm sexually unsatisfied and undisciplined, as I obviously overeat. And of course there's that stain on my shirt, level with my left breast because I was a bit careless when having coffee with Port earlier. Because Port made me spill it, big kid that he is.*

"Don't go trying to drive the price down," she said. "It won't work. Either you want the house or you don't. Either the house wants you or it doesn't. There's no middle ground."

She gave a small smile and enjoyed seeing the young woman's irritation. Franza was sure the woman was thinking she was completely stupid because she was behaving like such a sourpuss and not sucking up to her, something she really should do if she wanted someone to buy this house.

But perhaps, she thought with a small inner sigh, *the house doesn't want to be sold. Perhaps the house simply wants to stay ours.*

Her cell phone rang. The display showed Herz's office number. *Oh dear,* she thought, *not a good sign. Can't I take an afternoon off without people killing each other?*

"I'm sorry," she said. "I'm afraid I'll have to go. Perhaps you could call my husband. He might be able to show you around the house."

She took the call. They had found a body. September 12.

11

Herz's first thought was of Hanna Umlauf. *Maybe her husband was right to worry? Should we have taken him more seriously? Could we have done something—prevented something?*

"What are you brooding about?" Franza asked as she joined him in the car.

"Nothing." Felix smiled and patted her arm. He would tell her about Belitz later. Nothing could be done about it now anyway. "I'm sorry I called you, but I thought you'd want to be there from the start. Sold your house?"

"We didn't finish the showing, but I don't think she was really interested."

He laughed. "I'm sure you managed to put a wrench in the works. Like you usually do."

She gave him a sideways look, eyebrows raised. "Am I that bad?"

"Yes," he said with a sly grin, "that bad."

· · ·

They arrived. With its tree-lined drive and leafy surroundings, the house reminded Franza of her own.

As they opened the front door, Franza sniffed the air. "What's that smell?"

"Damsons," said Arthur, who was waiting for them in the hallway. "A whole load of damson jelly has been made here during the last few days."

"Oh." She nodded. "Where is it?"

Arthur quickly showed them the way. As soon as they entered the room, they felt the stillness they met at every homicide scene.

Franza looked around. The room was bright, spacious, with white kitchen appliances. There was a sideboard with a vast array of jars filled with dark red glistening jelly.

A table stood in the middle of the room, eight chairs placed casually around it, with newspapers, pens, and various items of general clutter at one end of it. Apart from that, it was scattered with a number of dirty dishes, water glasses, wine glasses, two coffee cups, a wooden chopping board with remnants of cheese and cold meats, and a half-finished loaf.

Between the sideboard and the table, the floor was scattered with broken glass. Recently filled jelly jars were now violently smashed, glass shards mingling with the fresh jelly and embedded in the partially congealed mass. There were dark red splashes on the white kitchen surfaces.

Franza's eyes finally came to rest on the woman. Slowly. Carefully. She was lying on the floor in a pool of her own blood. Long brown hair, early to midforties, mouth slightly open as if she still had something to say, but death had gotten there quicker. Light summer clothing, shorts and a T-shirt, tanned skin. In the middle of the blood, touching the woman's arm, lay an onion, as if it had not wanted to leave her on her own, as if it had wanted to be with her to the end, seeing as there was no one else.

"So it isn't her, after all," said Felix quietly. He let out a sigh of relief while wondering why he was relieved—after all, he didn't know this woman or Hanna Umlauf.

"Isn't who?" asked Franza.

"Nothing," said Herz. "Later."

Borger, the coroner, was already there, as were the other members of the forensics team. They nodded to each other.

Franza bent over the woman on the floor and felt the stillness that radiated from her, and as if everyone around her also noticed it, their voices became quieter.

Franza closed her eyes. *Let me feel you,* she thought. *Let me into your heart, only for a moment, and show me what moved you so much it killed you.*

I can't yet, the woman said in Franza's mind, *give me a little time.*

All the time in the world, Franza whispered back into the silence. *I'd give you all the time you need—to eternity, even—but I don't have time . . .*

She rose, smiled a little sadly at Borger, whose features had grown still, and listened for the sound like faint background white noise in the distance. Franza brought the thought to its conclusion: *But I . . . I don't have time . . . so help me . . .*

It was like it always was. A sense of hovering between the heights and the depths, reaching out, feeling, sinking into a stranger's life, a stranger's death.

What was it like? What was it like when you felt the blade of the knife on your skin? When it cut into you? When it slipped smoothly between your ribs and into your heart? As smoothly as a voice whispering into an ear: It's OK. It'll soon be over. Be calm. It's OK.

Then there was a high-pitched tone reaching up to the sky, penetrating the blackness of the night. Then she died. Then she was dead. With a knife in her breast, piercing her heart. With a pain that tore her apart and finally released her into gentle death. Perhaps she was astonished by this remarkable fact—the fact she was dead. Now. So suddenly. So unforeseen. In this place that was intended for life, not for death.

She fell and left her body. Her arm sank to her side, her hand opened, bitter white lines, blood.

Perhaps she felt a vast loneliness, perhaps she froze. Perhaps she still heard the blade as it clattered to the floor, perhaps she heard the sound in the air, then . . . nothing more. Death swallowed all noise, muted it, muffled it, killed it.

"Gertrud Rabinsky," said Arthur, who had already gotten down to work.

Franza abruptly raised her hand. He hesitated, and she took a deep breath and closed her eyes for a couple of seconds before finally turning.

"Now, go on," she said.

"Sorry," said Arthur.

"No problem," she replied.

He began.

"Forty-four years of age, married, an adult daughter with an apartment in town. A young son, who was spending the night with his grandparents, I believe, or with friends. In any case, neither of the children were at home. Her husband found her. I sent him away a little earlier. All he was doing was standing around in complete bewilderment. I'm sure he'll be breaking it gently to his children that their mother . . . you know . . ."

He fell silent.

Well done, Arthur, Franza thought, feeling a pang of tenderness for her young assistant. *You're doing well. Never allow it to leave you completely cold. Protect yourself, but don't be cold.*

She gave him a nod, and he continued. "She had a pottery shop in the town center. Near the cathedral."

"Ah, that's it," Borger said. "Now I know why she seems familiar. I bought some mugs from her. I watched her working and then I bought some mugs. It wasn't long ago. Lovely mugs."

Franza nodded. "Yes, I'm sure." She felt the beginnings of a smile.

A case took on a whole new strangeness if you knew the victim, however fleetingly. If you had met them even briefly when they were still alive, the shield of distance was suddenly removed.

"What have you got to tell us?" Herz was a little less sensitive, not always hearing, or wanting to hear, the subtle undertones. Franza was grateful to him for that. It was a way of building bridges between what was clear and what was indistinct. So often she found that the truth lay somewhere in the middle.

"Stab wounds," Borger replied. "Three. Inflicted with great force. Probably in quick succession. Typical of a crime of passion. People who know each other. Emotions running high. You've got the murder weapon here—a simple kitchen knife, which it looks like someone had been using shortly before to cut sausage and cheese."

He indicated the table, the wooden chopping board, the onion on the floor. "And perhaps onions, too. Not this one, though. I'll be able to give you a more precise picture when I've examined the traces in the puncture wounds." He paused briefly. "The place where she was found is without doubt the crime scene."

Herz smiled. "Thanks, Borger, but can you leave us something to do? Or have you already solved the case?"

"When did it happen?" Franza asked.

Borger tilted his head. "Judging from the degree of rigor mortis and the consistency of the blood, I'd say fourteen, fifteen hours ago."

"During the night, then." She did a quick calculation. "Around one. Around midnight."

Borger nodded. "I can tell you more precisely later."

"Did she try to defend herself?" she asked.

Borger shrugged. "Can't say yet. Apart from the stab wounds there are no immediately obvious injuries."

He picked up one of the dead woman's hands and indicated her nails. "What will I find under here? When I examine her, it's possible I'll find skin particles under the nails indicating a struggle. But I need a little more time."

Franza nodded. "Sure. Of course."

Borger sighed. "So you want it yesterday."

"Correct," she said, a smile escaping her. "I'm so lucky to be surrounded by such exceptionally intelligent men."

They took a quick look around the house, taking care not to get in the way of the forensics officers, who would soon be taking over the house—the crime scene—for themselves. But Franza and Herz were eager to gain some insight, some feeling for the people who lived here, for the dead woman.

It was clear from the house that Gertrud Rabinsky was a woman of taste, with a feel for shape and color, for warmth and light. In the family photos, however, she came across as slightly aloof, reserved, as if the camera were an alien intrusion, something against which she had to defend herself.

Herz picked up a portrait. "OK, we'll take this with us. Now let's go see her parents. They're all together, her husband, her children, and her parents. Arthur, you hold the fort here."

They left the house. Past the damson tree, still laden with overripe fruit. *They'll go rotten now,* Franza thought. *No more jelly, no damson schnapps, no cakes. What a shame.*

She'll have turned up, Felix thought. *Hanna Umlauf will have turned up and is probably safe on her way back to France with her husband.* He wondered whether he should call Hansen and ask him. Sometime next week. There was no hurry.

They drove back toward town, but before reaching it turned off into a valley, at the end of which was the house—no, the villa. That was a more fitting description. Tasteful. Idyllic. From the outside. But no longer so inside.

"Herz." He produced his ID. "Criminal investigation. This is my colleague, Oberwieser."

"It didn't take you long," said the man who opened the door to them. He was somewhere in his midsixties, wearing a shirt and tie. Perhaps he had been pulled away from his office. His face betrayed signs of exhaustion and deep sadness.

"True," Herz said. "That's part of our job."

"Brendler," the man said. "I'm her father. Come through; we're all in here."

They followed him through the house and finally entered a spacious living room. An elderly woman was sitting at the table, leaning on her elbows, shock visible in her features and in her bearing. Once again Franza was amazed at how quickly it all happened, how rapidly tragedy seeped into a person's body, how fast it spread and drained them of all strength.

Moritz, the five-year-old boy, was sitting on a sofa, and a man, evidently his father, was holding him in his arms. Franza guessed he was in his midforties. Dressed in jeans and a T-shirt, blond, glasses, moustache—his features were set as if the pain had not yet fully registered.

"I found her," he said. "I came home and found her. That's all. There's nothing more to say."

"Yes, there is," Herz said. "I'm sure you can tell us more. Just take your time."

Herz turned to Frau Brendler. "Perhaps you could take care of the little boy. He shouldn't hear all this."

"Yes, you're right." The woman stood. "Come on, Moritz, come with me!"

"What about your granddaughter?" Felix asked.

"We've called her," Hans Brendler said. "She's on her way."

They didn't find out a great deal. The evening before she was found, Gertrud's husband had been at a friend's birthday party that lasted until the wee hours. He had done the rounds with his colleagues, had drunk too much, and had gone to his office to sleep for the few remaining hours of the night. Late morning he had gone home, taken a shower, and changed, assuming that Gertrud had gone to her shop. He'd gone to the kitchen to fix a quick snack before driving back into town—and found her lying there.

"It says here you found her around twelve," Franza said, glancing at the notebook Felix was filling with an increasing volume of notes. "But you didn't call the police until half past one. Why leave so long? What were you doing for all that time?"

Christian Rabinsky stared at the floor, his elbows on his knees and his face propped in his hands.

"I don't know," he said flatly, barely audible. "Nothing. I wasn't doing anything. She lay there, not moving. She was really dead. Nothing could have changed that. I just wanted some time alone with her. That's what I did, I spent some time alone with her. Something I'm never going to be able to do again. Or, maybe . . . ?" He raised his head and looked Franza in the eye. "Maybe . . . ?"

"No," she said. "You're right. You're never going to be able to do that again. But nevertheless—"

She broke off. What had he said? She was *really dead*.

He was right. There was nothing that could have changed that. Nothing. Some time alone, him and her. Was there anything wrong with that?

Her attention was caught by a nearby movement, and she turned.

Felix was standing by the wall. The photos hanging there drew him. He'd been driven by curiosity, the instinct that led him through life. He did not know what exactly it was that attracted his attention, but it suddenly seemed as though the pictures began to glow, to wink at him as if they had something to tell him. He held his breath. A redhead. Did he recognize her? A memory. Radiant hair. Young. Could it be? Could it really be? Could it be *her*, her hair shining as if it were a matter of life and death?

"Who is that?" he asked, feeling a tingle, sensing a tension spread through his body.

"Who?"

Brendler's voice was louder than it had been. Felix turned and stared at the man as he slowly approached.

"Who do you mean?"

"This girl here. The girl with the red hair."

"Her? That's Hanna," Brendler said. "Why do you want to know?"

"And the one next to her? Gertrud?"

"Yes," Brendler said quietly and ran his index finger over his daughter's face, slowly, again and again. "That's Gertrud. My daughter."

"Hanna Umlauf? The photographer?"

"Yes." Brendler frowned, and Felix noticed the sudden alertness in his expression, in his voice. "Hanna Umlauf, the photographer. Why do you ask?"

"What's her connection to your family?" asked Herz tensely.

A rueful smile passed across Brendler's face. He turned and looked out of the window, out toward the trees, the garden. Green as far as the eye could see.

"Hanna is like my . . . our second daughter. She grew up here. Together with Gertrud. You could say we have . . . we had two daughters." He was briefly lost in his memories and then turned around, returning to the present. "Lovely days. Yes." Another short pause. "We haven't seen her for years. And now Gertrud's dead. I have to tell her. I must tell Hanna."

"That's going to be difficult right now," said Herz slowly. "Hanna Umlauf has disappeared."

"What?"

For a fraction of a second, Brendler and his son-in-law froze. Franza too. She came to her senses first. "What do you mean Hanna Umlauf has disappeared?"

"Just what I said." Herz's gaze moved between Brendler and his son-in-law to gauge what they were thinking and feeling. "Her husband reported her missing two days ago. I'm not sure of the current state of affairs, but looking at the situation here—"

"Her husband?" Brendler asked tensely. "Jonas? He's here?"

"Yes." Felix nodded. "He's here. So you know Jonas Belitz?"

"Of course I know Jonas Belitz." Brendler's voice sounded gruff and dismissive, but Felix was not put off.

"You do?"

"What do you mean by that?"

"Just tell me."

"There's nothing to tell. We grew up together, he was my best friend, until . . ." He hesitated, turned away.

"Go on."

Brendler turned back to Felix in agitation. "You're beginning to get on my nerves, you know that? What on earth does it have to do with anything? My daughter's been murdered, Hanna's disappeared, and you're asking me about a man I haven't seen for at least twenty years."

Felix smiled a little complacently. "Well, you could almost say he's your . . . son-in-law, so I think he's got everything to do with it."

Brendler calmed himself and sat back down. He thought for a moment. "Yes," he said wearily, "you would see it like that."

"So?"

"What would you say if your daughter came to you one day and told you she was going to marry your best friend, who is twenty-five years older than she is?"

Felix raised his eyebrows and took a deep breath. "Well," he said.

"Exactly," said Brendler. "And after that they didn't come to see us anymore."

Herz nodded. "OK, I think that's enough for now. We'll make enquiries. Missing persons cases aren't usually our area, but I'd say this is rather a remarkable coincidence." He turned to Franza. "I think we've got enough here for now."

As they were leaving, they opened the front door to find Lilli standing there. Franza recognized her on the spot.

"Lilli," she said in astonishment. "Lilli!"

What a surprise! The little kleptomaniac from the shopping mall was Gertrud's daughter.

"Yes," Lilli said. "Yes." She burst into tears. "I'd hoped that you . . . I really hoped!"

"Shhhh," Franza said as she hugged Lilli. "It's all right. It's all right." Even as she said it, she thought what a stupid phrase it was.

Frau Brendler came to the door and drew Lilli to her. "There, there, little one, come to me! Let's go in."

"Yes," said Lilli, wiping away her tears. More flowed in their place. Her grandmother drew her into the house and closed the door.

"What was that about?" asked Herz.

Franza waved an arm. "Nothing . . . nothing. We know each other, that's all. Ran into her by chance a few days ago. She went to school with Ben." She thought for a few seconds. "And this Hanna? What's going on with her?"

As they drove back into town, he told her about the strange coincidence that had found him stopping by Hansen's office when Hanna Umlauf's husband had come to report her disappearance.

"There's no such thing as coincidence," said Franza, giving Herz a friendly pat on the shoulder. "What's another word for it? Happenstance. Things happen for a reason."

And things were beginning to happen. The tingling had begun.

12

The black birds fly over the fields for the first time this year.

Shadows in the gray morning light. Cries.

Every morning I compare the pictures—the pictures on the screen of my laptop with the pictures in my head. Until I finally feel the flight of the birds in my head. In my body, too, but more in my head. And then I can feel myself dissolving, becoming black, growing feathers, raising myself up into the endless expanse of the sky.

I continue taking photos. I have my subject now. The ravens. When they make their early-autumn flights in black flocks above my head, cawing and noisy, I photograph the expanse of the sky with the ravens as the centerpiece, circling, swerving, turning suddenly and changing direction.

I watch them with all the yearning in my head and my veins, and when their cries grow quieter and fade into the yellow-gray of the morning sky, I close my eyes and send myself after them, falling into the past.

All those years we hadn't seen each other. Such a long time. I'm there, she's here. We were sisters. As good as. But in fact . . .

I didn't know then. Never. Only now. I didn't know she hated me at least as much as she loved me. I didn't know that she suffered so much because of me.

Before, before Tonio, long before. I didn't know that I tore her life apart, into the time before me and the time after me, and she had to get back at me when she had the chance.

I didn't know that I was really never her sister. Life is compulsion. And rarely fair. But don't we all know that?

The birds—at least the birds are beautiful.

13

No, she had not reappeared. Yes, she was still missing. A call to Peter Hansen at Missing Persons clarified that. Her husband had stopped by his office again the previous morning and they had opened a file. The wheels were set in motion, and now things were really moving.

"Is she the murderer?" Franza asked over a coffee in the office. "Or another victim?"

"Let's hope neither." Felix shoved the last bite of cookie into his mouth. They may not have had it down in black and white, only over the phone, but either way it was just as serious.

"I'll see you tomorrow." Franza picked up her purse and stood. "There's nothing more we can do today."

She took the photo that Hansen had quickly faxed over and studied the narrow face. It reminded her that she had wished for red hair herself when she was little. Not because she had found it particularly attractive at the time. No—because it would have been different. Made her stand out from the crowd. A counterpoint to the other girls.

The other photo. Gertrud. Also attractive, but in a different way. More reserved.

"When do you start to feel something like death approaching?" Franza stared at Gertrud's face, into her brown eyes. "What do you think, Felix? Do you think you start to feel it's time to go?"

He laid a hand on her shoulder, thinking it was typical of the questions she felt the need to ask.

"I don't know any more than you do," he said. "It's not something you get to practice."

No, it was not something you could practice: departing, dying. It was always new to those who did it, and the last thing they experienced. You could practice anything, all the things in the world, but not this.

"You're right, smart guy," Franza said with a smile. She looked at the photos again. "We need their histories. What else links them."

"We do," Herz said. "Herr and Frau Brendler will have to tell us more."

They left the office. It was a mild September evening toward the end of the summer holidays. A small boy and a teenage girl had lost their mother. Two men were missing their wives. And yet . . . it was still a mild September evening.

It never ceased to amaze Franza that death never changed anything. That the days and the evenings were exactly as they had been before. Mild or stormy, cold or hot, rainy or sunny. She looked up at the sky, trying to see a slight darkening, a clouding over, even fleetingly—but there was nothing.

A young couple passed by on the other side of the street, their heads leaned in together.

"It could be Marlene," Felix murmured, looking at them a little too eagerly and thinking of his eldest, about whom he knew so little.

"Yes," said Franza. "She's grown so pretty, your Lena. She takes after her mother." She parried Felix's raised eyebrows with a smile.

She thought of Ben, who had recently started writing song lyrics in the firm belief that he was going to make a career of it. Franza saw it as therapy for him and thanked God for Max's lucrative profession and his patients' perennial tooth decay.

The pair across the street were now kissing passionately. Franza and Felix watched them with a mixture of amusement and embarrassment. Franza thought about the early days of her relationship with Port. One summer's day, they had met in town and it began to rain in buckets. They ran to the porch of a church, the air hot and close, their wet clothes flapping, and they'd looked into each other's eyes, fallen into each other's arms, and begun to kiss. As their passion reached its giddy heights, a group of teenagers strolled past with wolf whistles and wisecracks. Franza panicked. What if Ben had been among them and had seen her like that? In shock, she buried her face in Port's shoulder, pressing herself against him as if to hide. She had sent up a quick prayer to heaven—not inappropriate, given their location.

She sighed and reached into her purse for a packet of cigarettes that she had bought three days ago and that was now half-empty. She lit up.

"Since when did you start smoking again? You'd stopped for so long. Three years, wasn't it?" Felix shook his head in surprise.

"I don't smoke," Franza said. "Only now and then. And only a little."

As she drew in the smoke, she imagined with a sigh how her lungs would be getting a little blacker.

"Since when?"

She shrugged. "Dunno."

"Give me one," he said. They smoked together in the twilight, puffing away in contented silence.

．　．　．

She knew. She knew very well by now. Since that night two weeks ago, when she realized.

She knew now that Max was not as mellow as he'd appeared for the last two years. On the contrary, he was jealous as a cat, which didn't suit him. She'd known since that night two weeks ago: he was a lover who wanted her back in his arms, by his fireside, in his bed.

She'd known since she and Port had run into him and Max had put away a couple too many. She'd gone to meet Port after a performance at the theater. As usual, he'd wanted to stop at the bar around the corner—a meeting place for him and his fellow thespians. Who would have expected Max to be there?

But there he was, for whatever reason. He had a twenty-five-year-old on his arm and a glass of beer in his hand. From his eyes, Franza knew immediately it was not his first. He noticed Franza as soon as she opened the door, and, beaming at her a little drunkenly, he made his way toward her.

Shit, she thought. She stopped short and felt Port stumble into her, then throw his arms around her and lay his head on her shoulder. *Shit,* she thought again, frowning and wondering what Max was doing there. Until now they'd always respected one another's territory.

"Franza!" Max said in honeyed tones. "My beloved, deserting Franza! Come to me, let's go home!"

He embraced her and laid his head on her other shoulder. Port looked up at Max in surprise and said, "What the hell . . . ?" as they stared into each other's eyes.

This was the first meeting of Franza's husband and Franza's boyfriend—and she was stuck between them like a piece of cheese in a sandwich, unable to move backward or forward. She was speechless and helpless—but only for a second. She extricated herself, grabbed hold of Max, and dragged him out the door. Port followed them.

"Is this . . . ?" he asked in amazement.

"Yes, this is . . ." Franza said.

"Does he always booze like this?" asked Port.

"No," said Franza. "No, he doesn't always booze. In fact he never does! I don't know what's gotten into him!"

"You!" Max snarled. "You've gotten into him, sweetheart! But sadly someone else has now gotten into *you*! Him! Him!"

And he lunged for Port, banging his hand against his chest, once, twice. Until Franza took hold of him, and pressed him against the wall.

"Ow," he said. "Ouch! You're hurting me!"

"Do I care?" she gasped, but loosened her grip slightly. "You're being such an idiot!"

"Let him go," said Port, getting hold of himself after Max's sudden onslaught. "Put him in a taxi and come back in. I'm hungry!"

You're an idiot, too, thought Franza. *You're a little egotistical idiot who thinks only of himself.*

"I'll take him home," she said, caressing Port's cheek affectionately. "I can't leave him to his own devices in this state. You understand, don't you?"

"Oh." Port was clearly affronted. "What about me? So you can leave me to my own devices, can you? No, I don't understand!"

"What a shame," she said, a slight smile twitching at her lips. "I really thought you were a big, grown-up boy."

She thought once again, *Yes, you're an idiot, too. But a sweet one.*

"Huh," said Port, now edgy and huffy. "How big and grown up is he?" He pointed at Max, who stood staring dimly ahead of him.

"He isn't at all," she said, eyeing her husband. "No, for some reason he isn't today."

She laughed softly, shaking her head.

Port was offended. "I'm glad you find it funny."

Franza shook her head, inwardly rolling her eyes.

"Of course I don't," she said, grinning in spite of herself.

"So, I see now," Port said in an injured tone. "Well, that's it for today! You know full well what you're missing, and I guess I've no need to be jealous, as he's not likely to get it up tonight!"

Max overheard that and turned in a flash. "You! *You!* I'll show you what I can get up! Come here!"

"Out of here!" snapped Franza, shoving her husband in the direction of a taxi. "Out of here! Enough now. We're going."

But Max was not to be put off. "My wife!" he yelled, waving his arms around. "Look here, this is my wife! With whom I'm no longer allowed marital relations. It's no fun anymore! No fun! No fun! No fun!"

"Poor bastard," the taxi driver said as they got in. "Why don't you give him a quickie?"

Franza gasped indignantly.

"Give me a blow job," Max wailed. "You haven't done that for ages."

"Oh, that's harsh!" the taxi driver said with a grin. "Go ahead. I won't look. Promise!"

That was the last straw for Franza. She waved her police ID in front of his eyes.

"One more word out of you and I'll have you both arrested for sexual harassment. Then I'll sit you together in a cell and he can blow you—blow his stinking boozy breath in your face."

"Oops, I see you're not one to be messed with! Understood, Inspector! So, where to?"

As they drove along the Danube, Max sniggered to himself, disturbing noises escaping him every now and then.

"I'll tell you one thing," the taxi driver said, "if he hurls all over my car—"

"Shut it," said Franza. "Just drive!"

The driver obeyed as Franza contemplated telling him to stop so she could tip him, his taxi, and her husband all into the Danube. But she was a police officer, and police officers didn't do things like that. Police officers brought people safely home, heaved them into bed, and tucked them in. Or at least they did when it came to cast-off husbands and the like.

As Franza finally closed Max's door behind her, she was torn between stopping for a bottle of wine or a pack of cigarettes. She went for the wine *and* a pack of cigarettes, and took them to Sonja's.

. . .

The next day, Max came into Franza's office full of remorse. He raised his hand in careful greeting to her colleagues and very carefully, as if the slightest movement would cause his head to explode, laid a bouquet of white roses on Franza's desk. He left as quietly as he had come, white faced and nearly transparent.

"What was all that about?" Felix asked, dumbfounded, following Max with his eyes. "What have you done to your husband?"

"Nothing," said Franza with a grin. "I don't believe he's feeling particularly well."

"Well, if I didn't know him so well, I'd say he was hungover. Is that possible?"

He looked knowingly at Franza, who smiled and said nothing.

Two days later, Port came out with the Vienna business.

14

Franza walked along the narrow promenade along the bank of the Danube. She did it regularly after work, especially if there was something she'd been unable to think through fully during the day. She didn't want to take her unfinished thoughts home with her. She wanted her apartment to remain untouched, a peaceful haven free from death and crime. But it rarely worked, and this time was no exception. The new case had already gotten under her skin, into her thoughts and feelings. The face of the murder victim was burned behind her eyes, along with the face of the missing woman.

Two mature women, one of them a little younger than the other, but there came a time in life when any age differences vanished. There was the thirties club, the forties club—she didn't like to think much beyond that.

What had Gertrud's father said? *You could say we had two daughters.*

It sounded straightforward. It sounded nice. But things were not always as they sounded.

Franza turned toward home. There, she unlocked the door to the building, made her way upstairs, turned the corner to her apartment, and saw her sitting on the doormat. She was leaning against the front door, asleep.

Franza gasped in surprise and approached her cautiously, observing her. Her young face looked peaceful and relaxed as she slept, but it would soon change when she awoke to find tragedy still all too real. Franza touched her cheek.

"Lilli?"

Lilli jumped, banging her head against the door and wincing at the brief pain.

"How did you find me?"

"You're in the telephone directory, Inspector."

"No need for formality."

Lilli nodded.

"Come, now." Franza reached out a hand and helped Lilli up. "Come in."

Lilli slipped cautiously into the apartment, like a cat on silent paws. *Like she's on the lookout for perfume,* Franza thought, smiling to herself. She had two or three bottles in her bathroom cabinet. Would they still be there in the morning?

"Are you hungry?"

Lilli nodded.

"OK, let's cook." Franza unpacked her shopping bag. "Apple strudel or apple strudel?"

Franza's love of baking knew no bounds. When she was in the middle of a case and came home tired, there was nothing like getting busy with complicated pastries and elaborate recipes. The next day the whole station would delight in the fruits of her labors.

As a change from the ubiquitous cookies, apple strudel was on the menu. The sweet-and-sour cooking apples on the grocer's shelves had caught her eye. The shiny red little devils whispered shamelessly to Franza, *Take us, take us, we're the pick of today's crop!*

Franza had taken them at their word—after all, apples were healthy and stimulated the brain. Because clear thinking was essential right now, the station would all be eating apple strudel the following day.

"Apple strudel," Lilli replied, tying on the apron that Franza passed her.

They worked in silent concentration, interrupted only by Franza's instructions and explanations, as Lilli had never baked apple strudel. She was amazed and delighted as she rolled the pastry out to a thin, translucent skin, spread it with butter and sour cream, sprinkled it with toasted breadcrumbs and cinnamon apple, and finally rolled it up with the help of the strudel cloth.

She maneuvered it into Franza's twenty-year-old casserole and placed it in the oven. Franza was pleased to see that the dark cloud hanging over Lilli had lifted a little.

As the smell of the strudel gradually spread through the apartment, they sat on the couch in the corner of the living room, drinking water and nibbling nuts.

"Why are you here, Lilli?" Franza asked carefully. "What is it you want to tell me?"

Lilli shrugged and remained silent.

"I don't know," she finally said. "I don't know. Nothing, probably. It's so confusing, so awful. I can't stand it at home any longer. They're all crying, they're all wiped out. So am I, but . . . ." She gnawed her bottom lip. "My grandmother was in a state about me leaving. She said the family has to stick together at a time like this." Her voice had become scornful, wounded, angry. "But we're not a family!"

"No?" Franza asked quietly. "Why not?"

"I don't know. We never have been, somehow," Lilli said curtly. "Moritz is my family."

"What about your father?"

"He's not my father. I don't know my father. I know nothing about him. She never told me anything. We were on our own for a long time, my mother . . . Gertrud and I. We had an apartment here in town. Sometimes she worked in a library, but mostly not. I think my grandfather supported us financially."

Was it longing that Franza could hear in her voice? Or a mixture of sadness and impatience? Impatience about what? A longing for what?

"Why didn't she work regularly? Especially when you were older, at school."

Lilli shrugged. "It's probably my fault. She got pregnant when she was just starting her studies. She never finished."

"Why not? Arrangements could have been made, surely?" Franza was amazed. "With your family?"

"Yes. They could. But they weren't."

Franza waited.

"She was supposed to become a lawyer." Lilli quickly corrected herself: "Or, she wanted to be a lawyer." She shrugged. "What do I know? You know about that, don't you? My grandfather and his law practice. A long-standing family tradition." She raised her hands theatrically. "She was a great disappointment to the old man. And as for me . . ."

"What about you?"

"I'm going to disappoint him, too."

Franza nodded. "He'll get over it."

"Yes, he probably will. In any case, he's got one last chance." Lilli grinned. "Moritz."

"And after that?" Franza tried to bring the conversation back to Gertrud.

"What do you mean?"

"What happened with you and Gertrud?"

Lilli thought briefly. "Then Christian appeared at some stage." She hesitated, thinking some more. "It was a good thing that he came. He liked her. Very much. She liked him, too. It . . . it did her good. She . . . needed it."

"How old were you then?"

"Twelve. Around twelve."

Wow, Franza thought, *still a child and so perceptive?*

"They got married, and my grandfather gave us the house."

"That was generous!"

Lilli laughed bitterly. "Generous? No, I don't think so. He merely brought her a little bit more under his control."

"Oh," Franza said in surprise. "That sounds harsh. How did you come to that conclusion?"

Lilli shrugged. "Dunno. That's how it is. Always has been. He pulls the strings and they all dance."

Lilli paused to think before qualifying her words. "It's not so bad, though. At least someone cares. He's just a bit . . . domineering."

"Was there anything worrying him?"

"Isn't there always?" Lilli sighed as she thought that she still hadn't told him she wouldn't be continuing her studies. She wouldn't be his successor.

"I mean, anything in particular. Anything . . . out of the ordinary."

Lilli bristled. "What's that supposed to mean? What do you want? Are you pumping me for information about my family?"

"I'm sorry." Franza raised her hands in appeasement. "Calm down. I'm not pumping you for information, honestly. But I've got a feeling you want to talk. Why else would you have come?"

Lilli shrank into herself. "I don't know why I came. It was probably a mistake. I should probably be with my family right now. But . . ."

She broke off and wiped a hand over her face. Tears. "Do you think it was one of us? Do you think we killed her?" She asked it quietly, barely audible, a tiny, horrified whisper.

"No," Franza said comfortingly. "No, I honestly don't believe that." She stroked Lilli's hair. "But it must have been someone, and everything you tell me will help us find out who. That's why it's a good thing for you to talk to me."

Lilli jumped up in anger. "What kind of a woman are you? Always digging for dirt! You insist on bringing it all out into the daylight, spoiling everything! Don't you ever think about the damage you're doing?"

"Of course I do," Franza said. "Of course I always think about that. Always. Every time. But I have to do it. It's a question of truth. Shouldn't the truth be brought to light? Often you find that things can't get any worse. And once something's out in the open, bare and hurting, it has a chance to heal."

They heard a beep. The strudel was ready.

Good, Franza thought as she stood and went over to the oven, *we need a break.* She pulled the casserole out, set it down on a wooden board, and went back to Lilli.

"Don't you want to know what happened to your mother?"

"Ohhh," Lilli snarled. "I hate you! Yes! Yes, I want to know what happened to my mother. I want to know, but perhaps it would be better . . ." She sank back on the couch and covered her face with her hands, whispering the last part of the sentence, ". . . perhaps it would be better not to know."

"Why?"

"Because . . ." She shook her head.

OK, Franza thought, *take your time, girl. I can wait.*

"Tell me about her. What was she like?"

"Gertrud?"

"Is that what you called her?"

"No, not really."

"Why are you calling her that now?"

Lilli shrugged, glanced up briefly, a dark flash in her eyes. "Dunno. I just am."

Franza nodded. "What was she like?"

"Lonely," said Lilli, the word shot out as if from a pistol. She nodded vehemently. "Yes, lonely." She smiled sadly, swallowed. "I always felt bad that she was . . . she was so alone. I always felt guilty when I went away. Even when I was a child, when I went to school, because I knew she was alone. Even more alone. And she would always freeze up."

Lilli remembered when she came home from school and saw her mother in front of the TV, huddled beneath a blanket. There was always that quick glance out of the window, looking to see whether anyone else was there, that Lilli had not been followed.

Lilli had once asked, "Mama, what are you frightened of?"

Gertrud smiled. "I'm not frightened. What would I be afraid of? I've got you!" She drew the child to her, hugged her, and whispered, "No one, you hear, no one will ever take you away!"

She intoned it like an oath, like a magic spell, and Lilli stroked her mother's back, saying, "No, of course not. Why would they? You're my mother." But she always sensed the coolness, the iron ring Gertrud had formed around herself.

Then Christian had come along. Things improved, but were never wonderful. Until Moritz was born—then things got much better. Even if only for short periods, for moments.

But she didn't tell Franza any of this.

"Let's eat," Franza said.

They ate, drank coffee. The strudel melted in their mouths. It was late, past ten, and darkness had long since fallen.

Eventually, Lilli said, "She was always on guard."

Franza was surprised. "On guard? Against what?"

She shook her head, shrugged, paused for thought. "I don't know. I wondered about it often enough. But I'm right, she was on guard. Always. As if she were afraid. For me. For herself. I don't know . . . Somehow she was never relaxed, never at ease, never happy and cheerful and relaxed. Like people just are sometimes. Like you *have* to be, or else . . ."

Silence.

"Yes," Lilli whispered eventually, aware of the dismay in her own voice. "That's the way it was. She wasn't happy. She was a woman who was never happy. Somehow . . . she wasn't free enough. Yes. Of course. She wasn't free enough for happiness. Trapped."

And Lilli knew then what it was. She'd known since earlier that evening, since that morning. She knew what had kept her mother trapped her whole life long, why she had not been free to experience happiness, for herself, for life—why she always had to be on her guard.

Lilli closed her eyes, thinking. Should she? Ought she? Tell Franza? Tell the police officer? So that she could use it? So that, eventually, the whole town would know?

Lilli's thoughts moved back and forth until, finally . . . she decided.

No, she would say nothing to Franza. She would tell her nothing— she had already said enough, too much. She shouldn't ruin the memory of Gertrud's life now, when it was all meaningless and much too late. No, that was something Gertrud did not deserve.

"Trapped by what? What do you mean? What are you trying to tell me?"

Franza's voice was gentle and enticing. She was offering a salve for her to sink into, to bear her up. Lilli considered it once again for a second, for a fraction of a second. It would do her good to tell Franza everything, it would be like a release. Franza would know what to do . . . but on the other hand . . .

Lilli cleared her throat, shook her head. "I don't know."

She wanted to go, wanted to stop talking, but she sat as if glued to this couch next to this woman who . . .

What a pity, Franza thought. *Lilli knows something, and she was on the point of . . . Such a pity!* She gave a negligible shake of her head and stroked Lilli's arm.

"You were young when you left home."

"Yes." Lilli nodded. "Straight after school. She kept me on a leash, but at the same time she looked at me like I was a stranger. She would hug me and I'd ask myself who she was."

Well, Franza thought, *that's not particularly unusual. I'm familiar with that.* She thought of Ben growing up and how she had sometimes

83

wondered, full of concern, who this person beside her was, this person whose thoughts and intentions she did not know.

"I just went," Lilli said with a shrug. "I couldn't stand it anymore, the restrictions, the ties. And then . . ."

She fell silent.

"And then?"

A quick glance, a rapid decision. Again. "Nothing. Nothing at all."

Shit, Franza thought. *What was she about to say? What have I just missed?*

"Lilli," she began. "Lilli, tell me what you know, what you're thinking! It could be important!"

Lilli laughed angrily. "Oh, stop all your police tactics! You're beginning to get on my nerves!"

Franza suspected it was too late. Lilli was not going to say any more. She made another attempt. "Hanna?"

Lilli jumped up and grabbed her coat.

"I'm going," she said, her voice cool and steady and full of arrogance. "I don't know anything about Hanna. She'd already gone when I came on the scene."

"Oh, Lilli." Franza stood. "Why don't you stay? It's late. You can stay the night here. I have a guest room. We don't have to talk anymore."

Lilli nodded, a small smile. "True. We don't have to talk anymore. So I'm going now."

And she went. Purple velvet coat, over-the-knee boots, a pretty, tough, sad-looking girl. Franza stood on the balcony and watched her walk down the street. The sky was dark, there was a rustling in the trees, the start of rain. September rain—you could hear it pattering on the leaves. You could hear the wind, September wind, and yet the night air was slightly warm, the balcony slightly warm. With a blanket around her, it was fine.

Women were always cold in front of the TV and on the balcony, Franza thought. She was no exception. But she liked the quiet depths of the night, when the sound of a spoon stirring a cup of coffee sounded like a small, gentle circular saw. She liked sitting on the balcony at night, the lamp throwing a circle of light into the darkness. She felt shut away inside herself, shut off from the world, she could allow her thoughts to run free. If they would only continue, but they stopped as the night wind gradually penetrated through the blanket to reach Franza's skin.

Tell me, Lilli, she had asked. And Lilli had told her—but not everything. She had gone, the little rascal who stole perfume, who grieved for her mother because she had not caught hold of happiness with a firm grip.

If Franza hurried, *she* could still catch hold of happiness that night. With a firm grip or even a lighter one—whatever she felt like. She had to grin as she imagined her happiness. It was made up of a taut, youthful torso, a firm backside, eyes that shone with a mischievous twinkle, and lips that managed to reached the most impossible places.

Franza jumped up, all her tiredness vanished, and reached for her cell phone. Yes, she wanted this happiness. Now. Always.

15

They sat on the spacious terrace. The housekeeper had served coffee and then quickly withdrew. It was September 13, the day after Gertrud was found.

"My wife will be coming soon," said Hans Brendler, who, they now knew, owned a large successful law firm in the town, where he employed a number of attorneys.

Brendler cleared his throat, leaned forward, his elbows on the table, his eyes flickering as they sought out the coffee cup. He looked tired, at a loss, which surprised Franza.

Perhaps it's because he's not in charge of this situation—clearly not in charge—and he's not used to that.

She arrived finally. Dorothee Brendler, his wife. She sat down with them, looking elegant, pearls at her neck. They gave Franza the impression they were choking her. She was surrounded by an aura of sadness, as immediate as autumn in the garden, and something else—Franza tried to sense what it was. Anger? Bitterness? Resignation?

"Start where you like, anywhere," Herz said.

Franza was moved by the gentleness in his voice and once again felt a deep warmth for him.

"Start where we like," Brendler said with a slight nod, giving his wife a look to which she did not respond. He cleared his throat. "Start anywhere. That sounds so easy."

"We have time," said Franza. "And we know how difficult this is for you both."

But of course it was not true—they didn't have time. Not an infinite amount. The dead were dead and could rest in peace, but there was still someone out there with whom they were concerned—at least one person. The murderer. Man or woman. And possibly another victim. Whom they could maybe still save.

Franza thought of the forensics team, who had returned to the crime scene to seek traces of another female, a red hair perhaps, lipstick on a glass that did not contain Gertrud's DNA.

Franza thought of Arthur, who had observed the forensics team when they searched the pottery shop and the surrounding area, and who was now feverishly on the lookout for anyone who had known Gertrud Rabinsky, anyone who had noticed anything strange recently—visitors, maybe, who had not been seen there before. Anything.

"We have time," she repeated softly, smiling a little. She turned her face to look at the pattern of shadows formed by the breeze in the leaves—sunny, shady, sunny, shady. It was still, so still. It was that early fall morning stillness that could calm the spirit.

There was a small clink of porcelain. Dorothee Brendler set her cup down and interlaced her fingers. "You took her into your heart," she said, and her voice was like porcelain. "More than your own daughter. I'll never forgive you for that."

There was a further moment of stillness, and the pain reached his face, too. It was quite clear for the first time, and Franza knew this pain would last a lifetime. Hans Brendler opened his mouth to say something, his eyes imploring Dorothee, but she was unrelenting. And distant. And she raised her hand. "No," she said. "Be quiet. I can't listen anymore."

Dorothee stood, placing a card on the table.

"You can reach me at this number if you need me." She nodded to Franza and Herz and left. Into the house. Into the stillness. Then they heard a car departing.

"She's leaving me," Brendler said emptily. "She's leaving me, too. She told me this morning. She was only here for your visit." He fell silent, and then said again, "She's leaving."

He listened to his own voice and stared at the French doors through which she had disappeared, as if he could still see her. Not so much as a shadow remained, not a single trace.

Franza looked up. The sky was blue, bluer than dreams of longing, bluer than the blue of memory.

16

Here again. I walk the old paths. I've been away for twenty-two years. Away from a life that, an eon ago, I thought would turn out well. But we deceive ourselves. Your world comes crashing down, and nothing can bring it back. I never hated you, Gertrud. I had forgotten you. That was far more effective. But perhaps I should have hated you.

. . . dear hanna . . .

That's what a letter like that can do to you. An ancient scribbling that would have been thrown away if it weren't for pointless sentimentality. Today people send e-mails that are quickly deleted so no one can find them, so they can't invade the security of a future life.

Here again. Walking the old paths. It was such a long time ago.

The river is still the river, as is the terrace outside the café. We came here, and here, and here. The tables are unchanged, the same pictures on the walls. The bathrooms have been remodeled, something that should have been done even back then.

So little has changed. The eyes of the young girls still sparkle on the dance floor, the lights shimmer. They feel light, as if they're floating, just as we did back then, as I did, feathers in the wind as the lights shimmered. Our high heels clicked on the asphalt. We were young, young as the summer and just as radiant. Our hair shining, we were curious, everything was so distant.

I stand here now. This is where it happened. My eyes are young, joyful, and shining. Tonio is holding me tight, sinking into me as I breathe in his breath that tastes of brandy and cigarettes. Everything is easy, everything is beautiful, love is a fountain, splashing but deep.

. . . and if one day we have nothing left, it will have been plenty—a truth between the lines, between us, the trace of a love, a vast longing . . . dear hanna . . .

Yes, I was *dear hanna*, and if I fell, Tonio caught me. But then he himself fell into the raging blackness of the sea, into the wind, into the storm, clear and direct, leaving no shadow, no shading.

17

"Do you have any children?" Hans Brendler asked. "Do you love them all equally?"

The officers made no reply. He wasn't expecting one. He sank into his memories, diving in and pulling one out: the story of his failure, his guilt.

"She was . . ." he said, trailing off. "From the beginning she was so . . ."

Hanna's mother had been his secretary. Some people suspected she had also been his lover, but that wasn't true. It wasn't an affair, nothing of the sort. He had no need for affairs. He was married to a clever, attractive, lovable wife whom he loved and who loved him. They had the daughter they had always wished for, both had good careers, money, a beautiful house—what more could they want?

But then something dreadful happened.

"She simply collapsed," Hans Brendler said. "She simply fell from her chair in the middle of a dictation and lay there. As if dead."

She wasn't dead. She came round a little but not completely. She moved her head, groaned. Her face was a strange color, had a strange expression. He hardly recognized her. He called an ambulance.

She survived but never fully recovered from the damage caused by the stroke. She was left mute and partially paralyzed, with no memory of her previous life. She was thirty-two and had no relatives. In recent years she had lived completely alone with the child, with Hanna.

What was to be done with her? With the child?

"My wife was the first to say it out loud. 'We'll take Hanna in,' she said. Just like that: 'We'll take Hanna in. You're a lawyer,' she said, 'you'll be able to arrange it all.'"

And he arranged it all. There was no registered father, no grandparents, no other relatives. The youth welfare office agreed immediately, and also to Brendler's agreement to bear the cost of permanent care in a nursing home for his former secretary. It was only possible because the law firm was a long-established one that had brought in a lot of money for his father and grandfather before him.

"And then?" Herz asked.

"And then . . ." Brendler echoed, tapping into his memories. "Then it all started."

He took a drink of coffee and peered into the cup before setting it down on the table.

"The early years were easy," he said. "I often didn't even notice them. Either of the girls."

He fell silent, smiling ruefully. "I know that doesn't sound quite . . . honorable, but maybe you understand how it is. You leave the house in the morning while the children are still asleep and when you come home in the evening . . . Well, as I said."

He shrugged.

Yes, Herz thought, *I know.*

Yes, Franza thought, *I know.*

"We had a housekeeper," Brendler continued. "A very respectable, warmhearted woman. Sabine. A real gem, you could say. She had no children of her own. She took care of the girls, since my wife worked, too. In the hospital, as an internist. And so they simply grew up—elementary school, high school. They were always side by side. Often I thought how lovely that Gertrud had gotten a sister in such a simple way, someone her own age in the bargain. Someone to share everything with, who saw everything from the same point of view, with whom there was no need to explain everything."

Someone who represented competition, Franza thought, *someone who could make life hell when it came down to it. Because she took everything you'd rather have had for yourself. Because she was always the first.*

"I remember one day when they came to my office," Brendler said. "It was a late afternoon in winter, already dark outside. They must have been around fourteen or fifteen. They had done some work for school, I can't remember what subject. Gertrud burst in first—she'd received the best grade and wanted to tell me about it there and then. She was so delighted. Hanna came after her slowly, a smile on her face, and sat on my desk, swinging her legs. She stretched a little, and for a brief moment the ceiling light caught her hair and lit it up like a fireball. She noticed me looking at her and looked back at me. At that moment I realized that she had let Gertrud win. With the grade. And with a number of other grades. Often."

He fell into a pensive silence, probably seeing her there, legs swinging in her blue jeans.

"For a brief moment it hurt." Brendler's face crumpled in momentary pain, then he composed himself again. "I believe I really saw her for the first time that day. And from that moment . . . always."

Asshole, Franza thought. *Stupid asshole.* She imagined Gertrud as she had been when she was a child, as a teenager, how it must have become increasingly obvious that she would be in the shadows, that her life had become a bad movie and that there would always be someone saying: Smile! Smile more brightly! Smile more convincingly! *Poor girl, poor little girl!*

Brendler shook his head, smiled an involuntary smile. "I don't know how that woman, my secretary, produced this child. She was a very ordinary woman, nothing outstanding about her, but her child, her daughter . . ."

Silence.

"Yes?" Franza asked carefully. "Her child?"

"Was blessed by the gods," he said slowly. "I can't put it any other way. Blessed by the gods. That's how it seemed to me."

"That's how it seemed to you?" Franza gasped.

"Yes," he said. "Yes. Everything she touched turned to gold. She tried everything, and she could do it all. It was a pleasure to watch her, a pleasure. She was . . . she attracted everyone's attention. And if that wasn't enough, she also had an enchanting way about her. She was lovable, funny, clever, full of life."

Suddenly, it became difficult for Gertrud. Suddenly, there was someone close to her who could do everything better. Who was developing better. Who was more beautiful. Gifted. A butterfly. A miracle.

"She was a real miracle," Brendler said. "She was a miracle to me and I began to compare the girls, and in making comparisons . . ."

He fell silent.

Asshole, Franza thought. "Wasn't Gertrud doing well?" she asked.

He shook his head, scarcely perceptibly.

"Gertrud wasn't doing well, in fact," he said in a whisper, as if he didn't dare to speak the words out loud, as if they were as poisoned as he was.

He stood and took a step toward the hedge.

"I never said anything to her," he said to the garden, and then turned back and raised his hands beseechingly. "You have to believe me, I beg you! I never said that to her! Never! But . . . she must have sensed it. And my wife did too."

"Did you and Hanna—" Herz asked.

Brendler raised his hands defensively.

"No!" he said. "Never! Never! I never got too close to her. Not in the way you're thinking. There was nothing erotic about this love. Not a spark. I never touched her. I loved my wife. I never had any desire for little girls. Never, at any time. Never. Ask my wife if you don't believe me. She would have annihilated me if I had." He nodded as if to emphasize his words, and then continued. "But Hanna . . . amazed me. I was so proud of her. I loved her. Yes. Like you love a daughter. She was my daughter. Nothing more and nothing less. My other daughter. My second daughter. My . . . special daughter."

He went quiet, suddenly feeling a great shame. Although that wouldn't change anything.

"She had so much . . . wisdom in her," he whispered. "Such wonderful intelligence. A certain clarity. I don't know. Something people just have. Or don't." He raised his eyes. "Do you know what I mean?"

Franza and Felix exchanged a look. Neither knew exactly what he meant, but they nodded. He continued to talk, telling them how the girls went to study in Munich and how as the years went by Hanna visited ever more rarely, that they grew distant. He had always regretted it and never knew the real reason for it. He guessed that during their time in Munich a rift had grown between Hanna and Gertrud, which must have been the reason for Hanna's ultimate withdrawal from the family. Or perhaps it was her marriage to Belitz, which he had never approved of.

He'd followed Hanna's career in secret and with pride, but no one in the family ever spoke of it. Brendler spoke only of Hanna, not of Gertrud.

Franza felt a cramp in her stomach. She longed for a cigarette and at the moment vowed to flush the remaining five in the pack down the toilet, although she suspected she wouldn't do it.

Poor Gertrud, she thought, *you really got the bad deal there.* She wanted to hear it confirmed one last time and dealt him the final blow.

"If you had had to choose between your daughters, which one would it have been?"

He stared at her. She saw the horror in his eyes. He was well aware of his betrayal, and he was still committing it, again and again. He was caught. He turned gray and shook his head.

"Please don't ask that question," he whispered, but Franza looked at him, merciless, impenetrable.

He lowered his eyes, slowly, the fight gone out of him.

"Yes," he whispered without having to think about it. "Yes. Hanna. It would have been Hanna."

Felix stood up in the silence that followed and cleared his throat.

"OK," he said. "At least we now have a basic outline of the situation. That's enough for today. If we need anything else, we know where to find you."

They went out to the car, and Brendler followed them, suddenly looking agitated and nervous.

"Do you really think these old stories have anything to do with the death of my daughter? And with Hanna's disappearance? Do you really believe that Hanna . . . ? That can't be possible!"

"We'll find out," said Herz. "You'll have to be patient."

But Brendler took no notice.

"Listen," he beseeched. "Listen, I've tried to make things right. I've really tried. But I don't know whether . . ."

He shook his head.

The detectives didn't ask any more. They had heard enough.

On the journey back into town they were quiet, each dwelling on their own thoughts.

"But Hanna must have needed it, this love," Felix said quietly. "A father. Something. Security. Everyone needs that. Otherwise you're living in a vacuum. She had nothing, after all. No mother, no father. Zilch. They had to share, Hanna and Gertrud. Sisters always have to. It's normal. People have to, don't they? Learn to share."

Franza nodded. "Yes," she said. "You're right. If that's how it was. But he'd made his decision."

Silence fell again. They reached the town center and worked their way into the Saturday afternoon traffic. Somewhere a blue light was flashing, uniformed colleagues on duty, an ambulance, an accident.

"The twins," Felix said finally. "They're everything to me." He thought of his youngest children. The lights of his life. They had done what he had believed impossible, given a new completeness to his marriage, his life, his sense of fatherhood. Not that he loved his other children any less for it, but since the twins had burst into their lives some eighteen months ago, everything had been a little different.

Franza laid a comforting hand on his knee.

"That's another story," she said. "A completely different story."

He looked at her gratefully.

18

She had arrived at nine, as she always did when she was on the early shift. She opened up the café and switched on the coffee machine—the usual routine. Vasco had long since begun cooking in the kitchen. She threw a final glance over the tables to make sure everything was in order, checking that the sugar dispensers were filled and the flowers in the vases hadn't wilted. She went outside to make sure everything was set up there, as the weather seemed good enough for patrons to prefer their morning coffee alfresco. It was only then that she noticed the frenzied activity in Gertrud's pottery shop. People she had never seen before were going in and out.

She stopped, hands on her hips, a frown on her face. What was happening? The shop was supposed to be closed for another week!

She and Gertrud had spoken about it on the evening before her holiday. She'd said she was going away for a few days—to the black beach on Kos, where her father had a house.

"I need to relax," she'd said. "Put everything to one side for a while. Without Christian, and without the children. Some me time, to get my act together. You know what I mean, Renate?"

"Of course," Renate had said. "I certainly do! You should do it. Enjoy yourself. A few days away and you'll be a new woman." She leaned back and sighed. "I could do with something like that myself."

Gertrud had nodded, and then started for the door. She hesitated, turned. "Why don't you come with me? There's plenty of room in the house."

A smile. One of those rare open smiles she sometimes granted. "What do you think?"

Renate's eyes had opened wide. What a wonderful idea! How tempting! But it wouldn't work. She sighed.

"Wow! That would be lovely! Yes, I'd love it, no doubt about it. But I don't have time. You see . . ." She waved a hand expressively around the café.

Gertrud nodded. "OK. It was only a spur-of-the-moment idea. But it's obvious you can't just drop everything and go. Would you keep an eye on the shop for me, please? I should be back next week. See you soon! After my holiday!"

She waved and crossed the street to her car. On a sudden impulse, Renate ran after her.

"Gertrud! Wait! Let me give you a hug! And wish you a lovely holiday."

They laughed and Renate hugged her. She felt good, soft but firm, the scent of herbal shampoo in her hair.

Then she was gone. Renate stood there for a moment and thought of Greece, of Kos, of the sea and the black sand. She had sighed again and briefly closed her eyes before returning to the café.

And now?

What was going on?

Hardly a week had passed. She ran a quick calculation through her head—no, it was only a few days, and there were all those people across the road. Not Christian or Lilli or Gertrud's parents, and no sign of Gertrud herself.

Ah well, Renate thought, running a hand through her short black hair as she impulsively crossed the street to the pottery shop.

"Can you tell me what you're doing here?" she asked, a little indignantly. The counter was full of papers, catalogs, and documents, which the men had clearly found in one of the cupboards. "Who are you? I'm going to call the police!"

She reached for her cell phone. The four men regarded her keenly. One of them came over to her. He looked young and dynamic and quite kind in fact, but she nevertheless took a step back. He raised his arms.

"It's OK, it's OK, don't worry. You don't need to call the police. We *are* the police. And you are?"

She froze. The police? What was going on? What had happened?

She gradually calmed down. "Can I see your ID?"

"Of course." The young man got his ID from his pocket. "I'm sorry."

Arthur Peterson, it said, but she forgot the name immediately in the face of what else she saw there, something far more important and, she slowly realized, horrific.

"What's happened?" she asked. "Please tell me what's happened. Has something happened to Gertrud?"

"Did you know her? Was she a friend?"

"A friend? Yes, yes. Sort of." She thought of the invitation to Greece. "We work more or less next door to one another. I run the café across the street."

She turned and pointed to the café. As she did so, she suddenly realized that he had spoken about Gertrud in the past tense.

. . .

Later they sat at one of the outdoor tables at the café. She had brought Arthur a coffee and a schnapps for herself. She sipped it now, and when customers approached, she said, "We're closed. Bereavement."

She thought of Gertrud and how they'd had little contact in recent years, only in the last few weeks—goodness knew why.

What would have happened if I'd said yes to Greece, she thought. *If I'd agreed to go, there and then. If I'd closed the café, switched off the coffee machine, and left Vasco to hold the fort for a few days. If I'd taken Gertrud up on her offer and we'd caught the next available flight? Would that have prevented her murder?*

Renate sighed and wiped away the tears that fell relentlessly. *Who knows,* she thought. *Who knows? Perhaps she would have drowned in the sea off that black beach.*

"I wanted to order some of those new cups she had," she said suddenly, raising her cup. "The old ones are all chipped. Where am I going to get my new ones now?"

Yes, thought Arthur, *this phenomenon. It's always the little things we miss first. The trip we planned but that never happened. The cups we'll have to get from another pottery now. The vase we broke and never got chance to apologize about.*

Arthur had not been on the team for long, only a little over two years, but he'd made that discovery quickly—when the pain began, it began with the little things. Was it because they were easier to grasp?

"You'll work it out, I'm sure," he said.

"Yes, you're probably right. How silly of me to be thinking of something so trivial."

She laid her hands across her eyes, and as she did so, she remembered the young man. The man who had come here for coffee two days in a row. He'd said he was visiting an acquaintance, and then he'd crossed the street and spoken to Gertrud. She'd looked shocked. So much so that it was visible from here, from across the street.

Was she guilty because she'd served Gertrud's murderer? Had it happened because she'd not been observant enough, not drawn the right conclusions? But how were you supposed to draw conclusions about a murder?

"Of course not," Arthur said, handing her a tissue. "No one would suspect anything of the sort. There's no reason to feel guilty. In any case, it doesn't necessarily mean anything. Could be sheer coincidence."

He took a drink of his coffee. "What did he look like, this man?"

She described him, and as she did so, she had a vague feeling that he reminded her of someone. But the more she racked her brain about it, the more the image slipped from her grasp. Perhaps it would occur to her again when she went to the police station to have a composite picture made.

"I'll miss her," she said as the young detective took his leave with a firm handshake. "She was a good person. Very reserved. Very quiet. You could say a little aloof, if you didn't know her. Almost shy. She didn't let people get too close too soon. But once you got to know her . . ."

Her voice shook. She ran a hand over her cheeks again.

"Yes," she said quietly, "I'll miss her."

19

He had holed up in his grandfather's apartment. He needed a new plan. There was a problem. A massive one. One that had not been foreseeable. He couldn't have imagined a development like that. All the signs pointed to a storm breaking, and he was right in the middle of it. But he wouldn't lose the game. Not him.

At night he lay awake for a long time, the image of the woman before his eyes. It was not a nice picture. The blood. Her outstretched hand. The sound of the knife as it hit the floor.

"Don't go," she had gasped, scarcely understandable. "Don't leave me here like this! Please!"

Then . . . there was no comma anymore. Period.

He had fled out into the night, back into town to the apartment. Hunger gnawed at him, but there was nothing to eat, not even a slice of bread. The fridge was as empty as his head. He found the remains of a pizza from *before*, which he had devoured as soon as he got home. But he needed food: bread, cheese, butter. First, he needed a plan. A damned plan. But his stomach was growling. And his brain was on fire.

He had seen many dead bodies before, a lot of death—it was part of his job—but this had been something else. More appalling. It had happened so quickly. It had been completely unforeseen because it had simply happened. It was something he had been unable to prepare himself for. In the face of death at the hospital, you could close off your heart and your head beforehand—create a makeshift defense, but a defense nevertheless.

In his panic he thought of Kristin. They'd met six months ago at an exhibition he'd gone to by chance. She was standing with a group of people in the middle of the room, and he had recognized her at once. They sometimes rode the elevator together. He knew she was quite a big fish in the hospital administrative hierarchy, a lawyer, which, given her age, was quite impressive.

Well, he thought as he watched her from his position of safety at the bar, *perhaps she simply slept her way to the top; she's not bad-looking. Maybe she's ready to sleep her way into a slightly lower bed. Let's see how it goes. There's always a chance.*

She had recognized him, too.

"You're the nurse who always gets out on the seventh floor," she said when they sat down together half an hour later. He nodded, grinning to himself at how much she recalled.

"Will you order me a glass of wine?" she asked, raising her eyebrows slightly in a way he found quite bold. It moved him.

"Anything for you," he said, waving the bartender over.

She was already a little tipsy, which excited him all the more. He wanted to match her, and so he downed three glasses of wine one after the other. Still, he knew he wouldn't catch up to her, as he was able to hold his drink too well.

"You're drinking too much," she said primly. "I don't want to be embarrassed by you. They all know me here."

She giggled and he laughed, too. He stood and walked past the rows of pictures, pausing before each exhibit. They all left him cold. He wondered if Kristin felt the same way. It was possible, he thought. But even if it were true, she would probably never admit it.

"They're crap, aren't they?" she said as he returned to her. "The emperor's new clothes!"

He was stunned, and when she laughed, chortling and squawking, it amused him all the more. She finally said, "Come on, let's go to my place. I have a lovely apartment I want to show you."

She smiled and twisted a lock of hair around her finger.

"Ah," he said. "A beautiful apartment. Yes, I'd really love to see it."

On the way she became serious, looking at him with blue eyes that had a certain depth, and pushing her hand into his.

At her apartment they drank some gin, and she opened a tin of caviar, which she spooned out for him as an accompaniment. He soon found himself licking the black delicacy from her navel.

They slept together, and she tasted just as she appeared: sober, objective, a little like the blue paper from the admin department, a little like a fake thousand-euro bill. But even a thousand-euro bill had its good side, there was no denying that.

Afterward, they lay quietly side by side and she said, "You're sweet. Really. I've had my eye on you for a long time."

During the next few weeks she stayed with him often. She liked his apartment, which had a chaotic, unfinished air about it. She enjoyed making him breakfast and even dinner—until Tonio ruined it all.

Kristin, Kristin, Kristin. He rolled back and forth on the mattress. *Should I call you? Tell you everything? About the apartment, about all the things I've found, about this dreadful thing that's happened?*

Perhaps she could help him, perhaps she knew of a plan in her clearheaded legal brain, a plan to get him off, to deflect everything a little.

He looked at the clock. Three in the morning—a bad time for a call for help, especially from someone who had behaved like an incredible asshole. She probably already had her eye on someone else, probably had for a while now—the head surgeon, for example, or the manager of the corner supermarket who liked to stare at her silk-clad backside.

He thought of her sharp business suit and the hot lingerie she liked to wear underneath. As the recollection stirred his mind and his loins, he groaned and rubbed himself to release. Finally, he fell asleep.

20

They searched without knowing exactly what they were searching for.

"Red hair" had been the instruction. "Maybe you'll find a red hair of some sort that belongs to neither Gertrud nor her daughter or her mother."

So they searched. A needle in a haystack.

"Concentrate mainly on the kitchen, the crime scene. But not only there. She could have been anywhere in the house. We just don't know."

So they searched. Cursing a little. Slightly unmotivated. How could a needle be found in a haystack like this?

Difficult. Time-consuming. Demanding. But they were used to it. And then they found it. The needle. On a pillow. In the marriage bed. A red hair. An actual red hair. So she had been here. Hanna Umlauf. In Gertrud's house. In Gertrud's bed.

21

I was there.

And as she stood there in her house that smelled of damsons, as she looked at me with shocked eyes, I knew immediately. I knew I loved her again. Loved her as I had back then.

We sat in her kitchen, among the late harvest of damsons from the big tree in the garden. There was so much to talk about.

22

"OK," said Herz. "We're on the second day. Status report. Let's take stock before we go any further."

Around the table in the meeting room were all the investigators involved in the case, or rather the cases—Franza, Arthur, and Hansen from Missing Persons. Borger, the coroner, and the district attorney, Dr. Brückl. Felix was at the head of the table. He stood and pinned Gertrud's photo on the bulletin board, writing her name beneath it.

"Our murder victim. Gertrud Rabinsky, forty-four years of age. She ran a pottery shop in the town center. Married to Christian Rabinsky. Mother of two children. Between Thursday night and Friday morning she was stabbed in her kitchen. We found the murder weapon next to her corpse. A kitchen knife, the kind used for chopping vegetables or slicing bacon. The handle hadn't been wiped and we found the fingerprints of three people. One set belongs to the murder victim. Unfortunately, the other two are still unknown to us. Do we know the precise time of death yet? Borger?"

"Midnight," Borger said. "As I thought from the start."

"Can you give us any more detail about the nature of the injuries?"

Borger nodded. "Three stab wounds were inflicted with great force, indicating a similar strength of emotion. All the stab wounds were in the breast region, and one went straight to the heart, which led to a quick death. The wounds were inflicted from above. May I demonstrate?"

He stood and looked at Franza. "May I have your assistance?"

Franza rose and stood before him. He raised his hand to head height, balled it into a fist, and brought it down three times in rapid succession against Franza's upper body. "Something like that."

They sat down again, and he continued, "If we can judge from the angles of entry, and there's no reason why we shouldn't, the perpetrator is a person between five feet nine and six feet in height."

"Hm," Franza said. "That doesn't narrow down the range of suspects much. It's quite a common height."

Borger shrugged regretfully. "Sorry."

"Does the force of the blows indicate a male perpetrator at all?"

Borger shook his head. "No, not at all. A sharp knife like this penetrates easily. And if someone's angry, acting in the heat of the moment . . . Yes, a woman would be capable of it, too."

"OK," Herz said, nodding slowly. "Anything else, Borger?"

"Well, it may not be relevant, but the knife was used before the attack to cut sausage—salami, to be precise—Emmentaler cheese, onions, and tomato. I found traces of them in the stab wounds. And she had eaten these things herself. Our victim. Her last supper, so to speak." He paused briefly. "I found them in her stomach. Fairly undigested."

They nodded. Borger's analyses of stomach contents were always very graphic.

"Another thing," Borger said. "I did actually find some skin particles beneath her fingernails."

"Aha," Franza said. "Can we assume that there's someone missing these skin particles, who now has corresponding wounds?"

Borger nodded. "Precisely, my dear—you've got it. Scratches. Someone must have clear scratch marks somewhere on their body. Unfortunately, I haven't found any DNA matches. So get to it, friends. A part of the puzzle is still missing."

Herz snorted. "There are still plenty of pieces of the puzzle missing, but we're smart and patient when it comes to putting them together. Do you have anything else for us?"

"No, not for now," Borger said. "May I go? I'll let you know if anything new comes to light."

They nodded and he left, leaving them to continue their team meeting.

"Next item," Herz said. He took out another photo and pinned it to the board. Hanna Umlauf.

"Hanna Umlauf," he said. "Also forty-four years of age, an art photographer, fairly well known, married to Jonas Belitz, a gallery owner, resident of Strasbourg, France, no children. Have I forgotten anything?"

Shaking heads and shrugs all around. Felix continued. "On the morning before Gertrud Rabinsky's death, Jonas Belitz reported his wife, Hanna, missing. I happened to be there when he first visited Peter's office."

"Is there a connection between the two women?" The district attorney had clearly not read up on the case.

"I'm coming to that," said Felix, nodding in Brückl's direction. "Peter, have there been any developments?"

"Nothing," Hansen replied. "Absolutely nothing. Her husband is completely out of his mind—you can't blame him under the circumstances. He's staying at the Hotel Babenberger, where his wife had also been staying. We made a thorough investigation of her room, but as you can imagine there was nothing—not a trace—to be found. The rooms are always thoroughly cleaned when someone checks out."

"Yes, unfortunately, in this case," Felix said. "Thanks, Peter."

He turned to Brückl. "The connection is that the two women knew each other very well. They grew up together. Gertrud's family was effectively also Hanna's family. There is official evidence of the guardianship. But in recent years there was hardly any or no contact, either between the women or between Hanna and her foster parents. According to her husband, Hanna hasn't been back to this area for many years. But they all knew one another. Jonas Belitz was also involved with the family in the past. He was a friend of Hans Brendler, Gertrud's father, when they were young."

"What do you think?" Brückl asked him.

Felix shook his head. "Nothing, for now. We're gathering our thoughts. Of course, it could all be mere coincidence, but we don't really believe that."

"Why did Frau Umlauf break off the contact?"

"We don't know yet. Only that there was a difference of opinion."

"Which could have provided grounds for murder?" The district attorney suddenly seemed wide-awake.

Franza had to smile to herself. As if they hadn't considered all that themselves!

"Possibly." Felix nodded patronizingly, throwing Franza a glance. "Could indeed be the case."

"So Umlauf could be Rabinsky's murderer? And she's now on the run?"

"Possibly," Felix said, apparently completely indifferent. Only the tiniest raising of his eyebrows indicated to Franza, who knew him well, that he was slightly amused. He was well aware that the district attorney sensed publicity, a moment of glory, glamour. Of course, a movie actress would have been a better catch, but an art photographer would do nicely.

"Of course, the scenario could be completely different," said Herz.

Brückl nodded rather brusquely. "Yes, yes. I'm not trying to do your work for you, Inspector Herz! Whatever happens, this case has high priority. Frau Umlauf is a public figure. You know what that means!"

"But of course we know." Felix sighed. "Don't we, Franza? We are aware of it?"

"We are." Franza nodded obligingly. "Of course we know, Herr Brückl."

Although she was in his home often—she had been best friends with his wife, Sonja, since kindergarten—they were not close. On the contrary, they were often at odds with each other.

"By the way, Sonja sends her greetings and asked you to pop by," he said, with a slightly embarrassed smile as though he suspected they could all see right through him.

"Thank you," said Franza. "Tell her I'll give her a call."

She thought of her last visit to the Brückls', the evening when a drunken Max had approached her in the theater café and she'd had to take him home. After dropping him off, she'd phoned Port to say she was free if he wanted to come by. But he had still been aggrieved and didn't come. So she'd taken the wine and cigarettes she'd bought at the gas station and driven to Sonja's, where they had sat on the terrace, drinking and smoking, while the district attorney worked at his PC in his home office. From time to time he came to the window, waved and smiled, and Sonja waved happily back.

"Is everything going well with you two?" Franza had asked, and Sonja nodded.

"Yes, we're fine. He works a lot, but that's OK—so do I."

"Yes," Franza said. "Don't we all?"

"It's better to be working than hanging around in some online chat room," Sonja said, and told her about a girlfriend who regularly logged in to chat forums under some pseudonym, getting to know men and even going on occasional titillating blind dates.

"Just imagine," Sonja said. "You get there and suddenly find yourself standing in front of your neighbor, who always seemed so nice and in love with his wife. How horribly embarrassing!"

Later that evening, at home, Franza had spent some time on the Internet herself.

"All right," Herz was saying. "If we've all got our private lives in order, can we carry on?"

Franza and Brückl raised their hands at the same time, indicating they were ready to proceed.

"So, to recap: Things could have happened as we've already described. As I said, we're gathering ideas here. Another possibility could be that Hanna Umlauf is another victim of the same perpetrator. Perhaps he enticed her to the area for some reason, probably in connection with the women's mutual past, and killed her. That would explain her disappearance."

He fell into a pensive silence.

"We do now know that they were together at some point, Hanna and Gertrud. In Gertrud's house, no less. We found Hanna's DNA there."

Brückl leaned forward in surprise. "Oh? What? Where? Doesn't this support my theory?"

Felix tipped his head to one side. "Our theory. Ours." He paused for a beat, then continued. "Yes, perhaps. Perhaps not. We shouldn't draw rash conclusions."

He glanced thoughtfully at the image of the photographer. "A hair. Bright red. Of course, the laboratory checked the DNA—Herr Belitz had one of his wife's lipsticks with him."

Arthur let out a gasp of surprise. "Who would have something like that? Had he assumed from the start that his wife was dead and we'd need DNA for some reason?"

"Well," Franza said. "He's bound to have seen some detective shows on TV. Whatever the reason, he's made our work unusually easy. Strasbourg is a long way away, after all. If he'd had to go and get the lipstick, we still wouldn't have our confirmation."

"Indeed," Brückl said. "So where did you find the hair?"

"Hm," Franza said casually. "In the bed."

"In the bed? In the guest room? Did she stay there after she checked out of the hotel?"

"No." Franza drew the word out a little. "Not in the guest room. In the bed of Herr and Frau Rabinsky."

"Aha," said the district attorney. "Ahaaaa." He also drew the word out. "You don't say! That's not a little indelicate. What do you conclude from it?"

Franza gave him her most winning smile. "As we've said: nothing yet. We're gathering our thoughts."

Brückl sighed and rolled his eyes a little, but seemed patient enough.

"At first glance it simply expands the range of people we're considering as suspects," Felix added.

"The husband!" Brückl exclaimed. "Jealousy. Frau Rabinsky catches her husband in bed with Umlauf, they get into an argument, the wife dies, the lover vanishes, and Herr Rabinsky plays the grieving husband."

He had been talking at full speed, shaking his head indignantly. "Honestly, if you ask me, infidelity always ends in tears!"

Felix raised his eyebrows. "Well," he said, "that's life. You can't do anything about it. Or do you have an idea about that, Herr Prosecutor? A new law, perhaps? Because we don't have enough laws?"

Brückl flushed slightly, shifting in his seat. "Pff," he said brusquely. "Nonsense!"

Felix grinned. "Of course extramarital coitus is not to be held up as exemplary behavior, but thank God that screwing around while in a conjugal state is not yet the stuff of a criminal act."

Wow, Franza thought, *how's that for a pompous statement!* She grinned and looked around at her colleagues' expressions, which were no different from her own. The district attorney didn't find it as amusing.

"Are you making fun of me?" he snapped. "Tone it down."

"No, I wasn't making fun of you," Felix said calmly. "Nothing could be further from my mind. But things are never as straightforward as they appear."

Brückl sighed. "Very well. I don't want to step on anyone's toes here. But a man's entitled to his thoughts, isn't he?"

He glanced at Franza, who responded with a radiant smile. *Asshole,* she thought.

Brückl cleared his throat. "So," he said. "Where were we?" He thought for a moment. "Oh, yes. Rabinsky, the grieving husband. Is he playing the grieving husband?"

"He's grieving," Franza said. "Whether he's playing a part is another matter. Hard to say."

"Anyway," Arthur put in triumphantly, "the list of suspects is about to get longer."

They all turned to him. He had drifted into the station right before the meeting, so no one else knew about the new witness.

"Frau Rabinsky had an interesting visitor," he said, enjoying being the focus of attention as he reported what the owner of the café had told him.

"OK," Felix said for the umpteenth time. "We now have quite a few leads, all in completely different directions. That's not necessarily a good thing. It certainly doesn't simplify matters. But that's how it is. Can't do anything about it."

He sighed. "We'll divide up the work. Arthur, you stay with the café proprietor, get a composite picture and all that. Can you also check out Rabinsky's alibi? Get the names of the people at that birthday party. Pump them for what they know. We have to determine whether there's a window when he can't prove he was seen by anyone. And whether that window was long enough for him to have gotten home, made certain discoveries, and committed certain acts."

Felix nodded to Arthur, then turned to Peter Hansen. "Peter, I'd like to ask you to speak to Belitz again. Find out if anything else has occurred to him recently. Any blind spots, skeletons in the closet, so to speak—you know what I'm saying."

Hansen nodded.

"As for you and me, Franza, we'll dig around in the past. Gertrud's past. And Hanna's. See whether there's anything else that overlaps. There will be, I'm sure. Intersection math, I believe it's called."

He grinned. Franza nodded, returning his smile. "Aye, aye, sir!"

"So I'm closing the meeting," Felix continued, stowing his documents away in a briefcase. "I wish you all a pleasant evening and a few new discoveries tomorrow."

He nodded, as if to confirm what he had just said, and stood up.

"But it's Sunday tomorrow," Arthur said, looking aghast.

"Hm? What about Sunday? It's a Sunday. And?"

"I just wanted . . ." Arthur stuttered, a little at a loss. "We just wanted . . ." He fell silent.

"Tut, tut," Felix sighed. "Hasn't she gotten used to it yet?"

Arthur shrugged, stood, muttered a farewell, and left. They all rose, nodding to one another.

"And you, Herr Brückl," Felix said. "You have a good Sunday, too."

They went downstairs together. Franza and Felix stood briefly by the door as the others vanished in various directions.

"Is it genuine?" she asked.

He looked at her. "What?"

"You know, the hair! The color."

A shake of the head. A frown. "Eh? What?"

Franza nudged him in the ribs. She knew him too well and was perfectly aware he knew what she meant.

"Don't give me that, man! Hanna's hair, of course. Natural or colored?"

He laughed, waved his arms dramatically. "My goodness! Women!"

She was unrelenting. "Just tell me!"

He laughed again, tilted his head and looked at her affectionately. "Natural."

Franza sighed. "I thought so."

"I expect you'd like to drop by for a coffee again, my dear Frau Oberwieser."

He waved his hands in front of her eyes, the broadest grin he could conjure up spreading across his face.

"He didn't say '*my dear Frau Oberwieser*,'" she said, aiming a punch at him. "At least not '*my dear*' . . ."

He laughed.

"In any case," he said, fending off her attack, "the apple strudel was heavenly! My mother never made it better. You'll have to make it again soon, sweetheart!"

He punched her arm and then held on to it.

"I didn't make it on my own."

"No? Which of your men helped you? Port or Max?"

"Neither of them," she said. "Lilli helped me."

"Lilli?" He sounded surprised. "Lilli Rabinsky?"

She nodded and told him about it. They both wondered about the significance of the visit, and Franza related how she had stood outside Lilli's apartment that morning and rung the bell, but Lilli had not answered so she had simply left the plate of apple strudel outside the door.

Franza sighed. "And as always, there could be a completely different explanation."

"I'm so glad I've got you," Herz said. "My clever Franza!"

"And as always," she said, "I continue to wonder what on earth my friend Sonja's doing with Brückl."

"Tsk," said Herz. "There's no accounting for love."

He gave her a hug, and she felt how warm he was, how much she liked him. He was truly her best friend.

23

Franza sat on her balcony in the evening air, sipping a coffee and resisting the desire to light a cigarette.

She was thinking about Gertrud and Hanna, about the case. The two women were in the prime of life, barely younger than she was. The next decade milestone was still a few years away, but it was a milestone at least one of them would not reach.

What could have happened? What had burst into their lives that had led to death?

Franza intended to call on Borger in the pathology lab on Monday, to be alone again for a brief while with Gertrud, to see if anything happened. Something always did. In Franza's thoughts. They softened, began to flow. Often in the right direction. She would see.

A breeze arose, and beyond the bushes in the river meadow clouds were heaped up like mountains. You would sink into them if you tried to climb them. Franza had to laugh when she imagined it. She shivered and went into the apartment. In the bathroom she undressed, took a long shower, then slipped into her bathrobe. She glanced in the mirror before turning away, then turned back and took a good hard look. A little stubborn, a little resigned, but not unhappy.

She was forty-five, and life showed on her face, had left its traces. But in fact . . . everything was good. Probably. She had no desire to be sixteen again. Or twenty. Not even thirty. This great freedom she felt, this calmness in herself and toward others, was a blessing of her forties. So life was good as it was. Mostly.

Her face. There were fine lines that had not always been there. Her hair. Needed a regular trim. But that was what hairdressers were for. Her body. Everything about it was a bit too soft, a bit too full, but warm and full of calm, a reflection of her life, which was sometimes a bit too hedonistic. She would certainly never be another Heidi Klum.

She sighed, turned back and forth a few times, and looked critically at herself. No, definitely not Heidi Klum, and if she were honest, she would never have managed it even before turning forty-five. It didn't matter. Didn't matter at all. She had never been sylphlike, and what was the point? Skinny women were probably no happier.

Sighing, she smiled at her reflection, nodded her affirmation, and tapped her brow. What crazy thoughts she indulged in sometimes!

Hanna Umlauf came into her mind. She was slim and svelte, and her hair—who would have thought it?—was still natural. But she had disappeared. Hardly ideal.

Her cell phone buzzed. Port. *I'd like to come over.* She leaned against the wall, looked up at the light. If he came, she wouldn't get much sleep. She would be tired in the morning and would have to bear Felix's tactless glances. *Yes,* she wrote back. *Come over! As soon as you can!*

As she waited for him, she lounged on the sofa, enjoying the peace, the softness, the warmth. The apartment was her retreat. Her oasis. It had been like that from the start. As soon as Franza had seen the high ceilings, the view from the windows, the balcony, the trees, the Danube that was shimmering a translucent gray on the afternoon of her showing, she had known then and there that it was *her* apartment and she would have no other.

It was quite a ways away from Port's apartment. Another district, another street, other trees outside the window.

"What do you think of it?" she had asked him, hoping for enthusiasm, for affirmation, but he had merely frowned a little blankly and said, "Yes. Nice. But why don't you just move in with me?"

She had smiled briefly and shaken her head. She knew what he had not yet seen clearly—that she had to set boundaries, that she couldn't get any closer to him, because at some point . . . at some point he would go—to another city, another life, and she would not go with him. So she had to keep the pain, which would surely follow, as minimal as possible. But it would hurt nevertheless.

No, Port understood nothing of all that and had suggested in all seriousness that she should move into his apartment with him, into the house with all the theater types, the artists, where someone was always singing an aria or practicing their lines or playing some instrument. It wasn't that she didn't like all that—on the contrary, over time she had come to like it more and more, had begun to let herself go and enjoy listening, smelling, tasting—but nevertheless, it was Port's world, and she was never quite at home in it.

"My apartment's big enough," he had said with a grin. "And I'd like to be able to snuggle into you in the mornings."

She had to laugh, gave him a playful punch. He raised his arms theatrically to fend her off, beginning a dramatic monologue at the top of his voice, something Greek or Roman—something ancient, in any case. As he spoke and gestured, he suddenly seemed so young to her, as in fact he was. Alarmed by the realization, she grabbed him, shook him, and silenced him.

"Ow," he said mockingly and drew away from her with a grin. "Are we feeling a little snappy today? A bit worried about something? Got out of bed on the wrong side?"

At that moment she had hated him. Only briefly. Only a tiny bit. But she had hated him. Such was life.

She heard the door, stood, went to him, and drew him to her. He buried his face in the hollow of her shoulder.

"Mm, you smell good," he murmured, pushing her in and shutting the door.

As always they landed—somewhere. As always it was dirty, thrilling, wonderful.

Wow, she thought, *it's been going on for so long now, two-and-a-half years or more, and I still love him and he still loves me and it was only supposed to be a few quick fucks, brief erotic dances, salt, chili, sugar all mixed in together.*

"You know what I love so much about you?" he murmured as his mouth explored her body.

"What?" she whispered, briefly holding her breath. "What?"

But he was busy. He had already latched onto her left breast, which was a tiny bit smaller than the right one, and which he therefore had to keep comforting, or so he said.

But she didn't forget what he'd said. As they were sitting on the balcony in their bathrobes, drinking coffee with whiskey, she asked him again.

He thought for a moment. "The fact that you know what you want. And also what you don't want." He laughed. "And that you want me. And that you know why. And that you know why you know."

"Aha," she said. "A bit complicated. What makes you think I know all that?"

He looked at her with a mixture of caution and devilment, waggled his head, scratched his chin. She had to laugh.

"Don't take this the wrong way," he said. "I don't mean anything bad by it. I'm just saying how it is."

She stopped laughing and waited, suspecting what would come next and knowing she shouldn't have asked.

"Because you're old enough to do that," he said and looked at her in such a way that she thought she would melt. He began to nibble her earlobe. "Women of your age know exactly what they want. And that makes you . . . so damned sharp."

She pressed him away, this sweet man. Who was so young. A fact that had once again been brought painfully home to her. "I hate it when you refer to me as a *woman of my age*. And besides, do you know so many *women of my age* that you're able to judge?"

He grinned and rolled his eyes. "Oh, God, not that one again! No, darling, I only know you! You're more than enough for me."

He jumped up and launched into an elegant bow.

"Fool," she said, and then sighed and let that sink into him.

He laughed and gently bit her shoulder. "Let me have a nibble at you. You taste so good!"

She sighed once again.

"For your age." He grinned.

She jumped up and hit at him, but he had anticipated her and held her tight, laughing all the time.

"There's only twelve years between us," he whispered in her ear later, "and I love you."

"Yes," she said softly. "Yes," she said again as she felt the sweetness of his words and his fearlessness, and explored her own feelings, the caution she had not yet let go. *Maybe,* she thought, and had to smile at the notion, *maybe, when I'm eighty-two and he's a youthful seventy, if he's still nuzzling around in my wrinkles, maybe then . . .* "Yes," she repeated with a rueful smile. "Because I'm old enough."

She thought how she sometimes hated being old enough, because every now and then it made her feel older than she actually was, but Port was unable to grasp that—only someone who was old enough could possibly know it.

"Yes," she said. "Yes, that's right."

She thought of the Vienna business and knew with that amazing, smart, lousy clarity of her forty-five years that there was more to it—that twelve years were not only twelve years, but . . . twelve years.

24

The Vienna business. That stupid Vienna business.

Of course Vienna would appeal to him, you could bet your bottom dollar on that. Of course it would hurt. But such was life—the old saying that always rang true.

"Would you come with me?" he had asked Franza two weeks ago, as she stood at his kitchen sink washing salad, cold water running over her fingers. "Would you?"

She had known at the time what it meant. She managed to stay calm for a moment. Then she turned the water off and left the apartment, ignoring his calls after her, his attempts to keep her there. She stretched out her hands, and it was enough. He let her go, suddenly speechless.

She drove along the Danube. It was evening, a Sunday, stillness hung above the river. She wanted the coldness of the water, so she undressed and went in. The waves gurgled around her, the cold gripped her, but none of it mattered. She stayed there a while, his *Would you come with me?* ringing in her ears, and she knew she wouldn't, and she knew it would be over—perhaps not straight away, but sometime, sooner rather than later. She knew that she had always known it, and cursed herself for being such a dumb little kid who wasn't capable of looking after herself or her heart.

How old was she again? Almost forty-six? Shouldn't she have finally learned to rise above things, to look down at the world from a distance as she went about her business?

When she arrived home, shivering with the Danube cold, he was sitting on her doorstep, watching her approach. She sat down next to him, laid her head on his shoulder, and murmured, "I'm sorry."

Later, he rubbed her hair dry, and they drank wine. He told her about the call from Vienna—a colleague had had an accident, they needed a replacement, and his name had come up. He was already familiar with the role, so it would not be difficult to step into the breach. In any case it would only be for a few weeks. His theater here was prepared to let him go, but he had to decide quickly. What did she think?

She said, "Wow! That's wonderful! A fantastic opportunity for you!"

As she said it, she thought that Vienna might as well have been Alaska, with three oceans between them, but she didn't say it out loud.

She sensed his excitement and his despair. It comforted her a little.

"Come with me," he said again. "Get some time off. It'll only be for a few weeks. Make some enquiries with the Austrian police. Police officers are in demand everywhere. Even in Austria. And you're actually Austrian, aren't you? Pay your homeland a visit." He was delighted by this idea. He beamed. "Yes! Go back home! What's keeping you here?"

She smiled and was touched by his euphoria, his desire to have her with him, so she said, "Perhaps. Yes, perhaps I will."

But she already knew she wouldn't. Her life was here and had been for many years. On these banks of the Danube, not the other ones, not the ones in Vienna. His life, on the other hand, would be there, because that was how it was meant to be.

"I have to do it," he said, and she nodded, because it was obvious, clear as day. "I simply have to. If I don't take this opportunity, I might as well give up right now."

"Of course," she said and laid her hand on his cheek. "Of course you must! I know. Of course you must do it."

Then they slept together, because it was the only thing that would give even a little comfort, and because it was the only thing that would make her even sadder.

Then she froze for three days, wrapping herself up in woolen jackets, in blankets, freezing.

"Are you ill?" Max asked when she visited him at his new apartment or his office.

"Of course not," she said. "I'm not ill. What makes you think that? I'm just a bit cold. I've been swimming in the Danube. That's enough to chill you through."

"Are you ill?" her colleagues at the station asked.

And she gave the same answer: "No, I'm not ill. What makes you think that? I'm just a bit cold. I've been swimming in the Danube. That's enough to chill you through."

But in fact she was a little ill, lovesick, sick from the love that should never have been but had materialized, creeping up unplanned, unintended. Not screwing, not fucking, not superficial eroticism—not anymore. Or not only that, anyways.

How it had all changed. Her assertiveness had dwindled and her tenderness grown. It was clear. Simple. Nice. It would hurt.

Later, while he was onstage, she spent some time in an Internet chat room. To distract herself. To arm herself. To defend herself.

25

Sunday. The third day since the body was found. September 14. Arthur cursed leaving Karolina's arms. But duty was duty, even if he didn't relish it.

"Ciao, love," he whispered in her ear, but she shooed him away like an irritating fly, rolled onto her other side, and went back to snoring softly. With a sigh of regret he tore himself away.

The café owner was waiting. Pacing up and down outside the police station, smiling at him as he hurried up.

"It's OK," she said. "No need to worry. It's Sunday, after all. I don't have anything else going on."

Yes, he thought, *it's Sunday. I don't have anything else going on, either.* "I'm sorry," he said as he opened up the station.

"No problem," she said. "I was a bit early. It's a habit of mine. I always get up early, even on Sunday when I don't have to go to the café."

"Yes," he said, rolling his eyes a little. "Sunday. Right."

She laughed. "You poor thing. I'm sure you must have had better things to do."

"Oh, you know . . ."

• • •

A little later they were sitting in the forensic team's office. The officer booted up the computer, and they could begin piecing together the composite of Gertrud's visitor.

She took her time. She had only seen him twice, so it took a while. But that was necessary sometimes. Make the eyes bigger, then smaller, then something in between. Hairline, brow, mouth, nose, chin. Gradually an image formed, a face. Again and again she trawled her memory to see whether it was correct, whether the face on the screen matched the one in her head. Eventually, finally, she was done.

She leaned back, looking slightly exhausted.

"I could use a coffee," she said.

Arthur jumped up. "Of course! I'm sorry. I'll nip over to the machine."

On his return he noticed immediately that something was different, that she was different. Tense. Wide-awake. And deeply shocked. She was staring at the composite in her hand, which the officer had printed out for her.

"What's the matter?" asked Arthur in alarm as he put the mug of coffee down in front of her. "You look as if you've seen a ghost."

"Yes," she said, looking up. "A ghost. I am actually seeing a ghost."

Arthur sat on the edge of the desk. "A ghost? Here in this picture? What do you mean?"

"This is Tonio," she said. "Oh my God, it's Tonio. How could I not have noticed? I can't believe I only just realized it!"

Arthur felt his skin beginning to crawl, the hairs on his neck standing a little on end, his heart beating faster. Lord, how he loved moments like this in his job!

"Who's Tonio?" he asked cautiously. *Not too quick,* he thought. *Give her time, don't overwhelm her, let her gather her thoughts.*

"Tonio." She hesitated and took a deep breath. "Tonio was the love of Hanna's life."

He whistled softly through his teeth. This was getting better with every moment. "Hanna? You mean Hanna Umlauf?"

"Yes," she said. "Hanna Umlauf."

"You know Hanna Umlauf, too?"

"Yes, I know Hanna Umlauf, too. Of course I know Hanna. But I haven't seen her for years. Not since the tragedy back then."

"OK," Arthur said, raising his hands to calm her. "Slowly now. From the beginning. I need more details."

She told him, slowly. From the beginning, in minute detail. Everything she knew. It was not as much as Arthur had hoped, but it was more than a little. You could say they were a few steps closer to an answer.

• • •

When the café owner had gone, Arthur sat there on his chair, shaking his head a little and smiling as the sweet feeling of knowledge flowed through him. *I have to call them,* he thought. *I have to tell them. They'll want to know all the details.* He took his cell phone and pressed the quick-dial button. Karolina answered immediately.

"Oh! Karo! It's you! I must have dialed the wrong number. OK, so I'll tell you first. A breakthrough!"

"What?" she asked. "What are you talking about? A breakthrough? Do you mean *breakdown*? You? That'd be nothing new, my little crazy!"

She laughed. He heard the affection in her voice and pictured her before him, stretching with a mysterious smile in the September sunshine. Alone. Without him. He immediately longed to be with her. Yet it wasn't as bad as it was before. At last he had made a breakthrough.

"No, I'm not having a breakdown! A breakthrough—me! Just imagine, my love, I've made the breakthrough!" He immediately qualified his words. "Well, maybe." Then he continued, on a roll, "I love you, honey, you know that, don't you?" He went even further, because it seemed so easy to say, the words somehow tumbling out of their own accord. "Will you marry me?"

As soon as the words were out, he realized what he had said, and that the ball was now in Karolina's court, and that, if she said no, he would look like the biggest idiot north or south of the equator. But he was anyways. Who but a complete madman, who but the biggest idiot north or south of the equator would in all seriousness ask the woman he loved to marry him over the phone?

I could kick myself, he thought. *I could really kick myself. Why doesn't she say something?* He started to tremble because she said nothing. She simply said nothing.

But then she spoke. "Yes, why not?"

She said, Yes, why not?

When he heard the words and heard the smile in her voice as she said them, he was delighted and began to shout for joy.

Later, he would say he felt like a giant at that moment, bigger than ever before, as though he were in a film. *Arthur,* he thought, raising a silent glass to himself, *Arthur, you really have a way with women!*

Then he finally called Oberwieser. She didn't reply.

26

Franza met Dorothee Brendler at the hotel in which she was now staying.

They walked through the park immediately adjacent to the hotel, stopping regularly, pausing in the conversation to gather their thoughts.

"Can you just tell me about your daughter, Frau Brendler?" Franza said, and Dorothee nodded.

"My daughter. Yes. I actually had two. Somehow there were suddenly two and . . . I know this sounds awful, but that was when all our troubles started."

She nodded, lowered herself down onto a park bench and shooed away the pigeons begging for food.

"Do you know the feeling when you know or suspect something's going badly wrong, but you're completely helpless, unable to do anything?"

Franza nodded. Yes, she knew that feeling. She thought of her son, Ben, and Marie, the girl he'd loved, who had died.

"My daughter, Gertrud," Dorothee began. "She's . . . she was a wonderful young woman with plenty of opportunities ahead of her. But she . . . she hadn't made anything of them for a long time."

"Your husband's already told us that—"

"He has? I thought as much. So you already know a lot. But maybe it's oversimplifying to reduce it to that." Dorothee shook her head. "Oh, I don't know."

A group of small children walked past, led by a teacher, another bringing up the rear. The children were holding hands and waddling along like ducklings. Lost in thought, Dorothee watched them go. "Is life still simple when you're that young?"

Franza shrugged. "I don't know. Do you think so? Doesn't every age have its worries?"

"Yes, you're probably right."

Franza's cell phone rang. She ignored it.

"You know," said Frau Brendler, "I was so pleased when the two of them had finally finished high school. I thought it would all be over then, that covert wrangling, which they never did openly. They carried it on in secret all those years, a constant fight, in which Gertrud was always the underdog. I thought, now at last they can go their own separate ways. One will study in this city, and the other somewhere else, and they can finally live their own lives. But no."

She shook her head and gave a brief, bitter laugh.

"When Hanna announced that she wanted to go to Munich to study photography, Gertrud said right away she would go with her. She was going to study law in Munich, and they could share an apartment."

She shook her head as though she still could not believe it, before continuing.

"I remember thinking I wasn't hearing her right. Hanna also seemed amazed, but she nodded and said, 'If that's what you want.' Later I took Gertrud to one side, begging her, 'Gertrud, please don't do it! Start living your own life!' But she looked at me like I was a complete stranger, and gave me a real dressing-down. What did I mean by that? Start living her own life? That was what she was doing, and it was her business. Why was I interfering? We should be happy she was helping us save money—this way we only needed to pay for one apartment. There was no point arguing."

"So they went to Munich."

Dorothee nodded. "Yes, they went to Munich together and shared an apartment, while I constantly asked myself why. Why was she doing that? Why wouldn't she let Hanna go?" She shook her head, incredulity in her eyes. "I took me an eternity to notice. I was blind. I probably didn't want to see it."

Silence. More head shaking. Franza began to suspect something.

"She was . . . in love?"

Dorothee was silent a little longer. "Yes, she was in love, my little girl."

Franza nodded cautiously. "With Hanna."

Peace in the park; the cooing of the pigeons; muted, far-distant voices; a soft singsong; a cyclist passing by.

"With Hanna. Yes. With Hanna."

Dorothee's voice revealed the cautious sadness of a woman who had seen something coming but could do nothing to prevent it.

"You don't happen to have a cigarette?"

"Yes, yes, I do." Franza rummaged in her purse. There were two.

"The first drag," Dorothee said quickly, blowing smoke from her mouth and nose. "It's always the first drag that gets to you."

Franza nodded. *Not only the first,* she thought and lit her own. They smoked, watching the billows swirling and vanishing into the air.

"You know," Dorothee said, "my Gertrud liked to care for people, even from childhood. First she took care of her dolls, and when Hanna came she took care of her. But Hanna only needed Gertrud's concern for a short while before she knew exactly where she was going and effortlessly overtook her."

Dorothee took a deep pull on the cigarette and continued. "Gertrud didn't notice it, not for a long time—the fact that we had a winner, someone who won everything, always. Someone who had only lost one thing in her life, and that was her mother. And then she'd decided she wouldn't ever lose anything again." She shook her head. "No, that's nonsense of course. Amateur psychology!" She laughed bitterly. "I sometimes wondered whether Gertrud hated Hanna because everything came so easily to her, even her father's love, but . . . I don't know."

Dorothee paused for thought, and then said, "I'm making it sound as though Hanna was a horrible person, but she wasn't—on the contrary. On the contrary."

Dorothee fell silent. Franza sensed her helplessness.

"At some stage," Dorothee continued, "Gertrud's feelings . . . changed. And then she simply couldn't let go of her."

Franza nodded, drew on her cigarette, blew the smoke out, waited. Nothing. Dorothee seemed sunk into silence. Franza asked cautiously, "What about Hanna?"

The woman raised her eyes, looked at Franza, and continued thinking, miles away.

"I don't know," she said eventually. "I really don't know. I never dared to ask. Not Gertrud, not Hanna. Perhaps she knew about Gertrud's feelings, or at least suspected. Perhaps not. Perhaps she even returned the feelings in some way. Perhaps not. Perhaps she simply allowed it to happen, tolerated it. Out of helplessness, out of . . . I don't know. The same way she simply accepted lots of things over the years. Probably out of gratitude toward us, because of a guilty conscience. But that would have been totally unfounded. We loved her. Even if it was . . . conflicting. Not easy. No. Of course she had a lot to thank us for. And then all our misfortune began with her."

Conflicting, Franza thought. *Yes, that's a good word: conflicting.*

"I know it sounds awful," Dorothee said, hiding her head in her hands.

"No, not awful. Just honest. Tell me more. Try to remember."

"Yes," Dorothee said. "Yes . . ."

27

Backthenbackthenbackthen . . . down the years . . . back . . .

"You look so beautiful." Gertrud looked at Hanna in amazement. "So beautiful."

Hanna laughed. "Oh, you're crazy! Me? Beautiful?"

"Yes," Gertrud said. "Yes, you are."

She reached out a hand and stroked Hanna's hair. Hanna flinched.

"Don't look at me like that, Gertrud! I don't like it."

She took a rapid step back, listened to the stillness, the pain she suspected Gertrud was feeling, and snapped the short thread of their togetherness. She turned. Turned on her heel like a spinning top with flapping arms and legs, and tore down the slope toward the river, with Gertrud . . . behind her, behind her, always behind Hanna.

"I'm an eagle," Hanna cried, laughing, running, flying. "Who is the wind's bride to carry me aloft?"

I will, Gertrud thought. *I will, let me be the one . . .* But she knew, knew with absolute certainty . . .

The river was still cold. It had rained a lot that year, with the temperatures well below the average, but the meadows were lush and green, and flecks of sunlight dappled their edges. Hanna jumped into the water, yelling and laughing to outsmart the cold.

"In the crimson waters the nettle banks sink deeper into the deeps!"

That was why Gertrud loved her—the way she yelled her word-paintings as she shook her wet hair like a dog and chased up and down the riverbank.

Gertrud loved Hanna because of her lightheartedness, her carefree nature, her courage, her generosity of spirit, and above all—above all she loved her because she had everything Gertrud lacked.

"I'm an eagle," cried Hanna into the red gold of the setting sun, spreading her arms wide. "Where's the wind's bride to carry me aloft?"

To love someone, Gertrud wrote in her red book during one of those glowing, hot summer nights that first year in Munich. *To love someone from the very first moment. To belong to someone from the very first moment. I have found the courage to let myself be touched by the facts, the realities. I have at last become immersed in love, at last—in love and in life and in light.*

The weather stayed hot and dry all summer long, but Gertrud rarely left the apartment. She only ventured out onto the streets and squares with Hanna, to explore the city in the twilight when it seemed golden and transparent.

In the mornings, after Hanna had left the house, Gertrud would slip into the bathroom, close her eyes and smell her. Only traces of her scent remained, but she breathed them in. *I will follow my beloved to the end of days.*

In Hanna's room she opened all the cupboards, boxes, drawers— touching nothing, only looking, driven to see, again and again, how, who, what . . .

Sometimes Hanna had left notes lying on her desk—*On someone's trail.* Since Gertrud *had* suddenly gotten on her trail, it shocked her, awakening guilt. Lying on the bed, she couldn't get the phrase out of her head. *Hanna, get on my trail . . .*

"Don't get burned," she begged herself. "Don't get smothered. Remember nothing is certain."

But it had already happened. If there had been a photo from those days, it would have shown how insubstantial Gertrud was.

28

A cell phone rang. A sudden ringtone, jolting Franza from her listening. It was the second time. Arthur again. It must be urgent.

"Excuse me, Frau Brendler," she said, "but I have to take this call."

She stood and moved a few steps away.

"I'm getting married," Arthur said.

Franza's eyes widened. "What? Have you gone mad?"

"Because I'm getting married?" he asked, sounding a little hurt.

She rolled her eyes. "Arthur, I'm really pleased you're getting married. Really. It's wonderful. But if that's why you're calling . . ."

"Oh," he said. "Of course not."

"Oh, get to the point, Arthur!"

"OK," he said. "Sorry. The point, right. Ask Frau Brendler about Tonio."

Franza hung up. *Fine,* she thought. *Tonio. Let's give it a go.*

"Tonio," she said. "Tell me about Tonio."

Dorothee Brendler looked up in surprise, shook her head. "Where did that come from . . . ?"

"It doesn't matter. Tell me."

"Tonio," Dorothee murmured, staring at the gravel at her feet. "He appeared out of the blue. A grown man. Almost thirty. Not a boy anymore, he'd made a life for himself. He came for Hanna."

29

It was at a small bar near the university called Renate's Inn. The place opened at noon and closed late at night. It was a students' haunt. Vasco, Renate's boyfriend, whom she had brought with her back from Spain, baked little cakes that were incredibly popular. They served Guinness, cola, water, and not much else, but the bar ran as if on well-oiled wheels, perhaps because of its simplicity. Its patrons said they played the best music ever. That was Vasco's department. At night he played whatever he felt like. Sometimes they brought in live bands, and people could dance if they wanted, or simply listen.

Hanna and Gertrud went there often. And then so did Tonio. One day he was sitting by the counter. Hanna entered the room, and Tonio saw her straightaway. And then she saw him. That was it.

The next evening he appeared again, and the next, and the third. As soon as Hanna arrived, the agitation vanished from his body. On the third evening Hanna began to dance, something she had never done before. She grabbed Gertrud's hand and dragged her onto the dance floor with her. Tonio sat at the bar, watching the girls, watching Hanna with penetrating eyes, a small grin on his lips. Hanna noticed and began to flirt with him over Gertrud's shoulder, coolly, with only her eyes and a tiny twitch of her mouth. Gertrud felt the change, turned, saw Tonio, and her heart stopped for a fraction of a second.

So I've lost Hanna, she thought. It hurt—really hurt.

"Hanna, is it?" said Tonio when he discovered her name and wound a strand of her red hair around his finger, raising it to touch his nose, his mouth.

She let him.

"I want to look at you, Hanna. May I?"

She let him. Later he sat five yards from her on his barstool, glass in hand, drunk, and she let him yell her name out into the thumping bass. Hanna smiled, and her teeth gleamed in the bright light.

30

It's raining.

I understand things now. A little. But to understand is not to forgive. The years flicker back, a gleaming carousel.

It's raining. The rain is warm and soft. I enter the water and swim out, the wetness enfolds me from above and below, the raindrops patter on the surface of the river, forming small circles and sinking into the depths.

Tonio. My Tonio. I hadn't thought about you for a long time. For all these years you were merely a tiny shadow in my memory, and now . . .

Nothing is lost, even if you shut it away in the depths of your memory and try to lose the key. At some point it all comes back. Stronger than before. What a mistake to believe that you can escape from your life.

Tonio was full of impatience. In everything. He lived life at such a fast pace. So different from me, so different from Gertrud. He came over us like a storm, unbridled, unrestrained. Wanted everything on the spot, unable to wait. Although . . . that's not quite true. No. He waited for me. Three whole days and nights. Waited until I noticed him. Until

I favored him with a glance. My smile. My longing. And yet . . . I gave him everything on the first day, in that first moment.

We were already away from home, we were already in Munich, Gertrud and I. There was this bar, like an enclave of our city, where we went on weekends. Renate's Inn was where all our friends met up, all those who had drifted away from the claustrophobic small-town scene. It was where we pursued life with Guinness, Bavarian pretzels, and Spanish cakes, and it was where Tonio found us.

It's difficult to remember. So many pictures in my head. The rain. Now I swim. The water bears me up so lightly, so naturally. It's amazing, but I never lost my trust in the water. The water has always remained my element.

Since I got the letter, Tonio's letter to me—one of his many letters—since his son, his son whom he never told me about, sent this letter back to me, the story has come to life again.

It's as though the gate to my memory has opened wide—it's all there again, every little thing, the tiniest detail.

Tonio was a good swimmer. He cut through the water with strong arms and legs. He was fast, much faster than I was. But he drowned. Now, at last, I know why.

You asked me whether I could understand it, Gertrud. Understand it? Understand that?

No. What can you understand in your head when there's a deep wound in your heart?

Now everything is an open book. Now I know, Gertrud, that at some point you stopped loving me like a sister. I may have suspected it back then, but I couldn't lose myself to you. Only to Tonio. Only to him. Only to his body.

Perhaps I should have said, "Go to Nuremberg, Gertrud! Or to Hamburg. Or to Cologne. Don't pin your life to mine. Nor your heart. It'll burn up."

But I said nothing.

I know your mother did. And she was right, Gertrud. But even she couldn't help us.

To understand means only to understand, not to forgive. Two people are dead now. But back—to the beginning. Or rather, to the middle. Back to Renate's Inn.

31

Renate's Inn.

Renate had to smile when she thought about it. It had been her first bar—the first bar of her own.

"What are you thinking about, darling?" Vasco asked, putting his arms around Renate's shoulders from behind her. She leaned her head back and thanked God for this man and his strength, this man who had made her life so much easier.

"You remember Munich?" she asked. "Hanna and Gertrud?"

"Gertrud. The potter." He pointed across the street. "The one who was killed. Of course I remember her."

"No, I mean do you remember her back then. In Munich. When I was running the Inn. She was always there with Hanna. Her friend. Or her sister. Whatever."

"Yes, you know I do," he said without hesitation. "They were there every day. I remember it well. Hanna was cool. Distant, somehow. Not my type at all. Always kept Gertrud at arm's length. And she found that difficult to cope with."

"You remember all that?"

She turned and looked at him in surprise.

He smiled. "Yes, why shouldn't I? I felt really sorry for her, that girl. She had no chance. Hanna really did have a heart of stone. Until . . ."

"Until Tonio came," Renate said, nodding. "Until Tonio came."

32

And then he danced, my Tonio. He really let go. He drank in the music, fell into it, moved beneath the flickering lights, saturated by the thumping beat.

Everyone around him was cool and alone—glittering, nameless night creatures. But not Tonio.

Tonio was . . . real.

I stood there as if struck by lightning. I stared at him, bewildered, stunned that someone could be so much himself and proclaim it so openly, shameless and unbridled. I was transfixed, unaware of time and space. It was as though he came from another world.

How lovely the water is, how beautiful this river is. I'd forgotten. How could I be away from here for so long? I'm only realizing now how much I missed it.

You were no longer very young, Tonio, and I liked that. I liked the fact you had a few years on me. I liked the traces of life in your eyes, in the lines on your face. I liked that.

And then, Tonio, you drew me into you. You took my hand and pulled me to you. But I had long since fallen in love with you, long since. In love with your cool, light hand that kept brushing the hair from my face, in love with your eyes. In love with you, Tonio. In love with you, body and soul.

Eventually we left the bar. You led me out, and we went down to the Isar, and stopped under some bridge.

"Just imagine this is the Danube," you said. "Just imagine this is our Danube. In our town. It'll make you feel more at home."

"But I feel at home anyway," I said, thinking, *now, here, with you.* I turned to the water. I couldn't bear your eyes on me any longer. They saw everything.

The Danube. The Danube, here, now. My river. I'm coming back to you. I'm leaving Jonas and coming back. Everything's been done. There's nothing new under the French sun. But here, by the cool Danube. Where it all began—even if it was actually the Isar. But he said: Just imagine this is the Danube. And it was the Danube.

I didn't dare turn to him that night beneath that bridge. I didn't dare turn from the water to him. He gave me time. He gave me all the time in the world. His eyes embraced me, singed the back of my knees, burned the nape of my neck. I felt it all. His eyes—like sharp arrows—hooked me fast, vertebra by vertebra, brushing my shoulder blades, over my neck, through my hair, transforming my brain into a mass of mushy thoughts.

You gave me time, Tonio, and then you didn't—all the time in the world, and then none. The world was so big, yet only the size of an almond. There was so much time, yet only a moment. I loved you from the very first second.

Finally he approached me, quiet as a panther. As his hand touched me, cool, light, stroking the hollow between shoulder and neck, I stood still, because it seemed so familiar and right, because it fulfilled my desire.

"You're so soft, Hanna," he whispered in my ear. "So soft, like a fresh cake."

I had to laugh, a little nervous, a little hysterical. The street lights were reflected on the water, breaking into dazzling orange pearls, as I felt his breath on my ear, as I heard him saying he wanted . . . he wanted so much . . .

"My Hanna," you said. "My Hanna, I've found you."

"My Hanna," you said, and your gentleness took my breath away. And so it began.

33

Hanna is the center, Gertrud wrote in the red book, *and that's nothing new. That's how it's always been. She is the point around which everything turns, around whom we circle like tigers around a piece of meat. I know I'll be the loser in the end, but the crumbs she gives me, because she's happy and radiates her happiness in every direction, these crumbs are worth any pain . . .*

They knew nothing of love or its power. They were young, still children in some ways. They had no way of foreseeing what they should have foreseen.

Three people, surrendered to one another in their helplessness, unsuspectingly destroying each other, excessive in their demands of life and love. All three of them were happy if only for a brief time—even Gertrud. She greedily took the enthusiasm Hanna radiated from her love for Tonio. He, an intruder, an interloper, had awakened a love the like of which had never been before, which permeated them all with the certainty that they had been made for each other.

They became dependent on one another, plunged into a feeling of imprisonment, which was deceptively weightless and clear. It made them happy, and if there was the slightest hint of fear and the inkling of a suspicion that this happiness couldn't last, they didn't want to believe it. They became dependent on the feelings they held inside. But dependence was the last thing they intended or wanted. *Freedom*—as Janis Joplin sang—*is just another word for nothing left to lose.* They now had a lot to lose. But they didn't realize it at first. The loss happened gradually, and for a long time they had no idea what it looked like, what it felt like, or how bitter it tasted.

Because they were happy at that time, every one for themselves, happiness at least seemed guaranteed. But was it guaranteed? No.

It's all in vain, Gertrud wrote in her diary while sitting in the departure lounge two hours before their flight to Greece. *All in vain. Hanna won't let me touch her, inwardly or outwardly. Her boundaries are clear as glass. I'm lost . . .*

And then Tonio died.

34

"Shit!" Felix exclaimed fervently when he and Franza met at a bar on Hollingerstrasse for a quick lunch and a brief team meeting, taking a table outside to make the most of the good weather. "Shit! She's simply vanished without a trace, this Hanna Umlauf! We've found nothing—nothing! Nada, *niente*, zilch!"

He'd been to the hotel and asked the staff whether they knew where she intended to go, whom she had met, what her plans were. But no one knew anything.

Checking the telephone records had yielded nothing. No interesting numbers on the telephone company's list, no one who might be the slightest bit likely to have anything to do with the case. She'd hardly made any calls at all. Jonas Belitz, on the other hand, had tried to make contact with his wife innumerable times, but without success. Since the night of the murder, her cell phone had been switched off, so there was no possibility of locating her that way. That was an additional cause for concern. It meant that either Hanna was dead or held captive somewhere, or that she didn't want to be contacted—which gave credence to the scenario in which she was Gertrud's murderer.

They had, of course, also checked Gertrud's telephone calls. Disappointing. There was only the usual contact with family. The only thing of interest was a number of calls from a prepaid SIM card, although that didn't really help, as it was not registered.

"What about you? Have you found anything new?" Felix asked, taking a halfhearted bite of his ham-and-cheese toasted sandwich. The cheese dripped, and Felix began to curse again.

Franza shook her head. "Now, now, calm down! Things are never as bad as they seem."

"They are," he snapped. "This damned cheese, for a start!" He rubbed at his mouth and chin with a paper napkin. "It's damn hot. Burned me!"

Franza waited a few moments for him to calm down, and then she told them about her conversation with Gertrud's mother.

Felix listened attentively. "Perhaps we shouldn't concentrate on Hanna as the sole suspect."

"No, of course not," Franza replied. "She could still be a victim. But of course she's a trail to follow. Did Gertrud's husband come to the station this morning? And the children?"

Felix nodded. "Yes, they came. We took their fingerprints. They're in for analysis now. But Robert thinks it could take a while until they've all been filed and sorted. In a family home like that, with children and visitors and all the comings and goings, there are a lot of fingerprints."

He thought for a moment, shaking his head. "This Rabinsky . . . I don't know. There's something strange about him. He knows more than he's saying. Perhaps Brückl's right after all. Jealousy has always been a strong motive. And that red hair in his bed . . ."

"Have you confronted him with it?"

"No, not yet. I thought we'd wait until we've checked out his alibi. Then we'll do it together." He grinned. "You know, good cop, bad cop. Sometimes we just have to live the cliché."

Peter Hansen joined them, carrying a beer.

He had no news either. He had questioned Jonas Belitz again, but he knew nothing about any stories from the past. When asked about his friendship with Hanna's foster father, he confirmed what they had already found out from Brendler—there had been no contact between them for many years. That was likely because Belitz had married Hanna, which was not met with great enthusiasm. But love rules all.

"He's really upset," said Hansen, taking a drink of his beer. "It's time we found her. The missing-person alert will be on the evening news. Let's see if that yields anything."

He studied the menu, which was rather scant, and finally ordered what he always did: egg on toast. "What do you think about the older man–younger woman thing?"

Felix had to smile, and Franza raised her eyebrows. Hansen hesitated. "Did I say something wrong?"

"No, no. Nothing wrong." Felix cleared his throat. "Well, to each his own, I say. Variety is the spice of life. Live and let live. That's what's so good about democracy and human rights, isn't it? Franza?"

He gave her a little nudge and grinned again. She nudged him back with a smile of her own. Hansen watched them in amusement. "Well, you two understand each other well enough. You're a good team, aren't you? It's enough to make me envious."

"Yes, it is," Franza said. "Oh, here comes the rest of our team. Just a word of warning: he's walking on air, don't drag him back to earth too suddenly!"

Arthur did indeed seem to float over to their table, his face slightly flushed, stars in his eyes.

"Jesus Christ!" Felix said. "What's up with him?"

"He's getting married." Franza raised her hands in the air. "But you didn't hear it from me."

"Oh my God!"

The men stood up to greet him, Arthur looking bewildered as they clapped him on the shoulder.

"So you've finally gotten your way with our little Karolina," Felix said and smiled.

"But how . . . ?" Arthur stammered.

"She couldn't keep it shut," Felix said affectionately, nodding in Franza's direction. "But don't be angry with her. You couldn't have hidden it in any case—it's obvious a mile away."

Franza punched Felix playfully, and then shrugged, her head to one side. She smiled remorsefully and gave Arthur a hug. "I'm sorry, fella, but it's no big secret, is it?"

"No, not a secret," Arthur said. "Just total madness!"

He thought of his hometown in the north, the moors and heathland—everything he wanted to show Karolina—and of his mother, who could be a bit complicated at times but was basically fine.

They eventually turned their attention back to Gertrud, to Hanna, and to the case.

"So, this café owner, Renate Stockinger," Arthur began. "She used to have a bar in Munich, a place Gertrud and Hanna often frequented. Then a man turned up, around thirty years old, Tonio. He was interested in Hanna and it turned into a passionate love affair. But then there was Gertrud, who, according to Stockinger, was inclined toward Hanna, in a romantic sense. So it looks like there was a bit of a triangle going on."

"Long live democracy and human rights," Felix said. Hansen and Franza nodded.

Arthur raised his eyebrows in question. "What?"

Franza shook her head. "Nothing. Inside joke. What else did she say?"

"One day, the three of them set off on holiday together. Greece, the island of Kos. Brendler has a holiday home there."

"And?"

"Only Gertrud came back."

"Because?"

"Tonio died and Hanna took off."

"Well, would you believe it?" said Hansen.

"That matches up with what Gertrud's mother told me," said Franza. "Did Frau Stockinger know any more details?"

"He drowned. He went swimming on a stormy night and drowned. Apparently he was an amazing swimmer, but it didn't help him that time."

"Why would someone go swimming in the open sea on a stormy night?" Hansen frowned and shook his head.

"Hopefully our Greek colleagues were able to find out," Franza said.

Felix nodded. "Indeed. But what do you mean, Hanna took off?"

"Well, Stockinger didn't really know. Hanna simply failed to return to Germany. She . . . set off into the world. She never saw her again. Unlike Gertrud."

"It's an incredible coincidence, isn't it? The café and the pottery shop being opposite one another. The fact that the two met again there." Franza sipped her coffee.

Arthur nodded. "It certainly is. Stockinger thought so, too. She was quite amazed when Gertrud moved in. It wasn't that long ago. Just over a year. Before that Gertrud had stayed home with Moritz. When Stockinger went over to greet her new neighbor and invite her over for a coffee, she found out it was Gertrud from Munich. It seems Gertrud wasn't particularly pleased to see her old acquaintance at first. It was a while before she accepted the coffee invitation. They weren't particularly close. In fact, it had only been in recent weeks that Gertrud had come over to the café with any regularity."

"She obviously didn't want to be reminded of the past," Franza said. "I'm not surprised, given all that happened. I'm not too thrilled myself to meet people who witnessed my past defeats."

Arthur shrugged, nodded.

"Well," Felix said. "We've got a lot to do, guys. A hell of a lot to do."

They stretched a little in the mild September sun, momentarily lost in thought. *The world seems to be constantly drifting a little toward the void,* Franza thought.

Felix took up the thread again. "Had that been Hanna's intention, do you think? To set off into the world?"

And back, Franza thought. *It also drifts back, but not everyone can rely on that.*

Arthur shook his head. "Stockinger didn't seem to think so. She was in the middle of her degree course. She hadn't graduated. It looks like it was a sudden decision. A reaction to the shock of her boyfriend's sudden death."

"Yes, that fits quite well with what Frau Brendler told me," Franza said. "Hanna traveled for a while, she thinks it was for around two years, but couldn't remember exactly. Then she broke off all contact and they were unable to get back in touch with her."

"What exactly happened in Greece?" Felix wondered. "I'd be very interested to know. Maybe that's the key."

"We'll contact our colleagues in Greece tomorrow via Interpol and ask a few questions," Franza said. "They must have investigated what happened at the time."

"I've already taken the liberty of initiating it, Boss." Arthur grinned, a little embarrassed.

"Very good!" Franza nodded her approval. "Good lad!"

Arthur spoke again. "I've got something else. You remember the guy who came to the café two days running and claimed to be visiting Gertrud?"

They all nodded.

"It was because of this man that Stockinger told me about Tonio. When we'd finished making the composite image, she suddenly turned quite pale and said"—Arthur paused dramatically—"she said it was . . . Tonio."

"Oh," Franza said.

"Wow," Hansen said.

Felix whistled through his teeth.

"But that's impossible, of course," Arthur continued, "because he's dead. Drowned in Greece twenty-two years ago. Besides, if it were him, she probably wouldn't even have recognized him. He'd be twenty-two years older and would have looked correspondingly different." He moved to stand by Felix and gave him an innocent smile as he aimed his words at Franza. "What I mean is, there's quite a difference between him and me, isn't there?"

"Yes, there certainly is!" Franza said with a grin. "Twenty-two years certainly makes a difference."

Felix gave Franza a dark look. "Traitor!" He turned to Arthur. "May you age badly, my friend!"

Arthur laughed. "Yes, Boss, I'll do my best."

They thought for a moment. So there might be a son—maybe a younger brother, but more likely a son. One from a previous life.

"Do we have a surname for this Tonio?"

"We do."

"Good. Find out about his relatives."

"It will be difficult if this supposed son has a different family name. Which isn't impossible."

"Well, perhaps we'll be in luck. You need a bit of luck sometimes."

Felix's cell phone rang. He took it out. A new smartphone.

"Oh," Franza said.

"Wow," Hansen said.

Arthur whistled through his teeth.

Felix gave a subtle smile, looked at the display, and moved to another table. He exchanged a few sweet nothings with Angelika, something he'd taken to doing recently. The others waited in a reverent silence. When he returned, he placed the gadget on the table.

"You're impressed, aren't you?"

"We're impressed," Hansen said. He picked up the phone and examined it from all sides.

"We're not *that* impressed," Arthur said, delving into his pocket. "I've got one, too."

"But we *are* impressed," Franza said. "Our Felix getting himself such a nice man toy? Are you entering male menopause, Herz? Or having a midlife crisis? I'd have thought you'd have gone for a bigger toy—a sexy convertible, for example."

They laughed.

"Or . . . ," Hansen began, his face lighting up, ". . . or a sexy . . ."

"Stop!" Franza said, raising her hands. "Stop right there! We don't need to hear it, Hansen!"

They laughed again, and Felix grabbed Hansen by the shoulders, giving him a light shake.

It's good to be here laughing, Franza thought, *and knowing they accept you as you are. You can be yourself. They take you seriously but know how to laugh with you. This is how you manage not to let it drag you down—this way you can stay afloat and face life.*

That was how it had always been—cases, obstacles. People tripped, went under, and then they arrived, the detectives, bringing things to light and finding answers. It was an eternal cycle, always in motion. A cycle which, to look at it pragmatically, assured their livelihoods, their income, their economic foundations. Everything had its place.

"OK," Franza said. "I think it's all coming together. I'm totally convinced of it. These aren't mere coincidences. This young man, Tonio. He appears suddenly. Gets in touch with Gertrud. She's scared to death. Hanna. She comes to this town for the first time in more than twenty years. And disappears without a trace. No, these can't be coincidences. It all hangs together, somehow connected with Gertrud's death. And her past. Once we know her past, her story, we'll see the motive. And we'll know why she died. And then we'll have the murderer."

"What could the motive be? What do you think?" Arthur asked.

Franza smiled. He was still so young; he knew so little of life.

"Love's the motive." She picked a bit of fluff from his jacket. "Hate, revenge. The usual stuff."

They were silent. A little reverential for a brief moment. The toasted sandwich on Felix's paper plate had long since gone cold. Franza had drunk her coffee.

"Aren't you eating anything?"

Felix looked at Arthur, who shook his head.

"Karolina's cooking."

"Oh my word," said Felix. "Then shouldn't you eat something first?"

Franza snorted with laughter and poked Felix in the ribs.

"Come on, now, there are women out there who can cook! Look at me. You're just unlucky!"

"True." Felix nodded in agreement. "You can bake, roast, cook—just about anything. A real gem." He gave Arthur a look of sympathy. "Well, kid, would you like my sandwich?"

Arthur frowned briefly. "I think she's making a . . . soufflé. It sounded . . ." He thought for a moment. "I'm not exactly sure."

"There you are." Felix pushed his plate toward Arthur. "You don't have to know all the details. And you don't have to put up with everything."

Franza smiled, closed her eyes, and let her thoughts wander. Business as usual. Death to one side, marriage to the other, and banter here. And then there were the people who suddenly found themselves . . . alone. When they had been . . . together for an age. Here they were, laughing and fooling around, although there was really nothing in their work to laugh about. Perhaps that's why they did it. Perhaps that's why they had to laugh, to keep their spirits up. They never knew on which side they stood, which way the pendulum would swing.

"There's a diary," Franza said suddenly, opening her eyes. "Gertrud kept a diary back then. Frau Brendler knew about it. Have we found one?"

"No," Felix said. "Not that I know of."

"Do people throw diaries away?"

"Not usually," Felix replied. "Angelika still has all hers."

"So do I," Franza said. "Hidden away in a drawer. I could never throw them away. They contain all my love stories from my past."

"Hm," said Arthur. "I'm sure they're fascinating—but what are you getting at?"

"That we should search again. Search thoroughly."

35

Lilli stared at the words until they swam before her eyes. She kept going back to them, again and again. The words that flowed over the pages of the diary wouldn't let her go, held her under their spell. Sometimes they jumped here, sometimes there. Sometimes they sounded full of happiness, sometimes optimism, before falling into despair.

"I don't want to continue my studies," Lilli had finally told her grandfather that day when they'd met for lunch downtown. "I don't want to work in your law firm."

He had nodded, taking in what she said. He simply accepted the situation. He had finally come to recognize that some things were inevitable.

"I've made a mistake," he said and wiped his mouth with his napkin. "I've made a big mistake."

She didn't ask what. A mistake. She didn't ask what he meant, whether it was about Gertrud or Hanna or even herself. She didn't want to know. She had suspected and discovered too much over the last few weeks and months. She didn't want to know any more.

"Maybe . . ." he began. She realized with astonishment that his voice was cracking. "Maybe, one day, your grandmother and I can—"

He broke off. *An old man,* she thought in amazement. *He's turned into an old, old man.*

"Yes," she said. "Maybe."

He looked at her gratefully.

She thought of the letter lying in the desk back home, right at the bottom of a drawer beneath her papers, all the other letters that had meant something in her life. She thought how it had lain there for a long time, and that she still hadn't opened it and so she still didn't know with any certainty what she had suspected for a long time. The letter had arrived shortly before she flew to England. She remembered how her heart had begun to beat faster. She started to open the envelope slowly, carefully, and felt a nervous flutter in her stomach. Suddenly, something caused her to hesitate, and she put the letter back down on the table. It lay there for three days until it was time to set off for the airport. When she heard the doorbell and Gertrud's voice—"Lilli, darling, I'm here! Time to go!"—she finally picked the envelope back up, the paper seeming to burn her fingers, and put it in the drawer. Right at the bottom beneath the other papers. Beneath the important letters. No, she didn't want to know what was in it. She still didn't want to look the truth in the face. Whatever the truth was.

"Here," she'd said to her mother, once they were out on the garden path. "Here's my key. Will you look after it for me?"

"Of course," Gertrud said and tucked it away. "I'll come by every two weeks to make sure everything's in order."

"That'd be great," Lilli said. "Thanks, Mama!"

Then she had flown to London. And then she'd returned, to find the letter still lying there where she had put it, right at the bottom of the drawer, untouched, unopened, unread.

36

Kristin was at the door.

The sudden ring of the doorbell had shocked Tonio to the core. He'd staggered backward and had to brace himself against the wall. So they had found him so quickly? So soon? It was incredible. Absolutely incredible.

As if in a trance, he felt all the blood in his body rush to his heart, and his heart began to pound and pound, his veins threatening to burst. Tonio held his breath and pressed his hand to his mouth, but the bell continued to ring. He expected to hear a cry of "Police!" and "Open up! We know you're in there! The house is surrounded! You don't have a chance! Give in now! There's no escape!" as he'd heard so often in the films.

And then someone did begin to shout. Loudly, impatiently. Loud enough to be heard throughout the whole building.

But it wasn't a harsh police officer's voice, it was a voice he knew. It was Kristin's voice. As soon as he recognized the fact, a new feeling struck him—surprise, a pleasant surprise even. He had yearned for nothing more fervently during those recent nights than to have her there, his comfort, his hope. He'd yearned to rely on her support in this desperate situation.

"Are you there?" she called. "Tonio! Are you there?"

Breathe deeply, he told himself. *Breathe deeply.* And he did, until he was at last able to push himself away from the wall and open the door. There she was, Kristin, head held high, hands on hips.

"You idiot," she said. "You stupid idiot! You dump my things outside the door and just take off! Are you crazy?"

"But that's what you wanted," he said, slowly coming back to his senses. "You wanted me to put your things outside the door."

She raised her eyebrows, shook her head, and snorted loudly. "Men! Impossible! Men!"

Silence fell for a moment, two.

"Are you going to let me in?" Her voice was suddenly gentle and a little shaky.

"Yes. Of course. Yes."

He stepped back and she entered.

He showed her the way. She moved tentatively, step by step, sensing she was entering new territory and taking due caution.

Later they sat at the kitchen table with two glasses of water in front of them. They looked at one another, twilight spreading through the room and muting the light.

"How did you find me?" he asked, thinking it must have been the power of his mind—he'd called to her and suddenly she was there.

"You don't seriously believe that I didn't write down the lawyer's name?" she said with a slightly shamefaced grin.

"Aha," he said. "So?"

She shrugged. "So what?"

"Well, there's a way to go between the name of a lawyer and the address of an apartment." He shifted his arm to the middle of the table and hoped she would do the same.

"You think so?" She leaned her head back against the wall and looked at him through sleepy, half-closed eyes.

He nodded.

"I don't," she said with a smile.

Tonio leaned forward.

"He actually gave the address to you?" He tried to imagine what the man had asked for in return. "Is he allowed to do that? Isn't that covered by lawyer-client privilege?"

She shrugged. "A lawyer is just a person with a sensitive soul."

He was stunned. "You little sneak! What did you do?"

Her smile grew mysterious. "You don't need to know everything."

OK, he thought, *she has a point. I don't need to know everything, I really don't. The main thing is, she's here.*

Sex, he thought. *Feel a bit of life first and then we'll figure out what to do. Or maybe not.*

"You clever thing, you," he said.

"Aren't I?" she replied.

"Sex. With you. Now."

He felt desire for her like never before, despite all the dreadful things that had happened. He sensed she felt it too, his desire, his arousal, creeping toward her across the table and settling on her skin, into her eyes, her thoughts, and feelings. She wanted it, wanted it so much. She had him now, had him at last.

"No. Something to eat. Hungry."

"Hungry. Yes. Right."

Hungry for her. For the truth. Whatever the truth was. For her. For the truth. For life. For her. In that sequence. In that order of priority.

"Red wine," she said. "Risotto and crispy fried fish. Caramel sauce. Cake. Chocolate. Then . . . you. And me."

"Yes to all those."

He stretched across the table, touching the ends of her hair, entwining his fingers with hers.

"Hungry," she said. "Very hungry."

"Yes," he said, wondering how he could ever have seen her as a thousand-euro bill.

37

I could call her, Lilli thought, poking small pieces of strudel around the plate with her fork before finally putting one in her mouth. It tasted of apple, cinnamon, sugar, and butter; it tasted the way it had in Franza's house, tasted of the scent wafting from the oven as they'd talked. Talked about childhood, about strangeness, about Gertrud, about Hanna.

No, not about Hanna.

Lilli wished she'd talked about Hanna. Hanna was claiming ever more space in her thoughts, the more she delved into the book, the more Gertrud's diary revealed to her.

Where would she say she got it from? That would have interested Franza, Lilli was sure of it. But she had no intention of saying anything about the diary. It weighed so heavily on her conscience that she kept it locked away—from herself and, even more, from the others.

Sometimes she longed to go into an expensive upmarket shop and pocket a perfume, a damned, cursed perfume, and then take it and pour it down the toilet before taking off. Maybe, maybe one day someone would notice, some filthy store detective, and finally get on her trail, track her down, and catch her. The dreadful events would be drowned out by the terrible news that Lilli was a thief. Perhaps death would then lose a little of its sting. Perhaps Gertrud's death and everything that went with it would be subsumed a little then. Perhaps it would be easier to grasp, perhaps it would no longer be *themostdreadfulthingintheworld.*

But it was *themostdreadfulthingintheworld*, and nothing—nothing—could drown that out, however much Lilli wished it. The images had burned themselves into her retina—the onion, the knife, the blood, the jelly jars, the shards of glass, the sickly smell of boiled-down damsons, of sugar and a dash of brandy—and Gertrud in the middle of it all. Lilli knew all those things would forever be associated in her mind.

She swallowed and swallowed, letting the tears flow, fervently hoping that sooner or later she would cry it all out. But that wasn't likely to happen anytime soon.

She had taken the diary for herself when that cursed night gradually drew to a close and she had gone up to her parents' bedroom, because . . . because . . .

She didn't know why she'd gone there. Impulse. Intuition. Perhaps she'd thought she would see her, see Gertrud there, her scent still clinging to her clothes, the pillows, just a little, a little . . . and so it was.

Lilli had entered the bedroom and stopped as if struck by lightning. The bedclothes were rumpled, clothes lay around on the chairs, books on the bedside tables. Lilli carefully ran a hand over them. Yes, Gertrud could still be sensed here, in all her things. Yes, she was still there, like a breath of air, like a brightness, like dappled leaves.

Lilli had suddenly had the feeling she was penetrating an inner order that was fragile as glass and shimmering like shadows.

Her actions became slow and gentle so as not to disturb anything, not to move anything, not to chase Gertrud away. She'd sat down hesitantly on the bed, on Gertrud's side, and it occurred to her that she had never lain there, never snuggled up to Gertrud in this bed. She'd been far too old for that when they moved to this house.

Now, she'd thought. *Now's the time.* She'd lain between the sheets, snuggled in, breathed in the scent that still permeated the pillows. She'd thought of Gertrud lying downstairs in the kitchen in a pool of her own blood, in the jelly, by the onion, by the knife.

When Lilli eventually awoke from her daze and rose from the bed, she'd seen it. It was lying there. On the floor. Bound in red leather, tied up with a blue ribbon, its colors faded. Lilli had picked the book up, and her heart had begun to thump as she felt, as she knew . . .

She'd untied the ribbon, opened the book, and begun to read.

I have a sister now, Gertrud had written in a child's handwriting on the first page. *A sister is for life. My sister is called Hanna.*

Lilli had felt the cover in her hands, felt its firmness, and known she was entering a secret world, known it could be dangerous and that the dreadful reality could get worse, as unimaginable as that seemed.

She'd quickly closed the book and started to put it back. *Put it down,* her inner voice whispered. *Don't read it, don't do it.*

But she'd had to read it. She couldn't do anything else. She opened the book again. *I have a sister now. A sister is for life. My sister is called Hanna. She arrived like lightning. Her hair is like carrots. Her mother is a ghost. If you lift her arm, it falls back down. Her skin is like the white paper we have in the kitchen.*

It had slowly grown lighter outside. Morning was on its way. Lilli closed the book, opened the window, and looked out. The garden, the trees, the damsons, jelly in the kitchen. All so familiar. Only three days ago she had been helping Gertrud cook them. The smell, the heat, Gertrud bending over the oven, sweaty and tired but strangely happy.

Forgive me, Gertrud, Lilli thought now. *Forgive me, Mama. I love you. I always loved you, but you became such a stranger, so distant, like a glass doll sometimes. You were like the curtains when you washed and hung them out in the garden to dry. I ran into the curtains, felt them flapping around me, slapping their wetness into my face. And that's how it was with you sometimes, Mama. You slapped my face with your panic at losing me. I didn't know why, but it made me afraid, afraidafraidafraid. Now . . . I know a lot, but still not everything.*

Franza, Lilli thought as she bent over the apple strudel. *You can't help me, either, Franza. No one can. You have to help yourself. Always. Perhaps it's the smell of apples. Perhaps that's what I've always missed, apples mixed with butter and cinnamon. Perhaps. Perhaps it was also the smell of damsons, mixed with sugar and cinnamon, and I didn't recognize it . . . No more, no more smell of damsons, no, no more.*

Eventually she'd left the house, stumbling out past the kitchen and out to her car, the red book in her pocket. Back into town, by the Danube, she'd begun to run, hurrying through the early morning—a shadow seeking herself somewhere in the world.

As she'd leaned out over the water and seen the glittering outline of her face reflected in the pale morning moonlight, the contents of her stomach had risen up, a forceful fountain shot from her body and spattered into the water, shattering her face into a thousand wavelets.

Later, in her apartment, the voice on the answering machine had made her shudder. The voice and the sentence that had driven her from the apartment almost three hours before, out of town and to her parents' house, to Gertrud.

She'd fled again from the voice, from the sentence, from the red book, fled into the bathroom and under the shower. She'd forgotten time and space as the water ran hot down her body and her head fell back, dragged down by the weight of her hair. All was full of steam. Eyes closed, Lilli had crouched under the shower, arms wrapped around her body as if to protect herself against life's evils, against all the dreadful knowledge, every dreadful idea. When she'd finally emerged, it was as though she was waking from a deep sleep.

She'd rubbed her softened skin dry, wound her hair in a towel, and gone out to the phone. Gertrud's voice was still on the answering machine, distorted by fear, distorted by her own terror.

"I've done something dreadful, Lilli. Come over, come to me, Lilli, my love. I've done something dreadful."

38

It was easy to find Tonio's family name. Arthur only had to call Renate Stockinger. Fortunately, the woman had an incredible memory. But that was where the good fortune ended. They soon found out that Tonio had no registered descendants; all they had discovered was a father, who had died not long ago, and some distant relatives in Italy.

Oh well, Arthur thought, having cursed away his frustration, *it's time for some new ideas. Tonio's old man must have had neighbors or friends. There's always someone who knows something to move us a step forward.*

Or maybe the man had had nothing but a dog, or a cat, or, even worse, a budgie. Maybe he was a grumpy old man who'd scared off all his neighbors.

We'll see, Arthur thought with a sigh. *We'll see, as we always do.*

39

Lars Beuerle, whose birthday Rabinsky and his friends had been celebrating, was a big man, a graphic designer who lived with his wife and children in a row house with a garden in the suburbs.

"Actually," he said, once he and Felix had sat down in the kitchen, "Gertrud was also invited. If only she'd come."

Felix nodded. *Yes,* he thought pragmatically, *then I wouldn't be sitting here, but at home with my twins in my lap.*

"Well, you never know about these things."

"No," Beuerle said. "You certainly don't. But why are you asking me? What do you think I can tell you?"

He's playing a little dumb, thought Felix. *Acting as though he doesn't have a clue.*

"We're interested in Herr Rabinsky's alibi."

Beuerle raised his eyebrows in surprise. "His alibi? Why? Surely you don't suspect him? That's laughable!"

Felix shook his head. "Purely routine. We simply have to consider all the possibilities. You do want Frau Rabinsky's murderer to be found, don't you?"

How often have I asked that question? he thought. *That very question. And now for the answer . . .*

"But of course I do!"

. . . the same answer as ever. Felix wanted to roll his eyes. *How often have I heard that?*

He curved his lips into a tight smile. "There, you see! So, please, will you simply tell me how you spent that evening?"

Beuerle scratched his chin.

He could do with a shave, Felix thought. *But so could I.* He rubbed a hand over his own cheeks and chin, feeling the scratchy stubble and suspecting he wouldn't be having any luck with Angelika that night.

A noise came from the other side of the door, and a woman entered, tall, slim—her breasts accentuated in a tight T-shirt.

A feast for the eyes, Felix thought, his hormones taking over momentarily.

"My wife," said Beuerle, turning to her. "Imagine this, Rieke, they suspect Christian in that business with Gertrud. Isn't that the craziest thing you've ever heard?"

"Well, well," she said. "But he has an alibi, doesn't he? Us."

She approached, greeted Felix, and sat down at the table with a smile.

"So," said Beuerle, looking slightly tense, "we were at FiftyFour from seven to ten and then at Jealousy, the night club in the town center."

Felix nodded. *Extravagant,* he thought. *You were really treating yourself.*

"We were there until about three in the morning," Beuerle continued with a shrug. "It's not your birthday every day, after all."

Why is he apologizing? Felix thought. *Partying all night isn't a criminal offense.*

"And you're sure that Herr Rabinsky was there the whole time?" he asked.

"Yes," said Beuerle without hesitation, glancing at his wife. "Of course I'm sure. There were nine of us. They'll all confirm it for you. All couples. Only Christian was alone."

"Why was that?" asked Felix. "Do you know why his wife wasn't there?"

"Hm," said Beuerle pensively. "I don't. Do you?"

He looked at his wife, and she nodded.

"Yes," she said. "I asked Christian, and he said Gertrud was getting ready for a trip to Greece. I must say I didn't think it was seemed right. She could have done all that the next day. But that's what she was like. You could never rely on her."

"Rieke," said Beuerle a little brusquely. "Please don't."

"Why?" she asked. "Because it's wrong to speak ill of the dead? But it's true!" She turned to Felix. "What do you think, Inspector?"

"If it's true, we want to hear it. What was their marriage like?"

She thought for a moment. "No idea," she said, looking at her husband. "You don't see behind the scenes. Not with anyone. Don't you think?"

"You're right, of course," Felix said, deciding it was time to get to the point and bring the conversation to a close. "So, to clarify: You're both quite sure that Herr Rabinsky was there the whole evening and that he didn't leave the party at any time for an hour and a half or so? I mean, that would be a long time, so I'm sure you would have noticed."

Beuerle shrugged. "As I've already said."

"And you, Frau Beuerle, can you also confirm that?" Felix asked, allowing himself a final furtive glance at her assets.

"As my husband said," she replied with a smile.

"You're both aware that it would be a criminal offense to tell me anything but the truth?"

Beuerle shrugged. "Why should I lie?"

"Precisely." Felix stood. "Why should you? Why do people ever lie?"

Because there's always a reason for it, he thought. *Always.* He smiled to himself.

"Well," said Beuerle. "That's almost a philosophical question, isn't it?"

"It is," Felix replied. "And because it always takes much too long to answer philosophical questions, we'd better not go there. I'll get going and not inconvenience you any longer."

"No, no, it's no inconvenience," Beuerle countered quickly, extending his hand to Felix and forcing a polite smile.

"I'll see you to the door," said Rieke Beuerle, leading Felix down the hallway. She opened the door to let him out, but before he could leave, she leaned toward him, the smell of her slightly stale perfume tickling his nose.

"Give me an hour," she whispered. "I'll meet you in the park by the ice cream shop."

He nodded in surprise. *That's one alibi smashed,* he mused. He thought of Moritz and Lilli. He felt sorry for them.

40

Felix saw Frau Beuerle from afar, pacing up and down by the entrance of the ice cream shop.

"Frau Beuerle," he said, smiling as he approached. "Was there something else you wanted to tell me?"

She looked good. A bit of a bimbo, perhaps. She even carried in her handbag a fashion-accessory dog, as Marlene, Felix's eldest, would have called the little yappy rat of a creature.

"Yes," she said. "Aren't you going to invite me for a coffee? Are the police allowed that kind of thing?"

"They certainly are," Felix replied. "If I may have the pleasure."

She destroyed the alibi, which did, in fact, make it a pleasure. Or perhaps not. He thought of the children again. No, it wasn't actually a pleasure at all.

· · ·

Over coffee Frau Beuerle told Felix that during the meal Rabinsky had been jostled by a clumsy waiter, causing him to spill a glass of red wine over his shirt and pants. She didn't know precisely what had happened, as she'd been in the bathroom when it happened. In any case, the soaking eventually made Rabinsky uncomfortable, and he said he wanted to pay a quick visit to his office, where he could shower and change into a spare shirt and pair of pants. He was gone for about an hour, perhaps a little longer. They were at Jealousy by the time he caught up with them.

When he got back, he was behaving strangely and got plastered, so drunk that by the end he was barely able to stand. Having said that, Frau Beuerle admitted that her husband had done exactly the same, as had the others. It seemed they had probably only taken their wives along to provide cheap chauffeurs for the drive home. Christian had ridden with them, and they'd dropped him off at his office, where, he said, he intended to spend the night because it would have been too complicated to go home at that time of night.

She paused at that point, took a drink of her coffee, and looked at Felix thoughtfully.

She hadn't wanted to tell him in front of her husband, she said, because Christian had called and asked them to provide an alibi. He'd assured them that he'd had nothing to do with Gertrud's murder, that he'd gone to his office, taken a shower, and changed, as they all knew, but he couldn't account for that hour to the police. There was no witness, and everyone knew how picky the police could be about alibis. He'd asked them all to be kind enough to help him—things were difficult enough as it was for the children. If he were a suspect, it would be even worse.

"Of course, we all believe him," said Frau Beuerle. "Christian would never kill his wife. On the contrary—he wouldn't harm a fly. But a lie is a lie!"

And, of course, it wasn't good to lie to the police, which was why she was now sitting here over coffee.

Felix watched her in fascination as the words flowed; the nut torte vanished elegantly, piece by piece, between her narrow lips, and her low neckline revealed tantalizing cleavage whenever she leaned forward to smile at him.

I'll be damned, he thought. What had Christian done to warrant this kind of vengeance? Had she been trying to flirt with him with that arsenal in her blouse and he'd sent her packing, perhaps because . . . because she'd been a bit too pushy with him? Grinning to himself, he leaned back in his seat and stretched out his legs. This day had brought some results, at least, he thought with satisfaction. Not least a bit of eye candy.

41

"Max," Franza said into the telephone. "Are you there?"

"Yes," he said, a little surprised. "You can hear that I'm here. What's the matter?"

"I mean, are you at home?"

"Yes," he said, "I'm at home. Do you want to come over?"

"Yes," she said, "I'd like to. Do you have any food?"

He laughed. "Ah, so that's the way the wind's blowing! Madame's hungry and has forgotten to do the shopping. Your cupboards are bare, I take it?"

"Yes," she said, a little remorsefully. "We've got a new case and I didn't get home till late yesterday and all the shops were shut. My stomach's rumbling."

"Should we go out for a meal?"

"No," she said. "I feel like the peace and quiet of home. Is that OK?"

He nodded, although she couldn't see it on the phone.

"Of course it's OK," he said. "Come on over."

She hung up, leaned her head against the headrest, and started the engine. She had been sitting in her car outside her building for a quarter of an hour, tired after a long day. She hadn't a clue what to do with her evening, and she was disappointed that Christian Rabinsky's alibi was thwarted.

Arthur and Felix had gone home, where their women were waiting for them with meals, probably pampering them a little. But there was no one waiting for her. All she could expect was an empty fridge, a vacant couch, and an evening's TV. She had no taste for any of it that night.

Port had a show, and afterward he wanted to go out with the company to celebrate the invitation to Vienna. Franza sighed. Yes, the Vienna business, that damned Vienna business.

A farewell . . . it would only be temporary, but a farewell nevertheless. Franza thought of all the other farewells, the wandering from one country to another with her Austrian parents because her father, an engineer, was needed here, needed there. She had spent the longest period of her childhood some twenty miles from here, in a house with the rushing of a stream in the background. Sonja had lived in the neighborhood. Her family was also Austrian, also career nomads.

Franza was twelve when her family returned to Austria. Her father had been promoted to a top position in his company, so for the next few years they lived near the capital, where they were from originally, by the Danube. As now. That was the same. The Danube. A constant feature. A fixed point.

Then came her student years, and Franza had felt a desire to see the world—a year in London, then Frankfurt, where she stayed a while. She met Max and Borger, and then Felix. Great times. A great life. Small loves, then the big one—Max.

Later came her final farewell from Austria. It was clear she wanted to stay with Max, that they would marry and settle in this town in southern Germany.

A little later, Franza's father died suddenly from a heart attack. Her mother grew lonely and spent a lot of time with Franza. As fate would have it, one day she discovered that the old house by the stream, where they'd lived when Franza was a child, was for sale—and she bought it. And renovated it. And moved in. She lived there until life on her own became too difficult, and then she moved to an old people's home, where she lived until she died.

Since then Franza had been the owner of the "little house by the stream," as she called it. She would sell it one day.

It was funny that over the years they had all somehow ended up here: Herz, Borger, even Sonja, her childhood friend from the days by the stream, now the district attorney's wife.

She and Sonja had never really lost touch, bound to one another like sisters. They had been in London together—Sonja had even stayed on for a second year. She studied languages and became a book translator.

Then, one day, she'd come to visit Franza, and while they were wandering around the town center, they'd bumped into Dr. Brückl, at the time about to launch into his illustrious career in the district attorney's office. Sonja had said she wanted a coffee and Herr Brückl had said what a coincidence, so did he. So they had all gone into a café, and by the end of it Franza had come to feel slightly superfluous.

Dr. Brückl's illustrious career had not taken off as he'd intended, and he was still chasing it, but he did find his partner for life—Sonja.

Franza was flabbergasted when Sonja announced she'd fallen head over heels in love, that he was the man she wanted to spend her life with, and that she was more certain of it than she had ever been about anything.

"You want to inflict that career-driven asshole on yourself?" Franza had asked her friend, aghast. Until that moment she had considered the whole thing a superficial dalliance. "You can't be serious!"

"Don't say that," Sonja had begged. "He's not like that. Not a career-driven asshole. You don't know him. He didn't have an easy childhood."

Franza had rolled her eyes. Didn't they all say that? Just an excuse for never growing up.

She didn't voice the thought out loud to Sonja, but apologized for her outburst. She didn't want to lose her as a friend. Besides, they had created a kind of Austrian enclave, which occasionally did Franza good in her German exile, as she sometimes jokingly called it.

When they were together, which they were often, they spoke in their dialect from back then, enjoying those small, special words that belonged to them alone. They still laughed when anyone tried to imitate them, especially when they failed spectacularly.

Yes, they were something like sisters, she and Sonja, so close. Fortunately they had never crossed swords when it came to their taste in men. Despite having so much in common, they had nevertheless always gone their own ways.

That was something that had obviously gone wrong with Hanna and Gertrud. You could have a sheltered childhood, Franza thought, with loving parents, money, a good education, and still be unable to find happiness, have no sense or gift for it. How sad that was, how painfully sad.

Max's building came into view. She found a parking space, went to the main entrance, and rang the bell. In the elevator she wondered how everything would turn out with Port and Max. Port was sure to want a commitment sometime in the near future.

She didn't want to think about it.

Would she become a fixture at Max's place, perhaps? Or would he at hers? Cozy evenings in front of the TV? Max would make a bacon sandwich, his daily evening treat, and ask: "Do you want one, too?" Or something like that. She'd reply: "No thanks, it's too late to be eating now." Or something like that. He'd shrug. "Up to you." Or something like that.

Then he would settle down on the sofa, switch on the TV, and begin to eat with relish. They would spend a while like that, Franza stealing an envious glance at Max's slim body that simply refused to put on weight, and at the bacon sandwich, which he sometimes garnished with leeks or radishes or simply salt and pepper. But she would resist. At first. But just when he had almost finished and it was nearly too late, her mouth would finally begin to water and her hands would twitch restlessly. It always ended with Max slapping away her fingers, then giving in with a sigh, standing, and going to make another sandwich, or sometimes two.

There would then be coffee and Franza's cookies, which were sometimes crunchy, sometimes moist, but always fresh and always perfectly decorated. There was always a moment of doubt as to whether they should be eaten at all, they looked so beautiful. But Franza invariably made sure there were plenty in stock, so they could be eaten without a guilty conscience.

It was no longer love, but friendship, a friendship that had grown from many years of living together. It was a friendship they'd only discovered once their mutual desire had faded and finally been extinguished.

This friendship consisted of TV evenings like that, of the wine they sometimes drank from a shared glass, both of them tired, both exhausted from a long, full day. They lay on the sofa, a movie playing, one of them nodding occasionally or jumping because the other had made a noise. Then they would grin, laugh, say, "Oh, you!" and soon drift back off to sleep.

Their friendship was made up of these little halfhearted phrases, the kind of phrases that belonged to the whole world, but also to them, those phrases such as "Leave it now!" or "Get on with it!" or "Calm down!" or "Get over it!" or "You're really getting on my nerves!"

It was also made up of moments of hatred, like when Franza stood in front of the mirror, contemplating her hips with a sigh, and he would walk past and comment laconically, "Well now, darling," which would make her want to hit him.

And it was made up of moments of remembering, the moments when she watched him secretly and remembered everything had been all right once.

It was the kind of friendship that came from being forced to live together "for the sake of the family"—no longer a couple but effectively sharing an apartment like in their student days. The other person's weaknesses required tolerance—those moments when they still hadn't showered, when their hair was in morning disarray, when mascara had run from too much crying or too much laughing, when tiredness furrowed their brows, when sadness consumed them and they wanted to capitulate before the harsh opposition of the world.

Each of them knew they could call the other if they needed help and the other would be there—perhaps not always or at all times, but mostly.

Franza had missed Max when she moved out. There had been those brief, empty moments of missing him, times when she had been about to turn round and call "Max!" and then realized he was no longer there. She would wonder as she stared into empty space whether she was in fact going crazy. Now that she was finally free of married life, how could she be missing her husband? After all, there had been many times when she'd wished him on the dark side of the moon. Not only the moon, but on Pluto at the farthest extent of its orbit. She suspected there were times when Max felt the same way.

Franza sensed that the time had come to take a further step, to create a little more distance from one another and from the things that had bound them, in order to finally gain her freedom. But those few last steps still seemed a ways off, and they seemed to give her a sympathetic smile, as if to say, "Well, come on! Take me! You still haven't taken me!"

Franza shook her head at the remarkable image that had popped into her brain, pushed it aside, and stepped out of the elevator. She did wonder whether going to his house was right, especially considering

Max's behavior in the theater tavern only two weeks ago—but hunger had gotten the better of her.

The apartment door was open.

"Hi!" Franza called. "It's me!"

She closed the door behind her.

"Come in," he called. "I'm in the kitchen!"

"OK, on my way."

He had raided the fridge and produced cheese, sausage, tomatoes, gherkins, eggs. Bread was already sliced into a little basket. No bacon today. He was standing at the table, laying out plates and cutlery. She watched him. He was tall and still slim, but his hair was thinning and gray and his shoulders stooped slightly. He fought against it, against gravity, against the pitfalls of aging that were irrevocably setting in. Not only for him, thought Franza wistfully. *It happens to us all.*

"Hello," he said, turning. "Everything OK?"

How amicable they were with one another these days. How relaxed and civilized. Friends. And yet it was clear to her that this was a fragile friendship.

What was that word that so perfectly described the vagueness between feeling and reason? Between that feeling in your belly and what your head told you?

Conflicting?

Yes, that was it. Who had said it? Frau Brendler? Conflicting.

Always. Everywhere. Everything.

Franza thought of the fights they'd had during their gradual breakup—those desperate attempts to find anything that might still hold the love of their early years.

They had been wild, those arguments, unpredictable, flaring up suddenly, flames that little by little burned up all they had had in common, including their feelings for each other. Despite all that, they had somehow managed to keep something, and she was proud of that.

She touched his back briefly. "Well," she said. "You know what it's like. A new case."

He nodded, didn't ask. He had never wanted to hear about the murders or the acts of violence that made up such a large part of her life.

"Wine?" he asked.

"I'd prefer beer."

They sat in his kitchen, ate, drank, talked about Ben.

Later it was coffee and the cookies that she still called *kekse* in deference to her Austrian roots, to the homeland she still missed in occasional unexpected moments. Then she would go down to the Danube, allowing her thoughts to be carried away downstream, leaving her feeling calm.

"Where's your sweetheart tonight?" Max asked as he stuffed another gingerbread cookie into his mouth.

"Show," she said.

"Vienna?"

"In a few days."

He nodded, and then grinned. "Do you remember how we met?"

"Of course I remember. It's not the kind of thing you forget. Baking cookies. I had dough in my hair. You tugged it out for me."

"That's it," he said. "Baking cookies. Your second passion."

She had to laugh. "What's my first, then?"

"Chasing after murderers."

"Ah," she said, a little disappointed. "And my third?"

"Ben."

"Ah," she said again. "And my—?"

"Men," he interrupted, smiling at her, enigmatic, wily. She looked him in the eye for a beat too long.

"Time for some wine now?" he asked.

She nodded.

"I sometimes think you might be lonely," he said as he returned with the wine and glasses. "More alone than before."

She chuckled and repeated his words. "More alone than before. Did you just make that up?"

He shrugged, smiled, and looked embarrassed, to Franza's amazement.

"Possibly," he said. "For you. It seemed appropriate."

"I'm not alone. Not even *more alone than before*."

"Then I must have been mistaken."

They fell silent, suddenly unable to think of what to say, merely sitting together wordlessly. Eventually she began to talk about Lilli. Then the wine bottle was empty, and she craved a cigarette.

"Since when have I been able to talk to you about something like this?" she asked as they sat outside on the balcony, puffing away. He shrugged.

"You always could."

She laughed out loud. "Wow," she said. "You haven't lost your touch for twisting the facts!"

He laughed, too. "Ah well," he said. "It was just that you obviously needed someone to listen to you today, so I did."

"Today?" she asked, thunderstruck. "I needed it today? And I never did before?"

"No, not before. Normally you're completely in control of things. You don't always need someone to listen."

"Oh," she said, still amazed. "That's very interesting. Is it something you've known for long?"

"Forever," he replied, looking at her. She let him. Silence like twilight, like a red light in the sky, like . . .

"I sometimes consider the eventuality . . ." Max finally broke the silence.

"The eventuality?"

"Of sleeping with you again."

He said it carefully, adding that he was afraid she'd take it the wrong way. After all, she was in a relationship. And her lover was a good-looking man. And probably a virile one too, considering his youth. And Max really didn't know if he could live up to him, but was it possible? With the lover soon disappearing over the horizon . . . Well, only for a few weeks and perhaps not *over* the horizon, but heading in that direction. Quite a distance away. If you thought about it.

She began to laugh. "Max, you're out of your mind!"

"Yes," he said, "it's possible. I'm out of my mind. I'm going a bit out of my mind with all these thoughts."

She was speechless. But she'd sensed it, deep down.

"Max, I . . ." she began, but he shook his head.

She sat in silence, looking up at the moon, that semicircle shining like neon.

He eventually continued. Lover-boy would be gone for a while. Think about it. Him. Yes. If he was being honest. About the eventuality. He'd been afraid of saying it to her, but now it was out, now the words were spoken. He was fed up with his life as it was, lonely, cold. Fed up with the female students the university sent him for internships, who knew nothing of life and nothing of love. They had certain abilities, sure, their hair shining, their lips smooth, their spirits gentle and unsullied and free from any corruption, and that was a good thing. She shouldn't misunderstand him—it was good; as things should be.

He paused, breathed deeply, ran his fingers through her hair, and continued speaking softly, saying he wanted to feel love again, deep in his bones. He might not be the smartest man in the world, but he understood things, and when he closed his eyes . . . When he did that, and he did it often, then he saw his life before him and he saw her in it—Franza.

She closed her eyes and shook her head imperceptibly.

"Don't say anything right now," he said. "That's not what I intended, you've got to believe that. I didn't intend to say all that to you, it just happened."

And then he continued, talking about how he wanted to make being alone more bearable for her, even though he now knew that she was not alone. They both knew that it was about him, Max, about his solitude, his loneliness.

He had never before in his life been so open, so damned open. Not even to himself. And he would love to see her regularly, and eat half her evening meal. Because she would surely regret it the following day if she ate it all herself. And then she'd stand in front of the mirror, overcritical of herself. Not that he thought she should. No, on the contrary. He had not forgotten her hips. How beautiful they were. Soft and lovely. And beautiful.

She held the glass in one hand and her cigarette in the other. It had burned out without her smoking it. She crushed it into the ashtray, set the glass carefully down on the table, and breathed deeply.

"I'm sorry," Max said. "I'm sorry. It wasn't meant to turn into a confession."

"We drank too much," she said.

He nodded. "Yes, we certainly did."

"People say things like that when they drink too much."

"Yes, they do."

She turned to him, looked him in the eye, the faint light falling on them from the living room. She placed her hand on his cheek and looked at him.

"Max," she said. "Oh, Max."

No, she didn't hold anything against him. Not now. Perhaps tomorrow, but not yet. Maybe tomorrow.

No, this eventuality was not an eventuality. Perhaps there was the tiniest possibility—an extremely tiny one. An extremely teeny, tiny one. But probably not. Or only in the moment. A moment when they had emptied a bottle of wine, no, perhaps even two, and smoked a pack of cigarettes and it was already so late, so damned late, probably already tomorrow, not today anymore.

What would she think about it tomorrow—or even today . . .

"Let's see," she said. "But probably not. Better not."

He moved toward her. She shook her head, but let him. He slipped his hand beneath her sweater, beneath her bra, and laid it on her left breast—he had always had a weakness for the left. His hand was warm and soft and as Franza remembered.

"Still the right size," he said, trying to make light of it. "Still as if made for me."

She smiled. "What you're doing there, it's . . ."

"I know," he whispered, burying his nose in her hair. "But it's so familiar." *Yes*, she thought. *Familiar, so familiar.*

"I have a lover," she whispered. "A boyfriend, a partner." She shook her head.

"I know," he whispered. "Of course I know. And I hate it."

She thought of Port and the fact he would be spending those few weeks in Vienna and what things would be like afterward, and she suddenly felt . . . that she was a little alone after all, more alone than before.

"Will you come to bed with me?" Max whispered. "Can we just lie together for a while?"

She thought about it, and thought about it some more, and then, her limbs heavy from the wine, she shook her head and nodded despite herself. They went into the bedroom, left the light off, undressed, slipped between the sheets.

They embraced, held each other tight, remembering how it used to be, before. For a moment Franza almost regretted it . . . but then . . .

"You've put on a tiny bit of weight," she said quietly, amazed, teasing. "A tiny, tiny bit. It makes you . . . almost soft, cuddly."

"Oh, well," he said awkwardly, but clearly delighted. "Time doesn't stand still. But you, Franza, you're beautiful."

She laughed a little sadly.

"Oh, get away," she said. "I'm not beautiful. We're all approaching our fifties." And it occurred to him that it would be her birthday in a few weeks.

"When I look at myself," she said in a slightly steely voice, "and I think of certain faces I remember from the old days and then see them after ten years or more, and I notice how they've changed, it scares me. It scares me so much. And then I imagine my own face, how it would look to me if I hadn't seen it for ten years, if I were seeing it for the first time in ten years."

He said nothing, merely stroked her hair. She smiled wistfully at him.

"But sometimes," she said, "sometimes, I feel beautiful. Now, for example."

They did not sleep together. Instead, they gave in to their sadness, their melancholy.

They thought of their failed marriage, of their son whom they saw so rarely, of Port, of the young women with whom Max had the occasional brief affair, of the house that, perhaps, would soon no longer be theirs.

"The house," he said. "They're going to take it."

Shit, she thought. *Shit!*

"Does it make you . . . ?"

"Yes," she said. "It does."

"Me too." They were silent for a moment.

"When?" she asked.

"As soon as we give the word."

She nodded. "Life is sometimes . . ."

"I know," he said.

Silence fell again. They were overcome by sadness. They lay in each other's arms to get through it. They felt a deep tenderness, an affection that enabled them to withstand the loneliness for a while.

"I wanted to kill you," she said.

He knew straightaway that she was talking about the young woman who had stayed with them as an au pair and, over the year, became his lover and then the mother of his second child. A lifetime ago, so many years—and still sometimes the same thorn in the same flesh.

"I know," he said. "Thanks for not doing it."

"It hurt," she said. "It really hurt."

"I know."

"I couldn't forgive you for a long time."

"I know. Have you been able to?"

She looked at him in the dark and smiled. "I'm going home now."

42

The weather had gotten worse. A slight drizzle was veiling the world. It was a tired Monday morning, the fourth day after the body was found. September 15. Christian Rabinsky had been summoned to the police station for questioning.

They now knew Gertrud's husband had told a white lie or two. It had not been easy to find out, his friends had closed ranks—the three couples Felix had interviewed after leaving Frau Beuerle had confirmed her husband's version of the events, but the information she had given Felix was enough to call Rabinsky in again.

He looked tired, his mood suiting the gray day and the drizzle outside the window.

"Good morning," Franza said as they entered the interview room, where Felix was already pouring coffee and water.

"Why am I here?" Rabinsky asked. "What do you want from me? I've told you everything. Why don't you leave me in peace? My children need me. They've just lost their mother, in case you've forgotten."

"No," Franza said, "we haven't forgotten. But there's something you've forgotten to tell us. Namely, where you were during the period between ten o'clock and midnight."

Rabinsky gasped. "So you actually suspect me of having murdered my wife?"

"We have to investigate all the possibilities," Felix said calmly. "At the moment we have the feeling you're not in a particularly strong position, Herr Rabinsky."

"I have an alibi," Rabinsky said. "I'll say it again—I spent the whole evening with my friends. You only need to ask them!"

There was a tremor in his voice. He noticed it himself and tried to suppress it, but failed.

"Will you please answer our question?" Franza asked. "Herr Rabinsky, you do not have an alibi for the time in question. Where were you?"

They saw him falter for a fraction of a second. They saw him fight for breath as he sought to regain his composure. They gave him time.

"How do you come to that conclusion?" he asked eventually, still with the tremor in his voice. Franza saw it spread slowly through his body.

"A witness," Felix said. "A witness refuted your alibi."

Rabinsky nodded. The fear that had settled in his eyes slowly disappeared, to be replaced by anger and a deep helplessness.

"Rieke," he said. "It's Rieke, isn't it?"

Felix nodded. "Yes. Rieke."

"But she's lying," said Rabinsky. "Rieke's lying."

"Why would she?"

"Because . . . because . . ."

"Yes?"

He shook his head. His shoulders drooped as he stared vacantly into space. He remained silent.

Franza leaned forward, her arms on the table. "We found particles of skin beneath your wife's fingernails that most probably came from the murderer. If a person is threatened, they defend themselves, injuring their attacker. Scratches. Grazes. Do you have any marks like that, Herr Rabinsky? Do you have any scratches on your skin?"

He swallowed.

"No," he said. "I don't. And I didn't kill my wife. I was away from home from seven o'clock. I went for a meal with my friends. We were celebrating Lars's birthday. A waiter spilled red wine over me. So I drove to the office, took a shower, changed, smoked a cigarette. I wanted a few moments to myself."

He fell silent, stared into his coffee mug, and then continued. "Then I went back to the others. To Jealousy. From there I went back to the office. And I came home the following morning. That's when I found her. But I've already told you all that. That's what happened. I don't know who killed my wife. Probably Hanna. Hanna Umlauf. I didn't do it. I loved her."

"Please, will you show us your arms, Herr Rabinsky?"

"Do I have to?"

Franza shook her head. "No, you don't have to. But you should if it could exonerate you."

He didn't react.

"Otherwise we'll have to ask you to agree to a DNA test."

He looked up. "A DNA test?"

"The skin particles. We'll compare them with your DNA."

"And if I refuse?"

"We get a court order."

He fell apart. Folded into himself. Sank into silence. They watched him go pale, his strength crumbling away like sunbaked sand.

"Very well," he whispered. "Very well."

He rolled up his shirtsleeve and held his arm out to them. It was covered in scratches.

"You can save the expense," he said. "No need for DNA comparisons. It's true. She did scratch me. The skin beneath her fingernails is mine. But I didn't kill her. She was alive when I left. And Hanna was still there."

"Where is Hanna now?"

"I don't know," he said wearily. "How should I know that?"

Franza stood and walked around behind him. She laid her hand on his shoulder, hoping she could transfer some of her calmness and warmth to him, stabilize him a little.

"What happened?" she asked. "Just tell us. It will do you good."

But he wasn't ready yet. Still needed time. He took three gulps of water. Four. There was despair in his eyes. He shook his head, incredulous. He supported his face in his hands, trying to still the trembling of his body. Then . . . at last.

"Yes," he said. "Yes, I was there. Shit, I'll say it again—I was there. I wish I hadn't been. I wish that stupid waiter hadn't spilled that damned wine . . ." He ran his hands over his face. "I wish I hadn't seen it. I wish . . ."

He broke off, shook his head, momentarily covered his eyes with his hands.

"What did you see?" Franza asked softly. "What was it?"

He remained silent, fighting with himself. A few more moments passed.

"They were . . . together. I saw them together. My wife and Hanna. They were lying in the bed on their sides. Gertrud behind Hanna. Gertrud had her arm around Hanna, her face laid on her shoulder. They were completely still, just lying there cuddled up. There was . . . a really peculiar tension. A really peculiar tension. Something very gentle, intimate."

His face was sad. *He's going to cry,* Franza thought. *It'll do him good.*

He cried. They let him. It did him good.

"I said nothing," he whispered. "I just stood in the open doorway and said nothing. I simply left."

"Left?"

"Yes. Left."

He pulled at a thread hanging from the fabric of his sleeve. "You know, I always felt that there was something, something going on inside her that had nothing to do with me. Nothing to do with me. I'm no prude, I can imagine a lot. But . . . she's . . . she was my wife. I loved her."

A painful tug around his mouth, a soft sob.

"What happened then?"

He shrugged. "They noticed me. When I backed away. I must have bumped against something. I went down to the kitchen. I drank a glass of water, I think. She came after me, Gertrud did. She said something like, I shouldn't have found out that way—something like that. I didn't want to listen. I wanted out of there. But she tried to hold me back. I pushed her away. 'You don't understand at all,' she yelled, 'you don't understand at all. It's all so complicated.'"

More silence, concentration. The detectives could see his mind working furiously.

"And she was right. I didn't understand. How could anyone understand that?"

He looked up imploringly. His expression contained a despair that made Franza shudder.

"She wanted to explain. I grabbed her hands, shook her, wanted to hold her, wanted to hold her—she was my wife, after all—but she . . . she suddenly said, so quietly, so clearly, 'I'm going away with Hanna.'"

There was amazement now in his voice, echoing the amazement of the moment he was remembering.

"And then we heard Hanna's voice from the top of the stairs. And she said no. She said, 'No, Gertrud, that's not going to happen. You won't do that. It's a misunderstanding. Don't send him away!'"

Another pause. He drank a mouthful of water. His hand was shaking.

"Gertrud froze for a second. Hanna came downstairs, came nearer. 'You're my sister,' she said, 'and he's your husband.' And that was when Gertrud flipped."

He shook his head. The amazement had turned to bewilderment. He kept shaking his head.

"She screamed, just screamed. No words. Only screams. And set on me. Like a Fury. She attacked me. Scratched me and hit me."

He showed them his arm again, and continued speaking. "Hanna came over to her and put her arms around her, holding her. As soon as she felt Hanna she melted on the spot. Started crying like a little child. I've never seen her like that before." He swallowed, sniffed. Tears flowed down his face. "Hanna finally said I should go. I should just go. It would all calm down with time."

He fell silent, wiped his hands over his face and laid them flat on the table.

"And I went," he said softly. "I went back into town, to my colleagues. Got tanked up. And when I came home the next day, she was lying in the kitchen, dead. And Hanna had vanished."

He breathed deeply.

"That's all." He leaned back, his arms hanging down limply as though they didn't belong to him. *Now comes the weariness,* Franza thought. *After the telling comes the weariness. I can see it now in his eyes.*

"And we're supposed to believe that?" Felix asked. "Isn't it rather the case that you were fighting and suddenly found yourself in the kitchen? And your wife said she wanted to leave you and you saw red. Suddenly, there was the knife in front of you—a sharp, gleaming knife. You picked it up and you stabbed her. Something like that happens suddenly. You lose all sense of reason, you're beside yourself, and then all it takes is one word."

Rabinsky shook his head.

"No," he said wearily. "That's not what happened. It *could* have happened like that, I'll grant you that, but it didn't. Believe me, please."

"What have you done with Hanna? Where's Hanna?" Felix's voice had an edge to it.

"Hanna? Nothing! I didn't do anything, I swear! Hanna sent me away. And I went." Rabinsky raised his hands. "I drove back into town, like a madman, like a lunatic. I just wanted to get away, away, away." He slumped into himself. "It must have been Hanna. There was no one else in the house. Hanna must have killed her. They probably got into a fight and then when she saw Gertrud lying there in a pool of blood, she got scared. And ran off. She's good at that. Running away. It's what she's always done."

He stood. "Can I go home now? I've got to get to my children."

Felix looked at him thoughtfully. Franza shook her head slowly.

"No," she said. "I'm sorry. We'll have to place you under arrest. You're suspected of having murdered your wife. The first step will be remanding you to custody."

He was stunned. His face turned pale.

"What?" he said. "What? Are you crazy?"

"The evidence against you is simply too strong," Felix said. "You've lied to us. You've given us a false alibi. You have the best possible motive anyone could think of—jealousy. And we're going to find your skin particles beneath your wife's fingernails. What would you think if you were in our shoes?"

"What about Hanna? Don't you suspect her at all? It's all cleared up, is it? I think you're oversimplifying things!" Rabinsky fought for breath.

"We'll continue looking for her," said Felix. "Don't you worry about that."

"And who knows?" said Franza. "Perhaps she'll be able to confirm your statement, Herr Rabinsky. Then, of course, you'll be free to go."

"What about now? Do you consider the case closed? Are you arresting me as the murderer? I loved my wife! I didn't kill her!"

He still couldn't grasp it.

"No," Franza said. "Nothing's conclusive. Would you like to call an attorney? And do you want to call your mother-in-law, so she can look after Moritz?"

"No," he said. "I can't. I just can't. How can I explain to her . . . ?"

He was like a helpless child who had given up defending himself.

"Then I'll do it," Franza said. "Don't worry about Moritz."

"Don't worry?" he protested once again.

"An officer will read you your rights," said Felix, summoning a uniformed officer in. "Take him away."

They watched him go down the corridor with the officer. Once he had gone from view, they sat down and looked each other in the eye.

"I don't know," Franza said. "I've got a bad feeling about this."

Felix said nothing.

They got it wrong sometimes. It wasn't unusual to get something wrong, to think it was all pointing in one direction, only to find that direction was false. To smell a rat, but the wrong rat.

They made mistakes, and for those who were the victims of their errors, it was probably the worst experience of their lives. They were caught up in a machine that ground, ground, ground them down, and in the worst cases did not leave much behind.

Both Franza and Felix wondered how you could know the truth on the spot, how you could always know what was wrong and what was right. How could they see the way if it was veiled in fog, a mist of uncertainty through which they could only penetrate gradually?

They had to stick to the facts, to whatever was tenable and provable in the course of their investigations. But facts were not always the truth.

"You don't want it to have been him," said Felix.

Franza nodded. "No, I don't want it to have been him. It could have been him—all the indications point to it—but, you're right, I don't want it to have been him. And I don't believe it was him."

Felix nodded. "I know."

"If only because of the children," she said. "They've had a terrible enough experience as it is."

"I know."

They were silent. What could they do? Nothing. Suddenly, Franza had an idea.

"Listen, on the road out of town there's a speed camera. I was caught by it once. If he really raced off like he said, perhaps we have a photo of him and could rule him out from being there at the time the murder was committed."

"Good idea. Let's see if he's had a bit of luck, the poor bastard."

They called the traffic department, who said they'd check and report back.

"I wonder if it was Hanna?" Felix stood and went over to the window.

"You're not getting prudish, are you?" Franza asked. "Don't you think two women should love each other?"

"Of course," he said, turning. "Love happens where it will. It's beautiful wherever it happens. But it isn't always a force for good."

She nodded.

"Are you hoping it was Hanna?" he asked.

"I'd rather it was no one," she said, her voice rising dramatically. "I'd rather the world was a happy and peaceful place where no murders are committed, no rapes, no muggings, no nothing."

He laughed. Softly. Thoughtfully.

"I know," he said. "A utopia of peace and happiness. But how would we earn our living then, my friend? Watering flowers? And how would all the other people who, one way or another, live off murder and death earn their bread? Police officers, lawyers, journalists, TV reporters, pencil pushers, actors, who knows who else. No, I'm telling you, however dreadful it sounds, it'd be missed by a lot of people."

She took a gingerbread cookie from the Tupperware box in front of her and threw it at Felix, who caught it and stuffed it into his mouth.

"Let me have my dreams," she said. "I don't have many left these days."

"All right, I will. I love it when you dream."

He smiled.

She shrugged. "Ultimately, it doesn't matter what we want or what our dreams are, does it? Ultimately, it's the truth that counts. Even if that sounds so dreadfully pathetic. So often you have no idea what the truth really is. It's made up of so many layers and perceptions."

She stopped talking, fixed coffees, and placed one in front of each of them. They ate cookies that crunched between their teeth and warmed their stomachs.

"Sometimes I do understand Sonja a little," she said. "Her marrying Brückl. The fact that she's happy with him. There's something good about his clarity and pragmatism. No layers, no 'Look for what you want and what you need, babe!' Pow! It is what it is, period."

Felix laughed. Then they went their separate ways. Franza to see Frau Brendler, to tell her the latest news, and Felix to see Hansen and ask whether there had, perhaps, been any developments in the search for Hanna.

43

"Come," she said. And I went with her. She looked at me as she had back then. With those eyes. She took my hand and I saw us as children. And I had this longing. I went with her into the bedroom, into her bed. She put her arms around me. She lay behind me and put her arms around me. It was lovely. We used to do that when we were children. When I felt alone after my mother . . .

I felt a longing—even if it was only for the past.

"We were happy," she said. "Back then. Before. We were happy."

Really? Were we happy?

I wonder now. Here in this quiet place, during these early fall evenings, in the prime of my life, so to speak.

If she was surprised when I turned up at her house that day, she didn't show it. She let me in, showed me around the house. We ate bread, sausage, cheese. We drank wine, and I thought how all the many years had hardly left a trace. Her eyes were still a gleaming brown like dark, milky coffee. Perhaps she had a little more flesh on her bones, I don't know. In the center of her brow, between her eyebrows, she had a deep furrow. Fine lines ran from her eyes, and her hair, though still long, was shot through with gray.

"Don't you color it?" I asked her.

Gertrud shook her head. "I'm having it cut off."

"Cut off?" I echoed. "What a pity. I can't imagine you without long hair."

We smiled at one another, felt our hearts beating in our throats, and recognized in each other the secrets of the years that we had not witnessed. I thought, *Nothing is lost if you carry it inside yourself.*

Evening came, and cool air flowed through the windows into the house. Although the summer was waning, its scents were still in the air. It tasted of damson jelly, elderberry jelly, and the windowpanes reflected a vague light, the last of the day, shimmering in the dusk.

Eventually we began to talk about back then, about *infinity*, or what we believed to be infinite back then. We talked about the frenzy in which we found ourselves, about that love that enfolded us with a vehemence we were no match for, which had brought us together but which in truth actually divided us—so craftily and carefully that we didn't notice it for a long time. Not until it was too late, not until death came to call.

"I don't understand," I said. "I don't know how we could have believed that this love would make us eternal. What a word, anyway. Eternal! What's it mean? Who would want it? To be eternal. Without end. Only children who know nothing."

There was a tremor in my voice. I paused and looked at Gertrud, whose expression was impenetrable. She didn't contradict me.

And I thought *backbackback*, twenty years back, more than twenty years . . .

The summer had settled in with its luminous colors, the evenings still glowing with that light that flooded the squares and streets, fountains reflecting the sun until it set, a golden disk that shattered when I threw in a coin and wished Tonio would be mine forever.

"Woe betide you if you don't make me happy!" I'd said, playfully threatening, dipping my hand in the water and splashing him. Darkness came to the alleyways late. Standing beneath an archway, I decided that I would have a daughter one day, and her name would be Lilli. She would grow up to become a woman, not a creature of seaweed and trinkets, but a woman. When she needed help, I would give it, I decided as I felt Tonio's breath on my skin. I was certain—God, I was so certain that I already spoke to her in my thoughts, chatted, laughed beneath that archway as Tonio brushed his lips over my neck, the hollows of my shoulder blades. I called her by her name, Lilli, even though she was light-years away, light-years—but at that moment I knew that sometimes dreams did come true.

Back in Gertrud's kitchen—drops of jelly on her knee—we talked about love and what we had taken for love back then. I shook my head, said, "No." That love was not really love, only a brief intoxication— nothing more. An unfortunate chain of unfortunate events. A mistake. Not wishes that had come true, no, never.

Gertrud didn't contradict me. We lay on the terrace. It grew cold, and we wrapped ourselves in blankets.

"Nevertheless, I never again loved anyone like I loved him," I said. "And I never suffered so much because of anyone else."

We wrapped ourselves in blankets and snuggled together. Because after those words we couldn't go indoors, nor could we look one another in the eye.

44

"I don't know whether Tonio would have been for life," said Dorothee Brendler. "I don't think so. But when someone dies at such a young age and in such a way, they become an unattainable legend."

Franza was sitting with Dorothee on the terrace beneath the damson tree. The last fruits were falling, rotting. Dorothee had left the hotel and moved into Gertrud and Christian's house to take care of Moritz. She was needed all the more with Christian in custody.

The place seemed normal, orderly. The kitchen floor was scrubbed. There was nothing to suggest that this had been the scene of a tragedy. Only the jelly jars, perhaps, which still stood in rows along the shelves, and the silence that lay like a black veil over the garden and over the house.

"Things seem back in order quickly," Franza said.

Dorothee shrugged. "What else could we do? Isn't it important to get back to normal? To get Moritz back to his life?"

"Yes, it probably is."

"He doesn't cry," Dorothee said, and Franza heard the absence of her grandchild's crying in Dorothee's own voice.

"Moritz?" she asked.

"Yes, Moritz. He doesn't shed any tears. He doesn't cry."

She shook her head, as though to erase her calmness and elegance, leaving her a person beginning to grieve, facing the ruins of a life she had believed was good.

"Give him time," Franza said, although she knew such things were easy to say but difficult to do. "Give yourself time."

"Yes. Maybe."

"I've talked to Lilli," Franza said. "She told me her mother always lived with a sense of panic about her. As if she didn't feel secure. As if she and Lilli were threatened by something. What do you make of that?"

Dorothee shook her head vehemently. "What garbage! What gives the child that notion? And you're mistaken about Christian. He didn't kill my daughter. I'd swear to it."

"What about Hanna?"

Another shake of the head. "No. Not Hanna either."

"Who, then? What do you think? Do you have any ideas? It must have been someone."

She shook her head. "No, I have no idea. Perhaps it was just an ordinary burglar and you're following completely false trails."

Franza was silent for a moment. She knew Dorothee didn't believe this theory herself, so there was no need to contradict it. Next question.

"Did you know that Tonio had a son?"

Dorothee Brendler froze for a fraction of a second, and Franza noticed with surprise that her eye twitched. But it was over in no time, and she looked as she had before.

"A son? What do you mean?"

Was Franza mistaken, or was there a tremor in Dorothee's voice?

"A son," she said. "In his thirties. Does that come as a shock to you?"

Dorothee cleared her throat. "No. No, not a shock. But I'm surprised. No, I didn't know. A son?"

"Did you know of any previous relationships of Tonio's? Before Hanna."

Dorothee shook her head. "No. No, I honestly didn't. I didn't know him particularly well. I rarely saw him."

"What was he like?"

Dorothee raised her head, gazed into the distance, looked up at the sky. "What was he like?" She smiled. "Well, as I said, I don't know much, but . . . he was rather . . . unusual. In every respect. Incredibly charming on the one hand. Very likeable. I can understand how Hanna fell in love with him. But on the other hand . . . he was a very difficult man."

Tonio had a fire inside him, a flame that scorched his heart and drove him to ask questions to which he was unable to find answers. Questions that plunged him into a loneliness he was unable to cope with, that tore him apart. His mother had abandoned him when he was ten. She returned to her homeland, to Rome, because Germany was too cold for her, because she was freezing all the time. He still had his father, who did his best. Every summer vacation he sent his son to Italy, where the extended family took him noisily into their arms. When the vacation was over, Tonio would return, warmed through by the sun, tanned—and the girls would secretly sigh with a desire to comfort his unapproachable heart. A heart that remained unapproachable until Hanna opened it up.

"Perhaps that was what linked them," Dorothee said. "The fact that they both lost their mothers so early. But this son you speak of. What exactly are you saying?"

"A young man has turned up," Franza said. "It seems he'd been trying to make contact with Gertrud. A witness said he had a very strong physical resemblance to Tonio. It's therefore highly probable that—"

"Oh my God!" Dorothee started. "Then perhaps he was the one who . . ."

Her whole body began to shake; she was unable to control it. Franza jumped up.

"Are you feeling unwell? Can I get you a glass of water?"

But Dorothee pulled herself back together and waved her away.

"No, thank you," she said. "Perhaps you could just leave me in peace now. Perhaps you should go. I'm simply tired. Exhausted. One new discovery after another. As if it weren't all bad enough already."

She turned inward.

What's she afraid of? Franza thought. *What's scaring her? And what isn't she telling me?*

"OK," she said. "I'll go now. Thank you for the coffee."

Dorothee nodded, but was no longer aware of her presence. Franza left, sensing her own tiredness, the sleep she was lacking. She thought about stopping to see Lilli but dismissed the idea.

45

"Nothing," Hansen said. "Absolutely nothing. The appeal on the evening news yesterday yielded nothing, either. A whole load of calls, but they were all to do with some photos of her in the paper. Not a soul has seen her since she checked out of the hotel. It's as though a magic spell has been cast."

"The perfect disappearance."

"Or the second murder victim."

"I don't know," Felix said. "Somehow I don't believe that. It wouldn't fit. If that were the case, we'd have found her body as well. Why would someone kill two women but only remove one body?"

"Because he was interrupted?"

"Hm. Possible, yes," Felix said. "Shit, time's marching on. Maybe there's a madman running around out there while we're just marking time."

"Or could it be that Hanna committed the murder? Out of some kind of desire for revenge from the weird love triangle they shared?"

"Or maybe it really was Rabinsky?"

They fell into a baffled silence. This damned case was turning into a jumble of disparate threads that refused to be pulled together. Too many people in the frame, too many possibilities, too much obscurity.

"Belitz is at the end of his tether," Hansen said. "Rapidly going to pieces. I think he's got some kind of illness, he looks so green."

Felix nodded. "Poor devil."

"Maybe his younger woman wore him out," Hansen said with a grin and a sideways nod.

Felix laughed. "Come on now, you're only jealous!"

His cell phone rang. Arthur. Interpol had been in touch, he said. The Greek authorities were going to fax over the old reports from Tonio's drowning, and Arthur was in the process of tracking down someone who could translate them from Greek to German. He was also going to check the address of Ernst Köhler, the father of this ill-fated Tonio.

"Excellent," Felix said. "Good work."

They agreed on a time for a meeting that evening and hung up. Felix glanced at the clock. Already approaching four. His cell phone rang again.

It was his colleague from the traffic department. They had a shot of Christian Rabinsky. He'd been caught by the speed camera driving back into town at around eighty miles per hour. It was ten minutes after ten. Gertrud had still been alive at that time. He couldn't be the murderer. He was in luck.

Felix felt a glow of satisfaction and rose to pass on the good news.

46

Herr and Frau Rabinsky. Hardly a picture of happiness. She was lying on a metal table in the coroner's lab. He was standing outside the court building adjacent to the detention center.

She had everything behind her. He'd just suffered hours of raging doubts and terror in which he had feared for his future. She had no future at all.

He looked up into the sky. It was dull, but it still suited him perfectly—his mood was also gloomy, even now that he had his freedom back and his innocence had been proven.

He'd been fetched from his cell to the telephone. Inspector Herz had been on the line, and he'd told him he could go back to his home and his children. He'd been photographed by a speed camera as he was driving back to town—when Gertrud was still alive. Lucky again, it seemed.

"Thank you," Christian had said. "Thank you."

He was bewildered and a little surprised that he didn't feel a hint of pleasure. It would take a while.

"No problem," the inspector had said. "We're only doing our work. We have to follow every lead. I'm sorry it caused you trouble. Take care now. If we need anything else from you, we'll be in touch."

Christian had nodded and stood for a while, the receiver in his hand and the beeping in his ears.

Yes, he had thought, *lucky, lucky again, yes, maybe, maybe a little. Even a little luck is still luck.* He suddenly remembered that on his return into town in the darkness that night there had been a quick flash, a brief flicker. Must have been the speed camera, but he hadn't taken it in, he was so caught up in himself. *Now I'll have to pay a fine,* he thought. For the first time in his life, he'd be glad to do so. He couldn't help smiling briefly and finally feeling a slight sense of pleasure, a slight relief.

He started walking slowly, eyes still turned to the sky, still gazing into the distance.

Gertrud would never look anywhere again. She was in the distance, somewhere so far distant it was impossible to imagine—such a wide, faraway distance. She had followed that quiet, delicate tone that suddenly filled the air, that had led her away from her life, that had whispered to her: *It's OK. There's nothing left to do here. Let yourself go. Let's fly away.*

They had closed her eyes, and her skin had taken on the pale color that Franza sometimes saw in her dreams, when she would wake and sit up with a start, switch on the light and breathe deeply. She would examine her arms, her legs, her body, checking that the color had not permeated her own skin, before falling back with a sigh and sinking back, relieved, into sleep. No, things had not gotten that far—she was alive. It was a good life, her skin was rosy without a trace of the pallor of death. Those hues were far away on the tables in the coroner's lab, at the crime scenes, on the corpses.

47

It's my fault, Lilli thought. *It's my fault, because my cell phone wasn't charged, because I always leave the damn thing lying around and the battery drains. If the battery hadn't been dead, she would have reached me that night and I would have gone to see her.*

And if she'd done that, her mama could have told her what it was all about, the dreadful thing she'd done. Could have told Lilli what she meant when she spoke into the answering machine—the same sentence she found in the diary. That last sentence followed by nothing, not on the answering machine, nor in the diary: "I've done something dreadful."

She wasn't there. When her mama had needed her, she was dancing, letting her hair down a bit, arming herself for the talk with her grandfather.

What was it? What was the dreadful thing you did, Mama? What could have been so dreadful that you had to die for it? And what does it have to do with Hanna, and with Tonio and why he went into the sea and drowned? And, Mama, who am I?

Half-truths didn't satisfy. They only awoke a hunger that gnawed at your insides and stopped you from sleeping.

48

Sometimes I can hear myself screaming. In the night. In my dreams. Not often, just now and then. I cry out his name, and he moves out into the water, into the storm, into the darkness. And sinks. Then I feel his cold skin beneath my hand, and the pain that tears me apart. Then I cry out his name, but no one hears me. Then . . . silence.

"Let the past lie," Gertrud said. "Let it go!"

But it doesn't work. It doesn't work anymore. It was because of the past that I came back.

"Did you send me the letter, Gertrud?" I asked her.

She shook her head and began to shake. Then suddenly Tonio was sitting by us. We felt him, his waiting, his silence. It gave me strength and *slowlyslowlyslowly* I could begin to think of her, to yearn for her.

49

The GPS had found the address effortlessly. Located on the outskirts of town, it wasn't a very good neighborhood. At least there was parking. Lilli parked and waited, without knowing for what. Just waited. For an idea. For inspiration. Anything. But all that came was a text:

Let's get coffee when you're free. Get in touch. Franza.

But Lilli didn't get in touch. Lilli didn't have time. Lilli was on the trail of the past. She turned her cell phone off.

She took the note from her purse. Yes, the address was right. The address had been there in the red book. Gertrud had written it down over twenty years ago, and now here Lilli was in front of the apartment building, outside the main door. When someone walked out, she went in, slipping quickly through the gap before the door closed.

It was an old building. She sniffed. It smelled of rotting vegetables, of sweat. She climbed the stairs slowly, second floor, third floor, third door on the left. No sign on the door, no name, no one in the corridor.

She raised her hand, and then froze, hesitated. She listened. *Half-truths don't satisfy. They only awaken a hunger that gnaws at your insides and stops you from sleeping.* She rang the bell.

Steps approached, and the key turned in the lock as a man's voice rang out: "Don't you have your key?"

The door opened. Silence.

They stood facing each other, staring. Neither had seen the other before, but they recognized one another—from the photos. From what they'd been told. From others' memories.

50

Arthur had the address. It wasn't a very good neighborhood. He switched on the GPS and drove off toward the edge of town, whistling softly through his teeth. He was in a good mood after the previous evening with Karolina. They had celebrated their engagement, without a ring, without champagne—he had not even gone to the gas station shop for a bottle of sparkling wine. He had been too tired, too exhausted after a long day's investigating. But she had welcomed him with a radiant smile, in a dress with a neckline that plunged almost to her navel.

Yes, things were going well! Fantastically well, and they had promised to treasure forever the little band of silver chewing gum wrapper he had given her in the absence of a real ring.

• • •

"You have reached your destination," the GPS announced.

Yes, Arthur thought, *that's true. In every respect.*

He parked the car and got out. No, this neighborhood was nothing special. Row upon row of concrete apartment blocks from the early seventies, few trees between the buildings. *Poor people's housing,* his mother would have said.

Arthur approached the door with the right number and glanced down at the name plates. Twenty families lived in the building, but none of the bell plates showed the right name: Köhler.

Damn. It would have been easy if that name had been there. He could have just rung the bell. And then the door would have opened and he would have been buzzed in and climbed the stairs. The apartment door would have opened, framing a man, Tonio Junior, who would have said, *Yes, it's me, Tonio Junior. I murdered Gertrud Rabinsky and abducted Hanna Umlauf. I'm the criminal you're looking for. Arrest me, Inspector!*

Arthur grinned to himself while his eyes roamed hesitantly over the name plates again as he continued to dream. He dreamed about receiving a commendation, maybe a personal invitation from the mayor, because he had rescued Hanna Umlauf, who, after all, as Dr. Brückl had stressed, was a celebrity. Arthur dreamed about being granted three weeks' special leave, three weeks in the Maldives or some such place, dreamed about Karolina going crazy and using her hot tongue to . . .

No, stop!

He cleared his throat and got a grip on himself. He couldn't have such thoughts when on duty! The main door opened suddenly, and Arthur's eyes widened—his dreams of a speedy conclusion to the murder case hadn't vanished completely and perhaps . . . But, no. It wasn't Tonio Junior leaving the building, but a young woman in a short skirt, tight blouse, shades. Sexy.

She gave him a brief stare, just for a second. As she moved past, he said, "Excuse me, could you just . . . ?"

She stopped and turned impatiently. "Yes?"

He drew the composite from his chest pocket, unfolded it, and asked, "Do you happen to recognize this man?"

She looked at the picture, looked at him, her eyes hidden behind the shades, and said, "No, I don't know him. I'm only visiting here. Excuse me, I'm running late. I really have to go."

And she was gone. Arthur watched her rapid retreat and felt a sudden impulse, but then the main door opened again and another woman appeared, a little older, with two whining children in tow. Arthur approached her, too.

"Excuse me," he said. "Police." He took his ID from his pocket. "Do you happen to recognize this man?"

She shook the children off and examined everything carefully— Arthur, the ID, the picture—and finally asked, "What do you want from him?"

"Merely routine," Arthur said reassuringly. "He may be a witness in a criminal case."

"Ah," she said and thought for a moment. "Well, he looks kind of familiar. Looks a bit like the guy who's been living here for three, four weeks in old Köhler's apartment."

It was as though something exploded in Arthur's head. *Fantastic,* he thought. *Fantaaaastic! A hit! Bull's-eye!*

"To be honest, I've been wondering who he is," the woman said. "Never says anything, not a word of greeting. A bit withdrawn. You could almost say creepy."

"Which apartment is it?" Arthur wondered if he should call the SWAT team straightaway or discuss it with Oberwieser and Herz first— they were the bosses, after all.

"On the third floor, I think," the woman said. "But perhaps old Frau Steigermann can tell you a bit more. She had a bit more to do with old Herr Köhler. She lives on the second floor."

OK, Arthur thought. *I'll go and see Steigermann first and then perhaps I'll phone the bosses.*

"Thanks," he said with a smile.

The woman nodded, gathered her children together, and left.

Inside the building Arthur was struck by a wave of stale air, a smell of boiled cabbage, stuffy heat. As he climbed the stairs, he phoned Oberwieser and Herz. Their instructions were "Wait." He should talk to Frau Steigermann and find out more about the apartment and the family connections here, but otherwise wait until they were there—no going in alone!

"OK," Arthur sighed. "No going in alone. OK, OK, OK." He felt a gnawing in his stomach. "Then I won't."

Second floor, outside Steigermann's apartment door. He raised his hand about to ring, but then he hesitated. Looked up the stairs. It wasn't far. Just a few steps. Couldn't he just . . . ?

He lowered his hand, turned. Softly, softly. Up the stairs to the third floor, quietly, treading carefully past apartment doors in a bare corridor, the names unknown . . . and then an apartment without a name plate.

Bingo, Arthur thought. *Bingo! This must be it.*

He listened. Nothing. Or was there?

He thought feverishly what to do. Ring the bell? With his gun at the ready? Perhaps there were children behind the closed door who would stare at him with wide eyes, traumatized for life.

But perhaps there was a murderer standing there, also with a gun at the ready, prepared to do away with him because there was nothing left to lose.

Neither of these two options was particularly attractive. No, the official regulations were there for a reason, and his bosses' instructions were clear. *Wait,* they'd said. *Wait for reinforcements.* So . . . !

Arthur closed his eyes briefly, took his hand from the gun at his belt, turned, and slowly went back down the stairs to the second floor, back to Steigermann's apartment. The door before which Arthur had just been standing must be directly above it.

Arthur rang once, twice. No response. No one home. But then a voice finally answered.

"Who's there?"

"Police," Arthur said. "I'd like to ask you something. Please open the door."

A brief pause, and then the door opened, and a woman of around eighty was standing there. She wore a dressing gown that once had been stylish, it was plain to see. She smiled, and Arthur took an immediate liking to her; there was warmth in that smile and in her face. Her permed white hair looked a little unkempt, as if she had not long since risen, and when she noticed Arthur looking, she smoothed it with her hand.

"I'm sorry," she said. "I've not quite gotten going today."

Arthur smiled. "It doesn't matter," he said, producing his police ID for the third time. "Nice dressing gown."

She giggled, took the ID, studied him carefully, and passed it back. "It is, isn't it? It's from New York."

"Oh, New York! Wow!"

Her expression grew a little more serious. "The police? What have I done wrong? Slept too late? Have the neighbors registered a complaint about my snoring?"

He had to smile, and she did, too. "No, no," he said. "Please don't worry. Will you let me in? I can explain."

She opened the door wide.

"Come in," she said, waving him through.

They entered a living room like Arthur's grandmother's—small, with neat photos of children and family on the walls, lace doilies, a shelf full of books. Arthur was amazed. He hadn't imagined a home in this building could be so cozy.

As if she could read his mind, she said, "You can make anywhere nice."

"Yes," he said as he looked at the photos.

"My daughter." She ran a finger over the face whose likeness at all ages covered the wall—from childhood through her wedding to adulthood with her own small family. "She lives a long way away. Up in the north. In Hamburg."

"Oh," he laughed in surprise. "What a coincidence—that's where I come from!"

She nodded and indicated for him to sit. Could she get him something? Tea? Coffee?

"Coffee, please." He sat at the ornate little Biedermeier table, hoping the similarly ornate chair he sat in would bear up under the weight of his workout-toughened body. It held without so much as a creak, and Arthur relaxed.

She vanished, and he heard the coffee machine. A few minutes later, she returned, now dressed and her hair combed, to serve coffee and cookies.

"Now, what can I do for you, young man?"

He brought out the composite produced from Renate Stockinger's description. "Do you recognize this face?"

She was surprised.

"Oh," she said. "This face? But of course I know him! Although I haven't seen him for a long time."

She stood and went over to a cupboard to take out a photo album that looked as though it contained photos from twenty or more years ago. She opened it up, leafed through it, and then held it out to Arthur.

"Here."

A young man, midtwenties, in jeans and a T-shirt, was standing next to the girl whom Arthur recognized from the photos on the wall.

"They more or less grew up together, my Johanna and Tonio Köhler from the third floor. When his mother went back to Italy, he was at our place all the time. I was a teacher, you see, and I'd taught him at school. He was a difficult child, even at that age, but a lovable boy. It was sad that he died so young."

Arthur nodded. "Yes, indeed. Died. So it's not actually him I'm asking about."

"No?" Her eyes were clear and confident.

"I mean the young man who's been living in the late Herr Köhler's apartment for a few weeks now."

She nodded, taking another look at the picture. "Oh, it's him. Yes, he does resemble his father. He's Ernst's grandson. Ernst left the apartment to him since his son had been dead for so long. He's also called Tonio, by the way."

She smiled briefly, but soon turned serious again. "But what do the police want with him?"

Arthur mentally wrung his hands in despair. This was taking ages. The old lady was very nice, but she was being pretty trying. Why couldn't people just say what they knew? Why did they have to ask their own questions all the time? And on top of it all, manage to pry out everything they wanted to know!

"He's a witness in a murder case," he said, trying to sound casual, "and possibly an abduction."

"Oh," she said. "Those two women. I read about them in the paper. Terrible. But I can't imagine he'd have anything to do with it. Not Tonio's son. No."

She shook her head vigorously, and then went to the window and gazed out for a while before turning back, a satisfied smile on her face.

"There are other things worrying him now," she said. "A friend's just been to visit him. A very pretty young woman. I saw her briefly. Very chic. Very elegant."

She sat back down. "Help yourself," she said kindly, gesturing to the cookies. "I baked them myself."

But Arthur was no longer listening. A young woman, he was thinking, just been to visit, and then . . . a thought exploded in his head.

Short skirt, tight blouse, shades, sexy.

"Shit," he exclaimed as he jumped up and ran from the apartment. "Goddamn it, they've tricked me! And now they've disappeared into the sunset!"

He was no longer aware of Frau Steigermann, or of her arms folding in satisfaction across her chest. He stormed out into the corridor and to the top of the stairs, from where he heard Franza's voice and Felix's laugh floating up. He dashed up the stairs to the third floor and heard Franza and Felix coming after him, also breaking into a run. He was finally outside the nameless door, hammering on it. With his knuckles, with his fists.

"Open up!" he yelled. "Open up! Police! Open the door!"

"What's happening?" Franza asked breathlessly, positioning herself with her gun in her hands. Herz did the same across from her. "Report!"

Arthur turned to them in disappointment.

"I don't think you . . ." he said, glancing at his colleagues' firearms. They followed his eyes, stowed the guns away, and then began to calm a series of neighbors who had come out in ones and twos onto the corridor, drawn by the commotion. Franza asked one of them to call the janitor.

Arthur told them what he knew. They listened in silence.

"You did everything right," Felix said as Arthur came to an end.

Franza nodded and clapped him on the shoulder.

"No going in alone," she said. "That's the number-one rule! And sometimes it means one slips through the net. For the time being, at least."

The janitor arrived. The usual procedure: IDs, the request to open the door, his dubious expression, the usual question: "Do you have authority for this?" and the usual reply: "Yes, we do." Finally, an unlocked apartment and the janitor hanging around—his curiosity knowing no bounds—needing to be forcefully sent away.

As they had suspected, the apartment was empty, the coffee machine still on, the birds clearly flown in panic. But the detectives discovered a lot, nevertheless. They unearthed another part of the story.

51

Tonio's death. And that which followed. We avoided it, didn't speak about it—not for a long time. Not until the end. Not until there was no choice.

It was September. It was September back then, too. Twenty-two years ago. Greece. Kos. The black sand. We dug ourselves in there.

Back to Gertrud's kitchen. She had boiled up the last damsons. Small beads of sweat shone on her brow as she stirred the bubbling jelly in the large pan. She said she had to do it before she left, she was flying to Greece, to the house, and she had to get everything in order before she went.

She was barefoot, wearing a short dark red dress, sleeveless. I rinsed the jelly jars, dried them, and lined them up on the shelf. We worked in silence, concentrating.

It was hot, although it was nearing the middle of September.

"Coffee?" Gertrud asked.

I nodded. She made the coffee, and its scent spread through the room. She took cups from the cupboard, milk from the fridge, sugar from the sideboard.

I watched her, my eyes gliding down her back and her legs, their shape outlined by her red dress, and tried to remember the old times, the Gertrud she had been back then.

A jelly-making session, I thought. *We're having a jelly-making session.*

We were silent, dwelling on our thoughts. *Happiness is dangerous,* I thought. *You cling to it and it deserts you and you don't know why. Contentment is what counts. Contentment is security.*

Gertrud's kitchen was bathed in late summer sunlight and the heat of the boiling damsons. She stood before the stove, which was speckled with drops of damson purée and damson jelly, and as she began to wipe and scrub, I finally realized that I had not thought about Tonio for a long time. Yet I missed him, missed him, missed him.

The evening hung on the air, and a drop of jelly fell in the fading humidity onto Gertrud's brown knee.

So that's why I'm here, I thought. *That's why. To remember. To become one again with my memories. To become one with myself. To be reconciled,* I thought. *As if doing a jigsaw puzzle, I'm slowly putting all the pieces inside myself together. Now the last piece should finally fit into place, too. But can I bear it? And Gertrud? Will she be able to?*

"Did you send me that letter, Gertrud?" I asked. "Was it you who sent it?"

She turned, brushed the hair from her brow with the back of her hand, and I remembered that she had always done that, always. Warmth flowed through me, and I wanted to hug her.

She looked at me thoughtfully, as if wondering what she wanted to say to me, and what not to say.

"Letter? No, I didn't send you any letter. It wasn't me, though I know who it was."

She sat down by me at the table and began to talk. About Tonio's son, whom he must have had with someone else, long before we'd met him. He'd appeared, searching for his father's past.

I was amazed. A son? Tonio had a son?

Gertrud nodded as if she could read my thoughts. "Yes," she said, "a son."

She fell silent, giving me time to get used to the idea.

"I saw him," she went on. "I told him everything I knew, and that's not much. I hope he'll leave us alone now. Will you come with me to Greece? Hanna? Will you come with me?"

Go with her to Greece? I hadn't been back since that time. I'd suppressed it all, forgotten it all, avoided that country, that island, that sea, without knowing why—I didn't want to go back down the trail of misfortune.

"Yes," I said. "Greece. Kos. Why not? Yes, I'll come with you. Maybe there'll be a seat on your plane, and if not I'll come later. It won't do any harm to see the place again."

Then the letter occurred to me again. "But how did he get ahold of that letter?"

"He inherited Tonio's father's apartment. And he found it all there. Our names. Photos. The letters. Tonio's father kept it all, and his son found it. Strange, isn't it?"

I still didn't understand it. How could Tonio's letter to me have ended up with his father? Gertrud explained. "I sent them to him. After I returned from Greece and you were off traveling somewhere in the world, I gave up our apartment in Munich. I didn't know what to do with all the things but I couldn't just throw them away. So I sent everything that involved Tonio to his father."

Silence. I must have nodded. Those letters . . .

"Did you read them?" I looked at her cautiously, hoping . . . but knew deep down . . .

She nodded. "Yes, of course I read them. But only your letters. Not his. But yours, yes. And the more often I read them, the more I got the feeling"—she struggled for the words—"the feeling that they were intended for me," she continued eventually. "As if you'd written them to me."

My breath caught in my throat. What was she telling me? She looked at me, her eyes impenetrable. I shook my head. The letters came into my mind, the exact words.

. . . *dear hanna . . . dear tonio . . .*

That was how they began, our letters, every letter always the same. I remember.

. . . *dear tonio . . .*

In the letters our days were empty and full of sorrow: I was waiting for him, my beloved, with every fiber of my being, wherever he was, whatever he was doing. I was longing for him. I wrote that I missed him as soon as he left the room, that his body was my pitcher, my jug, that my soul had found its place in him as had my heart, that without him I was a *small soft thing* that fell apart, unraveled . . .

Astonishment spread through me. What did Gertrud say? As if they were intended for her? As if I'd written them to her?

I shook my head vehemently. *No,* I thought. *No, that's impossible. They could never have been written for anyone other than Tonio and Hanna at that time, when our love was already coming to an end, when it was already driving us apart, in different directions.*

"No," I said, loud and determined. "No, Gertrud, that will never be true, never. Don't say that. It's not true."

Gertrud shrugged, turned away. I saw the letters before me, our handwriting, the color of the ink—changed according to our whims.

. . . *dear hanna . . .*

The days were empty and full of sorrow. He was waiting for me, his beloved. With every fiber of his being. Wherever I was. Whatever I was doing. He was longing for me. He missed me. He had always missed me. All his life. Always. And now. As soon as I left the room. My body was his pitcher, his jug. His soul had found its place in me and his heart had finally awoken. Because of me. He fell apart without me. And unraveled without me. As if he'd never been alive before . . . *as if I'd never been alive before . . .*

And he did fall apart. Did unravel. But at least he was alive. That was a consolation.

His death gradually came back to me. I slowly felt the blue swell in Gertrud's kitchen, a haze; perhaps it was only the damsons, the schnapps we drank on meeting again, that made us cheerful and happy. It was all like a play, a drama of life and death.

I suddenly remembered the newspaper photo in black and white, the picture that had accompanied me around the world: a dead man and me, Tonio and Hanna. It was a crumpled piece of reality that grew truer and more painful, the grayer the shadows that concealed him became. It was not until the journey homeward, that final journey, that I tore up the photo, and bending out of the train window, I watched the scraps of paper get caught up by the nighttime airstream and rapidly, irrevocably vanish from my sight.

And now?

Reconstruction of a death. Back then. Everything that happened. A pain that still hurts, a wound that still bleeds. In the middle of September we were afraid of the final eruption of the memory.

"Let the past lie," Gertrud had said. "Those old stories aren't true anymore."

She said it brusquely, almost nervously, and loudly enough to break the thread that tried to spin its way from back then to now. In the Indian summer the weavers of life spin their threads into time and time disintegrates and becomes as one.

52

They wouldn't be needing a translator after all. They'd found all the documents about Tonio's death in the apartment—translated police reports, letters, newspaper clippings—all translated and carefully filed by date and sequence of events. Ernst Köhler had meticulously documented the death of his only son for posterity, so that a picture could be formed of the accident that happened in Greece.

There had been three parties involved, none of them unknown to the detectives: Tonio Köhler, Hanna Umlauf, and Gertrud Rabinsky, or Gertrud Brendler as she was at the time.

The bare facts were that the three of them had spent a vacation on Kos at Gertrud's parents' house. The summer was coming to an end, and it was almost the start of the academic year. One night, two weeks after their arrival, Tonio, whom the proprietor of a nearby taverna described as nice and friendly if a little eccentric, had the crazy idea of going for a swim in the turbulent black sea. For several days there had been storm warnings—no swimmers and no boats out on the water. The fishermen cursed, the few vacationers still on the island at that time cursed, but people resigned themselves, it was the right thing to do. No one dared to pit themselves against the force of the sea.

Except Tonio. On that cursed night. First he got drunk, and then he staggered out into the water and threw himself into the waves, yelling and roaring with enthusiasm. He ventured farther and farther out, the waves bore him up, threw him back and forth until he was eventually dashed down beneath the surf.

Gertrud, who was recorded in the files as the only witness, had stated that nothing could have held him back, nothing. She had tried everything, but in vain. He had gone into the sea, in the storm, yelling and laughing. First the darkness had swallowed him up and then the sea.

Hanna had been asleep and had only found out about the accident the next morning. She was there when the coastguards retrieved the body that had been washed up on the beach. Before he was transported back to Germany, back home, they had tested his blood. The results showed that Tonio had 0.21 percent alcohol in his blood, but there was no trace of any other drugs. Recklessness was the final verdict in the files, fatal recklessness, brought about by excessive alcohol consumption. So it was self-inflicted. The records ended there.

"What a mess," Felix said. "A real tragedy."

"It must have been a great love between Tonio and Hanna," Franza said.

She held up the pile of letters that had been beneath the photos tacked to the wall. The top photo was of an old man, who must have been the grandfather, and immediately beneath it was a picture of Tonio, who bore an amazing likeness to his son. To either side were photos of the two women in their younger days, with Gertrud positioned farther away from Tonio than Hanna.

They also found photos with more recent dates among the stacks of paper. The pictures of Hanna were taken from newspapers or the Internet, while the ones of Gertrud must have been taken by Tonio himself. They showed Gertrud outside her shop, working or chatting with customers. But they also showed her in the garden outside her house, with her children and husband. Tonio had worked his way into Gertrud's life, spying on her, stalking her, an uninvited onlooker.

He had probably sat for hours in front of the little altar he had created around the photos. Was it here that he plotted his revenge? But revenge for what?

The fact that he had not had a father? That his childhood had been hard? And he now wanted to punish the women who had torn Tonio from his mother and therefore from him?

The detectives had no answers. Not yet.

"What now?"

Franza opened a window, positioned herself in front of it, and lit a cigarette.

"I have to calm my lungs after that race up the stairs," she said by way of excuse, grinning sheepishly.

Felix gave her the finger, but came to sit with her by the window and said, "Let me breathe some of it in. A little dose of nicotine every now and then—I just can't resist it."

"A minor rebellion against the nanny state?" Arthur's spirits had risen again.

Franza shrugged. "So where do we go from here?"

"A search, of course," Felix said, "with full fanfare. We have well-founded grounds for suspicion, so send the composite out to police stations nationwide. It should also be featured on the news. We also need a composite of his accomplice. Arthur?"

"What?"

"You know, what does she look like?" Franza asked. "You saw her, after all."

"She's a looker. Well, I think so." He pulled a despairing face as he realized how inane that sounded.

Franza rolled her eyes. *Men,* she thought. "Good-looking? Is that all?!"

"Well," Arthur stammered, "it all happened so quickly. She was wearing shades, her hair was . . ." He couldn't recall any more.

"Blonde? Brown? Red? Short? Long?" Franza prompted. But it was no use.

"No idea." Arthur sighed. "I'm really sorry. Long. No, short. Pinned up, perhaps. I don't know. I just exchanged a few words with her and then she was gone. I can describe the other one a bit better. I talked to her for longer."

"Except we don't need her," Franza said, trying to appear severe, but failing.

Arthur shrugged apologetically.

"Oh well," Felix said as Franza crushed the cigarette out on the exterior windowsill. "At least we have Clyde. Bonnie can't be far behind."

"We also need to extend the search for Hanna," Franza said. "What if he's abducted her, has her hidden away somewhere?"

They were silent for a moment, trying not to imagine what could have happened, the events that could be unfolding.

"Well," Franza said. "Let's go. There's a lot to do."

They made to leave, pausing only to pick up the toothbrushes lying on a shelf in the bathroom so they could compare them with the DNA traces found in Gertrud's kitchen.

They went by the apartment of Frau Steigermann again as they left the building.

The old lady turned out to be a tough nut to crack, insisting she knew nothing about Ernst Köhler's grandson—no surname, no telephone number, nothing about his life.

Perhaps it was true, perhaps not. It was most likely true. Why would Tonio Whatever-his-name-was spend his time going from door to door, giving his name and address to his neighbors if he intended to commit murder?

They left. It had gotten late, and tomorrow was another day.

53

It had been close. Very close. He'd been on the john. Thank goodness he had his cell phone in his pocket, so Kristin had been able to reach him. She had gone out to fetch something to eat; the cupboards were all bare, everything eaten. Then things started happening fast.

He had added coffee and water to his grandfather's coffee machine, one of the few things he hadn't gotten rid of, and switched it on.

Then a few quiet moments in the john, then the sudden phone call. He had cursed, knowing that it was Kristin—no one else had the number of the prepaid SIM he'd bought when he disappeared from his old life.

He swore. "Can't a guy even get a moment's peace in the john?"

He briefly wondered whether to pick up, but did.

"Police," she said, sounding only a little nervous. "They're looking for you. There's one here with a composite of you."

"Shit," he said.

"Don't lose your nerve. Stay calm. He's talking to a woman from the building who seems to know you. He's going to go in, I'm sure of it. Try and get past him. Get out somehow. If he takes the stairs, you get in the elevator. Do it somehow. Don't lose your nerve. We'll figure this out."

Her voice sounded like a metallic staccato in his ears, and he nodded ceaselessly, without thinking that she couldn't see him.

"Are you still there?" she cried. "Say something!"

"Yes." His voice was barely audible, as his heart was racing and there was a lump in his throat. "Wait for me by your car."

"Hurry up!" she said. "Move!"

Then she was gone, and for a brief moment he felt more alone than he ever had in his life. Worse than when he left home, and when he left his hometown, and even when Gertrud Rabinsky was suddenly lying dead on her kitchen floor.

He could feel himself trembling and commanded himself to stop. It worked, amazingly, and he crept to the apartment door, carefully opened it, and listened for sounds from the stairwell. The elevator was not moving. Voices drifted up from downstairs. The voice of a man he didn't know, the voice of a woman he did know—old Frau Steigermann from the apartment below. Then he heard a door, and the voices grew fainter until they could no longer be heard, swallowed up in the apartment.

He threw a quick glance along the corridor, felt a moment of regret as he suspected he was unlikely ever to return, stepped out into the stairwell, and silently closed the front door. No time to take anything with him, no time for sentimental good-byes. The elevator was there, no time wasted. He traveled down to the ground floor, cautiously pressed the button to open the door, saw no one; the way was clear. He slipped out, ran to the main door; it swung open, and he felt free—infinitely free.

Kristin was waiting in the car behind the building. He got in and she started it up.

"Everything will be fine," she said and drove off.

He thought of the girl. "Lilli," he said.

Kristin waved him off. "Doesn't matter. No time to worry about her now."

237

54

Tonio's death.

So sudden and unexpected. Not a natural death.

To think of it again, to experience it again, even in my mind, is hard. Still. Some memories weigh heavy. But I'm finally up to it.

Gathering the scenes together, looking for lost jigsaw puzzle pieces. Early autumn. Tonio's death.

A house in Greece, white with blue doors and window frames, near the beach, but not too close. Just near enough to the village.

All of us in that house, by that sea. Blurring of time.

The landscape no longer surrounded us with the glaring colors of summer. The mildness of fall was in the air, the sun red gold, no longer sharp and scorching. The sea was still warm, and it felt good, with a thousand shades of blue and green.

How beautiful the first few days were! The waves rolled gently in, spraying sea water onto the black sand, where the droplets gleamed like sparkling gemstones. Sometimes large ships steamed by in the distance, and the waves were lashed into wild breakers, spitting out bizarrely shaped stones.

"These stones are like messengers from another age," we would joke. "These stones are the dead, the drunks, the ancient Greeks whom the sea is spitting out again. Odysseus, maybe, and Helen and Menelaus and Cassandra the seer."

Perhaps that was too much. Perhaps we tempted fate and the gods wanted their sacrificial offering.

The storm came and nothing felt right anymore. There was no hanging around on the beach, no bathing. It was too cold, too windy. We were restless, and there was a bad atmosphere in the house. Tonio kept opening the windows, letting the wind in so you could hear the roaring sea and the storm around the house. The curtains billowed and the windows rattled in their frames.

The dishes piled up in the kitchen: plates with the remains of meals that attracted the flies, open wine bottles containing stale dregs, hardened bread.

I don't know why we didn't manage to keep the place in order. Maybe it was this outward chaos that got us all mixed up, too.

Tonio and I spent hours in bed, night and day, without a care for Gertrud, who took care of herself.

"Why doesn't she go to the village?" Tonio said in annoyance whenever I expressed concern that we shouldn't leave her alone for so long. "There's a whole crowd of single guys there. Why doesn't she just enjoy herself?"

I said nothing. I didn't tell him I could see in her eyes what she felt for me, could feel it whenever she was near. But Tonio probably knew it anyway. He became aggressive toward her, angry, surly. He refused to leave me alone with her, watched us continually.

Maybe Gertrud had also heard us in our room, in our bed. We were never quiet. We laughed, moaned, sighed. Tonio said, "That's what fucking's all about." And so it was. But maybe she heard us and it stirred up resentment, sadness in her.

And then it was that night. I know little about what happened. Nothing, really. I was asleep. And when I awoke in the morning, everything had changed. When I awoke, Gertrud was sitting on the other side of the bed. I saw her back, saw she was trembling.

You trembled, Gertrud, you didn't turn when I spoke to you, you didn't react. I sat up, turned to you. You cried, quietly, soundlessly, but in a way that shook your whole body.

I asked nothing, merely looked out of the window. I noticed right away that the storm had abated. I thought, good, we can swim again, perhaps not today, but tomorrow. Then everything will get back to normal, everything will be good again between the three of us.

But then . . .

. . . then I noticed the activity on the beach, over where we had always gone swimming, where the waves washed around us, lapped at our feet and gently splashed our legs.

There was activity on the beach. There were people there, lots of people, crowding around a single point. I got up and started walking, feeling nothing—slowly at first. But then . . .

I don't know why I began to run those last few steps up to the wall of people. I don't know why, Gertrud.

Then I saw him lying there, where they had laid him out. He was so still, so silent, already so stiff.

55

Dr. Borger, the coroner, enjoyed an excellent dinner and treated himself to a cigar, with an espresso and a cognac. It was then that he made a very interesting discovery.

56

"I hear myself cry out," I said in Gertrud's kitchen. "In my dreams some nights, I hear myself cry his name."

But no one hears me, least of all Tonio. I see him running. It all happens at breakneck speed. He runs and runs, out into the water, into the raging surf; he doesn't stop. He is alone. He is happy. He wants to feel the water on his skin. Feel the wind that has long since whipped up into a storm. How awesome it is to feel the water like oil on your skin, the wind like velvet—how often he said that.

His face glows brightly through the darkness. I feel his warmth from hours ago when I'd held him in my arms for the last time.

He'll die. I don't know it yet. I'm lying in our bed, sleeping. That's why he'll die. Because I didn't look out for him. Because I wasn't there. Because I was asleep. I didn't protect him from his own high spirits, from his own recklessness.

It's strange, but in my dreams everything always happens in slow motion. In my dreams Gertrud isn't there at all. I see Tonio die. I see the way the waves dash him down, the storm buffets him—all in slow motion, which makes it worse, because it lasts twice as long, because we feel the pain for twice as long—both he and I.

Everything is so much louder in the night. Every noise—the storm, the waves. The footsteps on the stones. His cry as he sinks into the water. Into death. Black air, black water. An ocean of distance.

He was a good swimmer, had been all his life—even in death. I see how he wrestles with the forces all around him, how he begins to feel surprise as he realizes that there is no use.

Eventually he is gone, the sea suddenly still, an oily black mass, the storm dwindled to a light wind. Everything empty, still.

As am I. When he disappears and stops fighting, I become as still as never before. When his heart ceases to beat; when his heart stops still. He disappears—his body, his warmth. And eventually . . . the memory of it, too.

. . .

The Danube. Here, now.

How beautiful it is. Smooth surface, the occasional shimmer as if the river is scraping along the sky. The sun is dazzling—the twin suns: the one in the sky and the one on the water. People walking in the distance move into the golden sunlight on the river, become black shadows, dissolve into dazzling shimmers. Gold light from behind the clouds, too. Two dogs, black and white, Pablo and Maja. The shrill cries of young girls float upward like white seagulls in the air.

I close my eyes and turn my thoughts back to Gertrud's kitchen. We drank wine; perhaps we were a little tipsy, which gave us the courage to ask the right questions, give the right answers.

"I ran to him," I said. "The next morning, after they retrieved him. They let me go to him. As soon as they saw me the circle silently opened up. I touched him and felt a momentary stillness inside, the stillness which came from his heart. I touched him again and again, stroked his body, felt the stillness, felt that his heart was no longer beating, felt that he was no longer warm, felt that he had already vanished, vanished into a faint shimmering, a dark beam of light.

"Wetness had pooled around him, the wetness of the sea, the wetness from the depths. I felt it on my hands and then the pain came, and it began to overwhelm me.

"I knew right then that it would hurt like nothing had ever hurt before. I knew it would take me to the edge, to a place where it's easy to fall over the precipice."

I halted, looked at Gertrud. She held her wine glass in her hands, looking into it so I couldn't see her eyes. I felt the faint scar inside me, the old pain.

"Yes," I said, without taking my eyes away from Gertrud until she turned her face to me, her eyes impenetrable.

"I knelt down, by Tonio's body," I continued, "and felt inside me that stillness which came from his heart, and which I didn't want to let go of for a long, long time. It was a protection, a shield. I took it with me out into the world. It accompanied me, made it possible for me to go, to begin my journey.

"At last they pulled me away from him, they spoke to me. There was a woman who held me in her arms, murmuring soft words, probably words of comfort, but I didn't hear them. I didn't understand her. I heard nothing. Only that his heart was no longer beating."

"Stop it, Hanna," Gertrud said. "I know it all already."

But I couldn't stop. I talked and talked. A light wind had arisen, murmuring in the trees. We could hear it through the open window.

"It was the last time I saw him, and apart from that . . ." I shook my head, listening inside myself. "I remember nothing."

Only that I set off then. I packed my backpack and disappeared. Away from the island. Away from Greece. Away from the black sand.

Gertrud nodded, and I looked at her cautiously. Her eyes were dark, her mouth a hard line. She looked like an animal about to take flight.

She looks old, I thought. *Suddenly, she looks old.* I granted us a break and put some fresh coffee on to brew. Milk, cups, sugar pot. With the coffee bubbling through the filter, I sat down again.

"Why didn't you come to find me, Gertrud?" I asked finally. "Why didn't you?"

Silence, only the bubbling of the coffee machine, a fly buzzing through the room.

"I don't know," she said at last. Her voice was a whisper, a breath, dying away. "I don't know. Stop asking. It's all so long ago. Leave the past alone. Let it go. Otherwise you can't live."

"Have you let it go, then?" I asked.

Silence again, then, "No."

I leaned forward, took a strand of her hair and wound it around my finger. She turned away, and the lock of hair slipped from my finger, pulling at her scalp a little.

"Where were you?" she asked. "After Tonio's death. All those long months?"

I shrugged. "Everywhere. Nowhere. No idea. Sugar?"

"Where did you live? How did you get money?"

I finally thought back.

To icy streets in cold lands, to smoke rising from chimneys, threads rising upward and cutting the sky in two, darkness falling rapidly. I thought of the rich green leaves of primeval forests, mangrove forests, sun, sea, oceans, foreign smells, foreign touches, and the ever-recurring cold, freezing until it was hardly possible to freeze anymore—all of it like a dream, but not mine.

At night, whenever I could, I slept with the door open, afraid of closed rooms.

"One day!" I would whisper then. "One day . . ."

I was always wishing for the future, and when the wishing grew too much, it drove me onward. Then I would stand on a station platform and choose from all the directions and destinations, blindly, without a plan, and send myself on my way, the main thing to be on the move.

The impermanence of velvet moments made life good. I liked to see the light reflected in a glass of red wine, to be enveloped by clouds of tobacco smoke making the light diffuse and gray.

Then I would smile myself and strangers into seventh heaven; I hung on to life or to whatever I considered to be life. I was not afraid of feeling a man's hand on my knee; on the contrary, I would grasp it, smoke my cigarette to the end, catch hold of the stranger's fingers, and guide them further.

It was as though I were standing next to myself and watching myself smile, laugh . . . and then cry. Because I suddenly recalled what warmth was. Because I suddenly recalled what . . .

I was moved by bodies that were good and wiry and tender. I smiled through tears when they immersed me in their language, of which I often didn't understand a single word, a single syllable—even when they scattered the incomprehensible sounds of their language over my body and continued to slurp them out, slurp them in . . .

I was always afraid of neglecting myself, no longer finding myself in the arms of happiness. I wanted to hold on to it, the happiness, hold it deep in my heart, but when morning broke on the diffuse fog of my intoxication and the traces of the night, the night itself could no longer be concealed, and I fled from the suffocation of my own alcohol-soaked breath.

Lipstick on the pillow and my face in the mirror of a wrecked bathroom, dirt-smeared and wrecked like the mirror itself, my hair straggly, my hands sweaty—my cold, thin, lost fingers.

In the bed sometimes there would be someone sprawled, a naked stranger, harsh as the morning, and I . . . I would take off again.

"He's dead," I would whisper into the mirror, and I finally knew it but kept forgetting it over and over again. "Dead and gone. No shirt will ever look good on him again—white, blue, or yellow."

And I took off. Again and again. Back to the sea. Another sea. Never back to that one. Stiff breezes. Squalls. Sand on the feet. Foaming white, mountainous waves. The line between sky and ocean lost in the twilight.

In all the images was a great stillness, deep cracks, and always the cold wet of Tonio's body on my hand. It had worked its way into all the pores of my skin—I would never be free of it.

I was on the edge, I thought, sitting in Gertrud's kitchen in the face of Gertrud's silence. *I was at the precipice, and the images I still have are those that led me back onto firm ground, like fine pins stuck in a map that is spread invisibly through my body.*

Another flash of light and more images, and the nearer I brought myself to home, the thicker and faster the memories came.

Finally, I lay on busy beaches in the Aegean summer. The days shimmered back into the sun as if they had never happened. At midday the seagulls were as if painted on glass, the sun shining through them, translucent around the edges, and the white feathery clouds seemed so close they were almost within reach.

It was there that I began to fall silent, that I crept into the stillness, wanting to unlearn all languages on the way to myself, to the wetness on my hand.

I dreamed of the days we'd had. They had been beautiful, beautiful. Splendid gems. If you could have tasted them, they would have melted on your tongue. Slowly. Solemnly.

I dreamed of the time that had dripped from the clock—invisible, intangible—time that had not been enough.

And then . . . I began . . . eventually . . . suddenly . . . to feel something foreign inside me, something that did not belong there—not inside me, not in my body. It made me afraid, a hazy terror. I wanted happiness once more, I thought, one more refill before I die.

I thought about Dorothee for the first time during all those months. Of Dorothee, who was my mother of sorts. I turned for home.

It was May, everything smelled of spring, of summer almost, but I was nauseated by all scents, unable to bear them. I descended from the train, shouldered my backpack, and walked along the platform into the concourse. All my desires seemed to be satisfied. For the sea, the wide expanses, the beaches. Again and again trains had spat me out, now here, now there, with cold monotony, cold regularity. Until nothing remained, only the amazement that I had not been drawn into their rattling, that the indeterminate remained indeterminate and the uncertain remained uncertain.

Tonio's death had come between everyone and everything. It was forever, I finally knew, like a death always is. But it also came between us, the living.

57

Dr. Borger had brought the medical record into town with him when he went to eat. He'd planned to enjoy it after his meal—the high point, as it were. With the last wisps of smoke from his cigar drifting up into the blue September sky, the espresso and cognac drunk, Borger opened the file and began to read.

When he had finished, he leaned back, took a deep breath, loosened the knot of his tie, stared into space for a moment, and finally raised his hand to summon the waiter. This piece of news merited another cognac.

58

It was dark in the room. Only the narrow strip of light from a streetlight fell through the window and brought out the contours of their bodies.

At seven that morning Port would be leaving for Vienna. His car was parked outside.

He stroked her face.

"Tears," he said. "You're crying? My Franza."

"It's for seven weeks, after all," she said. "And I've got so much to think about—Lilli, this case, you. Everything's getting a bit muddled up, you know?"

He said nothing, just stroked her face. She sniffled, and he wiped the tears from her cheeks, her mouth. She sniffled and had to laugh a little.

"You'll come, though, won't you? To Vienna. You'll visit me. Won't you? I'd like you to come. I really would. Otherwise these seven weeks will really drag."

"Yes, I know. I'll come."

They lay side by side, hand in hand. They laughed a little in the face of the imminent separation, in its salty, bitter warmth. Then he said, "I'm hungry."

He started to get up to go to the kitchen, to the fridge, but she held him back.

"Leave it. Stay here. I'll make you something."

She stroked his face.

"Oh," he said. "There's luxury! What have I done to deserve that?"

She shrugged, smiled. "You don't have to deserve everything you get. Sometimes you just get things."

By the time she returned, he had fallen back asleep.

She sat on the edge of the bed, the plate of open sandwiches in her hand. In the end, she ate them herself.

He slept in the strip of light from the streetlight. She gazed and gazed at him, taking in all his features, until the strip of light grew wider and wider, eventually overtaking the whole room because morning was gradually dawning.

She stood and went to her laptop in the living room. She knew he would be there. He always was at that time. Woken by an internal clock, he would be there. Waiting for her. For *alien one*. He was *alien two*. How stupid those names were. She had never questioned it. It didn't matter in the slightest. The words flitted across the page, like shooting stars—that was all that mattered.

At first she'd asked him what he was looking for there. After all, he was spoken for.

At the same moment she realized she could ask herself the same question, and as she did, she found she was unable to answer it.

He had tried to find someone.

He loved his wife. He felt committed to her for life. He would never leave her. . . . *but . . . there are some things . . .*

. . . some things . . . ?

. . . some things . . .

She left it at that, never asked more. Just as she never asked for a photo. Neither did he. But that wasn't important. They knew nothing about one another, only the basic facts: age, location. He was a little older than she was, they lived in the same town, he had dark hair, she was blonde. That was it. And that was how it should stay. Wolves in the night, howling occasionally at the moon.

He was waiting.

. . . i missed you . . . you weren't here yesterday . . .

. . . i was very tired . . . she wrote, *. . . i have a lot of work at the moment . . .*

. . . what . . . he began.

. . . don't . . . she wrote quickly, *. . . let's stay as we are, two aliens who met in Internet heaven, who will one day lose each other there too . . .*

. . . why do you believe that . . .

. . . because that's how it is . . .

. . . what if I don't want to lose you . . . he wrote.

She logged out suddenly. Shut down the computer. *No,* she thought. *Not those questions. Don't start.*

But it had already started. He would be there again tomorrow: *alien two.* So would she: *alien one.*

Tired, she went over to the balcony door. Lilli had not responded to her text. Earlier that evening Franza had tried to call her. Still nothing.

Rain was forecast, but it didn't look like it. Franza fetched a blanket from the couch, wrapped herself in it, and went out into the morning. The ravens would soon be arriving, swarms of black birds filling the sky, their cawing full of harsh faith in warmer days.

Franza sat down, turning her face to the cool morning sun. The rain had a gentle touch. It was raining now, after all.

59

There were photos on the wall above the dining room table. A little boy, a man, a girl. I looked at them, lingering over the face of the girl. My heart began to thump, wildly, racing; my throat tightened and a longing flowed through me, an incredible longing. So that was her.

"So that's her," I whispered. My voice was cracking, and I had to clear my throat. "Is that her?"

"Yes," Gertrud said. "Yes, that's her. Of course it's her. Who else would it be?"

I looked at Gertrud. Her face was ashen. We were silent. For a long while. It had gotten dark; only the small kitchen light was on.

"Maybe you'll simply return to Strasbourg," she said. "Perhaps that would be for the best."

I nodded. "Yes," I said. "Perhaps."

But I knew that wouldn't work anymore. She knew it, too.

"What was it like," I eventually began. I hesitated and had to begin again. "What was it like when she was growing up? How did you two get along?"

There was no hesitation this time.

"She was everything." Gertrud's words came flooding out." She held me together when I wanted to break apart. She calmed me. She's my home. It's through her that I've always felt I'm alive. She never left me. I haven't been alone ever again."

"Yes," I whispered. "Yes."

"Sometimes," she said, "it's difficult. Like everything is. But . . ."

I nodded.

Silence again. For a while. I wanted a schnapps. We drank a little.

Eventually she said, "Come with me." And she took me by the hand.

I went with her. It was lovely—her hand in mine, her arms around me, her scent. The night that glided over us finally gave me peace so that I was able to sleep. I fell asleep in her arms, like back when we were children and sisters.

But it didn't last long, the stillness. The sleep. It didn't last long. Christian arrived.

60

Franza was more punctual than usual. That was due to Port's early departure, after which she had showered, grabbed a bit to eat, and set off for the office, intending to arrive first on that Tuesday morning. But she found Borger sitting outside her door. He greeted her with a smile.

"Hey," she said, stopping in surprise. "You? Here? When all good people should still be asleep? I thought I'd be the first in today."

He inclined his head. "Sorry to have foiled your good intentions, my dear, but I've got some information for you, which might be important. So I thought—"

"Wonderful," she said as she opened up the office. "We need everything we can get. Any tiny detail that can move us forward somehow. Should we wait for Felix? He'll be here soon, knowing him."

Borger nodded and sat down. Franza put some coffee on, unpacked her Tupperware box, and got some cups from the cupboard.

When Herz arrived, he stopped in amazement, framed by the open door.

"What's this? A full house already! Borger? You?"

"I've got something for you," Borger said with a mysterious smile. Then he asked a question, to which both Franza and Herz replied with a resounding "Yes."

And then he told them about his interesting discovery, which floored them both.

61

Leaping in the sunshine, whirring in the wind, the gentle touch of the droplets, drizzle. I want to catch it all with the camera, capture it in pictures—experiments, trials; we'll see.

I'm playing a game. Tomorrow for tomorrow. Waiting for the rain. I'm lying on a blanket on the riverbank, camera at the ready, snapping and snapping, for as long as it takes. Then I put the camera back in its bag and lie flat on my back, surrendering totally. And I wait. For as long as I can bear to. Shirt up over my belly, sleeves pushed up, shoes off, pants off, to offer as much of myself to the rain as possible so it can rain down on me and leave traces on my skin.

At some point I always have to close my eyes. At some point I get a feeling as if the rain penetrates through my skin and into me, raining into my soul and into my brain. That's the moment when I have to leave, jump up, put on my clothes, grab the camera, pick up my bike, and return, freezing.

The girl. My girl. She's finally here.

62

"Gertrud Rabinsky," Borger asked, to gain himself a little time. "Gertrud Rabinsky had two children, didn't she?" A brief pause. "A daughter and a son, right?"

"Yes," Franza said. "Why?"

"Yes," Herz said. "Why?"

Borger shook his head. "But that isn't possible."

"What?" Franza asked blankly. "What isn't possible?"

"That Gertrud Rabinsky has two children," Borger said slowly. "Or, to put it another way, that Frau Rabinsky *gave birth to* two children, since"—he looked at the intent faces of the two detectives and continued—"since when little Moritz was born five years ago she was a primipara."

"A what?" Herz asked.

"Primi . . ." Franza thought aloud. "The first, first-time . . ."

Borger nodded with a smile.

"And *partus,*" Franza continued, "means birth."

"Good," said Borger. "Very good! Continue . . . What do you conclude from that?"

"A first-time mother," Franza said, catching her breath. "She was a first-time mother!"

"Bingo," said Borger with a smile. "Give her one hundred points. Once again, I'm full of praise for our educated classes!"

"Wow," Herz said. "That's quite something."

They were silent for a moment, taking it in.

"So?" Borger finally asked. "Do you want the details?"

Of course they wanted the details. Borger loosened his tie and began.

"So, after I found out that Frau Rabinsky had had a hysterectomy . . ." He trailed off, a teasing gleam in his eye.

Franza shook her head. "Don't keep us in suspense. Can you just get to the point?"

"But of course," Borger said. "Of course, my dearest Franza. So, hysterectomy, as I said. When I discover something like that it naturally arouses my curiosity—why, how, and so on—and I request the medical files. So I got them yesterday afternoon and there it was. Frau Rabinsky was admitted to the clinic five years ago on February 25 with severe pains, there was a vaginal birth, but it was followed by postpartum bleeding."

He paused and raised an eyebrow at Herz, who nodded. "Understood. I do know some things."

Satisfied, Borger continued. "Good. They carried out a curettage, a scraping of the uterus, in order to stop the bleeding, but it wasn't successful. So they decided to carry out an abdominal hysterectomy, that is, removal of the uterus through the abdominal cavity."

He paused briefly. "And in addition to all this information, the medical records also stated that she was at the time *primipara*. And therefore we can conclude that she could not have given birth to a child several years previously."

"And medical records don't lie," Herz said slowly.

Borger nodded. "That's right. Medical records don't lie."

"What about Lilli?"

Borger shrugged. "Whoever she is, she isn't Gertrud Rabinsky's natural daughter. The rest is up to you."

He took a gingerbread cookie from the tin, and was devouring it with relish when the door opened. Arthur.

"Oh," Herz said. "Here already?"

Arthur stopped, out of sorts.

"Sorry," he stammered, glancing at the clock. "I'm not *that* late. How come you're all here so early?"

"News," Franza said, and gave their younger colleague a quick summary.

"So, we have a new situation on our hands," Herz said when she finished. "Name of Lilli. And now we need to get to the bottom of it. Perhaps this is the key."

"What about Tonio? How does he fit in?" Arthur asked.

"We'll find that out, too," Felix said. "We always find out. Thank you, Borger, you've been a great help."

"My pleasure, as always." Borger rose. "I'll be off, then. Two postmortems waiting. Good luck with the rest of the case."

They nodded and he left.

"She knows," Franza said, scrabbling for her cell phone.

"What?" asked Herz. "Who?"

"Lilli," Franza said as she dialed Lilli's number. "That was what she wanted to tell me. That she knew, somehow. Or suspected. Of course. The strangeness. Of course! My God, how stupid am I? Why didn't I get it?"

"Don't stress," Herz said. "Something like that isn't necessarily something you get right away. I mean, you're not clairvoyant."

Franza shrugged as she waited impatiently for Lilli to answer.

"Arthur, you continue with the searches. Work with Hansen, arrange for photos of Hanna and Tonio to be distributed to the press," Herz said.

Arthur nodded.

"She's not answering," Franza said.

"We'll drive over," Herz said. He turned to Arthur. "And call Herr Brendler, tell him to go to his daughter's house right away. Tell him we'll wait for him there. Tell him it's very important!"

Arthur nodded.

"You're looking a bit delicate, by the way," Felix added.

"Didn't get much sleep," Arthur muttered.

"Business as usual, then," Felix said casually.

Franza grabbed her jacket.

"I can't wait to hear what the Brendler family have to tell us," she said. "Are you coming, Felix?"

"Aye, aye, sir!" He followed her. "You, too," he said as they went down the stairs.

"What?"

"A bit delicate."

She said nothing.

"Been on the chat sites again?" he asked.

"A little."

"You're crazy."

"I know."

63

Lilli wasn't there. They rang and rang, knocked on the door, called her name, but Lilli wasn't home. Or at least she wasn't opening the door.

"OK," Herz said. "Let's move on. Perhaps she's with her family. It's possible."

The detectives arrived at more or less the same time as Hans Brendler. Arthur had obviously impressed the sense of urgency on him.

"You again," Dorothee Brendler said as she opened the door. She looked tired and on edge. "What can I do for you this time?"

It was only then that she saw her husband, who had parked his car next to the detectives' and was slowly walking toward them. Her eyebrows shot up, and she was silent for a moment, a moment in which she hung in the balance between knowing nothing and only wanting to know nothing. But Franza could see she was already beginning to suspect that this conversation would shake another foundation.

"May we come in?" Franza asked. "Is there somewhere we can talk undisturbed? And is Lilli here?"

Dorothee was surprised.

"No," she said. "There's no one here. Moritz is at kindergarten, Christian's at work, and Lilli . . ." She stopped. "I don't know where

Lilli is. I hardly ever know where Lilli is. She's an adult, after all. What do you want with her?"

"Nothing," Franza said in an attempt to reassure her. "We only want to talk to the two of you."

Dorothee nodded. "OK. Should we go out onto the terrace?"

They went out. The terrace was covered, protecting them from the rain, a bright, light drizzle that gave the day a surprising glow.

"Can I get you . . . ?"

She stopped as she saw the detectives shake their heads.

"Please sit down," Franza said.

She hesitated briefly, then sat down, crossed her legs, and stiffened for a moment, looking at Franza with a questioning expression.

"Lilli," Franza said.

They were shocked. Both of them. It was obvious. They didn't want to be asked about Lilli. Dorothee gave a slight shake of her head. "What . . . what do you mean?"

"I think you know, Frau Brendler," Herz said.

She shook her head more emphatically.

"No," she gasped. "I don't know what you mean! What do you want from us?"

Hans Brendler cleared his throat and laid a calming hand on his wife's arm.

"Frau Oberwieser," he said, "Herr Herz, why don't you just concentrate on your work and find our daughter's murderer? What has our granddaughter got to do with the investigation? Why can't you leave us in peace? We're suffering enough as it is!"

"Herr Brendler," Franza said. "Lilli isn't your natural granddaughter. We know that. And of course you know it, too."

He was about to protest, making a great show of it. But his wife had finally had enough. She was tired and she wanted her life back, even though she knew that would never happen. She needed to rethink her approach. Everything would be changed by this truth that they had denied for all those years, but which had now come to light with unshakeable force. She accepted it now. She no longer had the strength to fight it.

But her husband did. He jumped up. "What are you thinking? I'm going to file a complaint against you! Don't you know who I am?"

His voice was agitated, and his face was flushed red. "How dare you assert that my granddaughter isn't my granddaughter! Do you want proof? You can have it—birth certificate, the lot!"

"Oh, I'm sure you can prove it," Herz said. "I'm completely sure of it. You're an attorney, after all. Who better than you, Herr Brendler, would know how to bend the law? But as far as we're concerned . . ."

Wow, Franza thought, *old Herz is really pushing the envelope! Take care, he'll file a complaint against you before you know it!*

She reached out a hand, about to lay it on Herz's arm to calm him down a little. But it wasn't necessary. Dorothee Brendler suddenly leaned over to her husband, motioning for him to sit down.

"No," she said quietly and firmly. "No more. That's enough. It's over. Let it be."

He looked at her for a moment in amazement, and then lowered his head and closed his eyes.

She stroked his hair. His face grew deathly pale and slack. Franza sensed his pain and the long years of deep uncertainty.

Dorothee gave a light shake of her head.

"I don't want to do it anymore," she said. "I can't. No more lies. Enough is enough."

She slid closer to him, laid her head on his shoulder, and began to talk, her face averted. Her husband put his arms around her and held her tight. Franza and Felix had to listen hard to understand her.

"I knew right away," she said. "There was no way I could fail to see. She stood before me in this ridiculous dress, her belly bulging out, and said, 'Help me. Make it go away. I don't want it. I can't cope with it.'"

"Who?" Franza asked. "Who, Frau Brendler?"

Dorothee was silent for a few seconds, took a deep breath, and said, "Hanna. Hanna, of course."

Silence reigned for a long moment. It was so silent that there was a thrumming in the ears, in the veins, in the air.

Dorothee Brendler finally continued, telling of the hours, the days, which had thrown her life off balance.

"She was away for a long time, Hanna was," she said. "A really long time—months—and we never heard a thing from her. It was as though she were dead. We were very worried. Gertrud had come home from Greece alone. Tonio was brought back a week later and buried a week after that. And Hanna had disappeared. You just can't imagine what we were going through."

She breathed in deeply, released herself from her husband, and leaned back in her chair, her face now a mask of stone.

"I recall I was completely alone that day. We had no help around the house anymore since the girls moved away. I was in the garden—I'd just been mowing the lawn—when a taxi drove up. And she got out, our Hanna. Skin and bone . . . except for that round belly. She looked ill, tired, completely exhausted."

Dorothee sighed, closed her eyes, and continued. "I went over to the car. She was standing there, an emaciated girl with a swollen belly. She fell into my arms and said, 'Help me! Or I'll die! It hurts so much, it's so hard. Make it go away!'"

Another pause. Dorothee thought for a while, picturing this starving creature with the swollen belly that she carried in front of her like a poisonous ulcer.

"My first thought was she needed a hospital. Of course. But she seemed so tired. I paid the taxi driver and put her to bed. She fell asleep immediately."

Dorothee looked at her husband, completely calm now, under control, sure of himself. "I called him, and he came and sat down by her bed. We were so happy to have her back with us, that she was alive. She slept for two whole days. In the brief periods when she was awake, we brought her food and drink. I monitored her blood pressure, her circulation. We washed her and fed her like a child. We took time off work to be there for her."

"Why didn't you take her to the hospital?"

She thought about it, listening to her inner voice. "I don't know. I really don't know. They were exceptional circumstances; the three of us were marooned. We weren't thinking clearly. We simply took care of her. The baby was lying high. There was no indication that she would give birth anytime soon. I thought we still had time. Two, three more weeks. And she was so happy to be home. She felt safe."

"What did she tell you?"

"Nothing. Nothing at all. She seemed to have put it all behind her, suppressed it. We didn't ask. We thought it would all come out when she was ready. In any case, she was asleep most of the time."

"And then?"

"And then . . ." She sighed. "Three days after she arrived, the pains suddenly began. It took us all completely by surprise."

She shook her head, still surprised by the memory.

"She was sitting with us on the terrace for the first time. She'd just eaten a bowl of semolina, her favorite from childhood. She seemed calmer, but still exhausted. I wanted to talk to her, to take her fear away. We'd decided we wouldn't take her to the hospital until later, until she really needed a safe place to bring her child into the world."

She hesitated and turned to her husband. "I'm thirsty. Could you bring me some water?"

He stood, went into the house, and returned with a jug of water and four glasses. She took a drink, continued talking. "But suddenly, so incredibly quickly, it all happened. Hanna suddenly cried out, grasped her belly, and screamed in panic and sobbed, 'I'm dying! I'm dying!'

And I said, 'No, no, Hanna, you're not dying, you're having your baby.' She looked at me in terror. 'But I don't want a baby!' she sobbed."

Dorothee looked at her husband.

"He took her in his arms, his Hanna, soothed her, and suddenly she was a little girl again. She had only known him as her father, no one else. I said, 'I'm calling an ambulance,' but he'd already lifted her up. She was groaning, moaning, and the pains were coming at short intervals. He said, 'We don't have time to get to the hospital. We'll take her into the house, into her room. You'll have to deliver the baby, you're a doctor.'"

She took another sip of water and put the glass back down pensively. "I'm an internist, I have nothing to do with midwifery, but she was lying there moaning and screaming in her bed. What could I do? Of course I helped her bring her child into the world. It was difficult. She was so unyielding—everything was hard and tense inside her. She was so terrified. But then the baby was there. Suddenly, she was there."

She smiled and tears began to fall, to run down her cheeks. She let them.

"At last the baby was born, a little girl. She was strong from the very first moment, wonderfully strong. She screamed bloody murder. She'd been determined to come into the world at any price. She'd roamed half the world with her mother and she'd been suppressed almost completely from Hanna's thoughts, her feelings, her awareness. She must have sensed that Hanna didn't want her, that Hanna rejected her; she had to let her do that so they could both survive, and then . . . and then she was there. And she saved her mother's life, I'm sure of that to this day. Without her, Hanna would have stayed somewhere, died, vanished. If that baby hadn't brought her home."

Her voice fell to a whisper. "A wonderful child. A wonderful girl, our Lilli. Right from the start."

She looked long at her husband and took his hand.

"He helped me," she said. "We looked after the baby, we looked after Hanna. You helped me."

They smiled at one another through tears, and they held hands.

"When it was finally over," she continued, "Hanna fell back into a deep sleep. She was fine physically, but she slept and slept as if she hadn't slept for weeks—for a day, a night, and another day. I can't remember exactly. And there we were with her daughter and no idea what to do."

She reached for her glass and closed her eyes, unable to say any more. Her husband saw it and took over.

"Gertrud came. She brought baby food, clothes, diapers—everything you need. I phoned her and she came immediately. She looked at Hanna, she looked at the baby, she picked the baby up. It was as though she had always had her. They fit so well together. I can't say it any other way. They fit so well together." He fell silent, a sad smile on his face. "It made her happy to be holding that baby. Yes, she suddenly looked . . . at peace, full of clarity, full of certainty. Like she never had been before. And the baby was also calm."

"What about Hanna?"

They looked at one another in silence.

"Hanna went to pieces," Dorothee Brendler finally said, quietly. "She couldn't find a way back into her life."

She recalled how Hanna awoke from her exhaustion and fell into an even deeper one. The images rose up in her mind.

•   •   •

Hanna had been away too long, been on the move too long. Too much had happened; she couldn't fit back into her old life.

"It's just a matter of getting used to things," her parents had said in the beginning, when they laid her daughter down with her. She'd looked at her with distant eyes and said, "Take her away! What am I supposed to do with her?" and pushed her away. The baby began to cry. Gertrud picked her up, and she became calm.

Dorothee and Hans stroked her hair gently, looked at one another, looked at Gertrud rocking the baby, began to wonder . . .

Two days went by.

"We have to register the birth," Dorothee said one morning as they were sitting to breakfast. The baby was asleep in her crib in Gertrud's room. "It's unforgivable that we haven't done it yet. Too much time has already gone by."

Gertrud suddenly said, "I want her."

Dorothee stared at her daughter. Her husband gathered himself first. "What? What do you mean?"

"I want her," Gertrud said again. "I want Hanna's baby. I'll be the best mother she could have, you know that. Hanna doesn't even want the baby. Just look at her. She belongs in the nuthouse. She's not in any position to look after her child. She starts to cry when she's anywhere near her. I want her. Give her to me. Let me have her. *You* owe it to me." She looked at her father. "You owe it to me."

They held their breath. Dorothee eventually said, "No, Gertrud, stop it! It's crazy."

But Gertrud didn't stop. She talked and talked, as if trying to get her childhood, her youth, out of her system. She had always been second best, always the loser, always in the shadows, burned, exiled.

"The way you looked at her! I hated it! You never looked at me like that. Never looked at me with that warmth, that sense of wonder, that enthusiasm. *She* was your daughter. Not me. She's always been the one, your daughter, in your heart."

It all fell apart in that moment. Dorothee felt it and could do nothing. Hans shook his head. "No, Gertrud, no! You're both my daughters, I love you both."

But Gertrud shook her head, sure of what she was saying. She clearly felt she was right.

"She was more your daughter," she said. "She was always more."

He moved to stand and go to her, to take her in his arms, but she stretched out her hands defensively, an impenetrable wall.

"No," she said. "I don't need it now. It's much too late. Give Lilli to me!"

She sprang up, ran upstairs to her room, picked up the baby—who was jolted awake but soon pacified—took her into Hanna's room, and sat on her bed, waiting.

"What's going on, Gertrud?" Dorothee had followed with her husband. "This is madness! What do you intend to do?"

"Wait," Gertrud said. She rocked the baby in her arms, listened to her making little sucking noises before falling back to sleep. "Wait for Hanna to wake up. I've done it before. Waited a whole night long."

They didn't have to wait long. It wasn't a whole night this time.

As if Hanna sensed a threat, she started awake, looked into Gertrud's stony face, and saw the little girl peacefully asleep in her arms.

"What," she stammered. "What . . ."

"Nothing," Gertrud said. "Nothing's happened, don't worry. Will you give her to me? Will you give me your daughter? Forever. So I can look after her. So I can be her mother. Will you do that?"

Hanna swallowed, leaned back slowly into the pillow, looked around. Dorothee was standing at the window, her back turned, and Hans was sitting at the little table by the door, his head in his hands.

"What," Hanna stammered again. "Why . . . ?"

"Because you won't be able to cope. Because Lilli's afraid of you. Because you're afraid of Lilli."

"Lilli?"

She had already called her Lilli. The baby already had a name.

"Yes, Lilli. That's what you wanted, too."

It all seemed so clear. So simple. So black and white. So heaven or hell. And Hanna was so tired.

"Give Lilli to me," Gertrud said again, her voice cutting the air like a knife, slicing through Hanna's thoughts, through her heart. Gertrud's voice brooked no argument; it had to be obeyed, simply had to.

Hanna's gaze roamed the room beseechingly, but found no source of help, as the others there were equally despairing and had no more idea of what to do than she had.

Hanna stretched out a cautious hand toward the tiny bundle in Gertrud's arms. She carefully stroked her finger over the baby's silky soft cheek, felt a warmth, felt for the first time a sudden joy tinged with pain, felt tears spring to her eyes, run hotly down her cheeks, felt as though she were seeing the child for the first time, feeling her only now, in the moment when she had to make her decision. "Let her touch me," she whispered. "Let her feel me."

Gertrud hesitated, but she finally laid the baby in Hanna's arms, and as if the little girl sensed the change, or was having a bad dream, she started awake and let out a small, angry cry. Hanna jumped. *Lilli*, she thought, *Lilli has decided. Lilli's afraid of me and yes, it's true, I'm afraid of Lilli. Then that's how it's meant to be. Let Gertrud have her.*

She nodded. "Take her," she whispered. "Take her! She belongs to you. I don't want her."

Gertrud closed her eyes. "Thank you," she said in a voice that sounded as though she'd been holding her breath for hours. "Thank you, Hanna. I promise . . ."

She broke off, hugged Lilli to her fast-thumping heart, and swallowed. "Go back to Munich, Hanna, finish your studies and then go back out into the world and take your photos. That's what you always wanted to do. Take photos. Be free. You're free again now. Free."

She left. She paused briefly in the doorway and looked at her father, who was slumped in the chair. "I'm sure our father will pay for it all for you," she said. "*Our* father . . ."

Maybe she wanted to sound scornful, but there was only sadness in her voice, and since she heard it herself and it brought on tears, she hurried out.

Dorothee eventually broke free from her daze and rushed over to Hanna. "Hanna, wake up. You don't know what you're doing!"

But Hanna had turned away. "Leave me in peace!"

They heard Gertrud's car drive away.

There was a note on the table downstairs. *You are witnesses. She gave her to me.* And it all fell apart. Dorothee felt it. There was nothing anyone could do.

64

I gave birth to a child. Her smile burned itself into my heart, into my soul, and I carried it with me. Her heartbeats tapped against my skin, as did her little feet, her hands. She loved me. She was one with me, but I . . . I sold her.

65

"What happened after that?" Franza asked.

Brendler shrugged.

"It was simpler than you'd think," he said tiredly. "We would have done anything to make the two of them see reason. But there was nothing we could do. Hanna refused to look at or touch the baby, and Gertrud . . . Gertrud wouldn't let her out of her arms."

"But Hanna was ill," Franza broke in. "In her condition she wasn't fit to make a decision!"

"Yes," Brendler said coolly, "you're right. But doesn't that justify Gertrud's argument?"

Franza shook her head in stunned amazement.

"Anyway," Dorothee said, "anyway. That's how it was. An unfortunate chain of events. So as a doctor, I signed the birth certificate. My husband looked after all the other official matters: he knew the right people, the right places. They congratulated him on becoming a grandfather. No one noticed anything strange. No one asked. Why would they?"

She looked at her husband, lost herself a little in his eyes—they, at least, had never fully lost their ability to calm her.

"No, it didn't strike anyone as unusual," Dorothee continued. "We didn't have a wide circle of friends, and Gertrud had been in Munich for a long while. She quickly sorted everything out there and looked for an apartment here. She took the first thing she found and moved in with the baby. With her baby. To all the world, it was her baby. Her daughter, Lilli. Father unknown."

Silence. It was monstrous.

"What about Hanna?" Franza finally asked.

"Hanna was ill for a long time," Hans Brendler said. "She couldn't have taken care of a child. She needed caring for herself. A friend of my wife's, a psychiatrist, gave us a lot of support. But the matter of the baby was never discussed, we never told her doctor about it, and Hanna . . . we never talked to her about it either."

"What about when Gertrud came to visit with Lilli?"

A brief pause. "Gertrud didn't come to visit at all. Hanna never saw Lilli again. It was only once Hanna was well again and had finally left that Gertrud gradually reestablished contact with us."

Franza nodded. *Families,* she thought. *A haven of happiness.*

"For how long was Hanna ill?"

"A long time. More than a year. Does someone with an illness like that ever really get better?"

They need that question, that justification, Franza thought. *They need it to excuse what they did.*

"What about Christian?" Herz asked. "Does he know?"

They both shook their heads.

"No," Hans Brendler said. "No one ever found out. Gertrud met Christian when Lilli was twelve, and Christian and Lilli took to one another from the start. She couldn't have had a better father, our Lilli."

"Yes, Christian was a stroke of luck," Dorothee added. "For Gertrud, for Lilli, and for us, too. When they got married, we gave them this house. And we were a family again. And then when Moritz finally arrived . . ." She paused to think. "But we were always fooling ourselves. It was a great bluff. An illusion."

And Lilli sensed it, Franza thought. *The bluff, the illusion.* "Didn't you ever think of Hanna? What you had done to her?"

Dorothee raised her head and looked up into the foliage of the damson tree. "We never stopped thinking of Hanna. Never. She's always on our minds. Every time I look at Lilli."

"It was like being between a rock and a hard place," Hans Brendler said. "I knew I'd lose one of them. And the way things were at that moment, it had to be Hanna. There was no other way."

His voice cracked.

"And it was definitely the best thing for Lilli," Dorothee said. "She had a wonderful mother. Hanna could never . . . never have managed that."

That too, Franza thought. *You have to think like that to justify yourselves.* Perhaps it was even true. She thought of what Lilli had told her. Perhaps it wasn't true.

"What happened with Hanna after that?"

Dorothee cleared her throat and began to speak.

"Hanna couldn't get herself right. She just lay in bed, never got up, didn't eat, didn't drink. She said she knew that sadness wasn't good, and she felt safer staying where she was. Everything had to be manageable, easy, according to a plan."

She insisted she wasn't sad, only tired. She didn't know why, but the tiredness had burned into her soul and it was incredibly difficult to shake off. But she assured them she would be all right, and that they shouldn't keep watching over her and worrying about her. She'd be back to her old self soon and would put it all behind her.

"She couldn't be bothered with cleanliness anymore," Dorothee said. "Whenever I cleaned the house she said I had no imagination and insisted that the true shapes of things showed through from under dust. And she'd tell us we had to look reality in the eye. You had to face up to misfortune, that was what counted. I said, 'No, Hanna, the will to seek happiness is more important.' But Hanna asked me what happiness really was, what I thought it meant, and said that you couldn't force happiness.

"To all intents and purposes, her room became an island. It was as though she had formed it around herself in layers, and eventually she placed an old doll from her childhood on her bed so that no one would desecrate it."

Her attempts to write cards, letters to friends from her old life, all failed. She made do with a signature on a blank sheet of paper. *Just letting them know I still exist,* she would say. *That's enough.*

She must always have held on to the feeling that she could continue, get out, into wide-open space, onto endless streets. *It's tearing me apart!* she would say, fighting for breath. *I'm cracking up.*

She took country drives in Dorothee's or Hans's car. She hungered for people, faces, life, because she couldn't face her own loneliness. Above all she hungered for freedom and hoped to regain it with wild breakneck drives along country roads. If a deer had jumped out onto the road, they would both have been killed.

She hardly spoke, merely sat or lay there, looking inside herself, seeing nothing around her. Sometimes she murmured what sounded like names, quietly, unintelligibly. Her life had not gone as it should have. The realization was bitter, and there was no way back. But where would that life have led? To a freedom that existed only to be given up, to the knowledge that freedom was not possible, that all the time, everywhere, there was so much to lose. She never asked about the baby.

"She finally returned to her life after more than a year," Dorothee said softly. "By then, it was more than we'd expected or hoped for."

It was January. Early-morning mist had risen from the meadows, froze, and made the streets and sidewalks slippery and impassable. The fog spread through the forest and the meadows, a greedy white animal.

Hanna had walked through the trees and noticed how the fog swallowed her up. It made her feel really light, so light—like a cloud, a feather, white, downy, gently floating—moving onward and upward. Onward and upward.

And then she turned around. Allowed herself to be spat out from the fog, with its white light that left her dazzled.

Allowed herself to be spat out, looking into bright eyes with her own bright eyes and, suddenly, she knew herself again.

"Yes," Dorothee said, "it was amazing. We were so happy. Then she went away. As Gertrud had told her to. Back to Munich. To continue her studies. At first we tried to keep up the contact. I called her regularly, but either she didn't answer or she was on the phone so briefly it was embarrassing. I eventually stopped phoning, asking her how things were going, inviting her here. I believe she preferred it."

She picked up the glass and drained it. "Perhaps we reminded her too much of Lilli. Although she never asked after her. Never. And to be honest, I was relieved that she didn't. I was terrified that she'd ask." She fell silent.

"We didn't see her after that," Brendler said. "Only sometimes in the papers. Once we went to one of her exhibitions. One of the first. *Waiting Halls*, it was called, I think. We saw her there, our Hanna, in those pictures. The way she was when she returned to us, her restlessness, her loneliness, her sadness. So that's what she'd been working up to all that time. Wonderful pictures."

Silence. They'd said all there was to say. Almost.

"Why didn't you go down the official route?" Franza asked. "You of all people—you're a lawyer! It would have been easy to initiate an adoption case."

They shrugged, shook their heads.

"It wouldn't have worked. It would have taken too long. You can't imagine—it . . . it was such a tense situation, so horrible. We were completely detached, like on an island. We couldn't wait. Gertrud couldn't wait. And what if Hanna had changed her mind? What then?"

"Fine," Franza said and rose. She didn't want to hear any more. It was late morning. The photos would be shown again on the midday news. The one of Hanna and the one of Tonio Whatever-his-name-was.

"We've still found no trace of her," Herz said. "And you know yourself that she had the best possible motive."

"It wasn't her," Dorothee said. "I'd know if it were."

"Really?" Herz said, unable to keep the light note of irony from his voice. "You would?"

She looked at him wordlessly.

"What about Lilli?" Franza asked. "What will you tell Lilli?"

"Lilli?"

Dorothee and Hans looked at one another, shocked. They hadn't thought of Lilli.

"She knows, by the way," Franza said. "I think she knows that Gertrud wasn't her natural mother. She suggested as much, but I didn't get it. And now . . ."

She got out her cell phone. No text.

"You'll have to answer for this, both of you," Herz said, also rising. "You do realize that?"

They nodded, remained seated, radiating exhaustion. The detectives left.

. . .

They drove back to the station slowly, no bad news on their cell phones, nothing new.

"Let's go by my house," Herz said. "You haven't seen the twins for ages."

"Yes, let's do that," said Franza. "A quick cuddle."

The twins, Justus and Johanna, trotted up right away. The little boy was half an hour older than his sister; the little girl quicker to find Daddy's arms than her brother. He soon followed, and the three of them swayed back and forth. Angelika and Franza stood in the doorway laughing, and Angelika asked quietly, "Has something happened? For you to come out of your way to visit?"

Franza nodded. "I'm sure he'll tell you about it tonight."

And they were off again, on their way to the police station, a meeting with Arthur and Hansen to round off the morning. What would the rest of the day bring?

66

They sat in silence for a long time. His hand in hers, cold and clammy.

"Aren't you feeling well?" she asked eventually. "Your stomach again?"

"No," he said. "I'm not feeling well. My stomach again. I can feel it. Can't eat anything."

"I can tell," she said. "You've lost weight."

He nodded. Silence fell again.

She thought of the many years they'd spent together, all the years during which things had been relatively good, during which they had not thought about *it*, not about Hanna and her daughter, and not about the fact that they had turned Hanna's daughter into Gertrud's daughter. But sooner or later the truth would come out.

"What about you?" he asked.

Dorothee shrugged. "I have to keep going. The children are still here."

"Do you ever cry?" he asked.

"Yes. Sometimes. At night. When I'm alone."

He looked at her. Her face was unreadable.

"I'm so sorry about everything," he whispered.

She nodded. "It doesn't change anything."

"I know."

He stood, her hand still in his. She looked up at him, slowly disentangling her fingers.

"Are you coming back?" he asked.

She heard the despair in his voice, the loneliness. *I'm lonely myself,* she thought. *I wonder, if two lonely souls come together, can they comfort one another?*

"I don't know," she said. "I can't tell you."

He nodded and leaned over her, her scent drifting up to him like a greeting from better times. He kissed her on the cheek, burying his nose in her hair for a brief moment. "I love you," he whispered. "I've always loved you. Every minute."

She swallowed, feeling like she was about to cry.

"I know," she said, so quietly that her voice could hardly be heard. "I know. But it doesn't change anything."

He nodded and remained motionless. *One more second,* he thought, *let me be with you for one more second.* And she let him. Then he straightened up and attempted a smile. She noticed how gray his face was.

"Where are you going?" she asked. "What will you do?"

He shook his head vaguely and shrugged.

"I don't know," he said. "Back to the office. Into town. Anywhere. It's all . . ."

He stood there for a second more, thinking. She looked at him.

No, she thought. *I can't even help myself, how could I begin to help him?*

He left.

She finally began to cry, and then called out, "We have to think of Lilli!"

But he had already gone.

67

Kristin had gone to the shopping center and bought food, a pair of sunglasses, and hair clippers. She'd also reserved a room in a motel near the autobahn. It was simple. There was no hotel clerk, just an anonymous machine you fed with money and it spat out a room key card.

Tonio had wondered for a few seconds how she'd known such a place existed, and how she knew such a place existed *here*.

As if she knew what was going through his mind, she'd said with a wink, "A popular meeting place for lovers who want to remain anonymous. Men deceiving their wives. Women deceiving their husbands."

She'd smiled.

"Oh," he said. "So a modern woman needs to know about a place like this?"

She shrugged and grinned. "As you can see, knowledge like this can be really useful."

"I think I need to keep an eye on you," he'd murmured, drawing her to him, and then grabbing her behind and gently biting her shoulder, causing her to cry out with laughter.

"Bonnie," he murmured.

"Clyde," she murmured back.

"Why are you doing all this for me?"

"Dunno," she'd said. "Perhaps because you belong to me now."

That had been yesterday. Today she cut his hair off. Today they would hone their plans.

68

Third row on the left, fifth grave—easy to see. It's still there, the cemetery on a hill beyond the noise, the busy streets. I went into the church to find the priest. When I mentioned Tonio's name, he immediately remembered the tragedy. It had attracted a lot of attention at the time.

"It was a beautiful September day when we buried him, young Tonio Köhler, beneath a clear blue sky," he said. "Did you know his father?"

I shook my head. "No."

The priest nodded. He said his father had been a broken man from then on.

"And his mother? Did you know her?"

No, even less. "I never met her," I said.

"An Italian," the priest said. She came for the burial, he said. An incredibly beautiful woman. The journalists' cameras had flashed away like mad. The regional papers were full of her and no wonder—she could easily have been a movie star, a Gina Lollobrigida.

His enthusiasm was a bit over the top, and I stopped listening.

"Yes," the priest sighed. "That's how it was."

He paused as though thinking back, as though dwelling on his memories, and then gave himself a mental shake.

"What about you?" he asked, studying me. "How did you know him, if I may be so inquisitive?"

He said that someone else had visited the grave a few weeks ago, probably pure coincidence. It was a young man who'd asked similar questions before standing a long time by the grave—it must have been more than an hour.

"Oh," I said. And told him I was a passing acquaintance traveling through the area and everything had come back to me. I'd thought . . .

I broke off, not knowing how to continue.

"And you thought he'd like that," the priest said, pressing my hand. "And I'm sure he would. Go over to the grave, commune with him. Take all the time you need."

And so I stood by the grave. Alone with you, Tonio. After such a long time.

It's well tended. Your name is on the gravestone along with the dates of your birth and death. Nothing else.

I should have flown home with you then. I could have come face-to-face with your mother, looked her in the eye, supported her, your father, too. But it wasn't possible.

"You didn't deserve it, Tonio," I said quietly. "Didn't deserve such a death, not like that."

I bent down and brushed my fingers over the cool white heads of the Michaelmas daisies.

They won't survive the first frost. The gardener will come and tidy up the grave, decorating it with twigs and wild forest greenery, ready for the winter. You would have found that funny, Tonio, wouldn't you?

"Here they come in their green uniforms," you would have said, braying with laughter, "with their weapons at the ready, and when the hopping hares hop around among the twigs and branches of the forests, they shoot them down and have themselves the finest Christmas feast!"

I had to grin as I imagined it. It was as though I heard your voice. It came down from somewhere up high, not up from the depths.

Where are you now, my sly fox? Where are you, my Tonio, my love?
Standing by your grave I felt a sob, a burning in my breast and throat.
Lilli came into my thoughts, my need to tell you about her.

"There are two," I whispered. "Just think, you have two children,
Tonio. A son and a daughter. And the son was already born back then,
and you never said anything."

I waited, I don't know for what. For an answer? No, probably not.
Perhaps for a hopping hare, but none came.

I thought about your daughter, Tonio. About our daughter.

And she's . . . so wonderful! Even though I still know so little about
her. Although I've hardly ever seen her. And you know what's so dreadful? That I never missed her. Never, Tonio. Not for all those years. I
never felt that . . .

Only now, Tonio, only now, since I've looked into her eyes, only
now do I know that it was never right, that I was fooling myself.
Because . . . I did miss her. Always. It's been such a dreadful emptiness
inside me. All those years, a terrible longing.

． ． ．

I went back and knocked on the priest's door.

"Come in," he called. "It's not locked."

I went in. The priest was sitting over his files and books. His parish
must be big, and he needed to run it properly.

"Come in!" He stood. "Come right in! Can I do anything else for
you?"

"Yes," I said. "I'd like to know who keeps the grave tidy. It's very
well cared for."

The priest nodded. "Yes, it is indeed. Do you like it?"

He indicated the glass of wine on his desk. "Can I get you a drop
too?"

I shook my head. "No, thank you. Very kind. But I'm in a bit of a hurry."

"Of course. I understand. It's the same for me, always in a hurry. Yes, yes."

"The grave." I smiled. "You were going to tell me—"

"Oh!" the priest said, and laughed. "Yes, of course. The grave. Yes. It's maintained by our gardeners, paid for by a middle-aged lady, if I may call her that. She comes here regularly, brings fresh flowers, candles. I just can't remember her name. Wait a moment."

I said Gertrud's name.

"Yes," the priest said with a nod. "That's it. That's the name."

He didn't yet know that she was dead. I told him. It affected him deeply. He said he had gotten home from vacation yesterday and there was still a lot of news he hadn't caught up with. I left.

69

They had lunch in the cafeteria, and afterward the schnitzel lay in Franza's stomach like a lump of glue. It was not the first time that she'd been unhappy with the cafeteria food, but hunger was hunger, and it was simply too expensive to keep going to the Italian place around the corner.

In the conference room, Arthur had made coffee, Franza's cookies were out on the table, and there was the usual array of water jug, glasses, and cups. They were ready for the meeting.

There wasn't much news apart from what Franza and Felix had to report. This, at least, held everyone's full attention.

Hansen told them that the photos on the previous evening's news broadcasts had once again led to numerous phone calls and his people were in the process of checking them all out, but after the failures of the last few days, he wasn't hoping for much. Of course, they would still be following up the tiniest of leads, but it seemed as though both people had vanished into thin air. But they shouldn't give up hope. After all, wonders never ceased, and he was sure they were all aware that hope was always the last thing to be abandoned. Hansen rolled his eyes and sighed deeply.

Then it was Arthur's turn. He reported that all the fingerprints had now been analyzed, but unfortunately this wasn't much help. Most of them belonged to family members. However, there were also many others that were as yet unidentified. This wasn't particularly surprising in a family house where there were a lot of people coming and going—friends, neighbors, relatives. On the knife, the murder weapon, they had found Gertrud Rabinsky's prints and those of two other people. Unfortunately, it hadn't been possible to identify these, although one was probably the perpetrator's. A small incidental detail was that Christian Rabinsky's prints had not been found, which once again ruled him out as the murderer.

Franza sighed. "Yes, but we already knew it wasn't him."

The others nodded, staring a little cluelessly into their coffee cups. Finally, Herz summarized it all once again. The situation to date was that the main suspect was Tonio Whatever-his-name-was, and he was clearly being helped by a young woman, who unfortunately remained nameless.

Hanna Umlauf's role in the case was still unclear. She could be a victim, abducted and held captive—maybe even killed—by the aforementioned couple. However, she could also quite easily be the perpetrator—she had the best possible motive.

But another one with an excellent motive, they now knew, was Lilli.

It was still complicated. They were running around in circles and getting no further.

Please let my cell phone ring, Franza thought. *Lilli, call me!*

And then there it was! Her cell phone!

It didn't ring, merely beeped, but all the same. Franza opened the text message immediately—and sighed. Not Lilli. Port. He had arrived safely in Vienna and sent his love. Lovely, but not what she needed right at that moment.

The afternoon went by in a flurry of routine and trivia. They chewed everything over again, from the first visit to the crime scene all the way through the clues they had found and the information they had gathered. They sounded everything out again and again. Had they overlooked anything? Was anything unclear?

The district attorney looked in, asking for an update. Herz gave him what he wanted and then walked over to Franza's desk.

"Have you seen him? Is he sick? He looks so pale."

Franza shook her head. "I didn't notice."

"Doesn't matter," Herz said. "Perhaps he's not getting enough sleep, either."

He went over to the coffee machine, got himself a cup, and came back to Franza's desk with a broad grin on his face. *Oh my God,* Franza thought with a frown. *Oh my God, what's he going to say?*

"Like you," he said, bursting out laughing.

She was confused.

"Like me? What do you mean?"

"Well," he snorted, "perhaps he's up all night in chat rooms too!"

Franza raised her eyebrows and tapped her temple, but couldn't help laughing. *It's my own fault,* she thought. *Why do I have to tell him everything? I'm such a stupid woman!*

She glanced again at her cell phone. Nothing.

Why am I so on edge? Franza thought. She knew as soon as she thought it that it was Lilli who was haunting her. *I have to get out of here. Give myself space to think—no office, no computer, no colleagues around me. No Herr Brückl on my back.*

Hairdresser or pedicure? she thought. *Where should I drift off to? Quality time for my head or my feet?*

She decided on the feet. Her hair was fine, and anyway, a haircut would cost a lot more. She called and got an appointment right away.

"I'm off . . ."

"It's OK." Herz gave her a nod. "Perhaps something we've missed will occur to you."

"You've got my number," she said, waving her cell phone at him.

"Of course. Off you go! Get inspired!"

I have to talk to Lilli, Franza thought as she waited for her appointment with the pedicurist. She closed her eyes and let the images flow. They were all muddled to begin with, but gradually settled into a clear structure.

"Annika," the pedicurist said, "can you get Frau Oberwieser into the footbath?"

The images in her head faded to another: the small, delicate Annika taking hold of the not-so-small-and-delicate Frau Oberwieser, and calling on all her strength to lift her up and maneuver her to the footbath. Immersing Frau Oberwieser totally in the little basin intended only for feet, causing everything to tip over—the water, the basin, big Frau Oberwieser, and little Annika.

"Thank you, Annika," Franza said, unable to suppress a laugh. Annika, who had just filled the footbath with hot water and was now inviting Franza to place her feet in it, nodded, probably mentally shaking her head at her client's weird sense of humor.

"Thank you, Annika," Franza said again, sighing luxuriously and imagining all the calluses in the world softening and falling away without the need for protracted scrubbing.

At last Lilli came back to mind, Lilli and the knowledge she was probably dragging around with her. She picked up her cell phone and dialed the number, but Lilli did not pick up. Lilli was not answering.

Lowering the cell phone, Franza thought that either she had completely botched it or something had happened.

Suddenly, it rang! Franza jumped in shock and picked up.

"Dorothee Brendler here. We can't get hold of Lilli! She's disappeared! Do you know where she is?"

Franza jumped up immediately, with Dorothee still on the line, and shouted into the telephone: "I'm coming! Where are you? Wait for me!"

She was out of the footbath, into her socks and shoes, past Annika's astonished eyes, and past the nodding of her favorite pedicurist, who had seen such behavior often and displayed a suitably unperturbed reaction. Franza had called out a quick "I'll call you!" in her general direction and was away, heading for Lilli's apartment, her heart thumping out an alarm. She called Frau Brendler again on the way.

"Don't worry unnecessarily," she said. "There'll be a perfectly good explanation."

It was as if she were trying to reassure herself.

There was a brief silence on the other end of the line, and then, "Do you really believe that?"

Franza closed her eyes briefly.

"No," she said quietly. "In this case I don't really believe it. We're almost there. Are you in the apartment yet?"

"No. We're afraid to go in."

"Good," Franza said. "Wait for us. Is your husband with you?"

"No. Only Christian." Her voice was expressionless.

"Have you tried to contact your husband?"

"Yes, but he's disappeared somewhere, too. Oh, I don't know. His cell phone's off."

"Good," Franza said, thinking what a stupid word it was. Nothing was good. There was silence on the line. Franza wanted to hang up.

"I'm suddenly thinking . . . terrible things," Dorothee said, and Franza sensed she was shaking, that the cell phone in her hand was shaking.

"No," Franza said. "No, don't do that."

"But you are," Dorothee said. "You're thinking terrible things, too, aren't you Frau Oberwieser?"

"There'll be a perfectly good explanation."

"Yes. Yes, I'm sure there will be." She paused for a beat. "If only I could turn back time and make everything different."

"Yes, I know. I know." She heard a click. Dorothee had hung up.

They all met outside the door to Lilli's apartment: Christian Rabinsky, Frau Brendler, Franza, and Herz, whom she'd called on the way. A strange coolness radiated from behind the door. *What's waiting for us in there?* Franza thought with a shiver and felt the unease that had been creeping around inside her all day, that unease that seldom deceived her.

"Can you give us the key?" Felix's voice was gentle, soft. Christian gave him the key and looked at him with a questioning expression.

"Perhaps . . ." Dorothee said, and then hesitated. "I'm so scared."

Franza nodded. *Yes,* she thought, *I can believe it.* "My colleague and I are going in. You wait here."

"But . . ." Christian objected. Franza raised her eyebrows, and he fell silent.

Felix and Franza went in, carefully, ready for anything. But . . . there was nothing. They called out Lilli's name. Nothing. Looked in all the rooms. Nothing. The apartment was empty.

Franza went to the door. "It's not what you feared, Frau Brendler. The apartment's empty."

Franza saw the relief in their faces. "Come in," she said. "Have a look round. Is anything different from usual?"

They entered the apartment, went slowly from room to room, looking around. The answering machine was flashing.

"That was me," Dorothee said. "I called at least five times and left messages."

Franza nodded. "We'll listen to them anyway."

Christian was in the bedroom. He turned pale.

"Oh my God," he said quietly, staring at the bedside table. On it was a little book, red leather bound, tied with a blue cord.

"What is it?" Herz asked tensely. "What have you seen?"

"That book," Christian said, his voice shaking. "That's Gertrud's diary. I last saw it in our bedroom, a few hours before . . . before she"— he hesitated—"while she was still alive."

No, thought Franza. *No, not that.*

"Are you familiar with it? Do you know what's in it?"

"No. No, I don't. I've no idea what's in it. I looked at it once, years ago. Picked it up. Gertrud freaked out. I had no intention of reading it. I just liked the cover, but . . ." He paused and continued with an effort. "She always kept it hidden, for all those years. I don't know where. It doesn't matter. I never thought about it. But that night it was lying on the floor by the bed and I recognized it."

"Are you sure? You could be mistaken."

He shook his head. "No, I'm not mistaken. I wish I was, but I'm not mistaken. I remember that I was surprised to see it again. I thought, *So it's got something to do with that. It's in there that she wrote about Hanna and their . . . love.*" He halted again. "And now . . . it's here?"

He turned, looked at Franza, looked at Felix, a question in his eyes. "Was she there?"

Dorothee's voice was tiny, a whisper, a breath. "Lilli? That night? No, she can't have been. It can't be true! You're mistaken, Christian. You must be. You must be mistaken! It can't be true! Gertrud must have given it to Lilli before she died! She must have!"

He turned to her and looked at her. She said nothing more.

"We really don't have any reason to worry yet," Herz said, after they'd sent Christian and Frau Brendler away almost forcefully. "I mean, what do we have here? An empty apartment. A young woman who hasn't been in contact with home for a few hours. You think that's unusual? Really? If that were the case we'd be on call all the time."

Franza had to admit that if you looked at it like that . . .

But then they listened to the answering machine messages. They also found a letter from a laboratory that said there was no genetic match between the two DNA samples examined, so there was no way that the two people in question could be mother and daughter.

And then when they quickly leafed through the diary, they found an address they knew. They sent Arthur to the address to ask whether anyone there had seen Lilli. Yes, someone had seen her there.

"Hm," Herz said thoughtfully, and cleared his throat. "Now we do have reason to worry."

70

Night fell quickly. The sky was cloudy, and it looked like rain.

Franza thought about Hanna and Gertrud, whom a quirk of fate had brought together so many years ago. They were still bound by these chains, these fetters, and in the middle hung Lilli, helpless and alone. They were tugging at her, each in a different direction, and Lilli cried and screamed, not knowing where to turn, feeling the shackles of her mothers tightening around her, hanging on her like a great weight, great enough to tear her apart.

With the Danube shimmering before her, a dark, metallic expanse, Franza remembered Port's text and realized she had not yet replied. She finally did.

He wanted her to come that weekend, but she suspected she would pass on it. She wanted him to fly in his theater heaven, his artists' heaven, wherever it took him—and she suspected she would never be able to fly there with him.

It began to rain. Franza stood for a moment, stretching out to feel the soft, refreshing wetness enfold her. *A vacation,* she thought. She needed a vacation—now, in the autumn, when the south had grown milder, the heat had faded, the sunburns had healed, and the memories of the woman whose fateful vacation would always mean painful recollection had vanished. *A vacation,* she thought—*as soon as we've solved this case, if we ever solve it.*

.   .   .

. . . sometimes it's all very difficult, alien one wrote late that night, when she was unable to sleep. Lilli, the little devil, had only trusted her with half a story. Franza had clearly not succeeded in doing what was necessary—earning Lilli's full trust, not just a part of it.

. . . yes, alien two wrote back, *. . . i know. . .* As if he really did know what she was talking about.

71

Gertrud told me everything. Everything. I didn't want to know any of it.

After Christian left, she cowered on the floor. I told her that she shouldn't send him away; she needed him. I was not an option, not for anything she wished.

It destroyed her. She stayed on the floor. Sobbing. Unable to calm herself. I went over to her and laid my hand on her shoulder. She shook me off, angry, raging in helpless pain.

"Gertrud," I said. "Gertrud, calm down! Let's talk. We can sort it all out. He'll come back. You can get your life back."

"Sort it out," she said, and I recoiled from the bitterness in her voice. "You really think there's anything that can be sorted out? Are you really that stupid? What kind of a life? What kind of a life do you think this is? Talk? What do you want to talk about now? Everything's over. Everything's been said."

"No," I said. "I don't agree. Nothing's over." Suddenly I thought of Lilli, my Lilli. "I wish I'd had your luck."

She laughed at that—nasty, furious, full of hatred. She stood, turned.

"Luck," she said. "You call it luck? I've been lucky? No, I haven't been lucky. Neither have you, that's true. But I . . ."

She closed her eyes briefly, her face tightening into a painful grimace. Then she took my hand and led me to the table. I don't know why, but I felt afraid. Horribly afraid.

"Come here," she said. "Sit down. I'll tell you something."

And then she told me. Mercilessly. Uncompromisingly.

She began with Greece. I'd thought there was nothing more to say about it. I thought I already knew everything. But I knew only the tiniest part, the least painful bits.

She began by saying that when all was said and done, perhaps Tonio had just been unlucky, perhaps he had just drawn the shortest fucking straw possible—by coming across us completely by chance and being crazy enough to fall in love with me.

"Yes," she said, "with you, Hanna. If you look at the big picture, you could say that all this tragedy is your fault. As for him, he was simply unlucky."

She laughed unhappily and fell silent for a while.

I didn't dare ask what she meant by all that. I should have simply got up and left. Up to that moment, it could have been OK. Nothing would have gotten worse than it already was. But her eyes were relentless. She showed no mercy, no kindness, and I knew she wouldn't let me go.

"Do you remember what he said? About the wind?"

I didn't want to remember. *Leave it alone,* I thought, *just stop!*

"The wind clears the head, he always said. He liked the wind. The wind never scared him. That was why it was so . . . easy."

So easy? What was?

My heart began to thump. I felt a coldness suddenly begin to seep through me, trickling down my spine, settling into my body. With difficulty I suppressed a shudder.

"What do you mean?" I said carefully.

She stood up, found a bottle of wine, and began to drink.

"It was easy. Everything." She laughed scornfully. "You had no idea."

The images from that holiday came into my head. I had not seen them for so long, but suddenly they were there. Like a blinding light. Like a flash of lightning.

"Let's go to the beach," Tonio had called out enthusiastically morning after morning. "Let's run around in the spray."

We lay on the crests of the waves, faces turned to the orange sun, floating and feeling so light. Those were the early days. The wind was bearable, with only the merest hint of the coming storm.

"You remember now, don't you?" Gertrud said. "You can see all the images again now, can't you, Hanna? All the images of Greece, our last time together. Do you want some wine?"

I shook my head, stood. "I should go. I've got to get in touch with Jonas; he'll be worried."

"No," she said, and jumped up, too. "You're not going now. You wanted us to talk. And that's what we're doing. Now it's all out in the open. Now it's all got to come out."

I tried to resist her. "Whatever you still want to say to me, Gertrud, I don't want to hear it. Leave me alone!"

She laughed angrily and swept her arm feverishly across the table, knocking over two jelly jars that crashed to the floor and smashed on the tiles. Jelly, still warm, splashed around, mixed with glass splinters. She ignored it, grabbed my arm, and forced me down onto the chair.

"It doesn't matter what you want," she hissed. "What's important now is what I want."

I closed my eyes. *OK*, I thought. *Out with it. I'm prepared. Whatever's about to happen won't touch me. I'm finally going to see Lilli tomorrow, so nothing can touch me.*

How I deceived myself.

She took a deep breath, trying to calm down. She began to whisper, murmuring words. ". . . blue-black the water permeates your dying, smashes your heart to pieces . . ."

I held my breath.

Silence.

"I couldn't stop thinking those words," she said, "like an endless loop, as I was sitting on the bed next to you, waiting for you to wake. You know. When he was already dead."

She picked up the bottle again, took a mouthful.

"And I still have them in my head. They won't go away. They'll never go away."

She smiled, stood again, went to the window. I drew my jacket tight around myself. It was no use; I was freezing from the inside.

She spoke the words again in a monotonous voice. Spoke them out the window. Spoke them into the depths of my being.

. . . *blue-black the water permeates your dying, smashes your heart to pieces . . .*

She spoke them into the depths of my being, those words, and there they would stay, I knew it. There they will stay, I know it, just as they stayed with her.

She turned. "He was lying with you in the bed. You were asleep. The red wine went to your head. It always made you sleepy. He was also asleep, but I went to him, woke him. He looked at me as though I were a ghost. I had to laugh. 'Shh,' he said, 'Be quiet! Don't laugh so loudly, Hanna's asleep. Don't wake her up.'"

She was silent for a moment, listening to her own thoughts—the echoes of her words. Then she repeated, "Hanna's asleep. Don't wake her up."

"Maybe," she said, "maybe that's what it was, I don't know. Maybe I just wanted a bit of peace, for it not to always be about you. I don't know."

She turned and stood in the twilight, in the half-light by the window, where the ceiling light didn't reach. I couldn't see her face, but I could hear in her voice that she was crying.

"I said, 'Come on, Tonio, let's have a little drink. I'm thirsty. I don't want to be alone.' He thought about it for a moment, and I was thinking he wouldn't come, he'd go back to sleep by your side until morning. Then I said, 'The wind's dropped a little. We could go to the beach for a little night swimming.' He tapped his temple and said, 'You're out of your mind!' But he got up, pulled on his shorts and a T-shirt. We crept out and he shut the door quietly behind him. The wind hadn't dropped. On the contrary it was roaring around the house, enough to scare you out of your wits. We took the bottles with us—schnapps and red wine, he liked to mix them up a little. I don't know what exactly I was planning. Whether I was actually planning anything. I don't think so. Things just have a way of happening."

She stopped speaking. I sat on my chair, unable to move, as if under a spell, as if tied to it. What was she trying to tell me? What was going to come now? She continued.

"'Awesome!' he said as we reached the beach. 'What awesome waves.'

"'Do you love her?' I asked him.

"He turned to me and asked, 'Love? Do I love the waves, perhaps? These huge, crazy waves?' And he began to laugh, split his sides laughing over that attempt at a joke.

"'Ha ha ha,' I said, 'Very funny. You could win a prize with that, for sure!'

"Then he grew serious and asked, 'You do, too, don't you? You do, too.'"

She stopped talking. A fly buzzed around the room, its humming clear. Gertrud only paused for a moment before whispering, "I hated him at that moment. And I knew I could kill him."

No, I thought, and felt a dreadful stabbing pain. *No, Gertrud, don't say that. Not that.* But she did. She said it.

"He was an asshole," she continued mercilessly. "A fucking, son-of-a-bitch asshole, but he was a good-looking asshole, and that's what you fell for, Hanna. It was a farce, that vacation as a threesome—that whole life we led as a threesome. Stupidity, a complete mess. For that alone he . . . he needed punishing."

Punishing . . . ?

Punishing . . . I thought, and for the first time this year I felt the oncoming autumn, how it ate into my bones with its dampness. So he needed punishing, did he? Really? With death?

"It was simple. So easy," she whispered. "We were standing at the waterline, right at the edge, the waves lapping at our feet. I could see the white surf even though it was dark. He drank. I didn't. He laughed and talked about his life, about you, about what a sexpot you were, what awesome orgasms he had with you, and how I shouldn't waste my time on something that would never be. I'd be better off looking for another lover, as I wasn't bad-looking at all."

She fell silent and slowly came over to me. I looked into her face and saw how sad she was, how lonely. She stroked my hair with her hand. I didn't move. I felt her so close to me and had a dreadful sense of foreboding.

"You can take everything I tell you and do what you want with it," she said tonelessly. "I don't care. I can't bear it anymore. Not a moment longer. It's been eating me away, tearing me apart."

I pushed her away, unable to bear her presence any longer. She backed off toward the window, into the darkness. Then she continued talking.

"'You won't do it,' I said. 'I'm right, aren't I? You wouldn't dare.'

"He looked at me, at first unable to work out what I meant. But then . . . 'You want to get rid of me,' he said, surprised, astonished. 'You little bitch, you want to get rid of me!' He laughed again, the alcohol already fogging his brain.

"I said, 'Yes, I want rid of you, but you're too much of a coward, you won't dare go into the water. You're a coward, and one day Hanna will see through you. She'll see you're all front and she'll press against you with her finger, only a little, and then you'll fall and melt away like butter.' I was so angry, but he merely laughed at me.

"'Like butter,' he laughed. 'Like butter! Gertrud, you're a real joker. I never realized!' Then he grew calm again, drank from the schnapps bottle, warbled some lines from a song, and sat down in the sand. 'Ugh! Cold, damn cold,' he said as the waves soaked him. 'So,' he said, 'You want me to go in right now, swim around a little. What am I supposed to prove to you? That I'm the biggest, the best? Don't we know that anyway? You don't seriously believe that I'm afraid of this, these little waves, these meager gusts of wind? Absurd!' He turned to me. I felt his eyes on me.

"'You've got nothing to prove to me,' I said. 'Nothing at all. Forget it. I knew you wouldn't dare.'

"But I knew he was a gambler, a risk taker; he couldn't walk away from a bet.

"'Both of us,' he said. 'Come on, go for it, no need to be scared. Nothing's gonna happen. This mild breeze, we can outsmart it. You're right. It's truly awesome weather for swimming.' He jumped up, undressed, threw his shorts and T-shirt in the sand and grabbed my hand.

"'OK,' I said, 'OK, give me a moment.' I slipped out of my shoes, out of my jeans. We set off, into the water, up to our ankles, up to our knees. You could feel the force of the wind, the force of the waves. He was already way ahead. I could hardly see him as the darkness gradually swallowed him up. And I . . . I stopped. Just stopped. He didn't notice. Or he didn't care. He yelled, shouted for joy, sang—all the time going farther and farther out into the water.

"*What an idiot,* I thought. *How did Hanna fall for someone like you?*

"He was really far out by then, at the point when the ocean bed falls away sharply, where you lose the floor from beneath your feet. He began to swim. Into infinity."

She laughed bitterly. "I could still hear him, his breathless shouting. I was still standing in the same spot, the water whipping up against me up to my hips, each time the waves broke, spraying me in the face. I knew he was already lost. In the sea, the wind, the darkness. Eventually I could no longer hear him. I heard the crashing of the waves, I heard the storm, but Tonio . . . I could no longer hear him. I don't know whether he struggled, whether it was difficult or easy. I only know that at some point I could no longer hear him."

Silence. She didn't turn, merely stood rigid, leaning against the windowsill, the blackness in front of the window like the blackness at sea had been back then.

I'm freezing from Gertrud's words, I thought. *I'm freezing right here and now.*

But you don't freeze that quickly, you hear the words and take them in, lock them into a part of your brain, where they rumble and rumble around until they explode and flood you with their truth. And then there's no escape.

"If it makes you feel any better, Hanna," Gertrud said eventually, "if it makes you feel any better, I lost my footing too. The same moment he did. And it was all so simple. So easy. And I backed away, slowly, slowly, step by step, out of the water and onto the sand. I stood there then. For a long time.

"'Big Sea,' I whispered. 'Big Sea, you're my friend, my accomplice, my partner.' I raised my hand in greeting, behind his back, behind Tonio."

Another silence and an intake of breath. The words penetrated my consciousness, her words—the ones she spoke at the beginning of her story, at the beginning of this dreadful truth.

Blue-black, I thought, my Tonio, *blue-black the water permeated your dying,* and I saw it, I saw the images, Tonio, your fight as the storm tore into you, threw you back and forth, as the waves broke over you and drew you down into the depths. I saw how amazed you were when you realized your strength would not be enough, that it would be the end, that it was the end.

I wanted to cry, to cry, my Tonio. She destroyed you, robbed you of your life, robbed you of me. The coast, such an expanse of beach. How you loved the black sand. Lilli came into my mind, your daughter, our daughter, and the fact that I'd . . .

She continued. Gertrud continued with the flood of her story, allowing me no respite.

"I came back to you, Hanna. Into the house, into the bedroom where you were sleeping. The empty space in the bed beside you, the cover thrown back, the pillows crumpled. You were sleeping, Hanna. You had no idea about his . . . going over into another world, wherever that was. I stayed sitting next to you, waiting for you to wake. Waiting for the morning, giving in to the flood that forced its way from me, that flood of tears that flowed and flowed and flowed. At last there was light over the sea, and suddenly there were people shouting: the German, the German! And, Hanna, you woke and sat up and you were shocked by the sight of me sitting on the bed, and you heard the voices and went out, down to the sea, where the voices were coming from. They had already found him, more quickly than I'd thought. He had washed up a little farther down the coast. They had laid him on a stretcher and brought him back for us to identify."

She shook her head. "The depths," she said, looking as though she were still amazed by it, "the depths didn't want him. Would they have taken him in paradise? Do you think so, Hanna? Do you think so?"

She turned to me. I said nothing. She nodded. "Are you crying?"

It was only then that I noticed I was crying. Yes, I was crying—wasn't there reason enough to cry?

She continued, slowly: "You went over to him, threw yourself on top of him, moaning and lamenting, your hair flowing over him like a sheet of copper. As for me . . . Nothing touched me anymore, nothing. Not the fact that he was dead, not your despair—only your hair, Hanna, your hair, that was spread over him like a cloak. *That'll warm him,* I thought, *on the long journey ahead of him. Hanna's copper hair will warm him.*"

She breathed deeply as if she'd been working hard. "And the next day you disappeared. Packed your bag, cleared out, vanished. Away, away, away."

She nodded, brushed both hands over her face. "And I . . . I was alone."

She went to the fridge, took out cheese and sausage, bread from the bread bin, a tomato, an onion, placed them all on the table, a wooden board, a kitchen knife. She cut the bread, the cheese, the sausage, and the tomato. She began to eat greedily, as if she'd eaten nothing for three days.

I looked at her. I wanted to go, wanted to get out of there—away from her, away from that house, away from that town. But it was as though I was paralyzed, and I knew that if I moved so much as a millimeter, I would begin to shake and never stop.

"Why?" I asked at last. "Why?"

She stopped eating and stared at me, suddenly shocked.

"Why?" she echoed. "Why?"

She thought about it, shrugged.

"I don't know," she whispered. "I don't know anymore. Perhaps because . . . you and him . . . because we both . . . oh, I don't know. It happened. It simply happened—the night, the storm, the things he said, the . . ." She let out a sob. "When I read those letters, Tonio's letters to you, it was as though I'd written them to you myself. I missed you, Hanna, missed you so much, always." She stretched her hand out to me. "You don't know it, Hanna, but you broke my heart."

It was enough. Too much. I started shaking. I stood and started for the door, to fetch my daughter at last, to go away with her, never to return. But Gertrud still hadn't finished. Her voice hit me in the back.

"And suddenly you were here again. And you were pregnant."

I stopped.

"Yes," I said. "Yes."

And the sadness overwhelmed me.

"With Lilli," she said. "With my Lilli. My grown-up, wonderful daughter. She saved me. I was able to stay alive for her sake." A pause. Then she said, "She never missed you. She never needed you. She's my daughter. You would never have been a mother to her."

I don't remember what I felt, I don't know what I thought. Nothing, perhaps. A vacuum. The vacuum of those many years. What an irony of fate, that she of all people . . . Gertrud of all people . . . She had taken everything from me—my lover, my child. I felt the sadness come.

"She'll never forgive you! A mother who sells her child. What kind of a mother is that?"

A mother who sells her child? Is that what I was? Had I . . .

For a moment I closed my eyes, thought about back then, thought about the apartment key, thought about the savings book that held so much money.

Hans had invited me into his study when everything appeared to be going well, when I was finally recovered, when I had decided to return to Munich and continue my studies. He looked at me awkwardly and asked me to sit. On the desk was a savings book, an apartment key, and a lease.

"This is all yours," he said and cleared his throat. "It should make things a bit easier for you. Because . . . It's because . . ."

He broke off. I looked up into his face, sensed his embarrassment, and was myself embarrassed. We didn't talk much more after that. He asked about my plans, and I told him I didn't have many to begin with, things would work out. I stood, took the savings book, the key and the lease, thanked him, and left.

Yes, I was a mother who sold her child.

I turned to Gertrud and saw she was beginning to fall apart. Like a tent that slowly collapses. Like a sandcastle that trickles away as sand dries out.

"She'll never forgive you for selling her."

She was right. That's how it was. Lilli would never forgive me. And I'd never forgive myself.

There was a smell of damson jelly. That smell filled my nostrils. Gertrud stood, stumbled against the wooden board, against the knife. It fell to the floor, clattered down by my feet. I bent down. Without thinking, I picked it up. Suddenly, I had it in my hand.

72

These fifty-somethings are a bunch of washed-up wimps, Kristin thought. *The only things worth knowing about them are their wallets.*

She had to smile. This adventure was getting fun—she hadn't had the slightest idea she had so much criminal energy in her.

Rummaging in her purse for her cigarettes, she looked around. It was an upmarket bar—it stank of money. The corners of her mouth turned down in recognition of the fact. It was upmarket places like this that made the world go round. She stood and went over to the door, where there was an ashtray on an artfully concealed stand. As usual, she couldn't find a lighter in her capacious bag. She waved a waiter over and asked him for a light. He fetched a book of matches, struck one, and held the flame to her cigarette before giving her the rest of the book.

"Voilà, madame," he said with a smile. She gave him a friendly smile back.

A cigarette, then another. Between them she drank a coffee. Her impatience grew. Where was he? They didn't have forever.

He finally arrived, later than yesterday, looking a bit gray and wiped out, as though he'd gotten some bad news from somewhere. He sat down at the same table where he'd sat the day before, ordered a sherry, didn't pick up a newspaper but merely stared straight ahead. He didn't notice her even though she'd been watching him here for two days now.

That piqued her a little. She looked great. Why wouldn't he notice her? *Men are stupid,* she thought, *thick as bricks. They deserve everything they get.* She grinned again.

Of course, sometimes something nice happens to them. But certainly not always. That wouldn't do. It would make life boring.

She laughed softly. Suddenly, the man raised his head and looked in her direction. She froze briefly, feeling a tingle run through her body. Would things get more exciting now? Had he *seen* her?

No, he looked through her like a pane of glass. His thoughts were miles away, his eyes vacant.

OK, she thought, *you can't say you don't deserve it. You're going to bleed.*

The man called the waiter over, paid, stood, and left. She followed him slowly. He went the same way as the previous day, unhurried, lost in thought, as though he had all the time in the world. No surprises. Boring. Washed-up old bastard.

Kristin felt sure of herself. The next step was in place. They didn't have forever; no one had that. But he—he had no time left at all.

The girl? The girl was out of the action. She would no longer be in their way.

73

He held the letter in his hands—if you could call it a letter. It was just a piece of paper in an envelope. *So it's all falling apart,* he thought. *Nothing left.*

He leaned his head back, shut his eyes, and sat like that for a while. Eventually he got out his cell phone, wrote a text, and pressed "Send."

74

"They're creeping into my head," Tonio said, looking out through the window at the fading daylight. "I can't stand them anymore."

"Who?" she asked. "Who are you talking about?"

She snuggled up to his shoulder. He had his arm around her, was playing with her hair.

"The patients," he said. "The patients on my ward. The dying. They're all dying. Sometimes two a day. Sometimes none. But they all die eventually."

She placed a finger on his lips.

"If I had to count them," he said, nuzzling it with his lips, placing little kisses along it without thinking, "if I had to count them, it would be never ending."

"So many?" she asked quietly.

"Yes. So many."

"Is that why you left? Why you vanished?"

He thought about it, nodded. "Yes," he said, "that's probably why. Because I couldn't stand it any longer. Because it wasn't working. Because I felt I was going mad. But here . . ."

It had all gone better. Almost gone well.

He told her about the anger that had grown inside him, which she had also experienced back then, and the fact that this anger had faded in his grandfather's apartment. As the apartment had grown ever more empty, ever quieter, he too had become ever more empty, ever quieter.

"Somehow they managed to rescue me a little, my grandfather and my father," he said. "And I know it sounds really pathetic, but somehow they've given me a new life."

"Yes," she said drily. "That's true. The life of a gangster with the police after him. That's certainly something. A shaven-headed gangster, too."

He grinned. "Well, you can't have everything. You're not complaining, are you, my gangster's moll?" He began to tickle her. She twisted in his hands.

"No," she laughed. "Help! No! Stop it!"

He obeyed, and they embraced again. Silence. She buried her head in his shoulder, felt his lips on her head.

"I'd never be able to do it," she said softly, "work on a ward like that. Looking death in the face all the time. I was always sure that I couldn't. And I admired you because you could. Do you know that?"

"No, I didn't know. On the contrary, I always wondered why a woman like you was the slightest bit interested in me. I didn't understand it at all."

"A woman like me?"

"Yes. Tough, clever, beautiful, ambitious."

"Is that what I am to you?"

She raised her head and looked at him.

"Yes, that's what you are to me. You just are. And you could have had someone completely different. Not some nobody of a nurse."

"But I didn't want anyone else," she said, stroking his chest and belly.

He smiled. "True," he said. "You didn't want anyone else. And now you've become a gangster's moll. Do you think your parents would like that?"

"So what?" she said with small grin. "My parents are just my parents, and I'm me, and I've never asked their advice about any of my guys. I've been grown up for quite a while now."

He laughed and stroked her face gently. She closed her eyes, savoring the gentleness of his touch. They remained silent as the daylight faded.

"Did you never see your father?" she asked eventually. "Never? Honestly? You didn't know anything about him?"

He shook his head. "No, never laid eyes on him. I knew nothing. He never existed as far as I was concerned. I only had my mother and my grandparents."

"And your mother never talked about him?"

He considered, realizing that he had never had such a conversation, that he was telling her things no one else knew.

"Yes, she did. Once. I was fourteen. One day, my grandmother handed my mother a newspaper and said, 'Look here. Read it. Does he look familiar?' My mother turned pale and went out. She came back two hours later. That was when I asked her."

"And?"

"She told me about him. That he was a crazy kind of guy. That she had fallen in love with him on the spot but she'd known from the start he wasn't a man who would stay. That she got pregnant."

"After that?"

He shrugged. "Nothing. I looked at that newspaper article. It said that he'd drowned in Greece. There was a photo of him lying there with a woman bending over him. You could hardly see anything of him. Only his legs and this woman above him, mostly just her long hair. But you know that photo. And the newspaper article."

She nodded. Yes, she knew it all.

"I never thought he was anyone particularly special," he continued. "He was merely my progenitor, not my father. I pushed it to the back of my mind, forgot about it. Or at least tried to."

He fell silent, smiled at her, lost in his thoughts. "And then that letter came from the lawyer and I found it all—the bundle of letters, newspaper clippings, documents."

Things had begun to snowball, moving faster and faster, out of control.

He pushed Kristin away gently, stood, and moved to the window. "I didn't want any of it, you know. I didn't want her to die, I didn't want . . . It all just happened."

She nodded. "I know. Of course I know."

"She . . . she could be my sister."

"We'll see," she said.

"She probably *is* my sister."

She heard the amazement in his voice. She looked at him, his back, his shaven head that she hadn't quite gotten used to yet.

"Yes," she said. "We'll see."

She wondered if he was someone who would stick around. She wasn't sure, but the question no longer concerned her, and neither did the answer—because she was beginning to love him.

75

. . . *yes* . . . *alien two* wrote back, . . . *i know* . . .

As if he really knew what she meant, as if he had the slightest idea what she was talking about. Franza was amazed. It couldn't be possible. It was an illusion. So much unfinished business: Port in Vienna, Max with his faithful-hound expression here, the red book with the blue ribbon, Lilli out there somewhere, and she herself was here, unable to sleep, simply unable to sleep . . .

. . . *i want to taste your skin and your thoughts* . . . *alien two* wrote . . . *i want your trail to interweave with mine* . . .

Franza jumped and at the same time felt overcome by an incredible sweetness, suddenly there on her computer screen, but then she recalled Lilli and the diary.

. . . *i'm sorry* . . . she wrote . . . *i'm not really with it—as i said, things aren't easy right now, i've got a whole load of unfinished business around me, nothing's easy, sorry* . . .

. . . *i know* . . . he wrote, . . . *as i said, i know. i'd like to meet you. now. right now, i'll wait for you* . . .

He named a bar that she knew; she went there now and again, formerly with Max, now sometimes with Port, sometimes even with Sonja. Her heart missed a beat because he was being bold and she didn't feel bold, and what did bold matter anyway. She didn't need any more unfinished business.

. . . i'll wait for you . . . he wrote again, *. . . i'm wearing a dark blue jacket, sitting at the bar, drinking a glass of red wine. i'll wait for you for precisely an hour and a half . . .*

Then he was gone, logged out, no reply possible. She sat in front of the PC like a wet kitten, shocked, shaky. Her eyes wide-open, she shook her head.

"What a madman," she muttered to herself. "What a crazy madman!"

She glanced at the clock. An hour and a half. What if . . .

No! She shook her head determinedly. No! She went slowly into the bathroom, slowly.

Hanna's copper hair will warm him, Gertrud had written in the red diary. Franza thought about that as she stared into the mirror, as she wondered whether she should perhaps, maybe, possibly . . . get ready for the *interweaving of the trails.*

She wondered what else *alien two* was thinking and what his skin tasted of. She wondered whether it tasted good or not, and whether she really wanted to taste it at all.

A prickling feeling settled in her stomach, and she wondered whether he had another name and whether she really wanted to know it. Whether he had a face and whether she really wanted to see it, or whether it might be better . . . to stay in their *alien* world with their *alien* names and *alien* faces—whether that might not be so, so much better.

Hanna's copper hair had not warmed Tonio, Franza was quite sure of that. When the water got into you, nothing could ever warm you again. Everything was cold and clammy, and your blood froze in your heart.

My heart, Franza thought. *I ought to protect my own heart a little. It's very vulnerable as it is.* She looked thoughtfully into her eyes in the mirror, and decided to leave *alien two* in the *alien* world. Shaking her head over the incredible silliness of the names, she settled down on the couch to read Gertrud's diary.

Poking about in the realm of his life, Gertrud had written a little pathetically, *everything becomes less clear and more involuntary. Big Sea, you're my friend, my accomplice, my partner.* She wrote that the water was like blue-black ink, like oil, a soft death perhaps, caused by the penetration of a little oil. That was a comfort, the only one.

Then there was the phrase on the voice mail and the phrase in the red book, the last one Gertrud wrote, faded a little over more than twenty years. *I've done something dreadful.*

No, Franza thought, *I don't want to read any more, I can't read any more. Why can't I sleep?*

She looked at the clock. Half an hour left—enough time. It would be tight, but there was enough.

She leapt up as if she'd been stung. Jacket, shoes—nice shoes. *I must be mad,* she thought. *Car keys. I'm out of my head, but I can't sleep anyway, so what the heck. I'm out of my head, but that's life.*

76

I come to the river every morning. Even though I come quietly, the birds hear me, rise up, and disappear into the mist, which still hangs thickly over the water. But I know the light will soon be here. When the birds fly off, they fly into this light. When I stand there and watch them go, I feel dizzy, as the mist has diffused all the contours and merged the sky and the water, leaving no trace—nothing to hold on to, no anchor, nothing, only the waterline. It holds me morning after morning, lapping at my feet with a quiet smacking sound. But I don't feel it. I'm drifting up, into the mist, into the white wall over the water. Everything loses itself—no orientation, no more knowing.

But somewhere at the limits of the mist, somewhere high above, the sun breaks through, a white disk with a pale light. It has so little strength, and that seems . . . familiar to me. That's why I love this sun, for the strength it lacks, for the light that doesn't catch anywhere.

I understand it; it's familiar to me. I understand it so well, so well. And so I spend morning after morning at the edge here. Ships sound their blaring foghorns as they pass, but even they are made small by the white thickness of this mist. In the background are the cries of the Danube gulls, dipping and weaving on light wings through the fleecy clouds of the mist, while fishermen let their lines whir into the water with a sound like pea whistles.

Yes, I'm drawn again and again to this boundary, lured by the river and the fog, where everything is indeterminate, vague, aimless. Here I can see Tonio sometimes—Gertrud too. They stand and wave me over, but I know they are nothing but hallucinations. When I've looked at them for long enough, I turn and look at the water meadows, the footprints in the sand. Back to reality.

What happened, happened. They go. Tonio. Gertrud. They go, lose their shapes, dissolve. It's the mist that causes it, covering them with its flurries, and then . . . It's a good thing that they go. It's time.

77

Blackmail, then. He had been seen. It didn't matter. It was all over, anyway. But he simply couldn't let her carry on any longer.

For two days he had been suffering nosebleeds. At first he had lain down and the blood flowed down into his throat, back into his body, and he had swallowed and swallowed, but then he had to cough, and saliva mixed with blood sprayed from his mouth, soaking the pillowcase with drops of his carelessness, his helplessness, his anger. Afterward, he had been enraged by the mess and thrown the pillowcases in the trash.

The next time his nose bled, he'd immediately bent over the sink in the bathroom, staring down at the bright red stream splashing up in a thousand tiny droplets.

"I'll tell her everything, and then she'll destroy you, your sacred Hanna," she had spat angrily into his face.

"And you?" he had asked. "Don't you have just as much to lose?"

"Me?" She'd laughed hysterically. "I'm already destroyed. I've already lost everything."

Then it happened.

In the giddiness of the evening light, he wanted to cry for her. He hoped for rain, to split the light into cold streaks. He wanted to cry for her in a cathedral, in the dim light of the candles as the faithful walked slowly and softly up and down the nave. The smell of incense would mix with the clammy scent of moisture evaporating from damp clothes. There would be the occasional raised voice, the occasional foreign language.

Oh, Gertrud, he had thought, as he'd stared into her silence. *One second,* he'd thought, shivering in the cold that had suddenly radiated from her, *give me one second to pull myself together. The eyes must be closed,* he had thought. *Oh, Gertrud.* He'd done it for her. *You were my Gertrud, too.*

She had been beside herself when he arrived, cursing him, attacking him, saying she would bring it all out into the open, unerring and clear as cellophane.

It had gotten to be too much. He'd lost it. Cried out like a cornered animal. As if his life depended on it. As if he didn't know that it was not about him, but about her—her life. He'd felt a heat rising in him, an anger, a despair. The knife suddenly in his hand. Amazement on both their faces.

He had no idea how it had gotten into his hand. It felt cool and real, and he himself was cool, calm, and clearheaded. Only a brief second's hesitation. A tiny moment. He saw the fear in her eyes as she began to sense that he was prepared to do it, that it wouldn't cost him anything anymore, only the slightest effort. She began to tremble.

"No," she said. "You can't do that. It's me. Me!"

He said nothing. He looked into her eyes, and their glint became powerful, growing to a storm, which welled up and beyond her and finally . . . finally . . . settled into stillness. He stabbed. She fell to the floor and lay stretched out, dying on the tiles in the kitchen.

She heard the blade as it clattered to the floor. Perhaps she heard a low tone in the air, and then she heard nothing more. No gasping, no moaning. Nothing. Death swallowed all her sounds, made her quiet, made her calm, made her still.

He froze—everything seared firmly into his brain forever. Her fall, her astonishment, her voice as she said, "Don't go. Don't leave me here like this, please." Her hand, that bitter white, her tearless dying that she perceived in amazement. No comma any more. Period.

Now he would wait. He would do no more. Only wait until they came. They would come.

78

That night Tonio had once again settled down to lie in wait. It had become a bit of an obsession. He knew he had to get a grip on himself, but he allowed himself this fixation about her life. What he was doing wasn't that bad. There were worse things.

All she had to do was tell him her side of the story, her version of his father's death, and then he'd disappear, leave her in peace again. Then he'd be off in pursuit of the other one.

Yes, he had settled down to wait. He had seen it all. Now he wanted to get some capital from it.

It had been like Grand Central Station around there. It had begun in the afternoon, when *she* had suddenly appeared, the red-haired one, the one with the letters, the one from the newspaper photo—Hanna.

He had been perplexed, hadn't expected it. Didn't she live a world away, in France? *What a story,* he thought, and had to fight hard to stop himself from shouting for joy. What total madness. His letter—or rather his father's letter—had had such an effect.

He shook his head in amazement. What a story he'd set in motion, what a crazy train of events!

He'd had to look at her twice to make sure it really was Hanna. Her long hair was gone, her long red hair from the photos of her youth and from the paper.

A pity, Tonio thought. *A real pity.* She had been so unique, distinctive. She'd impressed him with a wistful beauty that he was unable to describe.

So, she had short hair now. He had to admit he was disappointed. She was one of the images he liked to play with in his mind. They shouldn't just go out and experiment on their own. He wanted them to conform to the way he wanted them.

Ah well, he couldn't control everything. He continued watching.

They did what women always do: sat in the garden and talked.

From his hill he could see them well with his binoculars, but he couldn't hear what they were saying. He didn't dare to go any nearer. Maybe later, he decided, when it had gotten dark. He had to stick it out here, even as it got cold in the darkness. He hadn't brought a jacket, and he began to shiver.

Time passed slowly. The women talked and talked, and eventually went into the house. He scanned round to the kitchen and had them in his sights again. They were cooking—at least he saw Gertrud stirring something in a large pan.

Time went by. Nothing happened.

Why do women always have to chatter on? he thought. *Are you telling each other stories from the old days? You should be telling those to me!*

He moved nearer in the darkness.

He slipped down from the hill, toward the garden. The gate was still unlocked; it was simple. He crept toward the terrace, from which he knew he would have a good view into the kitchen, and the living room. This was not the first time he had been here. He'd already sounded it out a little. Perhaps there would be windows open or doors, and then he could hear, too . . .

But, nothing, nada, zilch, no windows open, no door.

Shit, he thought. *Shit, just my luck!*

So . . . what now?

Silence? No more stories?

No more stories . . . Gertrud lay her hand over Hanna's, and Hanna allowed herself to be led out of the room and up the stairs.

Yay, Tonio thought, out on the terrace, raising his eyebrows in surprise. *Yay, yay, yay—new developments?*

He listened. Nothing to hear from upstairs. Time passed, but not too much. He had no idea what was happening, what it all meant. He wondered if it made sense to stick around. He'd just decided it made no sense to stay, when . . .

. . . a car pulled up the drive and Christian Rabinsky got out, the husband. Apparently in a good mood, whistling a little tune, he unlocked the door, went into the house, and up the stairs . . .

Out on the terrace, Tonio held his breath . . .

Then . . . Noise. Shouting. Footsteps on the stairs—hurried footsteps. Followed by others. Christian hurtled through the kitchen to the sink, poured himself a glass of water, swallowed it down, tore the window open, and held his face out to the cool darkness. Scraps of words were heard in the background.

". . . you don't understand . . . complicated . . ."

Gertrud entered the kitchen, ran to Christian. He grabbed her hands, wanted to hold her tight, but she yelled that she was going. With Hanna. Her mind was made up. Something like that.

Then Hanna. Who turned it all around: "Don't send him away." She said that they were only sisters.

Then Gertrud flipped. Set on her husband, attacked him, shouted. She went crazy, lashing out, scratching. Hanna held her back, Gertrud collapsed, tears. Christian left the house and raced out of the drive, gravel spraying.

Silence in the house, silence on the terrace. Tonio, behind a bush, held his breath.

And then there was Gertrud's monologue. This heap of incredibly tragic knowledge, infinite guilt, that she painstakingly released from inside herself and dumped before Hanna as if before a judge, as if seeking absolution.

But Hanna gave no absolution. Hanna left.

Gertrud stayed. Destroyed. Her world in ruins. Heart broken in pieces. Everything.

The doorbell rang again. And Gertrud jumped up, full of delight, thinking it was Hanna. Still hoping for absolution, for a second chance, a second life.

But it wasn't Hanna.

Tonio had never seen the visitor before. But Gertrud seemed to know him well. Gertrud let him in, without a hint of surprise. Let him in to her kitchen. She appeared to be unafraid, to have no hint of doubt. As if it were perfectly normal for him to come to her house at that time of night—as if it were a daily ritual.

79

It was as if it were normal for him to come to her house at that time of night, as if it were normal for him to bring death with him. Because he did bring death. Not immediately. Not right away. He probably didn't even know it when he arrived. He was probably as surprised by the dreadful sequence of events, the awful dynamics of all the decisions that followed, as Tonio out on the terrace, as Gertrud.

It looked like a peaceful visit. They sat across from one another at the table, talking quietly. Tonio couldn't hear any of it.

He didn't dare come any closer to the window. They would have seen him: a ghost in the night, a shadow that didn't belong there.

Later, Tonio couldn't recall how the idea had come to him. Suddenly, it was there in his head and he gave in to it, quietly leaving his place on the terrace and slipping down the garden path until he reached the man's car. Tonio felt the hood. It was still warm. He nodded in satisfaction, and then took a picture of the license plate with his cell phone. Later he would do a bit of hacking, child's play. It was always good to know who he was dealing with.

Cautiously, he slipped back to the terrace.

The scene in the kitchen had changed. No longer peaceful. Gertrud had leapt up and was gesticulating wildly with her arms, her voice loud, shrill, cracking. She had been stirred up by the day's events, which had exposed her life like never before. She had been drinking, she had lost all stability—but the visitor couldn't have known all that.

From behind his bush by the window, Tonio heard his father's name, heard Hanna's name. He stared, transfixed and shocked. He saw the silhouettes of the two people whose voices had suddenly grown loud, who were fighting with one another. He saw the knife in the man's hand, as if it had arrived there by chance, and then saw his arm move . . . his hand . . . forward . . . toward Gertrud . . . who stood as if mesmerized . . .

. . . and then the pain spread, the cold, the gray of the in-between . . . she fell . . . lay . . . stretched out . . .

. . . the man . . . as if mesmerized, the knife still in his hand, Gertrud lying on the floor, stammering out words. The knife fell, clattering on the tiles, into the blood that flowed fast from the wound, spreading out around Gertrud, giving her back her stability, her contours . . .

Tonio thought . . . nothing, nothing . . .

The man in the kitchen eventually broke the spell that bound him, took a step back, looked around, breathed deeply, leaned briefly on the table with both arms, and gradually got control over himself.

And then, finally, he ran from the kitchen—out the front door, down the garden path, and through the gate.

Tonio sprinted after him, saw him get into the car and drive away, saw the rear lights of the car gliding away into the darkness and being swallowed up by the distance. His hand gripped the cool case of his cell phone tightly. He thought of the photo of the registration number. He thought that it would now be easy to find out to whom the car belonged. He felt his heart racing.

Later, back in the apartment, he began to shake. *So you're not so tough,* he thought, *not such a cool character.* For some reason that pleased him.

He lay down on the bed, but as soon as he closed his eyes, he saw Gertrud in front of him, lying in her own blood, with staring eyes and a new knowledge on her face.

Eventually he slept, and dreamed of Kristin.

80

The morning had been sobering. Franza had found it a great effort to force herself out of bed. *An old woman,* she thought, *that's what I am. I can't even handle two glasses of red wine and a few cigarettes.*

"Couldn't you sleep?" Herz asked when she reached the office.

She looked at him and saw that he didn't look any better. "You neither?"

He nodded. "The time always comes when they start to haunt you," he said with a sigh. "When that happens, there's nothing to be done about it. It's time for the final leg."

Franza nodded. "I don't think Lilli has anything to do with Gertrud's murder. I don't want to believe it."

"But she was in the house."

"Yes, I know."

"And she would have had a motive."

"Yes, I know."

They were silent. Then Herz began again. "What really worries me is the fact . . ."

". . . that she also turned up at Tonio's." Franza completed his sentence. "And what he could have done with her. And what he could have done with Hanna."

Herz nodded. "Precisely! And the fact that we've still found no trace of him."

Franza's cell phone rang. It was Borger. "The fingerprints on the knife. None of them belong to your young Lilli."

She breathed a sigh of relief.

"Is that a sigh of relief?" Borger asked.

She had to smile. "Yes, it is."

"And now you're smiling," he said with a grin.

"And now you're grinning," she said.

"You got it. But back to the point, I've got something else. We've run everything. All the things you sent us. So, there are some interesting patterns."

"Lilli is Hanna's daughter," Franza interrupted. "And Tonio is Lilli's brother."

"Yes," Borger said, sounding a little disappointed. "Yes, though I see you know that already."

"Don't be upset, Borger," Franza said, unable to stop herself from smiling again. "We needed confirmation. So you've been a great help to us."

"OK." Borger sighed. "Back to work."

"Well, at least it's something," Herz said, although he didn't sound too pleased.

"Let's go back to the Brendlers'," Franza said. "Perhaps there'll be some news. Perhaps our distinguished attorney will have reappeared. Perhaps . . ."

"Deep breath, Franza," Herz said. "Breathe deeply!"

But it wasn't so easy. *If you only knew,* she thought as they went out to the car. *If you only knew, my dear Herz!*

Last night there had been hardly anyone there—no wonder, given how late it was. He'd been at the bar, all alone, his back turned to her. Wearing a blue jacket. With a glass of red wine in front of him. All as he had described. It was as if he was giving her the chance to have a good look at him before approaching. But she'd had no need to look. She recognized him immediately. And fled.

Herz's cell phone rang. He switched it to speaker.

"One of you should come," Arthur said. "We've got Bonnie and Clyde."

81

They didn't actually have Bonnie and Clyde yet, but they had received an interesting call—a very interesting call. It was from the maid at a motel by the autobahn, who had been watching television on and off, her attention wandering. An item caught her eye—the missing-person announcement that appeared on the noon news. When they showed the composite, it looked somehow familiar—a customer she had seen fleetingly, very fleetingly.

He had seemed a little reserved, and she had also noticed hair lying around the toilet in his room. Not too much, just a small clump that she only noticed when she bent down to give the toilet and the area around it a thorough clean. She did this, she pointed out, because she was a thorough person. Always had been. She'd wondered where the hair had come from because the woman who was also staying in the room had light brown hair and the man had a shaven head.

There had been something about the picture on the TV screen that nagged at her, but she hadn't realized its significance immediately. Then she remembered the little clump of hair, dark, slightly curly, like the hair of the man in the picture . . . it had clicked.

She'd told them all this over the phone, first to some dumb duty officer with no responsibility, who was only doing his job, and then to someone who had at least a bit of responsibility, and finally to someone who had even more. And now two plainclothes officers had arrived at the motel, one introducing himself as Herz, the other saying he was the one she'd spoken to on the phone: Arthur Peterson.

"Heppner," she replied, refusing the proffered hand. "Sieglinde Heppner." She told her story once again, eagerly, in great detail and with some excitement.

She looked a little embarrassed as she came to an end.

"I hope I'm not getting anyone into trouble here, but"—she paused, as if examining her own thoughts—"but it seemed strange to me, is all. Odd. Yes, that's it, odd. They were behaving oddly, those two. As if they were hiding. And he hardly left the room. Only at night, when it was dark."

How does she know so much? Herz thought. *Is she always working, day and night?*

He sincerely hoped that he'd never find himself in a situation where others watched him surreptitiously and later described him as "odd" and "strange."

On the other hand, they had to be pleased that there were people like this Sieglinde Heppner in the world, who watched others observantly even if only to satisfy their own curiosity or out of boredom.

No! He shook his head. That was unfair.

Frau Heppner paused, looking irritated. "No? What do you mean?"

He laughed. "Nothing, Frau Heppner, nothing at all. I'm sorry, I was just thinking. Please continue."

"Yes, well," she said. "That's it, really. There's nothing more to tell. Do you want to see the room? I've got the key card here."

"By all means," Herz said. "By all means."

He gave her a friendly smile. *What will we find?* he thought as he followed Arthur and the woman. *What next?*

"Are the two of them still here, do you know?"

She shook her head. "No, unfortunately not. They left a while ago. You should have gotten here quicker."

Hm, Herz thought, *do you think we can fly? We're only human.* "By car?"

Another shake of her head. "No, they didn't have one. At least, not in the parking lot here. I"—she hesitated—"I investigated a bit. But I didn't dare follow them out onto the street."

"That's good, Frau Heppner," Herz said. "It's a good thing you didn't do that. That could've been dangerous. And it's not your job. That's our job."

She nodded, blushed slightly, and stopped outside a door.

"This is it," she said.

"Thank you," Herz said. "Thank you very much, Frau Heppner."

She stood there hesitantly. Herz sighed inwardly. The same old story. Burning curiosity. The reluctance to leave.

He smiled. "That'll be all, thanks. If you could just give me the key card?"

"Oh," she said. "Right. Yes. The card."

She gave it to him. "Yes, well . . ." she nodded, a little embarrassed. "I hope I've been helpful to you."

"You certainly have. Many thanks once again," Herz said kindly and offered his hand.

Once she had gone, the two police officers positioned themselves on either side of the door and slipped the safeties off their guns. Herz cautiously slid the card into the slot. There was a soft click, and the door opened. Herz pushed it wide and called loud and clear, "Police!"

Nothing moved.

The detectives entered the room cautiously, checking left and right. Arthur pushed the bathroom door open—the light went on, nothing. Just a gaping emptiness.

They finally stopped in the middle of the room, secured their guns, and slipped them back into their holsters.

"Once again they're ahead of us," Arthur said angrily.

"Well," Herz said, "at least this time we can be on the lookout for them and hopefully catch them. This time they don't know we're on their trail. At least I don't think so. In the meantime, let's look to see if we can find anything here. There might be something to help us."

They began a systematic search. Arthur started in the bathroom. Nothing particularly interesting: toothbrushes that looked as though they had just been bought, a few other toiletry items, scarcely touched. On the bed were a few plastic bags containing clothing, some of which still had the tags attached.

"It all looks new," Herz said.

"No wonder. They needed to buy everything new—they left the apartment in such a rush they didn't take anything with them."

He picked up one of the bags and emptied the contents out onto the bed. The last item that fell out was a set of hair clippers.

"Oh," Arthur said, "look at this! Look at this! What have we here? The hair clippers for changing his identity."

"That's right," Herz said. "Looking at all this, I'd say we've definitely hit on something."

"But why stay at a motel here? Why didn't they disappear into the sunset ages ago?"

They thought about it.

"Perhaps they're not ready yet. Perhaps they still have something to do."

"But what?"

"Hanna? Is she a hostage? And Lilli too, now?"

Arthur shrugged helplessly. "I don't know. No idea. I'm lost now."

"Courage, my boy," Herz said, sitting down on the bed and slowly gazing around the room once again. "It'll come. Believe me. It always does."

He suddenly jumped up, went to the desk, bent down, and fished something out from under it. He looked at it and held it up with satisfaction. A book of matches.

"It seems that one of them smokes," he said cheerfully. "That's great for us. Especially as there's something on it." He held up the matchbook and read out the name and address of a bar.

He smiled. "It's always nice when our birds sing. Let's get over there now."

He threw the book of matches over to Arthur, who frowned. "But it might not mean anything," he said sullenly.

"It might not," Herz said. "But it might! Might! And will! I can smell it. Or feel it in my bones. Whichever you prefer. Trust an old dog. Onward and upward. Come on!"

And he stormed out, hot on the new trail.

82

Back into the world?

Now?

Back from the peace and quiet?

Perhaps . . . yes, perhaps it's time to face things. I have to see Dorothee again, to talk to her. Not everything can have gone wrong.

I switched my cell phone on briefly a few hours ago, and the world has slipped a little closer. A lot of calls. A lot of texts. I'm not going to answer any of them. We've reached the end.

I don't know, he wrote. *I don't understand why anymore. I only know I have to die.*

Have to die . . . What a strange expression. Isn't that coming to us all?

The birds are flying south. I'm not going with them.

He asks me to forgive him. For everything. *Forgive me, Hanna. For everything.*

83

He ascended the stairs at his usual leisurely pace and asked for directions. They sent him to Oberwieser and Herz, but they were not there. He eventually ended up in Hansen's office.

"What can I do for you?" he asked.

"Nothing," the visitor said, mischievously. "You can't do anything for me. But maybe I can do something for you. Does the name Hanna Umlauf mean anything to you?"

He immediately had Hansen's attention.

He said she'd been at his cemetery. He was the priest of St. Peter's parish, and she had turned up there looking for a particular grave. He'd helped her to find it.

"So she's alive," Hansen said, filled with relief. "Are you sure?"

The priest frowned and stroked his beard.

"Yes," he said. "Yes. She was very much alive. A very likeable lady and very much alive. We had a good talk, but sadly not for too long. She seemed to be in a bit of a hurry."

The priest also had a good talk with Hansen. This one was also not for long. Hansen was also suddenly in a hurry.

84

"She's alive," Hansen said on the telephone. "Hanna Umlauf's alive."

He announced it twice, once to Franza and once to Felix. Both times he felt his colleagues' huge relief. He intended to announce it a third time, but that didn't happen because the call wasn't answered—the cell phone was off.

Hansen tried a few more times before finally giving up. He stared into space for a moment. And suddenly had an idea, as if pulled from the air. He began to investigate, without quite knowing why. And he made some surprising discoveries.

85

"Hanna's alive," Franza said after getting off the phone with Hansen. "We still don't know where she is, but at least we know with some certainty that she's alive."

"Thank God," whispered Dorothee, closing her eyes for a moment. "At least that's something."

"Maybe . . ." Franza said on a sudden impulse, ". . . maybe Lilli is with her."

Dorothee's eyes shot open, and she stared at Franza with a long, dark gaze.

Just under an hour ago, Franza had arrived and found Dorothee alone.

"Do you know where your husband is?" she had asked her.

Dorothee had merely shrugged helplessly.

"Why?" she asked now, with a choke in her voice. "Why would Lilli be with Hanna? And how would she have found her?"

"Perhaps it was just a question of logic," Franza said. "Yes, that's probably it—it's so logical that Lilli grasped it."

"But she doesn't know her at all." Dorothee was still trying to defend herself.

"Hanna is . . ."

"Hanna is Lilli's mother." Dorothee completed Franza's cautious statement for her. "Yes, she is. But there's no way Lilli can know."

Franza felt a small, sad smile rising inside her. Dorothee was doing what many people do: she was shutting herself off from knowledge that was already there, that had already crept into her heart and her mind. She had closed off, afraid of facing its power, afraid of facing what it represented, what it would change.

"Yes, she can," Franza said quietly. "She can, and you know that, Frau Brendler. All Lilli needs to do is put two and two together."

"If she's done anything to herself . . ." Dorothee said tonelessly.

Franza shook her head vehemently. "No, I don't believe she has! I'm sure she hasn't."

"If my husband . . ." Dorothee continued.

Franza shook her head again. "There wouldn't be any reason for it. We'll figure everything out. And until we do, you shouldn't think such thoughts."

But she knew people always thought such thoughts. People turned them over and over in their minds, and they grew into huge monsters that ate them up. Then they were trapped in their thoughts, in fear.

Franza knew it from her own experience. Yet she still tried to calm them when they were worried, tried to take away their fears, to relieve the agony of realization, of knowledge.

"So," she said, "let's start at the beginning. Have you called all Lilli's friends and acquaintances?"

Dorothee nodded. "Yes, we have. Christian and I. All of them. No one knows anything. She isn't with any of them."

"And you believe that?"

They heard the front door. Dorothee turned around, jumped up. Hans Brendler entered.

"Hans! Where have you been? I've been worried. I thought . . . Lilli . . ."

"What?" he asked blankly. "Lilli? What's going on with Lilli?"

"She's gone," Dorothee yelled. "Our Lilli has gone!"

"Our Lilli," he murmured. "Our Lilli will never forgive us . . ."

His expression was so empty that Franza was suddenly no longer certain that he wouldn't do anything to himself. He turned away, turned to his wife.

"And you thought I . . . ?"

She was silent, didn't look at him.

They're losing it, Franza thought. *Now they're both lost to one another.*

"Where have you been?" Dorothee asked.

He shrugged. "No idea. Somewhere or other. It's not important. I wanted to be alone. Get my head around it all somehow."

"I needed you," she said.

He didn't reply.

86

They parked the car around the corner. They wanted to remain inconspicuous, not rush in guns ablaze—no blue lights or sirens, a nice quiet approach. At least at first.

Arthur grinned. This was pure adrenalin, warming his veins and causing his blood to simmer. It was almost like sex with Karolina, so much fun. It was a kick, all right—showing up, talking, acting, if necessary. And he really hoped it would be necessary to act. To put dangerous murderers behind bars, a certain amount of commotion was certainly allowed, even expected. IDs out first. State the case. Explain themselves clearly, calmly. Then: *Pow!* Cut to the chase. Handcuffs clicking around Bonnie and Clyde's wrists after their weapons have been taken away. Later, he'd welcome the flurry of flashes from the regional press cameras—or even better, those of the national press—and finally a pat on the back from the chief of police and some words of praise for our capable young Arthur Peterson, the rising star in the police force, the nemesis of all criminal elements. Finally, the high point: Karolina would be waiting in the wings, her not-inconsiderable breast swelling with pride, and his mother, shedding a tear or two of joy.

Yes. That was how it should be. Arthur grinned to himself, but outwardly a little, too.

"Hey!" Herz said. "Boy! Daydreaming of fame and fortune again?" He smiled affectionately. "Keep calm, OK? We don't know what's waiting for us. Perhaps nothing. Perhaps zilch, nada, *niente*."

Shit, Arthur thought. *Caught in the act.* He blushed and lowered his head so that Herz wouldn't notice. But Herz noticed everything, as Arthur well knew.

"Yes," he said, subdued. "Yes, Boss, I know."

Herz smiled and touched the young man's elbow.

"It's all right," he said. "Nothing to worry about."

Then they were there, and it all happened fast. And unspectacularly—too unspectacularly for Arthur's liking.

It didn't begin too badly. They entered the bar and looked around. No familiar faces. The door to the terrace was open, and there were a few tables out there as the sun was still pleasantly warm.

Arthur recognized the woman immediately. His heart began to beat a little more loudly.

She was sitting at a table by the door—a woman in her early thirties, face turned to the Indian summer sun, soaking up the last vestiges of warmth before the gray of the approaching fall and winter. The wisps of smoke from her cigarette rose into the light, dissipating like fine dust motes.

Huh, thought Arthur with a slight feeling of regret, *smoking's just bad for your health; so bad for your health that—zap—it'll get you. What a waste.*

But she suspected nothing. Her eyes were closed as if she was waiting for something, for someone. It was as if she had all the time in the world, as if nothing or no one could want anything of her. She was an angel, beautiful, innocent.

Opposite her and turned slightly away, with his back to the police officers, sat a man with a shaved head. He was a little older than she was. He looked tense, restless, nervous, his head turning back and forth, his foot tapping the ground, beating out a rhythm that only he knew.

Arthur tapped Herz on the shoulder. Herz turned to him with a questioning look, and Arthur indicated the terrace door with his head.

"OK," Herz said softly. "Let's go. Quietly—we don't want to disturb the other customers."

Slowly, silently, they approached the table, their right hands poised inconspicuously over their holsters—out of sight of other patrons but ready to remove the safeties rapidly if needed, if the situation escalated. Their left hands held their IDs.

Felix stayed in the background to allow Arthur to step forward, a shadow falling in the path of Kristin's sun. She opened her eyes in irritation and blinked.

"Hi, Bonnie," Arthur said with a smile. "Lovely to see you again."

87

The computer spewed a lot of information onto the screen. Hansen sighed. Looked like a lot of work. Ah well, such was life. He thought briefly of his approaching holiday. Two weeks in Spain in the late September sun. He immediately felt better.

He quickly scrolled through the reports. He was convinced it wouldn't produce anything, but it was better than sitting there with a thousand thoughts about Gertrud Rabinsky's murder and Lilli Brendler's disappearance swirling around his head. It was a good distraction.

At first it was mostly uninteresting. A successful man, this guy—respected, wealthy. A perfect life. Almost. And then . . . suddenly . . . that little twist, that little niggle.

88

The detectives had everything under control. Kristin sat frozen in her seat, while Tonio jumped up.

Felix directed the proceedings in a sharp voice. "Police! Sit back down! Hands on the table! You're under arrest!"

Arthur pacified the other customers and the staff, showed his ID, and said loud and clear that they were carrying out a police operation. There was no reason to panic. Everything was under control.

Then he asked the head waiter for a quiet room where they could talk in peace with the pair under arrest. With a sigh of relief that the excitement was over, the head waiter guided the four troublemakers into a room that smelled as though it was a staff smoking room.

"Take a seat," Herz said, showing Kristin and Tonio where to sit. Already the cogs of Kristin's cool legal brain had begun to turn.

"What exactly are we accused of?" she asked. "Is it a crime to enjoy a coffee in peace?"

"No, no," Herz said in a firm voice. "That's certainly allowed, provided you don't also have any criminal intentions, or you haven't previously committed a crime such as murder."

Tonio leapt up. "What? Murder? You can't believe I'd—"

"We do believe it, yes," Herz said slowly, although for some reason he was no longer so certain. "You've already avoided arrest once by running away. We normally take that as a clear admission of guilt."

"That's garbage! Sheer garbage!"

"Prove me wrong."

Kristin stepped in now. "Since when has it been the norm in this country for respectable citizens to be required to prove their innocence? As far as I know, the opposite is true. You have to prove our guilt, and you can't do that! Because we're not guilty."

Herz suppressed a smile. *A fierce young woman,* he thought.

"Easy," he said calmly. "Easy, now! Let's just talk calmly to one another. That'll get us a whole lot further." He paused briefly. "So, what are you doing here? What, or rather *who*, were you waiting for here?"

They looked at each other, shrugged.

"Nothing," they said together. "No one. We were having a coffee here, enjoying the sun."

"Listen," Herz said, gradually becoming harsher, "we don't have all the time in the world. So, once again: What were you doing here? What or who were you waiting for here?"

They were silent for a moment before Tonio asked a question of his own.

"What on earth gives you the idea that I . . . could have murdered Gertrud Rabinsky?"

Felix smiled. "Well, that tells me that you do know what all this is about. Now, let's begin calmly at the beginning. So you admit that you knew Frau Rabinsky."

He hesitated. "Knew? No. You can't really say that."

"Well, it seems you knew her well enough to have—how shall I put it?—stalked her a little. I assume you're not really going to deny it."

Shit, Tonio thought. *Shit.* He shook his head uncertainly. "Now, you shouldn't take that the wrong way."

"So, in what way should it be taken?"

He said nothing, suddenly aware of how bad his position was.

Felix continued, "We've searched your apartment. And found a whole load of things. A whole load of evidence that suggests you've created a veritable list of grievances against Gertrud Rabinsky and Hanna Umlauf."

Tonio shook his head in amazement. "What garbage! Why would I have done that?"

"Because they effectively took your father from you."

Tonio laughed out loud. "Bullshit! No one took my father from me. He did that himself. I never knew him, never even saw him."

"So what *was* your motive for killing Gertrud Rabinsky?"

Tonio jumped up, stretching out his arms in despair. "None! Please believe me! I didn't have a motive. And I didn't kill her either! You've got to believe me!"

"Sit down," Felix said firmly. "We haven't *got* to believe anything you say. I hope you realize how serious your situation is. You should cooperate with us."

Tonio slumped into his chair, a picture of misery.

"I'll cooperate," he said. "I know when I've lost."

"Good," Felix said. "I'm listening."

Tonio turned toward him.

"I watched her. Yes, that's true. It became a bit like an addiction. Suddenly . . . you get involved in the life of another person and then you can't tear yourself away." He shook his head, as if unable to believe it himself. "It takes on a life of its own, everything starts moving so incredibly fast."

"Why were you watching her? Were you looking for something you could blackmail her with? And then, when you saw that wasn't working, you lost your nerve and grabbed the knife that was already there in the kitchen?"

Tonio shook his head again.

"No," he said. "No, honestly, that's not true. There was nothing I could have blackmailed her with. I simply wanted to . . . hear her story. I wanted to hear something about my father. I wanted to know what happened. How he died. How it was possible to drown in a sea like the Aegean." He broke off, laughed softly, a little bitterly. "I wanted to know whether he ever talked about me. Or about my mother. What we meant to him. Whether we were ever anything to him. Anything at all."

He fell silent.

Felix felt Tonio's nebulous pain and could suddenly understand why this lack of memories haunted him, why he wanted to know about his father, and when the opportunity arose, he . . .

Felix believed him. Gradually. Increasingly.

"Tell me," he said. "Tell me from the beginning."

And Tonio told his story: about the inheritance; about how this family suddenly erupted into his life, a family that was new to him, unknown and unexpected; and about how, at first, fear had been greater than pleasure.

He told them how all these people had suddenly emerged. First his father and then the two women. He'd been amazed at what a deeply rooted part of his father's life they'd been. He sensed that their traces ran more deeply and more forcefully than those of his mother or himself. If he were honest, neither he nor his mother had left any traces at all in his father's life.

That had hurt in a way that had taken him completely by surprise, because he had never imagined it would affect him like that. But now it propelled him to look into the past. He wanted to know, know, know.

And so he sent that letter to Hanna, who was living in France. And forced his way into Gertrud's life.

"And with your actions you set a lot of wheels in motion," Felix said.

Tonio nodded and hung his head. "Yes, I certainly did."

"Where's Lilli?" Felix asked.

"Lilli?" Tonio looked up, and smiled. "My little sister?"

"Yes," Felix said. "That's exactly who I mean."

"I have no idea," Tonio said. "Honestly! No idea. She came. We talked. She left."

"Where did she go?"

"She wanted to look for Hanna."

"And where's Hanna?"

"I don't know that, either," Tonio said. "I really don't! No idea!"

Felix nodded. And he believed him. There was no reason not to believe him.

"But you saw something that night."

Tonio sighed, glanced at Kristin.

"Canada," he murmured. "We can forget Canada."

She said nothing. A scenario began to take shape in Felix's mind.

"Doesn't matter," Felix said. "It's beautiful here, too. The trees change color in fall here, too." He smiled. "So, what did you see? And, most importantly, who did you see? Who did you see that you wanted to blackmail now?"

Tonio sighed.

"A lot," he said. "I saw a lot."

89

Hansen leaned back in his seat and stared at the screen. He was completely stunned. Fifty thousand was not an insignificant amount. Not at all. Having or not having fifty thousand made a difference. *A big difference,* Hansen thought. He found it remarkable that it could be obtained so easily. Just like that. And to get it from a source from which there had allegedly been no contact at all—no contact at all for years. Now he knew that wasn't true—they'd lied. There it was, just six months ago—fifty thousand.

Hansen leaned back, tapped his fingertips together, rocked a little on his chair, and thought about it.

So, he thought, *I think fifty thousand means something happened, something very powerful!*

He picked up his cell phone, typed a text, and sent it twice.

90

"He's in his room," Tonio said resignedly, waving a hand toward the window. "At least, he hasn't checked out yet. We'd arranged to meet him here, but the asshole didn't show up. Instead . . ."

". . . we did." Arthur completed his sentence for him. Tonio nodded. Herz had gone over to the window. "Over there? In his room?"

What was all this about? Some kind of distraction technique? Was this someone wanting to take the pressure off himself with vague accusations and wild speculation? But Herz had lived and seen and heard too much in his time. He wasn't about to fall for anything easily.

"Yes," Tonio said, "in the hotel. You can see the back from here. The Babenberger. It's a luxury hotel for the upper class. Don't you know it?"

Felix deliberately ignored the sarcastic undertone. The Babenberger? He thought for a moment.

The Babenberger. He knew it, of course, and he'd come across it recently, he was sure of it, but when?

There was a sudden beep from Felix's cell phone. He opened the text. Hansen. Stating that fifty thousand had been shifted from one account to another—quietly and more or less secretly. There was no business transaction connected to it, at least not one that a quick search had shown up. Hansen found it a little strange, given that they'd claimed there'd been zero contact for years. The money had changed hands six months ago, which meant a lie or two had been told. What could be the reason for paying someone that much money?

Maybe he was mistaken and it had little—or nothing—to do with the case. Or maybe it did. And now Belitz had also disappeared—turned off his cell phone.

Felix looked again at the back of the hotel.

Belitz? Jonas Belitz? Hanna Umlauf's worried husband?

And he suddenly remembered where he'd recently heard about the Babenberger. He turned.

"Belitz?" he asked. "Are we talking about Jonas Belitz?"

Tonio raised his eyebrows in surprise. "Yes. The very man. That's exactly who we're talking about."

91

"Fifty thousand euros," Franza said, whistling softly through her teeth as she closed the text. "That's quite a sum of money, don't you think, Herr Brendler?"

He glanced at her, and she could see that he knew what she was talking about. He turned away in silence.

Dorothee looked from one to the other. "What are you talking about?"

"You should ask your husband," Franza said. "I think he could explain it better than I can."

"What's happening? What do you want?" Hans said. "Shouldn't you be spending your time solving my daughter's murder instead of speculating wildly about things that have nothing to do with you, things you don't understand?"

He was angry, sad, bewildered—all at once.

"So can you explain it to me, please?" Franza said.

"Yes," Dorothee said. "Explain it!"

He closed his eyes briefly and shrugged. "Jonas called me about six months ago. He wanted to meet me in Munich."

"What? What are you saying?" Dorothee turned and faced him. "Why didn't you tell me? What did he want? Money, it seems!"

He made to stroke her hair, but she turned her head away, and his arm hung in the air for a second as if in free fall.

"I didn't want to worry you," he said quietly. "And yes, he wanted money. And I gave it to him."

"Why?" Franza asked. "Why did he want so much money?"

Dorothee laughed scornfully. "That's nothing. We've paid a lot more than that before."

"He wanted it for Hanna, as a kind of security," Brendler said, sitting down. "He told me he was very ill and didn't have long to live. Said he had debts from the gallery and that he could cover those debts with my money. That way, at least Hanna wouldn't have any financial worries if he . . ."

"Extortion, then," said Franza thoughtfully. "What with?"

Brendler shook his head. "No, not extortion. I gave him the money willingly. It was for Hanna, after all."

He looked at his wife.

"But you'd already paid him a lot more?" Silence.

"It's all come to this," Dorothee said flatly. "It's all come to this!" She turned to her husband. "Tell her. You tell her. I can't do it anymore."

He nodded, put his head in his hands.

"Jonas married Hanna and I couldn't prevent it. I would have, if I could. But it wasn't in my power."

"Why did you want to prevent it?"

"Because it wasn't right. Because . . . because it just wasn't right."

"You'll have to explain that to me," Franza said, leaning forward. "What do you mean by that?"

He said nothing. He simply sat there, staring at the table. Dorothee began to talk.

"My husband paid him money to pacify him. To keep quiet. Leave us alone. That was what he used to buy the gallery."

"So much money? Enough for him to finance a gallery? So much hush money?"

Brendler raised his head. "He turned up right after Lilli was born. You could call it chance or fate. Whatever. In any case, he was suddenly standing there at the door when Hanna's baby was three days old. Hanna was sick in her room and Gertrud had already taken the baby for herself, had already . . . become her mother. It didn't take long for Jonas to see what was going on. He was never short of imagination. What could I do?" He laughed bitterly. "He was my best friend. From way back when we were kids. We did everything together. I met my wife through him."

He gave her a long look. "We lived together when we were students. They were good times. Afterward, I came here and worked in my father's law office, while he tried to establish himself as a freelance photographer. He didn't do too well at first, but he didn't mind. He was a survivor. He always managed somehow, living here or there. Eventually he went to London, made a name for himself, and earned a lot of money. But he always visited us, again and again during that time. We never knew when he'd come. It was always a surprise. He'd stay with us, sometimes only for a couple of days, sometimes for a few weeks. That was also OK. The house was big enough and we liked it. They were good times. We were like extended family."

No, Franza thought, *an illusion of it at best.*

"He watched the girls grow up," Brendler continued. "He liked them, they liked him. He didn't have any children himself, so it was always a big deal whenever he came. They liked it when he stayed. He involved them in his photography, and that was the kick start for Hanna's career. He was a good friend. The best a man could wish for. Really. For all of us. But then he arrived at the wrong time."

He stood. "Anyone want a glass of wine?"

Franza shook her head. Dorothee didn't move. He went into the kitchen and returned with a glass and an opened bottle. "Maybe I should get used to the idea of drinking more. They say it makes everything more bearable."

"Only at the start," Franza said. "Only at the start. It all gets harder later on."

He nodded.

"I know," he said. "I know. It was supposed to be a joke. But this isn't the time for joking."

"Carry on with the story," Franza said.

He shrugged. "That was it, really."

"No," Dorothee said. "No, that wasn't it."

She took a deep breath. "I was so shocked when he appeared there suddenly at the door. We hadn't heard a thing from him for three years! And suddenly . . . there he was. He of all people. With his usual grin on his face. His lightheartedness. And there we were . . . with all that going on in the house."

She shook her head. "I didn't want to let him in. I told him it was a bad time. He should look for somewhere else to stay. He just looked at me blankly, pushed me aside, and was in. He asked after the girls. That was always his first question: 'How are the girls? Where are the girls?' I didn't know what to say. I went after him, and that was when he heard Lilli. She was hungry and crying dreadfully. Gertrud came down the stairs with her to make up a bottle. Jonas was thunderstruck. He looked at the baby, looked at me, looked at Gertrud. 'My daughter,' she said. 'My daughter, Lilli.' Jonas was shocked and said, 'But I had no idea that you . . .' And she countered with: 'Why would you? You haven't been here for ages.' That floored him—at first, but then . . ."

She took a gulp of her husband's wine.

"He settled in, as at home as ever. The next day it became clear that Hanna was also there, sick in bed. 'Why don't you take her to the hospital?' he asked, and I said, why should I—after all, I was a doctor. He said we should anyway, since she was so unwell—a blind man could see there was something wrong. And he looked at me as though I was a criminal. And I felt like one."

She fell silent.

"I'm pretty sure he knew by then," Brendler continued. "That evening he came into my study, sat down, said nothing for a while. Then finally he said, 'Nothing's ever as it seems, is it?' I didn't deny it. I was angry, asked him what these insinuations meant, would he kindly drop it. But he said, 'Enough! Don't give me that bullshit, Hans! I know you too well.'"

He fell silent, took a deep breath. "What could I do?"

"You did the wrong thing, Hans," Dorothee said.

He nodded. "Yes. The wrong thing."

He looked at her. There was no warmth between them anymore.

"I told him everything. Everything. I knew even as I was telling him that it was a mistake. I looked into his eyes, saw his horror, his disbelief, but I couldn't stop talking. And I felt such a relief to be getting it all out . . . to be unloading."

He fell silent, drank his wine, and poured himself some more.

"We sat there for a long time in silence. Didn't look at each other. Eventually he said he was broke. And that he'd had enough of roaming around the world. He'd found a woman who would stick with him and there was a gallery in Strasbourg he could take over. But that he was broke at the moment."

Wow, Franza thought. *Wow, so that's where friendships can lead—up a dark one-way street. Where there's no going back. Not a step.*

"I asked him how much. He named a sum. A substantial sum. I got out my checkbook, wrote a check, and laid it on the desk. Then I went to bed. I slept like I hadn't done for days."

He sighed deeply. "The next morning I went into my office first thing. The check was no longer there. And Jonas . . . Jonas was also gone, vanished, just as he had come. Three days later the check was cashed."

Silence.

I've had enough of this, Franza thought. *I'm tired of hearing all these goddamn stories over and over.*

"What happened then?" she asked.

He shrugged. "Nothing more. It was like a final blow. Our friendship was over. Neither of us tried to make contact again. He didn't come to the house anymore. And we didn't go to see him. We never went to that gallery in Strasbourg. It was the last time we saw one another."

"Until six months ago," Franza said.

He looked up, nodded. "Until six months ago. He looked bad. Ill. I hardly recognized him."

Franza stood. "Thanks for being so open. We'll be in touch."

She moved to go, paused, and then turned back and looked at Dorothee. "Weren't you ever worried that Hanna would come back to claim her daughter?"

A brief moment's silence.

"Yes," Dorothee said. "Yes. Always. Every second of the day." There was a dull grayness in her voice, resignation, the end. "But things were as they were. We'd made our decision. There was no going back."

Franza nodded. Yes, that was how some things happened. Irreversible. Some decisions were for life. Irreversible. No going back.

She was finally about to go, when Dorothee's voice held her back. "What about Lilli?"

"Just give her a bit of time," Franza said, pausing briefly. "And her mother."

Tears were running down Dorothee's cheeks, but Franza no longer saw them. Her cell phone beeped. It was a text from Sonja. *My husband's a goddamn asshole.*

92

It would have been so easy if she had just kept quiet. If she'd kept quiet like she had for all those years. Sometimes you just had to keep quiet.

But she had to talk, spill it all out. She had to accuse him—he, who, after all, had done the least wrong, who had just slipped into the story by a stupid chance.

He had only come to the house because he'd hoped she would know where Hanna was, since those incompetent police officers hadn't gotten anywhere with finding her.

But everything had gotten out of hand. And somehow he'd seen red. As she started her threats to tell Hanna that he'd accepted vast amounts of money, which meant his wealth was ultimately based on Hanna's misfortune, and that she'd never forgive him for it—on the contrary, she'd send him packing—he'd seen red.

"Send me packing?" he had asked. "Me?"

Suddenly, she had gone quiet, totally cold. He felt the chill as it drifted toward him. It made him think of the river, swathes of mist, frost on windowpanes.

"Are you scared now?" she had asked. "Are you scared that your precious Hanna will destroy you? That if she knows everything, she'll crush you underfoot like a small, hideous mealworm?"

He saw himself as a small, hideous mealworm. He saw the image like he always saw images—him in the dust and Hanna standing over him—big, powerful Hanna, her red hair gleaming like a bad omen.

He had to defend himself. Not against Hanna. No, not against her. Against Gertrud. Against Gertrud's coldness and her dreadful allegations.

"You made sure they bought your silence," she said. "Do you really think I don't know? You made sure my damn father bought your damn silence and you believed you could somehow make things right by marrying Hanna."

She paused, considered, and then shook her head. He thought everything would be all right. They could still make it right.

"No." He tried to contradict her. "I married her because I loved her. And I still do. And I wanted to be there for her, especially since she'd already lost Lilli."

He halted, helpless. "I also wanted it for you . . . And for your parents . . . We were friends, after all. We always were."

She had merely laughed, not loudly, not maliciously. It was a light, helpless laugh, but it was a laugh all the same.

"Friends?" she echoed. "You really believe that? No, surely you can't believe that. Your friendship vanished into thin air the minute you accepted that check."

"But what should I have done? Gone to the police? Denounced my best friend?"

"Yes," she said quietly. "Yes, maybe that's what you should have done. Maybe it would have been the best thing for all of us. Perhaps then we would all have had the chance to live honestly and sincerely, to be free. Perhaps that would have been your task, the reason why fate chose to send you to our house at that very moment."

She fell silent and folded her arms, lost in her own thoughts.

"And now?" he asked.

"And now," she said, "now you'll lose Hanna. Just like I'll lose Lilli. It's only fair."

That was the moment when his despair got the better of him. When he knew that he would defend himself with all his might. He wouldn't let anything else happen.

"You'll lose her," she repeated, her voice indicating such certainty that he began to shiver. "We're all going to lose."

That was what she said. She of all people. She who had benefited from it all, she who was the reason for all this . . . fuss.

He saw the last twenty-two years of his life pass before him. It all passed, it all faded: his longing, his concern, even the illness that was devouring him, the cancer that was destroying his insides, that had eaten its way into him over the years, like a silent animal that had recently begun to roar, leaving him ever less space.

But . . . it didn't matter. Nothing mattered.

The glint of the knife caught his eye. The silvery blade. And then . . .

93

She had to get rid of it all, couldn't keep it in any longer.

She said I was a plaything in an evil game, a chess piece moved back and forth. Jonas knew everything from the start and money changed hands. A lot of money. The gallery, in which my pictures hang. Where I spent so much time. Blood money.

It was so long ago when I met Jonas again. So long ago.

I'd known him almost all my life. He used to come to our house when Gertrud and I were still children. He was a friend of Gertrud's father. We liked him. He came and went at will, sometimes staying a long time, sometimes only briefly.

At one point he went to England, became a famous photographer, and exhibited in galleries all over the world. We must have been fifteen or sixteen; I don't remember. I thought it was all so wonderful—his photos, his traveling around the world. The years passed, studying in Munich, loving Tonio, holidays in Greece, on the island, Tonio's death, my own travels around the world, the pregnancy, Lilli. No dreams left to be dreamed.

What an effort it was to fight against my illness, to return from it, from that dark hole in which I had languished. How much energy it drained from me, but ultimately I emerged much stronger. I completed my studies and then I set off again, roaming the world again, searching again for pictures, impressions, life.

My first exhibitions, my first successes. And suddenly he appeared. Jonas. Elegantly dressed in black with a silk scarf around his neck. He had grown older and so had I, but I recognized him immediately.

Later he told me I was one of those women he found beautiful because they're hesitant, far from perfection, their heads not totally together. It made me laugh, and for some reason, I don't know why, I needed that so much. It did me such good, laughing with Jonas like that.

"Hanna," he said, brushing his hand against my face, nodding. "Yes," he said softly. "Yes." Nothing else. Something in him seemed to understand me.

"My photos," I said. "The exhibition. Can I show you them?"

He said no, I didn't need to. He knew my photos; he knew me, so he also knew my photos. Art shouldn't be explained.

I said nothing, a little hurt. He noticed that and tried to appease me. "Hanna, I came here by chance, just for the weekend. To think things over a little. Then I saw your poster and I had to come for a few minutes."

He waved toward the door, where a taxi was waiting. "I have to go, Hanna. My flight."

He shrugged regretfully, put his wine glass down on the shelf near the door, and left.

Years later, I received a letter. He had given himself a lot of time. *I saw you in the paper,* he wrote, *a wonderful photo, too. And I read your interview. Do you still remember me?*

I had to smile, while shaking my head in amazement. Did I remember him? *Coquettish,* I thought. *He's being coquettish.*

Even if I hadn't known him since childhood, even if he hadn't been in and out of our home, I would have known who he was. He was a big name in his field, at the zenith of his career. I was just beginning mine. To put it simply, you could say he was old and I was young. Later, much later, he would talk about himself as someone coming to the end, but I didn't let him get away with it.

His letter lay on my desk. I waited a few days, tapped it regularly with the nail of my index finger. Finally, I typed in the address in an e-mail window and wrote with trembling fingers. I said I was surprised by his message. That I . . . was pleased by it. I also liked myself in the photo, which was rare. And I clicked "Send."

His reply came immediately. He'd like to meet for a coffee—anywhere, in my town, in his, somewhere in between.

We went for the middle ground.

He talked. I listened. His life affected me. I listened. It all affected me. Fine pins and needles. I don't know why. I sat in that October wind, listening.

He looked a bit worn out, fighting for the last vestiges of a long-held love, battling lost dreams. He was full of the breakdown of his relationship. For years he had held the rip cord in his hand but never had the courage to pull it. Now his wife had beaten him to it, and surprised, he'd fallen through darkness, through hard times, and he had still not found his way back to the light.

"You've gotten thin," he said.

"No, not at all."

"You have," he said. "And your hair. So short."

"Yes."

The wind blew the ash from the cigarettes, put goose bumps on our arms. We were insufficiently dressed, not warm enough.

"I'll take you to the Tuscan sun," he said and smiled. I looked at him with shining eyes and shook my head.

He didn't relent. "But yes," he said. "It warms the heart and soul."

I laughed. "Quite the poet, Jonas."

He turned serious. "I'm not doing photography anymore," he said.

I hadn't known that. I hadn't seen any new works by him for a long while, but that he had given up completely was news to me.

"You mean you're taking a break."

He shook his head. "No, not a break. Finished."

"Why?" I was a little dismayed. He noticed that and gave me a placatory smile. He touched my arm lightly.

"It's not a bad thing," he said. "And in any case, we have you now. And you're better than I am. You've overtaken me."

I held my breath. What was he saying to me?

He nodded, as if to reinforce his statement, and smiled a little sadly.

"I have a gallery," he said. "It takes up a lot of my time. Yes, I've been settled for years. Will you visit me?"

We drove back, each to our own town, and exchanged a few e-mails.

I started traveling again, enjoying the flights, the train journeys. I enjoyed that which Jonas had long since grown bored of. Eventually I started taking my *Waiting Hall* photos. Sitting in airport departure lounges or station waiting rooms, resigned to hours of waiting because the flights or trains were delayed.

I took photos. Tiredness, hope. Sketches of waiting. Views of trains, airplanes, platforms, the broad corridor between the gates, passengers scurrying past, lonely footsteps in the darkness.

I often sat alone in the twilight, in the evenings or nights, my work done, commissions fulfilled, exhibitions over, hours away from home, laptop and notebook in my luggage. I felt the frequent specter of memory, the storm, the man, the child, her crying, but I never let it touch me, always pushed it quickly back and with it that tug in my belly and hands, that light pain in my heart. I would grab my camera and go out on the streets at night, taking pictures, as I knew that way I could bridge time, set time back to zero.

The strangeness of the flight passengers toward one another was like snowflakes that only touch one another when they land on the ground, when they fall onto one another and there's no going back.

French chansons sometimes played in the background; I found them fitting. It was as though they were about me—about me and my lover, about me and my child. The sad songs of failed lives and failed loves blended with the constant chatter of telephone calls playing out before me. Calls with friends, mothers, bosses. Agreeing to meetings, perhaps on Thursday, perhaps tomorrow, let's see what's in the schedule. The voices were sometimes young, sometimes old, sometimes tired, sometimes excited. Nothing was surprising: the dialects were familiar, a laugh was a laugh, astonishment was astonishment.

I stopped counting the hours spent traveling, eventually also stopped the exhibitions, and came to concentrate only on those moments at the airports and rail stations, waiting in readiness for the pictures, the photos, when they arose, when they were there before me. Snapshots merging into a long, endless journey inside me.

I had the clear, certain feeling that it was right, that I was on the move so that the photos could form their routes inside me, in my camera, in my eyes. All around me were people waiting to move on, the chatterers, the laughers, the newspaper readers, the telephoners, the texters, the online chatterboxes. Every now and then was the crackle and hum of alarms, of officials' radios.

Eventually, I chose only aisle seats, no longer window seats, no views of rain, fog, clouds, lights, sun, snow, whatever. I chose aisle seats so I could cross my legs, feel a little freer, a little more relaxed, not so alone. I could bear the loneliness of the hotel rooms, but it never became routine.

I always began to feel a little sad before the end of my journeys. The sadness of work completed, finished. A longing began to creep through me, displacing the magic of the beginnings.

Along the way I saw Jonas, who still wasn't taking photographs. It was as though I had taken over from him and now continued his work. He limited his activities to the gallery, curating excellent, highly regarded exhibitions.

"Things are slowing down with me," he said. "My career's in the process of decline. But yours, yours is taking off like a comet with these brilliant images of your restlessness."

He smiled, but I could feel his wistfulness. He was suffering, but I didn't know why. Perhaps he found it hard to come to terms with being the "prince consort" by my side, perhaps he was finding aging more painful than before, perhaps it was a thorn in his side. Maybe my success threatened his existence because it made him think about his own life.

I had the feeling that, on the one hand, he was grateful toward me, which he demonstrated with tenderness and with affection. But on the other hand, he knew that I didn't need him for my own career, and perhaps that was what caused him the most pain.

No, I didn't need him. I mustn't need him, for whenever in my life I had begun to need someone, they had been taken from me. Nothing was more important than to preserve my freedom.

And so we lived off one another, although we had never really lived together. And yet his reserve was unforeseen.

"Has it become a duty?" I asked him. "If so, we should end it. I can't be someone's duty."

He denied it. Vehemently. No, it wasn't a duty. What kind of a threat was I making?

But I'd always felt we couldn't follow each other into our different worlds; they remained apart, foreign worlds behind strangers' eyes. Despite all this, I eventually became his wife.

Not long ago a man was sitting by me at the airport in Munich. I felt his curious eyes taking me in, and I felt from his look that he was ready to approach me and strike up a conversation. *Very well,* I thought, *he can have it, I can manage that.* I looked up and found a warmth in those eyes that I had been missing for a long time.

"Are you flying to Cologne, too?" he asked.

"Yes," I said, "I'm going to Cologne, too." I surprised myself with the lightness in my voice. "Do you want a drink?"

"Yes, let's. Can I treat you? We've got plenty of time."

With a sigh, he looked up at the information board by the gate. *Delayed, Delayed, Delayed.* The flight would not be departing for another four hours.

We sat down in the nearest restaurant, and I don't know why, but I began to tell him of this strange love I was caught up in, which refused to be tied down to a time or purpose, which was doing my head in with this, I don't know, disembodiment. Yes, suddenly I could see it, suddenly I knew it with great insight and clarity.

I have no idea why I told him all that. Maybe because it was night-time and quiet and the clicking of heels as people moved along the corridors was louder than in the daytime. Maybe it was because this man was such a stranger to me and yet seemed so close. Maybe it was because I knew I would never see him again.

My voice was a little subdued, a little quieter than usual, like a shade in an in-between world. He listened to me as I talked, and I saw that he had curly brown hair, that he was wearing a business suit, a tie, that he carried the inevitable laptop, wore the obligatory dark coat, and had a wife and children, probably two, probably school age, at home. *Just like it should be,* I thought a little scornfully. *Just like it should be.* And I knew we would have sex.

We did it in the bathroom; it was quiet all around and I thought about the November fog outside.

We did it in the expected silence, with the expected concentration. My body had not experienced such intensity, such abandon, for a long time, and I felt as though I'd finally found myself again. I knew that it was good, that it was right, that it was fitting.

I realized at that moment that I had never stopped thinking about Lilli, never stopped missing her, and at that realization, my sadness was so huge that it moved me to tears. When the man in the business suit felt the tears around my mouth, he stopped in shock, but I held him tight, drew him to me, and said, "Don't stop. Stay, don't go. Hold me, hold me tight, don't let go."

I loved him in that moment, I loved his warmth, his calmness, his clarity, because I believed I could sense my daughter in all that, my daughter who was so far away, so far, and who, I was sure, knew nothing of me, would never know anything of me . . .

Later, we sat a distance apart on the plane. We met again only briefly as the carousel spat out our suitcases. We smiled at each other, and I knew what comfort I would gain from then on, picturing his hand on my breast, a hand that gave me support and strength. I knew that when I was next with Jonas, I didn't have to tell him anything.

Once at home I found my businessman's card, which he'd slipped into my coat pocket without my noticing. I felt a shiver, a warmth, that suddenly crept into me and filled me with a glowing, warming strength. I can't describe it in any other way.

I gave myself three weeks before I sent him an e-mail. I composed it carefully, in just a few words.

His reply came immediately.

. . . *Are you an enchantress?* he asked. *I still have an aura around me like a multicolored cloak. You've thrown a warm hood over me, so are you an enchantress?*

. . . *I miss you,* I replied. *I'll miss you for a long time* . . .

. . . *Then come,* he wrote straight back . . . *just come. Come to me, and stay* . . . That was the last e-mail.

I didn't write back.

Neither did he.

I told Jonas nothing of that incident at the airport, nothing of the fact that my body remembered many other evenings, nothing of the e-mail, nothing of question: *Are you an enchantress?*

Then Tonio's letter arrived. And I set off immediately.

Sometimes I'm a stranger in my own life, a hub of unrest, a wanderer between worlds.

94

He didn't resist, and he didn't deny anything. He admitted everything. The case was suddenly as clear as freshly polished glass.

The detectives had knocked at his door, after Franza turned up quickly and she and Herz had exchanged their latest information on their way over to the hotel.

The door to his room had been open, and Jonas Belitz lay on the bed, exhausted and at the end of his strength. They'd called an ambulance.

"She wanted to tell her," he had said in response to the detectives' questions while they waited for the ambulance. "She wanted to tell Hanna that I knew everything, right from the start. That I'd concealed everything, taken money. I couldn't let that happen. Hanna couldn't ever find that out."

They watched the vehicle take Belitz to the hospital. Arthur had gone with it. He would see to everything and make the arrangements that were required when a self-confessed murderer needed hospital care.

Bonnie and Clyde had also been collected by police officers and taken into custody.

Franza and Felix remained on the square in front of the hotel. Beneath the bright sky. And Hanna remained. Lilli remained. Wherever they were.

95

My little girl. Suddenly, she was standing there. My Lilli. Her despair was visible. Her helplessness, her bewilderment. Suddenly, she was standing there and wanted to know . . . and all I could do was nod.

"Did you . . . ?" she asked later.

"No," I said. "No. Don't worry about that."

"Whatever happened, she was my mother, for all my life. How am I supposed to . . . ?"

"I know," I said, "I know." I took her in my arms, cautiously, slowly, drew her to me, feeling all the long years that lay between us. I drew her to me and warmth trickled softly . . . slowly, cautiously . . .

Lilli allowed me to. I know the road will be long.

96

"Hanna's mother," Hansen said.

"Hanna's mother?" Franza asked.

They were back at police headquarters, drinking coffee, succumbing to the weariness of the long day.

"What do you mean?"

"Well," Hansen said, "I mean, her mother!"

Herz shook his head. "But isn't she—?"

"No," Hansen said. "No, she isn't—"

"She's not dead?" Franza asked, holding her breath. "Hanna's mother isn't dead?"

"No," Hansen said. "She isn't. We all assumed she was for some reason."

"Yes," Franza said, a little surprised. "We did. Although no one ever confirmed it."

"So," Hansen said, beaming a little, "I've done some more research, since everything with Belitz was, you know . . . a kind of success."

"And?"

There was a sudden tension in the air; suddenly all weariness had vanished.

"There's a rehab clinic a ways out of town, attached to a convent. St. Anna's. I happen to know it. My mother spent a few weeks there after her stroke. A very peaceful place, very good for contemplation. You can also stay at the convent. The rooms are very Spartan, but, as I said, also very good for contemplation. Maybe—"

"Maybe you could get to the point, my dear Hansen," Franza interrupted.

Hansen grinned. "Oh, Franza," he said. "Give yourself a break. Things are coming together."

She punched his shoulder, and he laughed.

"So," he said, "I won't keep you on tenterhooks any longer. A woman by the name of Rosemarie Umlauf has been in the care of this clinic for some thirty-seven years. She needs twenty-four-hour care, but she's alive. And she's currently got visitors. And she'll soon be getting some more. I've already arranged for you to go."

"Wow," Herz said, and stood. "Hansen, you're a genius!"

"You are," Franza said as she hurried to the door behind Herz. "I can only second that! Thank you! Thank you-thank you-thank you!"

Hansen laughed and called after them. "Glad to be of service. It'll cost you a beer!"

"No," Herz called from the top of the stairs. "It'll cost us two. Or even three. A whole night out, even."

Then they were on their way.

97

Lilli is doing well. I brought her into my mother's room and said, "This is Lilli. My daughter, Lilli. Your granddaughter."

Now Lilli is sitting on the bed, feeding her grandmother, who's like a little child. She has to be fed, washed, changed. She looks at us, but I don't know if she sees us. I read to her from old books that I found in the convent. As I read, I can feel Lilli's eyes on me, and I sense her thoughtfulness like a cool cloth. I know that one day she'll ask me why I didn't come sooner, why I didn't sense her doubt through space and time and the wind, why . . . why . . . why . . .

I don't know what I'll say; it makes me shudder. But it will work out, somehow. We're not alone anymore.

98

"Yes, we have a woman by that name here," the sister at the gate said. "Yes, she had visitors show up a few days ago. More than she had for all those years. First her daughter, then her granddaughter."

She smiled a little. "They're getting along fine."

Silence reigned in the corridor, a strange harmony, an aura of . . . Franza felt it in the air, an aura of . . . peace . . .

Maybe it would do me good to unwind here for a few days, she thought. *No, a few days on the Adriatic might be better. Although one needn't exclude the other.* And then she stopped thinking because they were outside the door behind which, in all probability, the remaining loose ends of the case could be tied up.

Lilli and a woman in her midforties looked up when they opened the door. They were sitting next to one another on two chairs by a bed. In it lay another woman—a small, skinny woman beneath a white sheet. Her gray hair and face suggested age, old before her time. Ancient, a face that looked as though it had borne a lot, endured a lot. But Hanna's features could still clearly be seen in it.

"Lilli," Franza said with a feeling of great relief. "Frau Umlauf! At last! At last we've found you."

"Yes," Hanna said. Nothing else.

99

Yes, Franza thought, *nothing else. A feeling of moving on, of not standing still, of heading wherever, you never know, you can't know, ever. But you keep going and going, even if it's only as far as the water meadows or the Danube. Then you stop and look down toward Vienna and beyond, to the Black Sea.*

It can work. Yes, I have a good feeling, she thought as she fought her way through the meadow, hop twigs getting tangled in her hair, dog rose thorns scratching her arms, and all around her the leaves of the bushes already beginning to dry up around the edges, a color between green and gray, between staying and forgetting. Through it all was the sun, a mild spectacle on the cusp of fall.

Three days ago she had closed the case, and two days ago she had booked her leave and bought a plane ticket. Yesterday she had set off toward Munich, heading for the airport.

About halfway there she had turned off the autobahn, looking for the little lake where she and Port had spent a weekend the previous year. Leaning against the car, she had smoked a cigarette. It was around four in the afternoon. The trees were resplendent in red and yellow, a flaming canvas against the clarity of the fall sky. A light breeze had risen, wrinkling the surface of the lake, glints of sunlight and the reflections of the trees in the water. Only the occasional fish jumping and splashing back into the waves disturbed the September stillness.

Then another cigarette before she took her plane ticket from her bag, looked at it, set it down in front of her on the car roof, took out her cell phone, and sent a text. She picked up the ticket, looked at it again, smiled sadly—and tore it up.

She ripped it into tiny pieces, threw them into the air over the water, and watched the scraps land randomly. The ones in the air were carried away by the wind, those in the water by the current. Franza imagined them washing up in Vienna, floating in the current of the Danube, or coming to rest by the Rochusmarkt in the Third District, where Port now lived. She imagined him bending to retrieve one of the scraps, lifting it up and wondering what it had been when it was still part of something whole.

Franza had to smile as she imagined the scene. She ran both hands over her face, wiping away the wetness, and breathed deeply. A sudden shudder escaped her, and she shook her head, got back into the car, and drove to see Herz. He asked nothing. He gave her a hug, and then the twins came bounding up and Angelika served coffee and cakes: delicious, moist, rich cakes full of explosive calories. Franza ate two pieces and knew she would be angry with herself tomorrow, as she always was, but tomorrow was tomorrow and today was today, and today it felt good.

They said nothing for a while, watching the children playing and fighting, fighting and playing, and nothing was right, but it was, really—a little. At some stage in the evening Franza went home, armed with good intentions—no more cigarettes, healthy eating, lots of exercise.

Nothing was over; she knew that. There was unfinished business that, if she looked too closely, would reveal pain—but it would be bearable, all of it, always, somehow. None of them was seventeen anymore. They were there, in the middle of their lives, constantly asking themselves, what happened? What's left?

At last she called him.

"What's up?" he asked. "Why?"

She closed her eyes, listening to his voice. It had sounded a little hurt, a little upset, a little sad. *Yes,* she thought, *that's OK.*

"You're my favorite actor ever," she said with a small smile, "and you always will be." She felt a sense of longing tug in her breast and didn't know how to continue.

"Why?" he repeated. "Tell me. I don't understand."

"You're there," she said, "and I'm here."

"So?"

She said nothing. He hung up.

She stood there for a while, the cell phone in her hand, and thought of the scraps of paper, wondering whether one had found its way to Vienna and whether Port had found it. She thought that was garbage, but it was nevertheless a nice thing to imagine.

Then she went to the computer, wrote Port an e-mail. . . . *Sometimes in the night the first snow winds have begun to blow . . .*

His reply was there the next morning. . . . *And you feel the damn cold in your bones . . .*

She smiled through her tears. *We're writing each other in farewell,* she thought. *Yes, that's what we're doing.* And she found it lovely. A little morbid, maybe, but lovely.

It suits Vienna, she thought. *Suits me, suits him.* She thought how it would be lost. They both sensed it. Even though they still gave in to one another, even though they still asked each other questions, gave answers, lost themselves in discussions, in long-winded explanations, in gentle controversies.

It was getting lost. They were losing it.

"Why do you cut everything off?" Sonja asked that night, when she'd dropped by Franza's. "You shouldn't, you know. I mean, it's only Vienna! So?"

"I cut everything off?" Franza retorted, and thought of *alien two*. She felt a distant gripping in her stomach. She looked at Sonja and . . .

"I'm not cutting anything off," she said. "I'm starting over."

"Why?"

She considered. "I don't know. Isn't it something you have to do sometimes? Start fresh?"

"You're so brave," Sonja said wistfully. "I wish I could be like that."

"No," Franza said softly, "I'm not brave. I'm crazy. I risk way too much."

She looked at Sonja, trying to convey how important she was to her. But Sonja didn't register it and hadn't been listening. Sonja was thinking of her husband, how he'd protested his innocence. What she was accusing him of was absurd. He would never, ever cheat on her. He wasn't an asshole. He'd been in that bar with a student friend, and OK, it may have gotten late but she could call him if she wanted. With all due respect, he found her mistrust disgusting!

"Oh, Franzi, my dear Franzi," Sonja said, throwing her arms around Franza.

Franzi! She had to laugh. Sonja was the only one who was allowed to call her that, and only every now and then at that. Franzi. A leftover from childhood.

"I've forgiven him," Sonja sighed. "Whatever happened, I've forgiven him. And now let's be naughty and smoke and drink!"

"And I'm getting a divorce," Franza said.

"Yes, I heard."

"He's been to see you?"

"Yes. He thought the two of you might . . . He was hoping . . ."

"I know," Franza said. "I know. But I have to make the break. Set myself free. I need clarity. Everything open. Not only for me, but for Max, too. And maybe . . . We'll see . . . I don't know . . . Maybe . . ."

Amazing, she thought. *So much moves on, so little remains. At some stage I'll notice that freedom can be cold.*

The doorbell rang. Lilli. "Can we cook something?" she said, a little embarrassed. "Do you want to?"

"Of course I want to," Franza said. "Sonja, come on, we're going to cook!"

They cooked. They cooked for hours. Roast beef with carrots, celeriac, and mashed potatoes, and as if that weren't enough, they added Franza's famous gingerbread cookies.

"You just have to be able to make this, Lilli," Franza said. "It's a hard life without this gingerbread."

They laughed, three women in the kitchen. They laughed.

Unfinished business everywhere, Franza thought, *but sometimes we have to spread our wings.*

Unfinished business everywhere, Sonja thought, *but sometimes we have to spread our wings.*

"Hanna can't cook," Lilli said. "Gertrud could cook."

"I know," Franza said, stroking Lilli's back, "I know."

"I'm going to train for the police," Lilli said.

Franza smiled. "Are you sure?"

"Yes," Lilli said. "Positive. As positive as it's possible to be."

"Let's eat," Sonja said, carrying the roast out onto the terrace. "Let's eat until we burst."

They sat beneath the evening sky, a yellow moon to their left among towering castles of clouds. They listened to Tracy Chapman, music from back then, music from their village days.

To be on the move, Franza thought, once she was alone, once the dishwasher was running and the fridge was heaving with food for three days, *to be on the move in life, me in my life, never quite arriving, full of longing and with no idea of where the search—the longing—will lead.*

Yes, she thought, *I'm still the same, still me, Franza Oberwieser, forty-five, detective, soon to be divorced, with a son. Fingers burned by life, but still hot and thirsty. Still prepared to believe in the only constant—change.*

Still prepared to rush out into the harsh depths of life, sometimes sweet, so sweet that you hope you won't choke on the sweetness.

Me, then, she thought. *Still, and yet again. This is how happiness feels. Like this. Sometimes. A small piece of happiness.*

She would spread her wings. Unfinished business everywhere, but from time to time she would keep spreading her wings. That's how it should be. Like that.

ABOUT THE AUTHOR

Award-winning writer Gabi Kreslehner lives and works in her hometown of Ottensheim, Austria, located on the shores of the Danube. She became interested in theater and writing at a young age and now works as a teacher. Her previous novel, *Rain Girl*, was her English-language debut.

ABOUT THE TRANSLATOR

Alison Layland is a novelist and translator from French, German, and Welsh into English. A member of the Institute of Translation and Interpreting and the Society of Authors, she won the 2010 Translators' House Wales-Oxfam Cymru Translation Challenge, as well as various short-story competitions for her own writing. Her published translations include a number of novels and nonfiction titles, and her own debut novel, *Someone Else's Conflict*, was published in 2014 by Honno Press. She is married with two children and lives in the beautiful and inspiring countryside of Wales, United Kingdom.